AURELIA

A Prequel to the Pendragon Cycle

THE PENDRAGON CYCLE
by STEPHEN R. LAWHEAD

Aurelia (a prequel)*
Book 1: *Taliesin**
Book 2: *Merlin**
Book 3: *Arthur**
Book 4: *Pendragon*
Book 5: *Grail*
Book 6: *Avalon*

*Available from Baen Books.
To purchase these titles in e-book form, please go to www.baen.com

AURELIA

A Prequel to the Pendragon Cycle

STEPHEN R. LAWHEAD

A Baen Books Original

Baen Publishing Enterprises
P.O. Box 1403
Riverdale, NY 10471
www.baen.com

ISBN: 978-1-6680-7234-9

First printing, January 2025

Distributed by Simon & Schuster
1230 Avenue of the Americas
New York, NY 10020

Library of Congress Cataloging-in-Publication Data

Names: Lawhead, Stephen R., 1950- author.
Title: Aurelia / Stephen R. Lawhead.
Description: Riverdale, NY : Baen Publishing Enterprises, 2025. | Series:
    Pendragon cycle ; prequel
Identifiers: LCCN 2024049559 (print) | LCCN 2024049560 (ebook) | ISBN
    9781668072349 (hardcover) | ISBN 9781625799982 (ebook)
Subjects: LCGFT: Fantasy fiction. | Novels.
Classification: LCC PS3562.A865 A93 2025 (print) | LCC PS3562.A865
    (ebook) | DDC 813/.54—dc23/eng/20241121
LC record available at https://lccn.loc.gov/2024049559
LC ebook record available at https://lccn.loc.gov/2024049560

Printed in the United States of America

10 9 8 7 6 5 4 3 2 1

To the memory of Jan Dennis,
who got me started.

 CONTENTS

CELYDDON
FOREST
● Goddeu

THE WALL

● Eboracum

● Deva Vitrix

● Ty Bryn

● Aberdyfi

● Viroconium

● Caer Myrddin

Venta
●

● Londinium

MOR HAFREN

● Ynys Avallach

LLYONESSE

THE NARROW SEAS

BRITAIN
Scale of Miles
0 20 40 60 80

● Constantia

ARMORICA

AURELIA PRONUNCIATION GUIDE
☩ ☩ ☩

While many of the old British names may look odd to modern readers, they are not as difficult to pronounce as they seem at first glance. A little effort, and the following guide, will help you enjoy the sound of these ancient words.

Consonants—as in English, but with a few exceptions:
  c: hard, as in cat (never soft as in cent)
  ch: hard, as in Scottish Loch, or Bach (never soft, as in church)
  dd: th, as in then (never as in thistle)
  f: v, as in of
  ff: f, as in off
  g: hard, as in girl (never gem)
  ll: a Welsh distinctive, sounded as "tl" or "hl" on the sides of the tongue
  r: trilled, lightly
  rh: as if hr, heavy on the "h" sound
  s: always as in sir (never his)
  th: as in thistle (never then)

Vowels—as in English, but with the general lightness of short vowel sounds:
  a: as in father
  e: as in met (when long, as in late)
  i: as in pin (long, as in eat)
  o: as in not
  u: as in pin (long, as in eat)
  w: a "double-u," as in vacuum, or tool; but becomes a consonant before vowels, as in the name Gwen
  y: as in pin; or sometimes as "u" in but (long as in eat)

(As you can see, there is not much difference in i, u, and y—they are virtually identical to the beginner.)
  *Accent—*normally is on the next to last syllable, as in Di-gán-hwy
  *Diphthongs—*each vowel is pronounced individually, so Taliesin=Tally-éssin
  *Atlantean—*Ch=kh, so Charis is Khár-iss

Ten rings there are, and nine gold torcs
     on the battlechiefs of old;
Eight princely virtues, and seven sins
     for which a soul is sold;
Six is the sum of earth and sky,
     of all things meek and bold;
Five is the number of ships that sailed
     from Atlantis lost and cold;
Four kings of the Westerlands were saved,
     three kingdoms now behold;
Two came together in love and fear,
     in Llyonesse stronghold;
One world there is, one God, and one birth
     the Druid stars foretold.

S.R.L.

Oxford, England, 1987

BOOK ONE

VENTA SILURUM

✠ ✠ ✠

"GOD'S TEETH, MERLIN! I hate this! I am sick to the soul with it." Uther, fresh from the saddle and still wearing his swordbelt and helm, storms into the big leather campaign tent, throws down a glove and falls into the nearest chair. He smells of battle—sweat and earth and blood—and the scent takes me back to a time when I, too, rode with a warband at my back, and I am again reminded that we tread a bridge no wider than the edge of a sword.

"There *must* be a better way." He glares at me and I mark the dark half-moons beneath those gray-green eyes. Our paths have only lately joined and I am still learning the measure of the man and his mighty moods—the passions that surge through him like the restless tide. And I ask myself, not for the first time: *Can this man and his brother really be the ones to unite our fractured land and all its factious peoples?*

"Bear it just a little longer, Uther," I tell him. "One more battle and the prize is ours. Just one more."

"Liar!" His fist slams down on the board, making cups tip and spill. "That's what you said *last* time!"

"Yes, well—"

"You said Vortigern was the only stone in our path," he complains. He takes up a cup and stares into it. "Ha! The path is nothing *but* stones!"

Uther is right. I had spoken my best hope: a mistake, more often than not. I should have known better—especially when dealing with a host of petty potentates and would-be tyrants clawing like mad rats for the High King's crown. Or, should I rather say *mice* mewling for a milksop? For, I swear, there is not a single lord of genuine stature or substance from Eboracum to Londinium. And those of the north who are worth their salt might be counted on the toes of one foot.

Yet, and yet, we had stood against the most powerful of those proud kings today. And this is the way of it:

Daybreak was still some way off as we labored up the hillside, thrashing our way in the dark by feel alone. Once we had gained the crest we formed the warhost, spreading out along the spine of the ridge. Then, we waited for the dawn. It was Uther's plan to have the light at our back, forcing Morcant's men to fight with the sun in their eyes. We waited, praying for cloudless skies—prayers heard and answered in full.

At the very moment the sun crested the hills, stretching its bright rays down the slopes and into the valley, Uther gave the command and the warband rose up, forming a single rank along the entire ridge. The warriors began beating their shields with spear shaft and sword hilt; they opened their throats to the battle cry: *Britannia! Britannia!* Coming in waves as a roar resounding from the hills: *BRITANNIA! BRITANNIA! BRITANNIA!*

Morcant's warband was caught unawares. Still shaking off their night's slumber, the first Morcant and his battlechiefs knew of the attack was when the clash of the shields and wails of the warriors rattled down slopes and echoed across the valley. Instantly, the camps were thrown into disarray as warriors scattered to arm themselves.

Uther did not linger to enjoy the sight of the enemy scurrying like ants dashed from a scalded hill. His upraised arm slashed down, the battered old battlehorn sounded, and the warhost flooded down the hillside, screaming to cry down the heavens. At the same time, Uther's brother, Aurelius, and his cohort of mounted warriors—his *alá*, in the old Roman fashion—swept in from the flank. Having ridden through the early hours to get themselves into position, they closed upon Morcant's forces before Uther and his troops on foot reached the camp.

The rebellious lord barked commands for his men to join battle. Some, only half dressed, cut their horses from the picket lines, threw themselves into the saddle, and raced to meet the attack. Having severed the picket lines however, many suddenly free horses bolted and ran, stranding more warriors on foot than were mounted. Meanwhile, their swordbrothers ran to their lord and clustered around him to make their stand.

Aurelius' men quickly surrounded the rebel king and his bodyguard but restrained the attack, allowing Morcant—wisely, I think—to feel the futility of struggling on. Several of the bolder defenders struck out: swords clashed, blood flowed, one man went down. Some among them shouted commands to rally and form the battleline, but it was already too late. In fact, the battle was over before the fight had properly begun.

The few skirmishes that had flourished when Uther's forces reached the valley, flashed briefly and were extinguished. In all, three men fell—all Morcant's, good men—and five horses. The injured warriors would live, but whether they would ever fight again remained to be seen.

I watched all this from the top of the hill with Pelleas beside me. And, yes, there was a time when I would have been at the sharp end of the fighting, matching stroke for stroke with the fiercest foe. But no more. Oh, I know well the ways of war and men, how battles can best be ordered, and so on. Yet, believe me when I say that I am far more valuable as an advisor at the king's right hand than merely another sweaty fist on a spear. That is not an over-proud opinion or idle boast, rather it is the work only I can do, and I will embrace it as my duty with the fierce devotion of the most loyal warrior.

In all, the battle played out before us just now could easily have been far worse: the fighting more desperate, the losses greater. But Morcant's heart wasn't in it; he knew himself outsmarted and outmanned from the start. Until he saw those warriors swarming down the hillside to him, I don't think he understood the true size of Aurelius and Uther's warband, or their iron resolve; if he had, he might have waited for Gorlas or Dunaut or Coledac to join him and mass their troops together. If Morcant had been better prepared, the brothers' simple maneuver would not have thrown his camp into such disorder and alarm. But arrogance is so often blind—and blinding.

Be that as it may, to pursue the conflict further would have been pure folly and not even Morcant, for all his haughty pride, was ever that much of a fool. When it became clear that Aurelius and Uther placed a higher price on victory than he was able to meet, Morcant quit the field and a contrite messenger was soon kneeling before Uther begging peace. Fortunately, the fight had not gone beyond recall. Indeed, other than a few inevitable wounds and injuries, I doubt either warband suffered any lasting hurt—which was a boon for all concerned. No mistake, we would need all the sound fighting men we could muster when we marched north to take the fight to the Saecsen invaders.

None of this prevents Uther from complaining about it, however. He is as irate as he would be had we lost.

"This is insane! How are we ever to trust these people?" Uther cries, his voice at once a challenge and a complaint. "Answer me that if you can!"

"What *is* all this shouting?" Calls a voice behind me. "You can hear it clear out to the tether line. You're scaring the horses."

I turn to see Aurelius stooping through the oxhide flap of the entrance. He sees me and then his glance slides to his brother. "What has Merlin said *this* time?" he asks, his voice a balm to soothe a heated temper. "Something utterly outrageous I'll warrant. What is it now? That we should smelt our swords for toasting forks? Our spears for kindling?"

The reference cheers me strangely. If only his winsome ways could win over the haughty royals of the self-satisfied tribes of the Southern Midlands; proud in their ancient power seats, they fret and brood in their noisome lairs, fomenting rebellion and nursing their hopeless dreams of kingship and empire. But even Aurelius' natural charisma, his fathomless charm, his manifold gifts of persuasion do not extend that far.

And so we must endure these heinous, pointless battles—maiming and killing, wasting the blood of men we would much rather welcome as swordbrothers in the fight against a superior and far more ruthless enemy. I swallow down the rebuke already leaping to my tongue, and instead tell Uther what I have told many another in the past. "Keep your eyes on the prize," I say.

"Good advice," says Aurelius, sliding into a chair beside his brother. He raises a cup to be filled.

"Eyes on the prize," Uther huffs with a snort of derision: he snatches up his cup and drains it in a gulp. "Aye, but is *any* prize worth the obscene price we are paying? Eh?"

"Never doubt it, Uther." Another has entered—and with a softer voice, but a voice I will soon come to know quite well.

I turn again to the tent flap to see a tall, slender woman of advancing years, her dark hair swept back and graying at the temples, and a face firm and lightly lined. Her back is straight, her eyes quick and sharp, but there is a thinness about her face that gives her a somewhat hollow look which, I suddenly realize, makes her seem older than her years.

"Mother—" Aurelius and Uther speak as one, as they often do. Both start up from their chairs, almost spilling the cups.

So *this* is Aurelia, I muse. With her, and close as a shadow at her side, is a servant. Mairenn, I will later learn, is a near-mute Irish girl rescued from the hanging tree—a mere waif of a thing: plain featured, inconspicuous, silent as snow. Mairenn is a ghostly presence, so easily overlooked as to be invisible. But, like her mistress, keen eyed. I suspect she misses nothing.

With them is a brown-robed priest—a young man of decent stature and the broad shoulders and hands of a warrior; his quick dark eyes lend him the air of a fellow ready for a fight wherever it finds him. Moreover, there is a familiar look about him, and it makes me think I have seen him somewhere before.

But it is Aurelia who commands my attention—though, in the flesh, she is not at all the person I imagined. The way Aurelius and Uther had spoken of her, I pictured a much more imposing figure: a winged Rhiannon, silver spear in hand; or a Modron, queen of queens. Anything but this well-aged woman with skin like parchment and liver spots on her hands. Aurelius' mention of the woman who raised him— much as one would speak of a she-wolf that ruled a pack of scrappy mongrels—does not at all match my mental image. Be that as it may, it is clear that both of these men are in complete thrall to her.

"How did you get here? When did you arrive?" Aurelius says. "Did you know she was coming, Utha?"

"No. I did not." Uther shakes his head. "You shouldn't be here, Mother. It isn't safe."

"Nonsense," she scoffs, in a manner so much like her son that I see at once where he came by it. "Do you think an armed camp is anything to frighten me? I grew up in a Roman garrison, son of mine."

"So did I," Uther mutters under his breath.

She moves to her son and gives him a maternal kiss, then pats his cheek. "Your concern touches my heart," she tells him, sarcasm edging her tone.

Aurelia's presence has instantly transformed the two brothers. Both men, so used to wielding the power of command over others, are no less used to being commanded by this woman.

I marvel at her effortless intimacy as she crosses to Aurelius, puts a loving hand to his face, and gives him the same maternal kiss on the cheek. "Hello, my heart," she tells him. "I don't see your crown. Have you lost it already?"

"You cannot lose what you do not have," he tells her with a laugh. "But my advisor assures me it is within my grasp." He nods in my direction. "Isn't that right, Merlin?"

The old woman straightens and turns to me. "Ah, the Wise Emrys," she says, her glance at once appraising and approving. "I am happy to meet you at last."

"The honor is mine," I reply, lowering my head in respect. "Aurelius and Uther have told me much about you."

"That I heartily doubt," she scoffs again, giving her sons a sideways glance. "Well, I hope at least some of it was true. Please, sit—all of you. Sit."

Though she betrays none of the deafness I am told she has endured the whole of her life, I mark that both Uther and Aurelius are mindful to face her when they speak and alter their tone accordingly. No doubt, Aurelia has become adept at hiding her impairment one way and another, either that or she actually hears more than she pretends. I do not know her well enough yet to say which.

"Uther is right," Aurelius tells her, resuming his seat. "This is no place for you. Anyway, we're moving camp in the morning and you'll—"

She raises a hand to stop him. "You need not worry about me. I've been very well looked after by King Tewdrig—"

"Tewdrig? Here?" cries Uther. Now I understand his bluster: years of speaking loud to accommodate his mother have made shouting his usual form of address. "Where is he? What does he want?"

"Peace, Utha," says Aurelius. "Let her speak." Turning to his mother, he smiles. "You say friend Tewdrig is here?"

"Oh, indeed. We met on the road. He is just now making his camp nearby and asked me to tell you that he will join you very soon."

"Why is he here?" wonders Uther, reaching for his cup. "Why now?"

"You will have to wait to ask him yourself," replies Aurelia simply. "But, he said something about securing pledges from the southern lords—whoever they might be."

"Humph," grumps Uther. "We need men and horses, not vows and pledges."

Bending over him, Aurelia strokes the back of his neck—a caring touch only a mother could perform with such practiced ease. How many times, I wonder, has she employed that same calming gesture over the years?

"Well, as I say, you can ask him yourself when he arrives, but from what I have gleaned, he is just as eager as you are to rid the land of Hengist and all his vile heathen brood—Tewdrig's very words. Not so, Mairenn?" The maid nods gravely, watching everything.

"That's all?" Uther sniffs, his anger and frustration abating somewhat. "He needn't have come all this way for that. He could have sent a message. Better still, sent men and weapons."

"Enough, Uther," says Aurelius, breaking in. "We'll speak to Tewdrig when he's ready." He reaches a hand to his mother and she takes it in her grasp. Seeing her hands in his—they appear small, fragile things in his powerful grip. "Pleasant as it is to see you," he continues, "Uther is right. It is dangerous on the road just now. You should have stayed in Armorica. You'd safe there."

"It is *always* dangerous on the road, my son—as you never tire of reminding me. But if I'd stayed in Constantia, I wouldn't have seen my boys." She pats his hand and releases it. "You've been away so long I wanted to see for myself if you still stalk the land of the living."

I feel a smile spreading across my face at this exchange. That these two battle-hardened chieftains, high-blooded and keen as new blades, kings in all but name, should bow before this aging woman who yet calls them her "boys" is both a delight and a wonder. I cannot remember when last I witnessed such matter-of-fact familial affection, such motherly devotion. Oh, but it is joy itself to see it now and share in the warmth of the moment. It breaks upon me then that I know little about this remarkable woman who raised such champions. Yes, and even that little is, I fear, very much mistaken: scraps patched together as it is from various fragmented accounts, rumors, and tales gathered from ill-informed sources. But here the living woman stands before me. I vow then and there to know her better and learn the truth from the only one who has lived it; and this, if time and heaven allow, I will do.

Pelleas enters the tent just then, bearing a jar of mead in each hand. I direct him to pour the cups. Mairenn moves to assist him, and Aurelia joins us and I introduce him to them. "Ah, the mother of our next High King," Pelleas replies, with a glance at me. As always, he knows more than he lets on, for little escapes his notice. "Your renown proceeds you." She beams at the recognition. "It is an honor to meet you." He indulges her in a little bow of acknowledgment and he and Mairenn carry the cups and jar to the board.

"You have Pelleas and I have Mairenn," Aurelia confides. "We are fortunate to have found such devoted servants."

I smile. "Indeed," I agree. "But Pelleas is more to me than a servant. He is confidant and friend, and more." I glance his way. "Truly, he is my guardian, my aide and advocate, my paraclete you might say." She wonders at the word and I add, "He has borne my burdens more than once." In truth, I have depended on his devotion more times than I can count.

As Pelleas and Mairenn fill the cups, and the others sit down to drink to the success of our fraught and worried cause, I turn to the silent priest standing nearby, greet him, and say, "I have the notion that I might know you, friend. Have we met?"

A ready mirth plays at the corners of his mouth. "No, Emrys, I confess I have not enjoyed that particular pleasure. But, I'm thinking you might have seen me at Caer Myrddin."

"Ah, that would likely be it."

"I am Ruan. Though, I think it far more likely that it was my brother, Rónán, that you saw," he quickly explains. "He is one of Lord Tewdrig's men and we are enough alike that we are often confused one for the other."

"Lucky, Tewdrig," I reply, "with two staunch men—a priest and a warrior—to serve him." I glance back at Aurelia chatting happily with her two sons.

Ruan sees my glance and explains, "The king has asked me to accompany her and serve her—which I have vowed to do as long as my assistance is required."

A gift, of a sort, from a most generous and thoughtful man. "I can see that she is in good hands."

We part then as he hurries off to fetch some food and drink for himself and Mairenn, the serving maid. Those gathered around the board begin to talk over the latest events, news and gossip; and, with cups in hand, gradually the heavy clouds of the day's troubles lift and drift away.

Watching Aurelius chivvy his brother into a better mood, I lean close to my elderly companion and say, "You've cheered them greatly—our Good Lord's own gift, I'm thinking."

She smiles. "I don't know about that. But I *do* know that I could not stay away another day longer. And if I had known Myrddin the Wise was riding with them, I would have come all the sooner."

"I have not been with them all so very long myself," I tell her. "Pelleas and I have been negotiating peace with the lords hereabouts, trying to prevent another battle."

"It looks to me as if you've failed."

"It looks that way to me, too." I shake my head and dismiss the thought. Instead, I say, "But you, Aurelia, how are you?"

"Old and getting older—and not long for this world," she says lightly. Despite her protests, she wears her age so loosely it seems to barely touch her—much as I do, though for very different reasons. In fact, now that I see her better, I realize that she is not as old as she appears. And I wonder at the pretense. "I'd heard you were with them," she continues, with a nod to the two warrior lords as they sit head-to-head with their war leaders, discussing the day's triumphs and disappointments. Pelleas, Mairenn, and some other servants with cooking pots enter with bowls and plates and begin laying out the food. The hungry warriors fall to their meal.

"Behold!" I say, raising my cup to them. "All that stands between us and annihilation by the Hengist and his Saecsen warhost."

We drink and she adds, "I hope and pray they are enough. I tell you the truth, Merlin, that has become my most fervent prayer."

I agree with her and tell her I believe her sons are the leaders raised up for this moment, and that I have pledged my life to their support. We drink again and, perhaps emboldened by the celebratory moment, I confess the grave error I made in the past and for which I must now make amends. "I was wrong about them, you know—very wrong."

"How so?" she cocks her head to one side.

"I believed them to be sons of Constantine, the High King. I thought—"

"Oh! *That* old lie," she huffs, "is almost as old as I am. I've heard it a thousand times if once." Suddenly earnest, with a flutter of her hand she waves aside my assumption as if it were a bad smell. "You'll do well to forget you ever heard that at all. My boys are no relation to that usurper," she snaps. "But they *are* well schooled, and that is an honest fact. The Good Lord knows their father and I did our best—despite what anyone says."

The comment together with her abrupt change of demeanor intrigues me and makes me wonder what lies behind it. "People say many things," I suggest. "You cannot prevent them talking."

"No, but you don't have to like it."

The bitterness in her tone betrays a long-lingering hurt. Something in me urges me to probe the wound a little. "You should hear some of the things they say about *me*," I tell her. "Most of it is fit only for the midden heap where it rightly belongs."

"Yes, well, *you* are not the mother of the next High King of Britain—the Good Lord willing." She turns her eyes from her sons and fixes me with a look both desperate and sincere. "Hear me, Wise Emrys, my sons are worthy of the throne they seek—never doubt it. There are those who would deny their claim because of me, but I will not have Aurelius and Uther defamed or dishonored because they lack royal pedigree. I will not have it, you hear? I will not see them slandered on my account."

Ah, we have struck the heart of her grievance. She is not wrong in this. The question of Aurelius' and Uther's birthright has been much discussed in the halls of the kings, and debated with the lords and chieftains I have attempted to win to our side. Upstarts, they were called, low-born mongrels, half-blood Britons, not British at all. It was even suggested that, given the chance, these two sly devils would side with their foreign kin; they'd sooner sell us out for the gold of the Saecsen Shore, and so on and on.

Of course, these slurs and insults were voiced most often by those trying to advance their own vaunted interests. Great Light, I do freely confess that I have also viewed Aurelius' and Uther's claim in error. And now it seems that I, too, have been mistaken about their lineage—succumbing, I suppose, to easy rumor and sly gossip where facts were not forthcoming.

Since entering the service of these two young firebrands, I have stopped my ears to all the mealy-mouthed complaints and self-serving protests of the small kings. If what their mother says is so and they are not in fact the sons of Constantine, they are still his heirs, so to speak. For, there is but one true path for Britain and no other. I see that clearly, and I will not be moved.

Be that as it may, I can also see that this question of birthright and noble pedigree weighs heavily on her mind, perhaps obsesses her in a way I do not rightly understand—and, likely, will not understand until I hear the full story. So, I poke a little deeper.

"Is there something you would like to tell me, Aurelia?" I lean back in my chair, cradling my cup to my chest. "If so, there is nothing I would like better than to hear it."

A sly smile curves her thin lips. "You may think otherwise when you hear what I have to say."

I nod, accepting her caveat. "There is but one way to find out."

Her eyes narrow as she favors me with that piercing gaze of hers and slowly makes up her mind.

Three of Uther's battlechiefs, having settled their warbands, come clattering into the tent, loud in their greetings and keen to share the victory with their war leader and lord; four more follow on their heels. Aurelia, seeing the men enter, rises from her chair. "Come to my lodging and we will talk." She bids good night to her sons, then she and Mairenn leave the warriors to their noisy celebration.

Later, as the camp slowly quiets for the night, I join Aurelia in the tent Uther has vacated for her. Mairenn has placed two camp chairs beside a small iron brazier and lit charcoal to chase away the chill that drifts in through the flaps and wind holes; rushlights burn in holders, casting a soft glow over us and scattering shadows everywhere. I have sent Pelleas to his rest in our tent across the way and I settle in to hear what Aurelia has to tell.

"Hear me, Myrddin, you will long outlast me and so I charge you to carry the truth of what I say. When I am ashes in my grave, I want it remembered."

I occurs to me that what I am about to hear is the cleansing of a wound that has festered for many years. No doubt, she has prepared herself, carrying it with her, working it over in her mind, polishing it over time like a stone of contention. She has chosen now to lay down the burden, and I am to bear witness. I wonder why.

Nevertheless, I do what I can to reassure her. "So long as I have anything to do with it, you will not be forgotten. On that you have my promise."

She takes up the tongs from the brazier and places another bit of charcoal in the embers. Then, having arranged her thoughts as she has arranged the fire, she turns her gaze on me. The rekindled light comes up in her eyes and she begins to speak:

"I want this known: I never was a slave. Never a captive, or tribe tribute, never a prize or trophy taken in battle, never a foundling abandoned at the garrison gate. God's truth, I am not a mud-sucking Saecsen slut left behind in a failed raid, nor a Picti maid married out of pity. I am Briton born. Noble blood flows in my veins. My great-grandfather was a prince of the Demetae, my grandmother a Silurian queen. My mother was the wife of a magistrate, and no mongrel Frisian urchin who sold goat cheese and duck eggs in some fly-blown crossroad dirt market as the gossips would have it."

"People love a good lie," I tell her. "I don't know why. But fly to them they do—like crows on a carcass."

She nods in agreement. "Aye," she adds, "they devour all they can and squawk for more. The things said about me—wicked rumors spoken behind my back when they think I can't hear. Falsehoods all—spun of pure malice and woven of jealousy.

"The cause of it? Nothing more than a hard fact they cannot stomach. And it is this: I was the wife of a titled official in the service of Rome. Great wealth and greater power lay within his command. My husband was Constantine Aridius Verica, Legate of Deva Vitrix and *Legatus Legionis* of Flavia Gallicana. The simple truth is that he could have had the choosing of many another willing woman to take as wife—and many more beautiful, more desirable, come to that. But out of all the others he chose me. And it is this raw lump the envious crones chew endlessly and cannot swallow.

"Let the nags and scolds gaze on me in their envy and flick their poison tongues as they will. I did not set out to seduce a man. I did not steal a husband. And God knows I did not murder Helena, the legate's first wife.

"Poor woman—she did not deserve her end. But I served her faithfully as handmaid, confidant, and friend. And I nursed her through those last bitter months. I was not forced. No bargains were struck for me. I served of my own accord, and I served her gladly. I was never under any bonds save those of friendship and affection.

"Hear me, and remember. I am Aurelia. Citizen by birth. Daughter of the Empire. Mother to the next High King of All Britain. My lineage is second to none, and I bow my head to no one in this realm or any other."

✠ ✠ ✠

1

THE SUMMONS ARRIVED in the red leather pouch along with all the other tag ends of parchment that fly back and forth among the emperor's overworked officials. One of these administrators was my father, Tullius Paulinus, Magistrate of Venta Silurum, which, I am in the habit of reminding people, was once a very important *civitas* on account of its central southern location and thriving market. While it may be true that Venta no longer enjoyed the eminence it possessed of old, the market was still busy, still thriving, and the magistrate was still an important official in the ranks of regional government. As magistrate, it fell to my father to decide what to do about all those scribbled messages delivered in the dispatch pouch: the grievances, petitions, appeals, demands, and reports. Who owed what in taxes; the price of grain in Londinium; the sorry state of some silted-up port or falling-down bridge; property disputes . . . and so on and on without end.

Each and every one of any of a thousand concerns arrived in that red bag and passed through my hands before ever they reached my father. This is how I learned to read and write, and how I got word of the world beyond the hills surrounding our small southern town. This is also how I learned about the summons that was to change my life.

The rider who had brought the bag had already departed by the time I came into the magistrate's chambers—one of two rooms facing the street at the end of our house. The larger of the two rooms was where official business was conducted; the smaller was where documents and such were kept and where I had a table to do my work.

I greeted the appearance of the dread bag with a sigh and resigned myself to spending the rest of the day reading those tedious, tight-scrawled messages until I became cross-eyed and numb with boredom. Of all my customary chores, this was the one I accepted, grudgingly, rather than enjoyed. Once read, I would then have to shepherd all these scraps into rough order for my father's attention. These tasks, among all the others of our busy little outpost, were duties my mother had once performed, but which I inherited when she died.

Morning had all but gone. Father was out and Augustus—his aging *adiutor*, his chief assistant—was about other business, so I had dawdled as long as I dared. I entered the work room to see the red dispatch bag on the table, waiting for me, taunting me. My heart sank. Not only had I missed the rider—a fine-looking young fellow who always had a word or two of gossip to brighten my day—but now I had a long, dull chore ahead of me.

With a reluctance bordering on despair, I loosened the straps and dumped the bag's contents onto the table. The tight-folded packets spilled everywhere—a spreading heap of monotony. As the little parcels scattered, I glimpsed a slash of red ink. *Well, well, what have we here?* I wondered. For, I had seen that mark on messages once or twice before and I knew them to be from somewhere high up the ladder of rank—higher, at least, than a magistrate's office.

Heart beating with anticipation, I reached into the pile and pulled out the special packet and held it up for closer examination. My father's name was written on the outside and, below it, a beeswax seal. I slid my finger under the seal, broke it, and carefully unfolded the parchment square. The rough-cut edges were marked in red ink and the writing was neatly penned. Ordinarily, I would have carried the message directly to my father. As I was alone, I read it instead. My father was being invited to join a delegation formed by Proconsul Esico to attend some sort of council in Viroconium. I gleaned little more than that, but the official tone and the detailed directions given made it clear that this was one invitation the magistrate could not refuse.

I knew that Esico was the chief administrator of our patch, the proconsul, and he commanded from the Civic House in Glevum, the largest town near us, bigger even than Isca. My father had dealings with him in one capacity or other often enough that it was not at all uncommon to receive messages from him or someone in his office. But, a red-edged summons—*that* was unusual.

I smoothed out the sharp folds and read the invitation again more slowly, stumbling slightly over the word "Viro-con-ium." I had heard of it, yes, though all I knew of the place was that it lay somewhere in the north and was considered a large and thriving town—a proper *civitas* in the grand old style. Why anyone would want to hold a council there was beyond me, but if it got my father out of the house and gave me a few days free from the incessant demands of the magistrate's office, I supported the idea entirely. Placing the message atop the pile of those he would read first, I set about sorting the rest.

"This is serious business," my father declared after he had returned and settled back into his chair. He picked up the red-edged message. "It's from Esico—the procurator himself will be there."

"It doesn't say that," I pointed out. "You knew about this already?"

"A marketplace rumor only, and you know how unreliable such things are. But this . . ." He tapped the summons with fingertip. "This confirms it." He gazed at the message again, nodding thoughtfully. "It could not have come at a better time." Then, looking up, he said, "I want you to go, too."

"*Me!*" The suggestion took me by surprise. My hopes for a few blissful days of freedom began to shrivel on the vine. "But, I cannot—" I protested, hardly knowing where to begin.

"You can and you will," he told me. Then seeing the stricken look on my face, he added, "Aurelia, listen, it's not good for you to shut yourself away behind these four walls all day. I want you to get out and see something of the world. Viroconium is a big town; they have markets—three of them. One just for clothes and shoes alone. You could buy a new pair of shoes." Unwilling to be bribed so easily, I crossed my arms over my chest. Tullius waved the summons at me. "See here, it is to be an official conclave—and those are rare. It's a chance to meet some important people, learn how things are done, gain some experience. It will be good for you."

"I don't want to meet important people. I want to stay here."

"Out of the question," he replied, dismissing the suggestion without a second thought. "I'm going and you're going with me. That is the end of it."

He picked up another scrap of parchment from the carefully arranged piles before him and began reading.

I watched him for a moment, then said, "Why?"

"Hmm?" he said without glancing up. "Why what?"

"Why is it out of the question?"

"Because I want you there with me." He put down the letter and looked at me. "Aurelia, my heart, the last thing I want is for you to sit here idling your life away in fusty little Venta with your nose stuck in a book."

"I like to read—is that a crime now?" Truly, I did like to read. In fact, I owned two books: one a history of Rome left in the house by a previous magistrate, and the other given to my mother by an aunt or someone as a wedding gift—a collection of Jesu's sayings and the Gospel of Mark the Apostle. I cherished both.

"You know what I mean," he said. "You were born for better things."

"Oh, was I?" I snapped, fire leaping up in me. "Then why was I born deaf? Tell me that!"

"You're not deaf," he sighed. We'd had this discussion many times before. "Hard of hearing is not deaf, darling girl. An impairment, perhaps—"

"Definitely!" I sneered. "An *impairment*, definitely. You don't know how hard it is."

I stormed from the room. Was I being unfair? Disrespectful? Selfish? Perhaps. Yes. But remember, I was only fourteen summers old and still very unsure of myself—all the more since my partial deafness made closed spaces and strange places with unfamiliar people very difficult for me. I had to concentrate so hard on everything just to understand what was being said, and often as not I mistook what I thought I heard and came away confused.

Attending a noisy conclave, whatever *that* was, could not but deepen the humiliation I felt almost daily. I liked our little Venta—I knew the people and they knew me. Safe behind the walls of our southern town, I could come and go as I pleased without forever having to apologize for or explain my lack of hearing. It was a place where everything was familiar and people accepted me for who I was.

All I wanted was to be left alone to do . . . what? I don't know. If you had asked me then, I could not have named what it was I wanted to do—but traveling a hundred miles and more to a boring old council meeting in a strange town somewhere up north was not it.

Something else I did not know—that the person who went to Viroconium would not be the one who returned.

2

TWO DAYS AFTER RECEIVING THE SUMMONS, I climbed into the cart beside my father and we rolled out onto the road. As we passed through the town gates, I turned for a receding look at Venta. Augustus was standing there, watching over our departure. I raised my hand in farewell then set my face to the low hills on the far horizon. I knew nothing of what the days ahead might bring—who does? Yet, even though I was going under duress, I determined to make an effort to please my father in the hope that his promise of new shoes might be fulfilled—and, if possible, improved to include a brooch or new comb.

We reached Glevum the evening of the next day, and stayed with a talkative old woman my father knew from previous visits; she offered lodging to travelers for a few denarii and a little company. Early the next morning, she gave us good broth and rusks to see us on our way, and we joined the travelling group already assembling in the square.

While my father hurried off to meet with the other officials, I walked around to stretch my legs and observe our fellow travelers. My futile attempt to remain unseen and out of the way failed when I happened to catch the eye of Coran, the proconsul's chief assistant. A large, overgrown oaf with a shaggy mane of brown hair, he was strutting around, shouting at people, and giving every appearance of being in charge of organizing the traveling party, if not the whole city. I had met him once or twice before and found him a puffed-up, pompous prig. He feigned surprise at seeing me and marched over to demand an explanation. "What are *you* doing here?"

19

I touched my ear to remind him that I did not hear very well. He drew breath and shouted, "I asked what you think you are doing here?" He crossed his arms in demand of an answer.

"Waiting for my father."

"You are not part of the proconsul's delegation."

"I am."

"No, you're *not*," he insisted. "Women are not allowed."

That remark was meant to sting, but I ignored it and looked away across the yard at the other carriages. "What's it about—this mighty gathering that's got everyone so ruffled?"

Happy to possess superior knowledge, he intoned, "Procurator Constantine has called for a general conclave."

"I know that already, Coran," I huffed. "That's why we're here. What's the gathering *for*?"

"Something must be done about the Saecsens in the north," he sniffed, as if this should be obvious. "Funding the army, building defenses, the usual things delegates find to talk about." He gave me a raw, disapproving look. "All the important people will be there—but not you." He made a show of looking around, then said, "Where's Augustus? Why isn't he here?"

I shrugged. "Ask Augustus."

"You think you're such a smart little twit," he sneered. "But you have no part in this and you're *not* going with us."

I gave him a fishy smile. "That will be news to my father. He wants me there. I'm helping him at the conclave."

This last part wasn't true, of course, as it was an open question whether I would be any help at all, or merely a hindrance and burden.

Anyway, I could see by the look on Coran's cocky face that he did not believe me. "Ha! A big help you'll be."

I touched my ear again. "What? I didn't hear that."

He made to reply, then gave up and stomped away.

"Good to see you, too, Coran," I called after him. "I do so enjoy our little conversations."

The arrogance of the self-important toad left a bad smell in the air and I walked around to put it behind me. Across the yard a two-horse carriage rumbled into the square. A single passenger got out and exchanged a word with the drivers, who climbed down and headed off to join other drivers idling nearby, leaving the young man to mind the horses. The carriage was a large, stately vehicle—much nicer than anything seen around Venta—so I sidled over for a closer look.

"Are you going to the conclave?" called the youth when he saw me approaching. Dressed in a faded green tunic tied with a leather horse strap around his waist, he regarded me as if expecting a reply.

"Are you talking to me?" I asked.

"I am," he said.

He mumbled some reply and I touched my ear and explained that I did not hear well. He moved closer and spoke more loudly. "I asked if you were going to Viroconium for the conclave."

"I am," I said. "Are you?"

"*They're* going," he said, nodding toward Civitas House. "I'm not." He looked me up and down. "Why you?"

I explained that I was accompanying my father who had been summoned by the proconsul.

"Who's your father, then? Somebody special?"

"Pardon?"

"I asked if your father was somebody very important?"

"Tullius Paulinus, Magistrate of Venta—that's my father."

He accepted my explanation with a gloomy nod. "Well, I suppose it's to lend more weight to the cause."

Not certain I had heard right, I asked, "*Claws*, did you say?"

"Cause," he corrected. "The cause of southern sovereignty." At my empty look, he added, "Sovereignty—for the south, you know."

I did not know what he meant, but the way he said it made it sound like something I could do little about and could care less. A muddled sound drew my attention just then and I glanced across the square as a troop of legionaries rode through the gate: eight soldiers—four burly veterans, three lean young legionaries, and one who looked like a commander of some kind—splendid in their armor: helmets gleaming, swords and breastplates burnished bright, leather shined.

"It looks like they're going, too," I observed, indicating the soldiers as they dismounted and led their horses to the water trough.

"Looks like it." He sighed heavily. "Everybody's going but me."

The surly youth turned to his duties, leaving me to meander around the square until my father returned.

Among those assembled in the square were four merchants along with their servants, one or two each, and two big wagons to haul their goods and supplies. The wagons were covered with heavy cloth to protect their wares and prevented me from seeing what kind of merchants they might be. All in all, it was a sizeable delegation and I warmed to the idea of being part of it.

At last, the proconsul and the other officials—my father among them—emerged from the Civitas House and as soon as a few last provisions were taken on, we set off. Proconsul Esico and his wife—Mona, I think was her name—traveled in the elegant carriage; two other magistrates and their servants shared one; the insufferable Coran and two others of his ilk had the use of a third; and my father and I rode in a fourth carriage along with another magistrate from the southeast somewhere—but I did not catch his name, nor much of what he said in his low, soft voice. The soldiers on horseback led the way and most of the servants went on foot alongside the wagons or piled on top, taking it in turn to sit on a mounting board, or behind one of the drivers.

I know everyone complains about the roads and how far they have fallen from earlier times. Sorry to say, it is true. There are holes and gaps where weather has eroded or, worse, folk have looted stones for building; great stretches overgrown by brambles and shrubs; ruined bridges, washed-out fords, and so on. The old roads *are* a shameful disgrace. But the new roads are no better, and in many ways and most places very much worse. Anyone who has ever had reason to roam beyond the fields he can see from his own rooftop knows this only too well. So, we traveled by the old roads wherever we could. Though it can make the journey longer it is often faster in the end.

I will not relate how we fared along the way—only to say that the weather held good and we suffered no mishap. Not even river crossings and fords slowed us overmuch, and we arrived safe, tired—I could have slept standing up—but, all in all, no worse for the ordeal. That said, no one was more glad than me when the carriage rolled through the great wooden gates and into the largest town I had ever seen—so big I could not take it in all at once. I grew dizzy trying to understand what I saw and vowed that the next day I would explore as much of it as I could.

Once through the southernmost gate of Viroconium, we proceeded up a wide street lined on each side with houses, and finally rolled to a stop in a small square. Another delegation had arrived before us—we had met them on the road a day or two earlier—so we drew up beside them and gladly quit the carriages. The merchants of our travelling party made their farewells and moved on. Shaking off my fatigue, I stretched my legs and looked around. We were soon hailed by a town official who, along with some of his men, had been charged with arranging lodging for all those attending the council.

A busy little man, he welcomed us in the name of Prefect Fotunato and delivered his prepared address of instructions in a stilted singsong fashion of which I made out little; he then passed among the delegates, handing out little purses containing coins. "Your delegate *per diem*," he said, then made his farewell—he clearly could not wait to see the back of us—and left us in the care of several barefoot boys hired to lead us to our various lodgings. Our little group broke up; some went one way, some another. My father and I were led by a lad with a malformed hand who spoke with such an odd inflection I could make out only one word in three.

Still, our young guide was smart and eager to please, and started off at a pace. Up the street and down a narrow lane, he soon brought us to a low house with a pitched roof. Modest in appearance, it was an old house built in the Roman style, with many rooms opening off a small central square enclosed by stone walls and an iron gate. The gate was open and we were ushered inside to a tiled courtyard not unlike the one we had at home—only this one had a stone bench beside a tiny pool with fish in it.

The owners of the house—a balding man named Seno with a white beard and a fat, smiling wife named Betrys, I think he said—welcomed us with a sort of stiff formality I expect he thought suited the occasion. Aware that they were hosting a dignitary, albeit a very minor one, the two seemed overanxious to please. Seno gave us sweetened wine, and Betrys produced a plate of good salty olives stuffed with almonds that she said had come all the way from Lusitania—wherever that might be—and a serving girl passed around a little plate of fluffy sweets made of honey and the whites of eggs. Apparently, Seno was a trader of some sort—cattle, maybe, or grain.

We sipped our wine politely and my father employed his well-honed talent for winning the friendship of strangers. I just tried to keep up with the conversation. The wine and hospitality did their work and soon everyone was smiling and laughing like old friends. Seno and Betrys did appear glad for the company as they lived alone with only a servant or two and were more than happy to have fresh victims to hear the local gossip about various scandals and events in the region. Later, we shared a good meal of grilled beef on skewers and beans stewed in beer with various seasonings, and then we were treated to a warm room and clean, straw-filled pallets nestled in wooden frames. I pulled the coverlet over me that night and slept better than I expected, in a strange bed, in a strange house, in a strange new town.

Indeed, I slept so well that I awoke the next morning to find my father already up, washed, and dressed; he had broken fast and was ready to be about the day's business. It fairly chafed him to wait for me, but I dragged myself out of my warm nest, groomed myself as best I could without a brush or mirror, snatched at barley cake from the little plate and followed him out into the street.

"Where are we going?"

"Anywhere you'd like," he replied. "This is our day to see the town. First, of course, I'd like to find the basilica where the conclave will meet. After that"—he waved a hand to the street stretching before us— "we'll go wherever the fancy takes us."

Now, I know what you're thinking. Londinium is said to be an enormous great *civitas*—and maybe it is. But in those days Viroconium still boasted a basilica, a forum, and even a bathhouse. There were two fine churches and three market squares—one for food, one for craftsmen of every kind, one for livestock. The town had expanded far beyond the large garrison outpost of former times so that there were many streets outside the protecting walls and all of them filled with houses and shops and taverns and squares, and the whole was surrounded by farms and fields in every direction to the horizon over the river flatlands. Just the thought of living in such a place made me giddy, yet I could feel myself beginning to appreciate the bracing charm of the place.

As I say, with so much to see, so much to discover, I began to understand why my father had insisted that I come with him. Together we strode out with quick, eager steps. Tullius was his best self. Lighthearted, engaging with the locals as he inquired the way, he showed a side rarely seen among the citizens he served. Amidst crowds of strangers, the worthy magistrate became an enthusiastic and carefree explorer. We passed churches and food stalls, craftsmen and vendors of every kind until we turned a corner and found ourselves in a wide street leading directly to the basilica. I spied its enormous red-tiled roof even before we came in sight of the great entrance doors. Though the building was old and in obvious need of repair, it had not yet been dismantled and its stones carted away for building material. The basilica still held pride of place in the crowded center of the town, not far from the baths and almost directly opposite the spacious, stone-paved square of the forum. "This is where the convocation will meet," Tullius told me, indicating the enormous edifice. "We have to see it."

"Do we?" I whined. "I'd rather go to the market."

"A quick look, that's all," he promised. "It won't take but a moment."

We moved on and entered the forum to find that many other official delegations had already arrived and, in tents and curious lean-to booths, had made camp. Many were dressed in ways we would have laughed at back home. For example, many of the women wore their hair in intricate braided coils, or swept back to hang in gathered tendrils. The men, for the most part, shaved either the back of their heads, or the sides; the better, I suppose, to show off their long braids. For the most part, the women wore mantles that left their lower legs bare, and others—men and women both—wore long, loose, floppy shirts and breeches in garish colors cinched with wide leather belts. I saw some displaying big bronze or silver brooches on oversized cloaks and, here and there, the gleam of a gold armband, bracelet, or necklace. I'd never seen such a vivid array in one place. By this, I guessed that they had come from more remote regions and, like me, had the look of folk half dazed by all they saw around them.

Upon reaching the enormous building we saw that the huge wooden doors were unbolted and open wide. Four paces inside I stopped to gape openmouthed at the largest room I had ever seen: a vast empty space—large enough for a horse race, I imagine—with a vaulted roof so high above the floor it made me dizzy looking up at it. The floor was paved with cut-and-fitted limestone the color of butter, stretching from one distant wall to the other. In the center of this limestone field a low wooden platform had been erected, and this was where the delegates were gathering in clusters.

Two men stood inside the entrance—officials in red-edged cloaks charged with aiding those arriving for the conclave. We approached and my father identified himself and asked where the conclave would meet. One of the officials pointed to the distant end of the great room. We made our way toward the place where we found perhaps a dozen or so men had gathered—our proconsul Esico and Coran among them. They greeted my father and, taking him by the elbow, led him away to meet some of the others.

I trailed after, gamely determined to take in as much as I could. But with hundreds of people all speaking and shouting to one another inside the stone walls of this enormous barn, it sounded like the roar of an ocean to me and made it impossible to make sense of a single thing that was said. Even so, it was clear enough to me that my father was being welcomed here and afforded genuine esteem by men who were reckoned of some account by those who reckoned such things. I didn't need to hear to know a matter of some importance, even urgency, was being discussed; the lowered brows, taut jaws, and creases of concern on the circle of faces told me all that and more.

All at once, the group broke up. A decision, it seemed, had been made. Tullius put out a hand to me and led me off to one side. "It was proposed to send a small delegation to see the procurator." He indicated the group of men he had been talking to. "They just received word that Constantine agreed to meet—in private." Before I could think what this meant, he added, "I've been invited to join them." Just as I was beginning to think that I might also meet this exalted person, my father put his head close and confided, "Constantine is not in the town. He's lodging at a villa outside the walls. It's a fair distance away, so we must leave at once."

My heart sank. The thought of spending the day thumping around in a carriage on a rutted road with a gaggle of pompous officials and another incomprehensible meeting at the end of it was not in any way my idea of a pleasant day out. I was on the point of launching a protest when he quickly added, "I'm sorry, Aurelia, but you'll have to stay here."

"I'm not to go with you?"

Mistaking my expression of relief for disappointment, he said, "Just think—you can spend the day looking around all the shops and craftsmen's stalls, like I promised. Maybe even buy those new shoes. Whatever you wanted."

"Well, maybe," I said, as if willing to be persuaded.

"I wouldn't do this, if it weren't so very important. The chance to make our case directly to the procurator may never come again. I'm sorry to abandon you, dear heart—I really am." He gave me an apologetic smile and put his hand to his belt and pulled out his *per diem* purse. "Here, take this," he said, fishing out a handful of silver coins and some bronze. "There should be enough for you to buy something to eat and anything else that takes your eye."

He poured the coins into my hand. Then, unfastening the silver brooch he always wore when on official business—an imposing wreath featuring laurel leaves with, oddly, blades or spearheads, with a square yellow stone in the center—he pinned it to my cloak and put his hands on my shoulders. "There," he said. "You are now a deputy of the Magistrate of Venta, and are hereby granted the freedom of the *civitas* of Viroconium, as decreed by the procurator. Now," he said, smiling, "go and enjoy the day."

I looked at the brooch and though I'd seen it a thousand times and more, I'd never been allowed to wear it. Suddenly, I felt as if I might be a magistrate indeed.

"I'll meet you at our lodging when we return," he said, eyeing me with concern. "Do you think you can find your way back alone?"

"Of course," I replied, feeling my newly gifted authority, "I'm not a child."

"No, you're not," he agreed, kissing me on the forehead. "Tell Seno and Betrys that I will return this evening to take supper with you." He smiled. "God willing, I'll have much to tell you then."

I gave him a kiss and tucked the purse under my belt. Tullius was already deep in conversation once more by the time I reached the wooden dais in the middle of the floor. I glanced back and gave him a little wave, which he returned, then made good my escape.

3

MONEY IN HAND and the day suddenly open in front of me, I decided to make the most of the shops and stalls I had glimpsed so briefly along the way before returning to our lodging house to meet my father on his return. With no better plan, I meandered here and there wherever fancy took me. Down one street and up another, I wandered around the town and soon caught myself imagining what it would be like to live in this house or that one, trying to choose the place that best appealed to me.

Upon turning one corner, I found myself at the entrance to a market filled with shaggy cattle and odd little black-nosed sheep with curly horns. I had a brief look, but the noise and stink did not invite me to loiter, so I moved on.

At the end of another street, I spied a church—so grand and big and faced with pale stone, it made Venta's tidy red brick structure look like a crossroad shrine. Just the sight alone lifted the heart and, since there was no one to prevent me, I went inside. It was empty as an eggshell and just as clean. New swept, even in the corners, and the walls freshly whitewashed, it smelled like churches everywhere: pungent incense and holy oil. The stone altar on a low dais at the far end of the room was bare and unmarked, save for a carving of a vine with bunches of grapes and leaves entwined around the legs. The real treasure lay in the center of the floor beneath the domed ceiling: a mosaic of tiny *tessera* in red and white, brown and black, forming pictures of the Holy Family, angels, and Jesu in his torments on the cross. Oh, I had seen mosaics before, on the floors of dining rooms in villas and houses of the wealthy, but this one was easily the most amazing thing of its kind anywhere—thousands of tiny tiles covering the entire floor beneath the high-vaulted roof.

How long I stood there gazing at the intricate designs, I cannot say, but finally stirred myself when two women came in to sweep—though there was nothing at all to whisk away—saying a small prayer before moving on.

More paths and lanes, more houses, and people in all kinds of dress: town folk in colored mantles and old-fashioned tunics and robes; country folk in rougher homespun; and some from, as I supposed, the wilder places wearing elaborate trousers and cloaks of many colors, and animal skins. Just seeing them all going about their affairs as if they saw nothing odd in this made me feel like I knew nothing about anything beyond my front door. A few days outside Venta's protecting walls and I was seeing things I never imagined. Who were these people? Where had they all come from? How much more was there to see?

Some while later I encountered another market. This one, however, was kinder to my senses, for instead of animals it was filled with artisans making and selling craftwork adornments of various kinds: elaborate jewelry—necklaces, earrings, arm bands, rings—many decorated with glass, polished stones, amber, and one or two with tiny pearls that must have cost a fortune. There were ornate cloak pins in bronze, silver, gold—shaped like animal heads, or birds, or the strange twisting, swirling tribal designs; also buckles for belts or horse trappings; decorative discs and bosses for shields and such of every description. Like the town fool, I wandered through the lanes filled with tiny shops and covered stalls, gawping everything until my legs threatened to give out.

Besotted by all that passed my wondering gaze, it wasn't until I found myself standing in front of a shoemaker's stall that I remembered I had money—at least enough for a new pair of shoes. Under the gaze of the watchful cobbler, I began examining the wares in earnest—looking at one pair after another. Finally, when I had seen enough, I decided on a pair of the high-laced variety made of supple leather attached to sturdy soles. These I waved to attract the shoemaker's attention. "Yes? Yes?" he said brusquely. "You decided. At last you want to buy, eh?"

"Yes," I told him. "I like this pair, and—"

"You like them so . . ." The rest was lost in mumbles.

"Sorry? I didn't hear that."

"I said"—he raised his voice—"you like them, so buy them. I'm a busy man."

"I'd like to try them on first."

He rolled his eyes and shoved them at me. I quickly slipped my foot into one and decided it fit well enough. "How much are they?"

"Ten denarii," he said.

"Ten!" I was shocked. That was twice what I would expect to pay in Venta. "Too much," I blurted.

"Buy them, don't buy them," he huffed. "Ten denarii."

I had encountered this type of merchant once or twice before, so I said, "Five—I'll give you five."

He snatched the shoes from my hand. "The price is ten. Stop wasting my time."

"Shoes like that cost five in Venta," I pointed out.

"So, go buy them in Venta." He made a motion to wave me away. I watched him replace the shoes on the peg over the bar of his stall.

"Seven," I said.

He turned back, shoes in hand. "Eight denarii and we discuss it no more." He looked at me and then at the shoes. "I suppose you want a bag."

I nodded, and with a snort of derision, he disappeared behind a curtain at the back of his stall and returned with a bag of woven grass of the kind I had seen in the hands of other shoppers I'd passed. I counted out the coins from my purse, and he shoved the bag at me, took the money, and turned away without so much as a thank you. The rudeness of the shoemaker stole the fun out of my purchase, but at least I had succeeded in bargaining down the asking price. Somewhat bruised by the exchange, I threaded my way out from among the tangled labyrinth of stalls and booths.

I must have lingered among the shops and stalls far longer than I knew, for when I finally emerged onto the street once more, the clouds in the sky were thickening and the sun had passed midday. Footsore and flagging, I decided to start back to our lodging house. Only then did I realize I had wandered without regard to where I was going and now had no idea where I might be. It occurred to me that it might be quickest to return to the basilica and make my way from there. All roads in Viroconium lead to the basilica, the largest and tallest structure in the town. I asked directions of a salt seller and, following his advice, was soon back at the forum. The area around the great edifice was busy with late arrivals to the conclave and local merchants hawking their wares to the newcomers. I paused a moment to reorient myself. And as I stood trying to locate the right street, I felt someone bump into me from behind, almost knocking me over. In the same instant, the grass bag was snatched from my hand. Startled, I spun around to see a skinny-legged boy in a dirty tunic running away with my shoes, and something else: my purse.

I gave chase, but the boy was nimble and quick—and he knew right where he was going. He flew across the plaza and into the forum and was quickly out of sight. I stalked around for a time, searching among the many alcoves and tents for the thief, anger and frustration mounting with every step. I was on the point of giving up, when I spied my bag lying beside a pillar. With a quick look around, I grabbed it up. Likely, in his flight, he had discarded the bag. The money and the thief had vanished, but at least I had my shoes.

Well, that is what I thought until I opened the bag and found that although it did indeed contain shoes, they were *not* the shoes I had purchased and tried on, but an entirely different pair! The disagreeable shoemaker had switched the ones I'd bought with a cheaper—and, to my mind, uglier—kind. The ones in the bag were thicker, heavier, more like something a stone mason or farmer would wear to work, not me.

Lied to, stolen from, my heart pounding from the chase and from rage, my ears ringing and head aching, and frustrated beyond endurance by my loss, the last threads of my frayed composure snapped, and I sat down against the column in the forum portico and let go the tears. The forum, the activity in the square, the basilica, the world entire dissolved in a floodtide of misery as I sat there sniveling— wondering why I had ever come to this horrible place and vowing never to go anywhere else ever again.

"What is the matter, child?" A woman's voice floated down from somewhere above me—loud enough, but with the odd, singing lilt of the north that I have since come to know so well. Then, such speech was new to me and it took me a moment to understand . . . *Child*?

What! Nearly fifteen summers old—and it was that long since anyone had called me *child*. I was jerked back to awareness. I smudged away the tears with the palms of my hands. "A beggar boy just stole my purse," I blurted before I'd even so much as glanced up.

"Well, perhaps he needed it more than you," came the reply.

The answer surprised me. Looking up, I took in her features for the first time to see a handsome woman—young still, with fair, even features. Dark eyes beneath arching, gull-wing brows gave her an intelligent and thoughtful look. Some might even have called her beautiful. Her long dark hair—impeccably braided and arranged in artful coils—was adorned with tiny gold pins. Her mien and manner, and her rich blue gown of costly material, spoke of wealth and rank. "Do you know what I think?" she asked.

I shook my head and she replied, "I think you are far too pretty to be sitting here crying in the public square where every cold eye can see you."

Pretty is not a word I often hear when folk speak about me. So, for the second time in as many breaths, I was brought out of myself. *Who is this woman? Why is she even speaking to me? Did I hear her aright? What does she want?* Suspicion raised its chary head.

She said something more, but I lost the words and, touching my ear, explained, "I'm a little deaf. But, if I can see your lips—"

"I understand." She turned her face to me and repeated, a little louder: "I said I admire your hair." She waved a manicured hand to one of my many wayward strands. "Such a wonderful color. I don't think I've ever seen red like that." Then, indicating the bundle in my lap, she asked, "What have you there?"

Full wary of this stranger now, I held the bag a little tighter. "Shoes."

"Oh, let's see them."

I carefully peeled back the coarse-woven bag to reveal my unhappy purchase. "Oh, now, well—" Her look betrayed surprise—I suppose because I'd bought something so unbecoming. "I have something similar—for working. Very sturdy." Then, "I love the smell of new leather, don't you?" She then turned her attention to me once more. "Your accent—I'm not familiar with it. Where are you from?"

Although she seemed friendly enough, I did not know her and could not imagine why such an obviously wealthy woman should take any interest in me. I got up to leave. "I have to go," I told her.

"Yes, so do I." She did not move, but stood before me, barring my way. "The brooch you are wearing—"

"It's not mine," I said quickly. "It's my father's. He gave it to me for the day." I turned away and started off.

Ignoring my rudeness, she fell into step beside me. "A brooch like that—he must be very important."

"He's Magistrate of Venta Silurum," I told her, hoping that his title would lend me a little authority.

"Venta... Venta Silurum, did you say?"

"It's a small town in the south. You won't have heard of it." *Why was I telling her this?* "Please, I should go."

"Your father—what is his name?"

"Tullius," I replied, edging past her. "Tullius Paulinus. You won't have heard of him, either."

"No, you are right about that." She turned with me. "But I expect my husband knows him. He knows everyone." She looked me up and down. "You're here for the conclave, aren't you."

Like everyone else in town, she knew about the conclave. My wariness increased. *What did she want from me?*

"We're here for the conclave, too—my husband and I, that is." Before I could reply, she hurried on. "My husband is Aridius Verica, Legate of Deva. Do you know Deva?"

Not certain I had heard correctly, I shook my head anyway. "Please, I must go."

"So must I," she said. "I shall accompany you—part way, at least. A young girl cannot be too careful in a place like this."

How well I knew it! Still, I hesitated. But, since there did not seem to be any way to dissuade her, we started from the forum together. "I'm Helena. What is your name?"

"Aurelia."

"What an enchanting name. I like it."

We made our way through the crowded forum. Upon reaching the entrance, a sudden dizziness made me sway on my feet. I put a hand to my head and paused. My self-appointed companion regarded me narrowly. "Have you eaten anything at all today, Aurelia?"

In my wandering investigation of the town, I had not thought to stop for a meal—not even a sip of water.

"Well, have you?"

Too embarrassed to answer, I shook my head.

"Ah, then your luck is with you," she said breezily. "As it happens, I was just on my way to sample the offerings in the market. I want you to join me." Seeing my hesitation, she added, "It will be my pleasure, and I will take it as a personal insult if you refuse. Have you ever had a pie?"

"P-pie? Is that what you said? I don't think so."

"Then that is where we will begin," she decided. "I know a man in Baker's Lane who makes the most wonderful pies. Don't look so forlorn—you'll like it." She gave me a smile which, combined with the softness of her mouth and the warmth of her eyes, told me kindness was as natural to her as breathing. Any resistance I had maintained until then simply melted away. "This way—it isn't far. Come along."

Without waiting for an answer, she started off and I fell into step beside her. From that moment, our fate was sealed.

4

LEAVING THE FORUM, we walked out onto the street and soon came to an area of tall houses, each one higher than the next. At the end of this street, we turned down a narrow lane lined either side with cloth and leather awnings of craftsmen and merchants. Helena moved easily among them, and even exchanged a word or two of greeting with some of those we passed. We rounded a corner into another narrow street and stopped outside one of the first booths we came to: a bakery. Much like the ones I knew in Venta, this one had a wide opening onto the street to reveal a room containing a table with a stone top, walls lined with shelves and, against the far wall, a large hot oven. Inside, a fellow in a white linen tunic and a sweat-stained brown cloth cap wrestled a mound of soft dough at the flour-dusted table. On the shelves were loaves of bread and many another thing he'd made. One entire wall of the room was taken up with the oven, next to which was a neat stack of firewood. The heavenly scent of baking bread wafting out of that shop brought the water to my mouth.

A wide sort of rail, or bar, fronted the open stall where patrons stood to conduct their business. A woman with an infant on her hip was just concluding a purchase and, as we stepped beneath the awning, the woman moved off and we took her place. A young girl stood at the rail to make the sales and collect the money. She dropped the woman's coins into a little box and looked up at us with a gap-toothed smile.

"Hello, you," Helena said to the girl, then called to the man, "Hello, Petus! Do you remember me?"

35

"Papa! Your friend ith here!" called the girl. Turning back to us, she said, "I'm Feli-thia." The youngster's lisp was pronounced and I had to work to understand her.

"Of course, you are. I remember now," Helena assured her. "Hello, Felicia. You are helping your father, I see." Again, I marveled at her easy way with people. "One day I hope I have a daughter like you to help me. Tell me, is he treating you well?"

The girl, who could only have been seven or eight summers at most, beamed proudly. "He tell-th me everything," she replied. "All his theecreths."

"Not *all* my secrets," called the baker, glancing up from the stuff he was kneading. "Not yet." He grinned and wiped his hands on his tunic. "Oh, Helena, it is you. Back again so soon?"

"Hello, Petus," she replied nicely. "Busy as ever, I see."

Stepping around the table, he came to the rail to greet us. "You're well, I hope. And your good man? Atticus, is it?"

"Aridius," she corrected.

"Ah, yes. What brings you to our town this time?"

"Official business—as usual. The conclave this time. There are delegations from all over, I'm told. You must have heard about it."

Baker Petus made a face. "True, true. Serious business, it seems. They say Constantine himself is coming—maybe even here already. All I know is that the town is overrun with so many important people you cannot move about the streets without being jostled by a prefect or vicarius. They've been arriving for a week already—and for a week, I'm working night and day. Not a moment to sit down."

"You complain about the work," Helena chided lightly. "But never about the money. Why is that?"

Petus put back his head and laughed. "Is this the wife of Legate Verica? Or is it *my* wife who speaks to me like this?" He seemed to notice me standing silently beside my benefactress. "And who is this you have with you?"

"Forgive me," replied Helena smoothly. "This is my new friend, Aurelia—all the way from Venta. She is newly arrived here with her father for the great conclave—"

"Like everyone else." He glanced a smile at me and rubbed his flour-dusted hands. "What can I get for you? What would you like?"

By way of reply, Helena addressed the baker's daughter. "Tell me,

Felicia—what do you have for two hungry ladies who have not had a single bite to eat all day?"

"The pieth," the girl replied without hesitation. "They're my favor-ith."

"You're a mind reader, Felicia." Helena laughed. "That's just what I was thinking. Two pies, then. What kind do you have?"

The girl's round face clouded in thought. She turned to her father and whispered, "What wath it?"

"Meat with onion," the baker whispered back.

The girl repeated what her father had told her, and looked at us expectantly.

"It sounds splendid," Helena told her. "One for each of us, then."

"An excellent choice," declared the baker. He nodded to his daughter who scurried off to select two freshly baked pies.

A pie, as I soon discovered, is a pouch made of a kind of puffy flat bread; shaped like a half moon and wrapped around some kind of filling—chopped pork, I think. These crisp parcels are brushed with fat or oil and baked until golden brown. Helena took one and passed the other to me and, as I can now faithfully avow, it was delicious. Then again, ravenous as I was, I could have happily devoured the whole pig raw.

Even so, my first tentative bite led me to believe that I had never tasted anything so good in my entire life. I had wolfed down half the pie before I knew it and forced myself to slow down and not to gorge.

"I expect we're going to be here a few more days at least," Helena was saying as she put coins into the box. "No doubt I'll be seeing you again very soon. God with you both, my friends."

We retraced our steps to the street, pausing only to buy a cup of wine mixed with honey water from a vintner. A little further along we found a small stone fountain, sadly dry, and perched on the rim to finish our pies and sip the cool, sweetened wine. Helena maintained a friendly chatter as we ate, and I felt better for having confided in her. At one point, she said, "Tell me about your family." She remembered to raise her voice when not facing me.

"My family?" I said, and shrugged. "What would you like to know?"

"Anything," she said. "Your mother. Is she here, too? Any brothers or sisters?"

"It's only my father and me. I don't have any brothers or sisters. My mother died when I was little."

"I'm sorry to hear it. You must miss her."

"It was a long time ago." I took a last drink of the sweet wine and looked into the empty cup.

Helena offered a thoughtful nod. We finished our little meal in silence, then returned the wooden cups to the vendor and thanked him. We continued on, wending our way back to the basilica. "What will you do now?" she asked as we passed along stalls selling lamps and candles.

"Now?" I shrugged. "Go back to the lodging house and wait for my father. He should return soon."

We talked of other things and arrived back at the basilica just as a party of delegates swept into the square. We moved to one side and scanned these new arrivals as they passed, but I did not see Tullius. We were still searching among them when someone called out, "Helena! Helena!"

A tall, well-made man strode quickly toward us. As he came nearer, I was surprised to see how young he was; his old-fashioned clothes made him seem older than his years. "Ari!" she shouted. Then, to me, she said, "It is my husband."

He joined us and was welcomed with a quick embrace and light kiss from his wife. Helena, taking his arm, turned him to address me. "Dearest, I want you to meet my new friend Aurelia. Now, her hearing troubles her, so speak up." To me, she said, "Aurelia, this is my husband Aridius."

His dark curly hair framed a broad, open face. "At your service." He gave me a little bow. "Aurelia—what an enchanting name—I'm happy to meet you."

That the Legate of Deva Vitrix was a most imposing man, few would deny. Not the most handsome, no—his nose was too big, and his hair, thick and tightly curled as it was, had seen neither brush nor comb that day. He had large hands that were always in motion, and his voice was a little too soft. But his dark eyes were quick and intelligent, and he stood a head taller than most anyone else likely to meet him.

He looked around quickly. "There goes Gaius Marcellus. I must speak to him a moment—"

But Helena held firm. "Oh, no you don't. You've had all day to speak to him, it is our turn now." She nodded to me. "Aurelia is here for the conclave with her father. I told her you would know him."

"Oh?" He stopped and looked at his wife, then at me. "Who is your father?"

I told him. "Tullius Paulinus . . . ," he repeated, arching his eyebrows in surprise. "The Magistrate of Venta? *He* is your father? Yes, I know him—not as well as I'd like, perhaps. But better than I did this morning. How not? I just spent the entire day with him."

"Where were you all day then?" demanded Helena, a slight edge creeping into her voice.

"At a private meeting," he said quickly. "A group of regional administrators went out to the villa of Maglus Tegern—the wine merchant. Constantine is staying at the villa and we wanted to meet with him in person to present our special concerns." Aridius glanced at me. "Proconsul Esico and your father were with us. We broke bread together." To me, he added, "Good man, your father. I like him very much."

"There, you see?" said Helena, giving my hand a squeeze. "I told you my husband would know Tullius." Indicating the group passing on down the street, she added, "But I didn't see him with you."

"No." Her husband shook his head. "He and some of the others stayed behind to speak privately with the procurator—about more local matters, I should think. Still, I don't expect them to be far behind."

That was some comfort at least, but not as much as I had hoped. I thanked Helena again for the pie and drink, made my farewell, and started away. I had not gone far when I heard Aridius shout, "Aurelia!"

I turned to see them still standing in the street, watching me. "Where are you lodging?"

"With Betrys and Seno," I replied.

"Do you know the way?"

"I think so." I paused and indicated the way by which I had come.

"Wait." Aridius looked around, then, raising a finger, said, "One moment." Some of the group from the villa meeting were lingering nearby, and he called out as he approached them.

I glanced a question at Helena. "Just wait," she told me. "He knows what he's doing."

I watched as he spoke to a thin young man with the scraggly

beginnings of a beard and a large cloth bag slung over one shoulder. They exchanged a word, then Aridius returned with the youth in tow.

"This is Rhin—one of Prefect Alban's men," he said when they had joined us. "He will conduct you safely home." He handed the youth a coin and said, "Make sure you see her in the door. Understood?"

The fellow peered at the coin dismissively, but tucked it quickly away. "Understood." Turning to me, he held out a hand indicating the direction. "It's this way. Follow me."

I thanked the two for their help and we parted, pledging to see one another again soon. The shadows were already thickening, melding into one another as we started off. "Do you know my lodging place?"

Rhin said something I didn't catch.

"What?"

Without looking at me, he repeated what he'd said, but with the street noise and his mumbling speech, I still couldn't make sense of it. I asked him to say it again. He stopped walking and turned to face me. "What are you—deaf?"

I cupped my hand to my ear in my habitual gesture, and said simply, "Yes, I am."

He rolled his eyes and muttered something.

"I only asked if you know the way to the lodging house of Seno and Betrys..."

"I know it," he grumped. "I know *all* the lodging houses." He started walking again and I hurried to catch up. "It's near Watling Gate." He gave me a sideways glance. "Come on."

Clutching my cloak around me, we hurried on, the shadows deepening around us. Rhin was not the most agreeable or forthcoming fellow—but at least he didn't try to rob me. We passed through the town at a fair pace, eventually arriving at a lane where we turned and...there was the house with its iron gate on the street.

"Here," Rhin said, pointing down the lane.

Before I could thank him, he was gone, leaving me standing in the street. "Don't worry about me!" I shouted after him. Then, seeing as I was alone and it was getting dark, I dashed the last little way and was soon through the gate and into the tiled courtyard. The villa door opened as I came near, and Betrys looked out, saw me, and looked beyond me—but, seeing no one else with me, shouted, "Dear girl, are you alone?"

I nodded. "My father was called away on another errand. But he said he would join us for dinner."

Betrys allowed that was often the case with official functions and hurried off to see about preparations for the meal. I went to our room to rest a bit and wait for Tullius to return.

Well, we were still waiting long after the meal was finished. As my father had not appeared when everything was ready, Betrys called her husband and said we would sit down together now and the latecomer—who had probably eaten with his friends—could have something when he finally turned up.

So that is what we did. I confess it was a little awkward at first, but as the meal progressed we grew more easy in one another's company. They delighted in telling me all about Viroconium and it was clear they were well used to housing strangers and making them feel welcome—and even if I sometimes struggled to hear everything they said, I was grateful for their hospitality. Yet, as the meal concluded and my father had still not arrived, it was suggested that I must be exhausted and longing for bed.

What could I say? I was already so tired I could hardly see, and the food and wine had me yawning. The thought of putting my head down somewhere peaceful and quiet was simply irresistible. I thanked Betrys for a wonderful meal and accepted her kind offer and went off to our room. A servant had lit a rushlight for me and I fell into bed and into a sound sleep—and likely would have slept the whole night through if not for a hand hard jostling me and a voice loud in my ear. "Wake up!" The voice was urgent, frantic, and loud.

"Girl, wake up! You are needed!"

5

I WAS PULLED FROM MY SLEEP by Betrys' servant girl who
jostled me awake, threw my cloak to me, and told me to hurry. I was
led back through the house and out into the small courtyard—now
crowded with men lit with the glow of flickering torches. Several were
kneeling around something shapeless on the tiles and as I approached,
a way opened for me. The onlookers parted and I saw a man lying on
a pallet. Closer, I saw two things: the man's tunic was sodden with an
ugly dark stain and the man was my father.

I gave out a little cry and rushed to him. He saw me and struggled
up onto an elbow. "Aurelia," he said, wincing with pain. "Aurelia, my
love. There is nothing to fear."

"You're bleeding!" I gasped. "What happened?"

Before he could reply, I felt strong hands on me and a stern voice
loud in my ear. I was all but lifted out of the way. "Step aside. The
physician is here."

A man pushed forward and took my place beside the pallet. He
knelt, gently felt the sodden clothing, and spoke to my father in low
tones. Then, rising, he turned and said, "Take him into the house. And
bring some light." To those standing around, he said, "Go on . . . go on.
Make way."

The pallet was taken up and carried inside, and I was left standing
in the courtyard with the others who all began talking at once. I could
make nothing of the babble of voices. "What happened?" I demanded,
pulling on the sleeve of the man nearest. "What happened?"

One of those who had helped bring him back replied, "There was an attack. That's all I know."

An attack! My mind went blank. I tried to think what this meant. My father . . . an attack . . . My eyes welled up and my hands flew to my mouth. "I don't understand. You say my father was attacked?"

"That's your father?" Another man regarded me for a moment, then said, "I only know what I heard. The proconsul's party was returning to town and they were ambushed by thieves on the road. Proconsul Esico and two others were killed, and three more were wounded—including your father. The raiders were driven off by some of the procurator's soldiers who came upon them shortly after the attack."

"But they survived," I insisted, my voice shaking with fear. "They all survived . . ."

"Did you hear me? I said Proconsul Esico is dead—and two of his men. Your father is one of the lucky ones. He's alive."

I started for the house. "I must go to him."

The man put out a hand and grabbed my arm. "Stay here. Don't get in the way."

"My father needs me!" I said, my voice pinched with pleading. Several of those standing near glanced my way. "I have to be there."

"You will. Soon," he told me. "Not now. Let Lucius work."

He pulled me a little further away. As we turned, I thought I heard someone utter the word *Saecsen.*

"Is that right?" I asked. "Was it Saecsens?"

"Most likely. They made off with the horses and weapons—that's what they do." His voice grew thick with derision. "Barbarians." The word was a curse in his mouth.

I looked to the door where people clustered around the entrance. "I'm going in."

Before he could prevent me again, I dashed forward and plowed through the onlookers. My father lay just inside the vestibule. His eyes were closed and his jaw tightly clenched. Lucius, the physician, knelt beside him with two small oil lamps to light his work. The top half of my father's mantle had been cut away to reveal a gash in his side—a narrow wound, raw, ragged, oozing blood in the lambent glow of the lamp. Lucius dipped a roll of cloth into a bowl of vinegar water and gently dabbed the bloodstained flesh to wash it. I watched how patiently, how carefully he applied the astringent. Satisfied that the wound was clean, Lucius took up a thin bronze needle attached to a threadlike length of catgut and, with studied precision, began drawing the ragged edges of flesh together. Tullius moaned as the needle pierced the severed flesh; he put his arm across his face as the needle bit into him time and again.

Appalled by the sight, I gasped aloud. I could not help it. I put my hand over my mouth. Lucius paused and glanced back over his shoulder, saw me, and said, "Go away!"

I fell back a step—still staring at the horrendous sight of that awful gash.

"Someone get her out of here," the physician snapped.

I fled the room. What else could I do?

The others were watching from the doorway. Rather than face them again, I made for my room, brushing by Betrys on the way. The kindly woman stood in the passageway, distraught, wringing her hands. "Oh, Aurelia. I'm so sorry." She shook her gray head. "So sorry. That this had to happen..."

"Just leave me alone!" I mumbled, and hurried on.

"Yes, yes," she called after me. "You go lie down and I will come for you when the physician is finished."

I rushed to my room, slammed the door, and threw myself onto the bed where I lay staring up into the darkness—now heavy, pressing down on me like a dead hand. Though I did not want to imagine the worst, all I could think was: *What if my father doesn't recover? What if he dies?*

I lay there thinking and the tears came. Again—for the second time that day!

I wept in the darkness, inconsolable. I must have cried myself to sleep, because the next thing I knew Betrys was leaning over me and speaking. I opened my eyes and turned my head to better hear her. "He's asking for you." I sat up. "Your father's awake. He wants to see you."

Throwing aside the thin woolen coverlet, I leapt out of bed and followed Betrys across the dark courtyard to my father's bedside. They had carried his pallet to the dining room and placed it on a low bedframe near the hearth where it was warmest. He raised his head and held out his hand as I came into the room. I knelt beside him on the stone floor and glanced down at his injured side. "Does it hurt very much?"

"Lucius gave me a tincture for the pain—opium, I think," he said, his voice rough but steady. He raised a little glass bottle of milky liquid. "It helps, but I think I could use a little more—perhaps an entire lake." He smiled and something of his usual humor returned, though his color remained pale gray. "Well, here we are, eh?"

"What can I get for you?" I asked. "Tell me what you need."

He swallowed hard and said, "Aurelia, listen to me carefully. I am wounded and in pain. Lucius tells me that I must remain in bed for a day or two, and let the stitches settle and heal. I'm afraid this means I cannot attend the conclave—"

"Of course not," I agreed quickly. "You must do all you can to get better."

"And I will," he assured me. "But it means you are going to have to attend the conclave for me."

"No!" I reared back. "I can't."

He countered my refusal with a wave of his hand. "Yes, dear heart, you can," he said, his voice hardening. "You must be my eyes and ears there. I need to know everything that happens. Venta is depending on it. Otherwise, we came here for nothing."

"Father, please, no," I managed. "It's too much. I don't know what to do. I can't—"

"I need you there, Aurelia."

Horrified, I stared at him.

"You can do it, Aurelia," he insisted. "I know you can. You're stronger than you feel."

"Don't make me . . ."

"I will depute you to stand in my stead. You will attend and report back to me—everything you see and hear. I trust you."

Oh, yes, I thought. *Trust a deaf girl to be your ears at the most important conclave ever.* "Trust me? Proconsul Esico might have something to say about that," I pointed out. "He will not look kindly on an unlearned deaf girl attending his great—" I realized what I was saying and stopped.

"Esico is dead. Did they not tell you?"

I nodded. "I forgot. But, what about Coran?" I suggested. "He's the proconsul's assistant. He can go—" The pitying expression on my father's face brought me up short.

"Aurelia," he said softly. "Coran was killed in the raid."

"Not Coran..." Though I detested the fellow, a queer feeling shivered through me. How could he be dead when I only saw him a day or so ago?

"Listen to me, Aurelia." Tullius raised his voice so I would not miss what he was saying, and I could see the strain in his eyes and the cords standing out on his neck. "Concentrate, now. This is important. Until I am strong enough to resume my duties, you are going to have to do a great many things you'd rather not. But you're going to do them—for me, and for the people of Venta. Someone must be there for us."

I accepted what he was saying, but desperately tried to think of another way, any other way. Something akin to panic began to rise within me as the full weight of responsibility began to settle upon me.

"I need to know that you will do whatever I ask."

I nodded, relenting at last.

"Say it."

"I'll do it—whatever you ask."

"For me and for the folk of Venta."

"For you and for Venta."

"Then all is well." He closed his eyes and his features relaxed. I saw how much our talk had taxed him and how very fragile was his strength. "I knew I could trust you, Aurelia." I barely caught this last as his voice fell. "Ahh," he sighed. "I'll sleep now...a little...."

I waited a moment, but he said no more. He sank into sleep almost at once. There was nothing to be done, so I rose and crept silently away.

6

THE REST OF THE HOUSEHOLD WAS QUIET, so I crept back to my room and lay down for awhile. Fretting over my father and what lay ahead of me drove any thought of sleep far away. When at last the first rays of daylight lightened the sky outside, I gave up any thought of rest and got up, took my time washing and dressing. I put on my good green mantle and blue embroidered belt. In a nook beside the wash basin, I found a small, round mirror in a carved wooden frame, and polished the surface with my sleeve. The face looking back at me did not inspire confidence. My long, ruddy hair hung in confused tendrils and there my pale blue eyes were red-rimmed from lack of sleep. I fetched my comb from my pack and dragged it through the mess of tangles and tried arranging it into something resembling an acceptable manner. I pinched my cheeks to raise a little color and rubbed my lips with some beeswax from my pot.

By the time I stepped into the courtyard, the day had brightened with a few scattered clouds, chill but warming as the sun rose higher. I stood for a moment in the light of that new day, looking at the clearing sky and wondering how the world could appear so calm when all inside me was in upheaval? I crossed to the little stone bench and had just sat down when Betrys appeared, looking drained and weary. Like me, she had slept poorly, agitated and worried by what had happened. She hurried over, sat down and, laying a hand to my arm, told me everyone was alarmed by the raid so near the town. "It is all anyone talks about," she said. "The procurator will have to do something about this...this outrage—these raids," she said. "He simply must."

We talked a little more and she went off to see to the morning meal. No sooner had she gone than Lucius, the physician, arrived. A slim, white-haired man with a little paunch beneath his tunic, he greeted me gruffly, then softened somewhat when he remembered who I was. He spoke to me, but in a voice so soft I did not catch it.

I touched my right ear and said, "I'm part deaf."

He nodded and repeated, "Your father—did he sleep?" Unslinging his heavy bag, he placed it between his feet.

"I don't know. I think so. He's sleeping now."

"Good."

"He will get better," I said. "Yes?"

"Time will tell." He picked up his bag. "I will go in to him now."

I rose and followed him across the courtyard to the door leading to the dining room. He opened the door and stepped in, then turned to me. "It is best you wait outside." So saying, he closed the door, leaving me outside.

I returned to my bench beside the pool where I sat and watched the fish while I waited for the physician to return. That is where Helena found me.

"Oh, Aurelia, dear girl," she cried and rushed to join me on the bench. She hugged me and then, taking both my hands in hers, looked hard at me, studying my face, my eyes. "How are you?"

Before I could reply—or even think how to answer—she said, "I came as soon as I heard what happened. What a terrible thing! How is your father? And the wound—is it very bad? Has the physician seen him? What does he say?"

I could hardly decide which question to answer first. "Lucius is with him now," I told her.

"Oh, that is fortunate. Tullius is a very lucky man. God must have been with him to survive such an ordeal."

I will never understand why people say that. Perhaps it comforts them somehow. "If God was with him out on the road," I pointed out, "he would never have been wounded in the first place. And no one would have died."

She regarded me sadly, then lightly brushed my sulky comment aside. "You've had a terrible shock."

"How did you know where to find me?"

"I didn't. But I knew where to find Rhin. He told me."

I nodded. *Oh, of course, Rhin . . .*

Helena was speaking, concern in her dark brown eyes. She said something I didn't catch.

"Pardon?"

"I asked what you plan to do," she repeated.

"My father wants me to attend the conclave. He says that our people should be represented. With Proconsul Esico's death there is no one else . . ." My voice trailed off as I remembered what the day held for me. "I don't even know how I'm going to get into the basilica."

Helena sighed. Somehow she understood. "Well," she said after a moment, "that, at least, is something I can fix." She became all efficient and competent. "Just you leave it with me. I'll make sure you attend, never fear."

I felt a weight lift off my shoulders. "Thank you, Helena. Thank you." Her kindness and willingness to help melted something inside me and I started tearing up. Despite my best intentions to remain strong and show some fortitude, the tears began to leak out and slide down my cheeks. "I'm sorry," I blubbed. "It's just so hard to know what to do."

"Ah, no, no. Don't cry." She slid her arm around me and pulled me close. "All will be well. Now, listen, I will go and tell Aridius that Tullius wants you to represent him at the conclave. He will see to it that you are admitted."

I thanked her again and she kissed her fingertips and pressed them to my wet cheek. I watched as she hurried across the courtyard to the gated entrance, then called after her, "Why are you doing this?"

"Doing what?"

"Helping me? Yesterday and now . . . this."

She smiled and lifted a palm toward me. "You were there and so was I. It is as simple as that."

True enough, but I know it is never so simple.

Helena moved to the doorway. "Now, I must go. There is much to do. Farewell for now, Aurelia. I will send someone for you and we will talk again after the conclave."

With that, she was gone. I sat in the courtyard for a time, thinking, waiting for Lucius to reappear. When he emerged a few moments later,

I hurried to meet him. "My father," I blurted, "how is he? Can I go in and see him?"

Lucius adjusted his bag on his shoulder, and turned to address me full face so I would not miss what he was about to say. "Tullius tells me that he slept well, and he does appear better rested. His color is returning and that is a good sign. He still has some pain, but that is to be expected."

"But he will recover?"

"Yes, I think so." He raised a finger in admonition. "For that to happen, the wound must be kept clean with soft rags soaked in vinegar. Also, he must avoid strenuous activity, to be sure, and eat to regain his strength. But keeping the wound clean is of utmost importance."

I heard the warning in his words. "Otherwise?"

"He will die," he said bluntly. "It is the corruption that kills."

At my horrified gulp, he placed a comforting hand on my shoulder and added, "I'm sorry, but it is the truth."

"I understand," I assured him.

"Good." He gave me a fatherly smile. "He must rest and allow healing to take hold." Adjusting his bag, he took his leave, saying that he would return later in the day to examine and bathe the wound again, and that I should take care to keep my father comfortable and make sure he did not move or try to get up as he might tear the stitches.

Before Lucius reached the gate, I was kneeling beside my father's low hearthside bed. His eyes were closed; he had taken more of the opium potion for the pain, I guessed. Still, he woke and smiled hazily when he saw me, and said, "There you are, dear girl. Are you ready to take your place at the conclave?"

"Helena was here. She told me she would speak to Aridius and he would arrange a place for me." I reached out and took his hand, squeezing it hard. "But I want to know about the attack—what happened, how you came to be wounded, and poor Coran and the others... all of it."

He shook his head on his pillow. "There is little enough to tell. I hardly know what—"

"No," I told him, crossing my arms. "Aridius said you and some others had stayed behind to speak to the procurator alone. Start there."

"Yes, yes," he sighed. "That is so. Esico wanted to speak to

Constantine about easing the *civitas* tax imposed on Glevum and other towns in the region—that, or increasing the number of available soldiers. Esico and the others had gone to see the procurator to appeal—because he felt the north received more than their share at the expense of the south. I was invited along to lend my presence to the party." He smiled wanly. "Strength in numbers, yes?"

"What did Contsantine say?"

"He had agreed to hear us and said that he would consider our request and let us know his decision in due course. That was all," Tullius explained. "We thanked him for hearing us and took our leave. It was late and we were in a hurry to catch up with the main party and get back to Viroconium before dark."

He seemed to drift off a little then, but I was determined to hear it all. "And then what happened?"

Passing a hand over his eyes, he drew breath and continued. "We came around a bend in the road where a stand of trees had grown close by. The first I knew anything was amiss—the first anyone knew, I expect—was when we heard a shout. One of the soldiers riding a little behind the carriage had seen something moving in the wood. He cried a warning of some sort—but it was already too late. They were on us before we could even turn around. Seven or eight of them, maybe more, I don't know. Big men. Barbarians. Long hair and beards. Four on horseback, and others on foot. All of them screaming and slashing with swords and spears. Esico and two others joined the soldiers to fight off the attack."

Tullius motioned to a cup of water that had been left for him. I held the cup and he took a sip, swallowed, and continued. "The rest of us—we had no weapons—tried to flee. I was caught by a spear as I climbed from the carriage. I fell, but the man behind me—one of Esico's, I think—took the next thrust in the stomach." Here my father fell silent.

"And then?"

"It was over. The raiders only wanted the horses. They got what they wanted, left us bleeding beside the road. It was all we could do to struggle back to the safety of the walls. I don't remember much after that."

Our short conversation had already tired him and the opium was making him drowsy. His words were becoming slurred and I could see the his strength waning. I thanked him for telling me. "You should rest now, Father," I said. "Helena is sending someone to fetch me for the conclave. I should go and make ready."

"You do that." He reached out to me and the movement made him wince. "Give me a kiss, dear heart, and promise you'll come back as soon as it's over and tell me all about it." '

I assured him I would, and advised, "And you must promise to eat something while I am gone. Yes?"

He nodded and closed his eyes. I think he was asleep again before I reached the door. Betrys, or her servant, had been busy while I was out of my room. A plate of sweet polenta cakes and dried figs had been left for me. As the day was still a bit cool, I decided to wear my cloak; I folded it carefully and arranged the folds so they fell just right, and pinned them in place with the brooch my father had given me—the one he wore on his official rounds—a big, somewhat ungainly thing, but he thought it lent him a little more authority.

By the time I entered the courtyard again, a boy was waiting to take me to the conclave. I had half expected to see Rhin again and was surprised to find myself disappointed that it was only a ragged, barefoot messenger boy. He knew the city and together we hurried through street crowds and markets, and every face I saw seemed to wear the same fraught expression of concern. My young guide delivered me to the basilica and to a man in a long white mantle who was standing at the wide-open doors of the great brick building. The man gave the boy a coin and the lad darted off again.

"Aurelia? I am Festus," said the man in a deep rumbling voice. "The legate has instructed me to wait for you and find a place where you can see and hear the proceedings. You're deaf, yes?" He passed a critical eye over me and I did not get the feeling he was much impressed by what he saw. "And very young."

I bristled at this. "Is that a problem?"

"I shouldn't think so," replied Festus with a shrug. "This way if you're ready. Aridius is already inside."

He turned on his heel and led me through the towering doors. We had taken but three steps when I was stopped again—by one of those men in a red-edged mantle; he carried a sort of black rod in one hand, and a short blunt sword in the other. "This conclave is closed to the public," he told us, looking directly at me. "Leave now."

"We are here at the command of Constantine Aridius Verica,

Legate of Deva Vitrix," replied Festus with stiff formality. "We are members of his delegation at his command. He requires our presence."

The gatekeeper considered this for a moment, passed his gaze over me, then gestured with the rod for us to proceed. The vast room was crowded with men—old and young and in-between—ranged around a dais that had been erected for the procurator's chair, an elaborate thing made comfortable with several stuffed cushions. Festus spotted Aridius near the foot of the dais. Threading through the crush, I shoved up beside the legate, who greeted me with a smile and a light squeeze of my arm. "Your father—how does he fare?"

"He is in pain, but will be better for food and rest. Thank you for helping me."

"It is nothing."

Anxious to make good on my promise, I looked around at all those serious, important men gathered there and noted their manner and dress so I could make a good report. I heard voices raised behind me. "Oh, I know. Terrible," said the first. "Just terrible. Something will have to be done." There was mumbled agreement from others, and more of the same—it did seem that everyone was buzzing away like worried bees over news of last night's attack.

Aridius gave me a little nudge with his elbow and directed my attention to the dais where a tall, lean man now stood. "The vicarius," he told me. The official held an iron-tipped staff with a golden eagle perched on top—the procurator's symbol of office. Raising the scepter, the official struck it three times on the stone floor of the basilica. The resounding *thwack!* echoed like thunder through the great room. "Silence!" he cried. "Silence for Procurator Constantine Flavia Gallus."

From the rear of the basilica came a small procession: three soldiers holding upright spears, two priests bearing croziers, and an official of some kind in a short tunic and trousers. They approached the dais and a hush descended upon the floor of the basilica as the entourage took their places behind the big, throne-like chair. The procurator seated himself on his cushions and passed his gaze across the assembly, a frown on his fleshy face.

I do not doubt that Procurator Constantine was a powerful man. But inspiring, no—much shorter than I imagined, and with a shaven head that gleamed as if his skull had been oiled. He affected the old

Roman style: robe and wide red leather belt with a gold-edged cloak folded over one arm and the opposite shoulder. The scepter-wielding vicarius called out something that sounded to me like the words my father sometimes read out to me from old documents and the odd roadside shrine. Then Constantine rose to address the conclave.

7

THE PROCURATOR SPOKE FORCEFULLY, and he spoke long. An able orator with a voice both strong and supple, he easily filled the enormous cavern of a room. Much to my surprise, I had little difficulty hearing him, missing a word here or there, but understanding most all he said. This, more than anything else, caused me to revise my first opinion of him. What did he say that was so important that he summoned everyone here to tell them in person?

Procurator Constantine told us of his recent journey to Rome to seek an audience with the emperor and his petition, his plea, for financial aid and the necessary troop support to reverse the ongoing deterioration of Britain's legions and garrisons, and to stem the incoming tide of invaders. "I asked for soldiers," he said. "I asked for weapons. I asked for money to repair the fortifications across our lands. I asked for the help and support of Rome. And do you know what the emperor told me?"

Constantine looked out over the assembly as if daring us to guess. "Can you imagine what the emperor said to his most loyal procurator?"

The basilica fell hushed; the gathering waited with breath abated.

"Emperor Johannes looked me in the eye, and the supreme ruler of the greatest, wealthiest, most powerful empire the world has ever known told me that he could not spare a single legionary. He could not spare a single sword, a single spear, a single shield. He could not spare a single denarius to pay for a single brick or timber for a single gate or wall. He told me he could not . . . would not help us."

These words were met with an angry murmur and several shouts of denunciation. The faces of those around me convulsed into expressions of anger, anguish, and disbelief. Raising his voice to knee-trembling strength, Constantine shouted, "Our Great Mother has forsaken us! Are we *nothing* to her?" His gaze became sharp and hot with anger. "Are we nothing to Rome? A trivial plaything to be discarded when pleasure palls? Refuse to be swept away and burned on the rubbish heap?"

Suddenly, the great hall convulsed with the shivering thunder of voices raised in rage and despair. The shouting mounted, growing ominous, belligerent. I could feel it like thunder in my chest. Constantine raised his head and looked to the high-domed ceiling as if expecting some answer from on high. Then, slowly, he lifted his hands, palms outward, for silence. "My friends," he said, when the hall had quieted enough to be heard, "we have been scorned, yes, and discarded. Some of you will know that this is not the first time this loyal province has been rejected. But I stand before you today and tell you that it will be the last."

He began to pace back and forth along the edge of the dais as if to order his thoughts. When he was ready, he said, "My grandfather was a commander of the Second Augusta when the Emperor Honorius replied to our governor's urgent request for aid with the phrase you will have heard repeated time and again. '*Look to your own defenses.*' We have done that. In truth, we have ever done that.

"And now, my friends, we must rise to the challenge once again. But this time it will be different. As Procurator of Britannia, I declare that from this day we cease payment of all tribute and tax to Rome, and that any and all such monies will be directed to the building up of our own forces, for our own defenses and protection."

This decree was received to great acclamation with shouts of approval and stamping feet. The sound came in riotous waves and roared on for some time. Constantine, his face hard, stalked back and forth across the dais until the acclaim dwindled enough for him to be heard once more. "Many of you will have heard that last night a heinous attack was made on members of this body within sight of the very walls of this *civitas*," he continued, to shouts and jeers of defiance. "Proconsul Silverius Esico and his *adiutor* were killed and others were injured—the Magistrate of Venta Silurum among them."

At the mention of my father, my heart quickened and I gasped. Constantine was still speaking. "This contemptible and cowardly act of cruelty was executed by Saecsen raiders who strike with impunity and often without reprisal." More jeers and cries for justice. "In former times, our roads were well maintained and travel safe. The citizens of our towns and villages slept secure in their beds at night, protected by an army of well-trained soldiers who kept the peace and enforced the laws and edicts of an invincible empire."

The procurator came to the center of the dais and paused, spreading his hands in supplication. "My friends, I need not tell you that time has past... long past. No longer do traders and travelers journey without fear. No longer are our garrisons fully manned with well-trained soldiers. No longer are we safe in our beds at night. No longer are marauders, invaders, barbarians taught the utter folly of defying the strength of Roman justice and might. Their outrages of violent brutality go unpunished."

These words brought another gale of protest: cries for the restoration of the garrisons, building new fortresses, swift punishment of all invaders who plunder and kill... demands for justice and revenge in bellows of such rude hostility it made me blush with embarrassment.

"Today, fellow citizens, Britannia will look to its own defense, and we will protect our own. No longer will we live in fear within our own homes. No longer will our taxes go to fill the treasure houses of emperors who care nothing for the lives of their people." Constantine raised his hands. "Our homeland will be free once more."

The procurator resumed his throne then and the vicarius read out the official decree and invited the delegates to voice their support. Aridius, standing mute and motionless beside me, stared resolutely ahead as the tempest broke around us: a maelstrom of attitude and argument. Every delegate, great and small, seemed determined to have a say, with one after another dignitary holding forth at length until my head throbbed with the strain of trying to remember the most considered opinions so I could repeat them back to my father. But one thing was clear: the ship Britannia would sever the last remaining ties to Rome and sail out into the world alone.

The clamor was nowhere nearing its end when I felt a nudge at my side. With a nod, Aridius indicated the basilica doors. We made our way back through the gathering and into the street. Once outside, we both took a deep breath, and Aridius looked back. "Remember this day, Aurelia. For good or ill, we are on our own. God help us all."

We entered the street and he asked me what I wanted to do now, and I told him I would go back and tell my father all that I had heard and seen at today's session. Aridius approved of the idea and said, "There will be more of this in the days to come. There is much to discuss. Go now and rest while you can." He then summoned a boy—messenger lads were always swarming around the basilica—and paid him to guide me. He sent me off saying, "Tell Tullius that I will look in on him this evening."

My father was asleep when I returned to our lodgings and Betrys reported that he had dozed on and off all day. The physician had been with him earlier to cleanse the wound again and change the dressing, and left more of the opium tincture and a warning that we were to remain vigilant and make sure Tullius did not exert himself in any way. They had also moved my father to a small room across from the bedroom we had shared. I thanked her for her care and told her to expect Legate Aridius later that evening when, no doubt, he would have more to tell.

Tullius must have wakened and heard us talking because, on my way to my room, I heard him faintly calling to me. With some apprehension, I put my head in the door to see him lying on his pallet looking pale and drained of life. Nevertheless, he wanted to know what had happened at the conclave. I told him briefly about the procurator's decree and the storm it had unleashed and would have told him more, but Tullius was groggy with the pain potion and marked little of what I said, so I told him to rest and that we would talk more later. "Aridius said that he will come this evening, and he can tell you more then," I said, then, leaving him, I went to my room and lay down for awhile to close my eyes and clear my aching head.

Some little time later, I awakened—having slept longer than I intended. The sun was a mere smudge of fading orange in the western sky and tiny black swifts filled the air, dodging and diving over the courtyard, when Aridius came calling.

On the arrival of his visitors, my father roused himself and made to throw off his coverlet. "Help me, Aurelia," he said. "I want to get up."

"Oh, no," I told him as firmly as I could. "That is the one thing you will *not* do! Your physician has given strict instructions that you are not to be getting up and prancing around. You must remain quiet."

"I have been *quiet* all day, my stubborn daughter," he said. "And I have never *pranced* in my life. I promise not to start now. Help me up, and let us go receive our visitors like civilized human beings."

He was determined and would not be opposed. I suspect the opium addled his mind and made him feel as if he could ignore good sense. As he refused to listen to reason, with great reluctance I helped him to his feet and made him lean on me as we shuffled slowly out into the courtyard and then sat him down on the stone bench beside the little pool. Legate Aridius honored my stricken father with an old-fashioned bow of deference and then settled beside him on the bench. While the two men reviewed what had taken place at the conclave, Helena joined me to discuss other things.

She said something I did not catch, and then remembered my difficulty and repeated the question loud enough for me to hear, but not so loud as to disturb the others. "Have you considered how you and your father will get back to Venta?"

Nothing like the thought had entered my head. "So much has happened, I . . . I. No," I confessed, "I haven't thought . . ."

"Well, never mind," she continued quickly. "I have a plan. In a few days, when Tullius is well enough to travel, you can both come home with us." Her easy intimacy was such that I felt I had known her forever. If I had a best friend, she could not have been more effortlessly familiar with me, or more understanding. "Come to Deva."

My puzzled look drew a little laugh from her. "Well, I suppose that may sound a bit strange. Let me explain." She paused to order her thoughts, then began, saying, "It is in my mind that Deva is far closer than Venta. Two days' travel—three at a restful pace. Then, Tullius can remain in comfort and allow himself to fully recover before undertaking the journey to Venta. See now, we have a villa in the town with many rooms and servants. My husband is legate, after all, and we are all well used to hosting guests from all over the province. To have you with us would be a thing of no consequence whatsoever, and you would be more comfortable there than you are here."

"My father's recovery," I said. "I don't know how long it will take."

"What of that? You can stay as long as needed," she replied. "Stay as long as you like. You both need to get some rest after all that's happened here." She smiled and put her hand on my arm. "Please, do come."

The offer came with such warmth and compassion, I was touched. "If it was my decision to make, I think we would be there already," I replied. "But this is for my father to decide. We will do what he deems best."

"Of course," she agreed happily. "But what do *you* think?"

"Me? I would like nothing better."

She smiled. "Then you will speak to Tullius about it?"

"Yes, but . . . perhaps the offer would sit better coming from you— or maybe your husband."

"As to that," she said, glancing at the two men beside the pool, "Ari is no doubt suggesting it even as we speak. But I wanted you to know you would be welcome with us—if your father should ask your opinion."

"It's been known to happen," I allowed.

She patted my arm. "Good." She turned her head and looked across the courtyard toward the house, sniffed the air, and said, "I smell bread baking and I'm starved. Let's go see what Betrys is preparing for our meal."

8

"YOU'RE NOT LISTENING, Aurelia," Tullius insisted. "The invitation is attractive, and kindly meant. That, I do not deny. But—"

"You could rest," I argued. "Recover your strength. Allow your injuries to heal. That is more important than anything else."

"I must return to Venta without delay," he said "Proconsul Esico's death is a calamity—an enormous loss to the province. The upheaval will be tremendous. New officers will be appointed, new assignments made, new positions. Truly, I would not be surprised if Constantine chose *me* to take Esico's place."

So, this was in his mind: a promotion from magistrate to proconsul, and it was shaping his judgement.

"Do you really think that likely?"

"Oh, I think it more than likely." He did not take offense at my question. "Who else? After all, I know the people. I have long cultivated trust and loyalty throughout the region among the tribes and leaders. Everyone knows they can rely on Tullius Paulinus. He's a man of his word."

I had never known my father to be an ambitious man, but he was nothing if not practical. All sentiment aside, it seems he saw a chance to make an important advance for himself and his people and he meant to take it. He would risk his health to gain this laurel and, to him, that was a risk worth taking. Further argument would be pointless, I decided. He had made up his mind.

Such were his powers of persuasion that he even succeeded in convincing stern old Lucius to agree that he was well enough to quit his bed and make the journey, providing he did not allow himself to become overexcited—whatever *that* meant. He declared that the injury was not healed—far from it—but father was recovering and well on his way to regaining some of his old vigor. With a final admonition to keep the wound clean, the physician gave his consent. So, Tullius paid the physician and, over my oft-repeated misgivings, arranged for our immediate departure.

I had hoped to see Helena to thank her for her remarkable kindness during our stay in Viroconium. This was important to me, perhaps excessively so because I had no mother, no sister. And, as a girl growing up, I did not have many friends. I like to think that, in another life, Helena and I might have been friends—maybe even more than friends: sisters, perhaps. I think I would have liked that. At any rate, I dearly wanted to bid her farewell one last time before we went our separate ways—knowing full well I would never see her again.

Alas, that was not to be. The day before our departure, Tullius had arranged for the two of them to come to us that evening to share a meal; but, the evening came and went and they did not. Nor did they appear the next morning. I waited while the proconsul's carriages were brought to us and our travelling company assembled in the square near the south gate.

Mona, Proconsul Esico's wife—widowed now and stoically grieving her loss—resolved to make the return journey with us rather than remain behind to make whatever funeral plans she might in a strange town she would certainly never visit again. Poor Esico's body was hastily cremated to make the journey possible; his wife would travel in their carriage with his ashes in a small ceramic vase. One of the merchants who had traveled with us to Viroconium would also return to Glevum; with him was a servant who drove the wagon. For escort, we had the proconsul's soldiers—only six now, for one had succumbed to wounds received in ambush, and another who was still recovering—but all the other folk who had come north with us elected to stay a little longer in town.

Thus, our travelling party, much reduced from the one that had originally set out, departed Viroconium as soon as provisions had been taken and secured. "Come, Aurelia," my father called from his seat in the carriage. "We must make a start."

Still, I hesitated, searching the busy square for a glimpse of Helena hurrying to bid us farewell and send us on our way.

"What are you waiting for?"

"I thought Helena would come," I told him. "I wanted to say good-bye."

Tullius, impatient to be on his way, grumped, "She's not coming. But *you* must. Come now, get in the carriage."

"Please, just a little longer."

"Obviously, something has happened. They were not able to come last night, and we won't see them this morning—otherwise they would have been here by now."

"Please. We could send a message. We could tell her we're leaving. We could—"

"No. We must make a start," he said, his tone taking on an edge. "You are making everyone wait—and to no purpose. Helena is not coming."

Reluctantly, and with aching regret, I discarded any hope of seeing her again and mounted the step into the carriage.

The day passed in a bleak gray mood. Though the sun was bright, the sky speckled with clouds, and the fields green and ripening, for me it was all a dreary blur. My supposed friend—whose care and friendship I had no doubt exaggerated in my mind—had cast me aside without a word. And I felt the sting.

The journey to Viroconium from Venta took ten-and-a-half days; Tullius hoped to make the return in eight. Unrealistic as this might be, the aim did inspire optimism and lifted his spirits which, I considered, was no bad thing. The first three days on the road passed easily and the milestones receded behind us. Even so, the miles could not pass quickly enough for me. Sullen, forlorn, and grumpy, I would not have wanted myself as a companion. Try as I might—not that I tried very hard—I could not rise above my disappointment at Helena's rebuff of our budding friendship. My father gave up trying to coax me into a sunnier mood and just let me stare at the passing countryside like the spoiled child I was.

The view was as bleak as my outlook—or so it seemed. Once beyond the settlements surrounding Viroconium, an array of empty heathered hills stretched away on every side with few settlements or holdings of any kind to be seen save in the broad green valleys alongside the fresh-running streams and rivers. The sky arched overhead in a vast blue dome through which clouds drifted endlessly, without cheer, devoid of delight.

The desolate view suited my gloomy mood so that, finally, out of frustration, Tullius suggested that I might write Helena a letter. *A letter*, I thought. That was a magistrate's answer to everything! And even if I did write, what would I tell her? I'd tell her . . . I don't know. Something. Anything—a word or two to express my disappointment, I guess.

Though I scoffed at the idea at the time, it worked away the next few days until it finally won me over. Though I refused to let on, I vowed that this is what I would do; once decided, I felt better for it.

Even an improved attitude could not improve the road. The further we progressed into the hill country, the worse the roads became and the constant bumping, lurching, juddering motion of the carriage over the broken stones and rutted surfaces had my father grimacing and groaning through clenched teeth—occasionally uttering an indecent oath beneath his breath. Poor man, he braved the pain until he could bear no more at which point we were forced to halt our march to allow him to recover. Tullius would then imbibe a bit of the opium tincture Lucius had provided for the journey and, after a little sleep, we would resume our journey. And so it went.

Indeed, this became our established practice: start early and travel until midmorning, rest, move on again until midday, rest, move on until time to make camp or take refuge for the night. Travel was tolerable—until we entered a stretch of poor weather with gusty wind and lashing rain.

The carriages and wagons were covered, of course, and thus kept out most of the water, but the soldiers and horses were drenched, sodden, and miserable for three days on end. One storm would cease, the sky would clear briefly, and the next squall rolled in. Those on foot walked with their cloaks and shields over their heads—not that *that* helped very much. Those of us fortunate enough to remain under cover in the carriages offered space inside and the footmen took it in turn to share our leaky ride with us.

Our soggy party struggled to advance beyond a few miles each day. And even that poor effort ground to a halt when we came to one of the deeper fords to find that the stream, now swollen with rain, had burst its banks to become a swirling torrent. Until the storm surge calmed, there would be no crossing. With no other choice, we took shelter in a nearby wood and hunkered down to wait. And it was here that the disaster we had so far avoided finally caught us.

They came riding out of the early morning mist. The rain had stopped, and the stream had fallen in the night. We had only just awakened and were preparing for another day's ordeal.

Because of the storm, Tullius and I had been spending our nights in the carriage, which was not warm and offered little comfort, but at least proved somewhat dryer than the sodden tents. I had risen to wash and make water in private in the streamside brush, and was about my business when I thought I heard someone shout.

I paused, held my breath and listened hard, and heard it again—a cry. I could not make out the words, but understood the urgency. I hurriedly threw on my mantle, snatched up my belt and ran for the carriage where my father was attempting—slowly, carefully, painfully— to scramble out. And that's when I saw them: raiders, swooping down from the hilltop, screaming as they came.

The dull flash of their naked weapons as they careened in a rush toward our little camp induced a tremble in my gut like that of faint thunder. One of the legionaries came running to me. "Saecsens!" he cried, and raced on. "Take cover! We are attacked!"

My heart stopped. I flew to the carriage and helped Tullius down. "Hurry!" I shouted. "We must hide!"

"Where is Mona?" He paused, glancing furiously around. "Find her—and merchant Giddis. Find them!"

"I'm not leaving you here!" I told him.

Another soldier rushed past, slapped me on the arm and shouted, "Take cover!" He raced away again as he and his fellows prepared to meet the attack.

I snatched at my father's sleeve. "Hurry!"

"Go!" cried Tullius. "I'll follow."

Stubbornly, I refused. I stayed with him, taking his arm to support him as we fled. Gasping with pain and cringing with every hobbling step, he made what speed he could as we hurried to conceal ourselves amongst the fringe of rushes and bracken lining the banks of the stream. Sounds of the fight soon reached us. I heard the muted ring and muddled clash of blades, the unholy shrieks of the raiders and wild neighing of terrified horses. A woman's scream.

"Mona!" gasped my father, pressing a hand to his injured side. "Did you see her? Did she get out?"

"I don't know," I whispered. "I think so. Maybe."

There were more shouts, more sounds of the fight—a confusion of jumbled noise in my dull ears—and then ... after what seemed an eternity, the low rumble of hooves as the raiders rode away. We waited, hardly daring to breathe, then Tullius heard one of the soldiers call out that the attack was over. "They're gone," he told me, and we crept from our hiding place and took in a sight that shocked and outraged us both: carnage.

The trader's wagon had been looted and the goods plundered; all that could not be carried easily away was strewn everywhere. Two horses were dead on the ground. Fortunately, no one else had been killed. Or, so I thought.

The merchant Giddis was missing. A quick search of the area located him, face down in a little ditch with the back of his head carved off. And Mona, the proconsul's widowed wife, was still in her carriage, clutching her vase of ashes—a spear thrust through her breast. As she would not leave her husband behind, she would join him in the afterlife.

Though I hardly knew Giddis, I still grieved him. He was a good-natured soul, friendly to all, and his death was as senseless as it was lamentable. Mona, however, I did know. Her death struck me like a blow.

The soldiers had survived the raid unscathed. Moreover, they had acquitted themselves bravely, driving off the raiders with skill and courage. Though they complained that they would like to have made a better account, their prowess proved enough on the day.

"Who were they?" asked my father. Wheezing with the effort and pressing a hand to his side, we joined the soldiers as they picked through the supplies and provisions they had managed to save from pillage or destruction. "Was it Saecsens?"

"Maybe," replied the commanding legionary, a grizzled veteran named Claudius. "All barbarians look alike to me." He passed his flinty gaze around the devastation. "I'm sorry, Magistrate. We could not save everyone."

"It could have been worse, *equitum*," my father told him. He raised a hand to grip the man's shoulder in salute; the movement pained him and he winced. "We are alive thanks to you." He turned to the other soldiers. "I will make a report of the action here and suggest a commendation for your service."

"Put 'em to the sword, I say," a legionary spat. "Stinking rotten thieves, the lot of 'em."

Assessing the damage, the commander made a quick calculation. "We best move on before they come back. We've lost two horses—"

"And the raiders stole one," added one of his men.

"So, we'll leave one of the carriages," suggested Tullius. "Throw everything into the wagon, and let's be gone."

"Giddis and Mona!" My voice broke on the words. "Giddis and Mona . . . dead."

Commander Claudius' reply was terse. "They are, and unless we want to join them, we dare not stay here any longer." To his men, he said, "Put the bodies in the wagon along with everything else. Once we're safely across the stream and away, we'll attend the bodies."

The soldiers gave him a nod and hurried away to make good our retreat. The merchant's servant and I set about helping retrieve any useful gear or supplies we could scrape together and bundling it all into the better of the two carriages before deserting our camp. Thankfully, the soldiers dealt with the corpses, wrapping them in their cloaks and laying them in the wagon bed. Soldiers, men of war, are used to such things, I suppose, but I was not and I was grateful to be spared that chore.

That was quickly done and the horses were soon hitched and ready. I climbed into the carriage with my father; Giddis' servant drove and we rolled to the ford. The stream still ran fairly high, the current nearly as strong as before, but we chose to risk it. Water seeped up through the carriage floor boards and our feet got wet to the ankles, but after all that had happened, I took no notice. When we reached the opposite shore, I realized I had been holding my breath.

Once across, we did not pause a moment but pushed straight on to put as much distance between us and the raiders as possible. It was a headlong race, I can tell you, and rough. The carriage bounded over the pits and holes, hurtling from one hollow to the next, swaying dangerously, but somehow lurching on.

We reached the downward side of a steep hill and saw a line of trees some way ahead. Claudius made for the shelter of the trees and here, at last, we stopped to catch our breath. "We wait here to see if we've been followed," he informed us, putting his head into the carriage as we rolled to a stop. "You can get out if you like."

I was only too glad to take his advice. I flung open the door and leaped down, then turned to help Tullius. It was then I saw the crimson stain spreading down the side of his tunic.

"Father, you're bleeding!"

9

TULLIUS LOOKED DOWN and saw the blood soaking through his clothes. He made a halfhearted swipe at it as if to brush away the ugly stain. His hand came away red and wet.

"Oh," was all he said, as if noticing a trivial inconvenience.

"Get back in the carriage and lie down," I suggested. "We will see what can be done—at least try to change the dressing."

"No time for that now," Tullius objected. He looked around as if confused by what was going on around him. "Why have we stopped? We should keep moving."

"Your wound has reopened," I said, fear making me shrill. "We have to stop the bleeding somehow."

"Later—once we're safe," Tullius replied. To Claudius, he said, "We move on."

Claudius regarded him and, with a glance at me, said, "The horses must be watered. The dead should be buried—" He indicated the shady grove around us. "This is as fit place for a grave as any."

"Listen to him," I said. "Claudius is right. We will move on and we cannot take them with us."

But my father held firm. "The proconsul and his wife were important people and were well-liked by the folk of Glevum. They were Christians and should be accorded a proper burial on consecrated ground—Giddis, too. I'll not have it said that we left them beside the road like muck swept from the stable."

He was adamant and when roused I knew better than to try to

change his mind. There was no reasoning with him when he got like this. "Nobody would say ever that," I countered and did a quick calculation. "But we're at least five or six days from Glevum, maybe more. We have to do *something* with the bodies. What would you suggest?"

Claudius and I looked to him for an answer. Tullius' mouth worked silently as he considered, then said, "Let them travel with us as far as the next settlement. We will make provision for them to be collected by the proconsul's people and taken to Glevum for a funeral."

"Let it be as you say," Claudius said, accepting the decision. "And pray God the raiders do not return."

The commander turned and began shouting orders to his men. Tullius allowed me to help him to his place in the carriage where I prevailed upon him to lie down and let me examine the wound. He at first refused, of course, but my persistence won out and he grudgingly gave in. Also, I think the ache had grown more acute and his strength had begun to flag.

With some difficulty, he eased himself to the floor and stretched out as best he could in the confined space and closed his eyes. I gently raised the side of his tunic. The bandage holding the dressing wad had soaked through, and the pad itself was a sopping crimson mess. I untied the binding knot and gently, gently pulled away the pad—stifling a gasp as I glimpsed the extent of the damage. In the exertion and excitement of our desperate retreat, many of Lucius' neat stiches had ripped away allowing the wound to reopen. It now gaped raw and ragged and weeping blood.

"How is it?" asked my father.

"Not too bad," I lied. "At least, not as bad as I feared."

He said something, but his face was turned away just then and I had to ask him to repeat what he had said. He did, and for the first time, I heard a note of genuine distress creep into his tone. "It hurts, Aurelia."

"Drink some of your potion," I told him, "and I will make a new pad and bind up the wound again. When we reach the next settlement, we can maybe get better help." I prayed inwardly that better hands than mine could attend my father—and soon.

Lifting his tunic, Tullius lay back. He closed his eyes, and drew his arm over his face, bracing himself for what was to come. I gave him a sip of opium from his little flask and set about tearing a few strips from the hem of my mantle. One of the soldiers had fetched water in a jar; I drank some and made my father do the same, then used the rest to wash away as much of the blood as I could. I folded the torn cloth to make a tidy pad, and then carefully positioned this over the nasty gash in my father's side. That done, he struggled up and, while he held the crude dressing in place as best he might, I wrapped the binding around him and tied it. I tried to wash some of the blood out of his tunic, but that only served to make it worse, so I pulled it over his head and hung it over the side of the carriage to dry until we started off again. Then I covered him with my cloak.

"Thank you, Aurelia. You are a blessing."

"Rest now if you can," I told him. He had lapsed into drugged sleep before we resumed our journey a short while later. Despite the lurching and rattling of the carriage, he slept on, moaning softly every now and then when one of the wheels hit a hole or rock.

The day was waning before we finally reached a holding of sorts: not much more than a large house surrounded by several smaller dwellings and a cluster of barns and storehouses arranged around a bare dirt yard, constructed on an older style with split-pine logs, and a steep, high-pitched roof with deep eaves and thatched with river reeds. The smaller buildings were likewise made of pine and thatch, save for one red brick storehouse.

We could see the holding from the road and turned onto the lane leading to it. I don't even think the place had a name at all. If it did, I never knew it. In any case, the settlement was home to several families of the Carvetii, if I heard right—or maybe the Coritani. Prosperous and orderly, the farmsteading was dominated by a single large dwelling—one of those called a lodge house—and the whole surrounded by large fields of that stubby rye they grow in the north. The folk were hospitable if slightly wary, but once we had explained who we were, made proper introductions, gained their trust, and offered to pay for our stay—and for the transport of Mona and Giddis' bodies—they could not do enough for us.

There was no physician. That would have been too much to expect. But one of their womenfolk served as a healer and knew much about wounds of various kinds. Claudius fetched her to meet us. "I am Agnese," she said when my father haltingly emerged. He had bled through his bandage again and stood leaning against the side of the wagon with a hand pressed to his side. "What has happened here?"

After I had explained about my deafness, she asked again and I told her what I knew of my father's injury and how he came by it. Agnese listened intently, then agreed to examine him and apply her skills. She had kind eyes and an easy manner, and I warmed to her immediately. "I would be most grateful," I told her. "We both would."

She went to where Tullius stood half collapsed beside the wagon, spoke briefly, and returned only moments later. "Your father has refused my help."

"He can be stubborn."

"Maybe you could you speak to him? Reassure him? It really would be for the best."

I led my father to one of the long log benches lining the side of the lodge house and sat him down. Gray-faced now, his features drawn, he leaned to one side. I knelt before him. "Father, hear me. You must let Agnese tend you," I told him, placing my hands on his knees. "She is a healer and you need help."

"I need nothing—save to be left alone," he said curtly. "I just want to rest."

"Why are you behaving like this?"

"I *hurt*, Aurelia!" he snapped. "Is that so difficult to understand?"

"Then do something about it!" I snapped, exasperation making me sharp. "It may be Agnese can give you something to better ease the pain. If nothing else, at least let her change the dressing."

He made to get up—as if to quit the discussion—but sat back down. "Oh! Oh!" he groaned. "It hurts."

I stood up and signaled to Agnese to join us. "She's going to examine you and that's the end of it."

She was with us in an instant with her cloth bag of medicines and, as my father took her arm and limped into the lodge, I was dispatched to her daughter for some clean rags and her jar of ointment. The girl was maybe a year or so older than me and knew her mother's ways very well. She wore her long dark hair in heavy braided plaits and, like her mother, was dressed in a simple yellow mantle and a green girdle with a pattern of swirls and spirals embroidered in silver thread. A handsome piece and I told her so.

"I'm Justina," she said and, after I told her my name, she ran off to gather the requested items. Meanwhile, I returned to the carriage and fetched the last bit of opium potion Lucius had given Tullius. It was almost empty, but I snatched up the flask and returned to the lodge where Justina joined me a few moments later. We went in and I watched while the two of them persuaded my father to lie down on one of the bench beds lining the walls of the great room; they removed his tunic to expose the injury, and then bent to their work.

Hands clasped beneath my chin, I watched as they poked here and there, doing this and that; but, since I could do nothing save interfere and worry, I drifted back outside. The westering sun was warm still, and bathing the soft air in a golden, honeyed light. The split-log bench outside the lodge door invited me to sit, so I obliged. The morning's tumult, fraught and frantic and terrible as it was, felt as if it had happened half a lifetime ago—possibly to someone else. I sat back and closed my eyes to enjoy the peace of the soft air and warmth of the sun on my skin. I allowed myself to forget, if only for a moment, the long journey still ahead.

Do not worry about tomorrow, for tomorrow will worry about itself. Today's trouble is enough for today.

This is what Tomos—my wise friend, and one of Venta's more venerable priests—always tells me. Actually, he says, "Be not therefore solicitous for the morrow; for the morrow will be solicitous for itself. Sufficient unto the day is the evil thereof." But it means the same thing. And as I sat there in the sun, I thought: *How right he is!*

Mulling this over in my mind, I heard someone approaching and opened my eyes. It was Claudius, our brawny *equitum*—still in his fighting gear, or most of it—and wanting a word.

"Here—sit," I invited. "There is room for two on this stump."

He wavered on the edge of declining, then relented and took a seat beside me. He was tired and smelled of stale sweat. He folded his hands in his lap and, after a moment, said, "The burial is finished. The headman here gave us a little timber to line the graves."

I wondered if I had heard him correctly. "Timber?"

"Aye, that will make it easier to retrieve the bodies," he explained. "When the time comes."

"Oh." I had been so anxious about my father, I had put the burial out of my mind and now felt bad for my lapse. I thanked him for taking on that necessary chore.

He accepted my thanks and said, "Is there any word?"

"About?"

"About the magistrate—his wound?"

Of course, he knew that the healer had been called. "Not yet. Agnese is tending him now. She will be finished soon, I hope."

"I'm wondering what orders to give the men," he said. "They want to know if we're to be moving on tomorrow. The way things are..." He let the thought go. "I didn't know what to tell them."

"Tell them that the troubles of the day are sufficient unto the day, and that tomorrow's worries can take care of themselves." I offered a smile. "How's that?"

He regarded me for a moment, then gave a little chuckle. "That'll do."

We sat in silence a little while longer and then he got up and went back to his duties and his men. The next time I saw him, he was with his soldiers in the company of some of the holding's men who were leading them to one of the outbuildings—the bakehouse which, I suspect, was also the brewhouse.

The yard grew quiet then and the smell of wood smoke drifted into the air. I got up and went to the door where I met Agnese coming out. "Ah, there you are." She smiled—I took that as a good sign—and led me back to the bench. She settled close beside me and looked out across the yard where two boys and a dog were playing with a stick.

"How is he?" I asked.

"I was able to stop the bleeding and I've given him some of the opium potion. I have also applied a poultice of comfrey and thyme mixed with a little honey." She told me how this mixture should be prepared and how it should be used if I had need of it later. A natural teacher, I think she could not help herself imparting what she knew, and she concluded, saying, "The herbs draw out the poison most wonderfully—"

"And the honey?"

"The honey helps all wounds heal more quickly." She nodded. "This is useful to know. And if I had any fresh willow scrapings I would make a tisane of that to ease the pain."

"Also useful to know," I mused. The talk of honey reawakened my hunger and my stomach gurgled.

Agnese smiled and put her hand on my shoulder, a natural,

motherly gesture. "I don't think you've had anything to eat today." She raised her eyebrows in appraisal. "Am I wrong?"

I shook my head. "We wanted to get as far away from the raiders as possible."

She gave my hand a pat. "I'll have Prisca bring some bone broth for him." She smiled again and stood up. "And a little something for you, too—until we can sit down to a real meal later."

I rose with her. "Maybe I should go in to him."

"Justina can look after him. You stay right where you are," Agnese ordered. "It is a fine evening and you have difficult days ahead of you. Why not enjoy the peace while you can?"

I could not disagree, so I sat back down. I was sitting there, soaking up the serenity, when a woman appeared with a steaming bowl in one hand and, in the other, a small, seeded barley cake and a cup of milk on a little plaque of cedar wood. I accepted the food gratefully and soon wolfed down the sweet cake and drained the cup. I stretched my legs out before me and closed my eyes. I must have dozed, because I did not stir again until I heard voices echoing across the yard.

The sun was down and the folk were gathering for their meal at day's end. I saw Agnese holding the hand of a little girl, no more than four or five summers old. They paused before me. "Dari," she said to the girl. "This is Aurelia. She is staying the night. Shall we ask her to sit with us at table?"

The little girl gave me a wide-eyed stare and then nodded. Agnese said, "You run along in and find us good places." She smiled as the girl flitted away—a bright little sprite, darting among the adults.

"Your daughter?"

"My granddaughter." She sighed. "It is so hard sometimes." I wondered at this, but then she added, "Everything is changing so fast. I fear for her—the world she will inherit."

I did not expect such morose talk from her and it took me a moment to find my feet. "Was it ever any different?"

Agnese shook her head. "No," she said, brightening again. "I suppose not."

The meal that night turned into something of a feast. Visitors to the settlement were rare enough that the inhabitants considered us special guests and they laid their best table to mark the occasion. Having slept a little and feeling better, Tullius did not care to disappoint his hosts, so joined us at table. Under the approving eyes of Claudius and his soldiers, our hosts brought out wine from Gaul and a good fat haunch of pork, onions and greens gathered from a plot behind the house, and fresh brown bread in tiny loaves. The moment we gathered, it seemed that they were all eager for news of the procurator's edict which they had caught word of. The men all wanted to hear the legionaries' stories about raids and battles. The women wanted to know about the markets in Viroconium and what it was like in Glevum and Venta in the south.

My father held his own for a time, but as the talk grew louder and more boisterous, he made his excuses to leave. I rose to help him back to bed, but he bade me stay and uphold the family honor. What he meant by that, I could only guess. But, as the wine was sweet in my cup and my companions pleasant, I was happy to try my best. For their part, our hosts treated me like a princess from some exotic distant realm. Their innocent deference touched me, going a long way toward restoring my bruised and broken soul. Thanks to the convivial company—and the food and cups of wine—the horrors of the day receded like the vapors of a bad dream touched by the warming rays of a new day's sun.

When at last we quit the table to go to our beds, we rose as friends. The settlement boasted no guest house, but a corner of one of the smaller houses had been made over for my father and me. The soldiers would stay in the lodge house with some of the younger men. For my part, I was glad not to have to share a bed—though, tired as I was, I do not think I would have noticed in the least.

Tullius was already fast asleep by the time I stepped through the leather curtain dividing the room. I lay down on my pallet and, exhausted by the adventures of the day, the fog of sleep soon stole the world from sight and mind.

We were to overnight at other settlements before reaching Venta, but it would be a very long time before I enjoyed the rustic splendor of a night like that again.

10

AGNESE SENT US ON OUR WAY the next morning armed with a pot of stuff to make the healing poultice and instructions on how to prepare more; she took pains to teach me how to apply it properly. I paid close attention to everything she said and, pressing her hands warmly, expressed my gratitude for all she had done. Tullius appeared better rested after a more comfortable night; he thanked her and Justina profusely and, in gratitude for their skill and care, bestowed the entire remains of his *per diem* allotment on the little settlement—much to the surprise and delight of the residents. With a last, lingering look, I climbed into the carriage and steeled myself for the way ahead.

A few days later, we entered Dobunni territory and came in sight of our destination. Road weary, exhausted, provisions low and our mood lower, we reached Glevum at the end of another long day. Squalls of rain had made us damp and dejected, so that even the crimson sunset of a clearing sky did little to cheer us. That bright setting sun faded quickly—just like the broad welcoming smile of Esico's deputy when he learned that the proconsul and his wife were no longer to be numbered among the living.

Good man that he was, the assistant gave our legionary escort money to buy themselves food and drink in the town inn, and invited Claudius, my father, and me to his home where his wife and servants prepared a simple but comforting meal. Of course, he wanted to know all about the raid that had taken his superior's life and listened intently—time and again shaking his head in disbelief and genuine grief—as Claudius and Tullius relayed a detailed account of the twin attacks that had taken Esico and Mona's lives. They told him everything, including some things I had not yet heard.

Then they fell to devising a plan to retrieve the bodies for a funeral in the town and what that might entail, and so on. But when the talk turned to what was to be done to fill the sudden vacancy in the proconsul's office, my thoughts began to wing homeward. When I finally could not keep my eyes open any longer, I quietly crept off to the pallet prepared for me by the *adiutor's* servants.

Annoyingly, we spent the next day in Glevum, too. There was much that Tullius wanted to do and people he wanted to see. This took up the entire day and threatened to stretch into the night. I had nothing useful to do, so the day dragged on and the waiting grew wearisome while I idled around doing nothing, finding interest in . . . nothing. That was bad enough, but I saw that all these talks and rushing around were plundering my father's limited store of strength. Each meeting, every discussion took a little more out of him. When I mentioned this toward the end of the day, he told me we would depart for Venta the next morning and he would rest on the way. And this from a man who had just journeyed all the way from Viroconium! As if travel was no more taxing than sitting in a chair by the hearth. Truly, just enduring the ruts and holes in the road for half a day is a labor worthy of Hercules.

Leave the next morning we did. The thoughtful *adiutor* allowed us to continue homeward in the proconsul's fine carriage and provided the use of a driver and servant. So, all things considered, we made the last miles of the journey in whatever passed for comfort on the road. Nevertheless, between Glevum and Venta, something changed so that by the time the carriage finally creaked to a stop in the street outside our house, Tullius was clearly worn through like cheap cloth and in considerable pain.

Faithful Augustus came running to greet us and welcome us home. Aghast at Tullius' dreadful color and condition, he swallowed his questions and disbelief and instead busied himself helping me get my father into the house and into his bed; he paid the driver and servant, and arranged for their lodging. Then, he scurried around preparing a meal to celebrate our return. As it happened, Augustus had a woman friend who, I strongly suspect, had been staying with him in our absence. Since our return had not been anticipated—how could it? Tullius had not sent a messenger ahead to tell anyone—the two of them had not had sufficient warning to hide the telltale signs: a pot of scented ointment, a fine fringed shawl left on a chair, a second pair of sandals outside the door.

None of that mattered to me. Others might have made much over such, as I know only too well. Scandal mongers are a greedy lot and Tullius—forever mindful of his repute and careful to avoid any taint of misconduct or wrongdoing—would no doubt have frowned upon this sort of thing. Even so, Augustus was such an amiable fellow and had long since endeared himself to our little town that most people were prepared to overlook this indiscretion, or at least pretend not to notice.

Her name, I soon discovered, was Dorcas and she was a gray-haired widow who lived with her sister; similar in age to Augustus, she was a plump little woman with a sweet round face and a fluffy, somewhat dithery air. She appeared in the passageway leading to my father's room looking a little flustered and uncertain. I think she had been in the cookhouse when we arrived and now tried to make it appear as if she had just called in to visit on her way to the market. She asked if there was anything she might fetch for us to better celebrate our return.

In order to forestall an awkward situation, and save any further embarrassment, I asked her if she would be willing to stay on to help with my father's recovery. I told her we would welcome any help she might be able to provide until Tullius was well again.

"Of course, I would be honored to aid the magistrate in any way I can," she said.

"We will pay you, of course."

"No, no," Dorcas replied, raising her palms as if to ward off any suggestion of reward. "That is not necessary—"

"Please," I said, "we could not permit it otherwise. My father could not have it said that he traded on his position as Magistrate of Venta to impose upon his citizens in any way." She cocked her head to one side as she considered this. "Also, I am thinking I would like you to reside here in the villa with us. It might be easier that way—for you, I mean. There will be much to do until my father is hale and healthy once more, and I know I can use an extra pair of hands."

"If you think it best . . . ," she replied uncertainly.

"I do."

She nodded, and I saw something like gratitude come up in her eyes.

"Then it is settled," I confirmed swiftly, lest she change her mind. "I will speak to Augustus at once and let him know that he can count on your help. And I'll have him arrange a room for you."

She gave me a smile and went away happy and, I think, greatly relieved. I was proud of myself for turning a likely problem into a genuine benefit. Truth be told, it was not Augustus I was thinking about, but myself. After all, *I* was the one facing a lot of extra work until my father had recovered, and just the thought of all that would have to be done in the days ahead made me tired. Also, I considered that it would be no bad thing to have another woman in the house—another pair of hands to help with the chores and my father's recovery, and someone who might more nearly share my thoughts and feelings.

In this, I was not wrong. For as the next days unfolded, my father failed to thrive. The first few days after our return to Venta, he rose early and attempted to paw through the heap of official business that had accumulated in his absence. Even with my help, the effort proved more difficult than either of us might have guessed because he tired very quickly and had to take frequent rests. On the third or fourth day, he did not wake until almost midday, complaining that he had not slept well. On the fifth day, he remained in his bed until the evening when he said he wanted to go stroll in the courtyard.

Our courtyard is small and would not afford much of a walk, but the day had been fair and the sky still alive with sunlight and swallows, so I helped him up and took his arm and we shuffled around our little square. "I should not have stayed so long abed," he said, drawing air deep into his lungs. "Aurelia, you must not let me sleep so long tomorrow. There is much to do."

"Perhaps you needed your rest," I told him. "Anyway, Augustus and I can deal with most things—if you let us. The little things at least."

"Oh, are you magistrate now?" he said.

"I am a magistrate's daughter who has sat at the feet of a magistrate all her life. Besides that, I can tell my left hand from my right. What else is there to know?" Tullius laughed at this—a soft chuckle only. But even that small movement sent a wave of pain through him. Yet, my heart warmed to think I had cheered him. "You have survived two attacks by Saecsen raiders, and a very serious wound. You can allow yourself time to heal. Why not rest while you can?"

"Glevum will not long remain without a proconsul," he replied. "Constantine will not allow it. I must show myself to be ready."

That again! Still uppermost in his mind.

"All the more reason to rest and let your injury heal completely before you charge into a new position."

We spoke of it no more and contented ourselves with enjoying the gentle evening air. Dorcas found us a little later, sitting on the bench together, Tullius absently stroking my hand. She had come to tell us that our meal was almost ready—a special meal, she said, of baked fish, beans with onions and greens, plums stewed in sweet wine and, of course, bread in small round loaves. I could tell she was making a special effort to impress her new employer as she stood wringing her hands expectantly. "Would you like some wine for the table?"

"Why not?" said Tullius. "I think I would enjoy sharing a cup with my wise and resourceful daughter."

Smiling, the elder woman hurried back to the cookhouse and, a moment later, Augustus dashed through the courtyard on his way to fetch a jar of good wine from the merchant. "Wise and resourceful," I mused. "Which daughter of yours is that? Have I met her?"

"Met her?" He gathered me to him and kissed the top of my head. "In a mirror, perhaps."

We did enjoy a meal with wine that night. My father was his best self—laughing, telling stories of his early days as an official and life with my mother and myself when I was an infant. And even though it was just myself, Augustus, and Dorcas, he presided over the meal as if it had been a banquet for hundreds.

The next day Tullius did not rise again until evening. And the day after that he did not rise at all.

BOOK TWO

TÝ BRYN

"TELL ME, MYRDDIN . . . Or, is it Merlin—which do you prefer?" Aurelia wonders.

"I answer to many names. I always have," I reply with a smile. The way my names and titles increase with the years—and stories with them—amuses me." I spread my hands in deference to her. "It seems to be the way of things."

We are sitting together on a rock beside the road, overlooking a shimmering freshwater lake nestled in a curve of the green valley stretching below us into the misty distance. While Pelleas and the carriage drivers are striving with a broken wheel hub, Brother Ruan and Mairenn have led the horses down to the lake for water. It appears we may be detained for a while; although, it seems to me that if muttering and bickering and gesturing could repair the damage, we would already be strolling the streets of Venta Silurum. Still, it is a fine day with the sun bright and high overhead and not a cloud in sight, and we are traveling south on one of those warm, gladsome days for which this part of our most-favored island is renowned.

This journey was my own suggestion. What with Uther and Aurelius urgently pursuing the campaign to win over the last of the defiant tribes and rally them to a united defense of Britain, it was clear that Aurelia could not long abide the warrior camp. Three days after her arrival, two more warbands from the south joined Aurelius' forces and more were expected any day. The brothers were increasingly engaged in negotiating with their lords for supplies of food and weapons and planning the assault on Hengist and Horsa and the barbarian strongholds on the Saecsen Shore.

When Uther suggested that she return home to Armorica to await the outcome of the campaign to secure the throne, she complained, "There is little for me to do in Constantia—now that you and your brother are here. At all events, I want to see how you are faring—not hear about it a month later, if at all."

Uther drew breath to make a hasty reply, thought better of it, and simply looked to me for help.

"There are difficult days ahead," I said. "And much to be done to prepare for battle."

"And the last thing anyone needs is an old woman poking her sharp nose into it," Aurelia replied primly. "I understand."

Uther denied the assertion. "It is just that we cannot—"

"Allow yourselves to be distracted." She finished the thought for him. "I do understand, believe me. But you needn't worry about me, my son." She reached up and patted him on the cheek—anyone else would have lost a hand. "Now that I am here, I have it in mind to visit my old home. I would like to go to Venta and see the town of my birth once more."

She recalled that her father had purchased a house or some land there and thought that she might pursue a claim which would provide a modest retreat. At best an unlikely prospect, I considered. Still, it could do no harm to satisfy her curiosity—if adequate safety and comfort of travel could be secured. It would hardly do for the mother of Britain's next High King to fall victim to some mishap on the road. For, if he could not even protect his own mother, what hope for the rest of Britain?

"Why not allow me to accompany you?" I offered. "If I might be spared here..."

"Yes! What could be better?" Uther seized on the solution—not least, I think, because it would keep me out of his hair for a few days.

"You would do that?" wondered Aurelia, a little taken aback by the thought.

"It would be my complete pleasure," I assured her.

We decided then and there that Aurelia would undertake a visit to her childhood home and that I would escort her, with Pelleas and Mairenn to look after her on the way; we would leave her in Venta in the company of a local worthy of good repute to await the result of the battles to come. Indeed, I was not lying when I professed myself happy to assist since it meant I would have a chance to learn more about the lives of the men who, I was more than ever certain, would be vital to Britain's survival.

With both her sons' enthusiastic approval, we departed at sunrise the next morning, enjoying the comfort of a legate's carriage to smooth the journey—that is, until a wheel struck a hole in the road and the much-abused axle gave way.

So, here we are: sitting on a rock beside the ruined road, our progress delayed while the damaged axle is repaired. Aurelia, though somewhat subdued after leaving her sons behind, seems as intent on learning about me and my kinsmen as I am about hers. "But which of your many names do *you* prefer?" she asks again, bending her head near to hear my answer.

"Whichever fits your fancy," I say. "Truly, they are all one to me."

"Then I will call you Merlin."

"As does Uther." I nod. "Mother and son agree."

Before she can say what is on her mind, a loud crack rings out followed by a heavy thump as something gives way and slams onto the stone cobbles. The men shout and curse, venting their growing frustration, and ever-patient Pelleas does what he can to calm them, and work continues.

Smoothing out the wrinkles in her mantle, she gives a little rueful laugh and says, "Folk grumbled much about the roads when I was a girl. But I'm here to tell you those roads are even worse now!" She glances around at the men working on the carriage. "I do believe we'll account ourselves fortunate to make it to Venta in one piece."

"It seems we are to be here a little longer," I observe. "Tell me more about your time in Armorica."

She sighs at the thought, and then brightens. "I have a better idea. You are a bard, are you not?"

"Once upon a time, perhaps."

"Then why don't you tell *me* a story instead?"

I smile at the thought. How long has it been since anyone asked such a thing of me? "I don't have my harp to hand," I tell her. "A bard always sings with his harp. Maybe another time."

She looks around at the stranded carriage where the men are working. "We have time now," she observes, adding somewhat wistfully, "and we may never have another chance. Please?"

I relent. "What tale would you hear?"

"Any you like," she said. "You choose."

I nod and consider which of all the old songs I know might suit the moment. "Well, since you ask, I will tell you one of my favorite stories. My father, Taliesin, was the Chief Bard to King Elphin ap Gwyddno," I explained. "I am told by those who heard him that he sang this song often in the court of kings. It is known by other titles, but my father called it *The Blemished Prince*. It goes like this."

She folded her hands in her lap and settled herself to hear and, closing my eyes, I rekindled the memory and began:

"Hafgan, Chief Bard of Britain, accompanied his king on a circuit of his realm. They were in the Region of the Summer Stars when night came upon them and, having journeyed long, they climbed a hill, rolled themselves in their cloaks, and fell asleep before the fire.

"It seemed to Hafgan that he had merely closed his eyes when he heard a sound like that of a thousand swans in flight. He stood up and looked around; camp and king were gone, and gone, too, the sacred mound. Instead, he saw a silver sea stretching out before him, shimmering in the pearl-gray dawn. On the strand was a boat, with neither oars nor sail, bearing a single passenger: a tall and slender woman dressed all in green and gold, whose grace and elegance far surpassed that of any beauty he had ever known.

"A single look and Hafgan knew he beheld one of the Tylwyth Teg, the Fair Folk race who held the Island of the Mighty long before mortal men wakened and walked the land. The lady beckoned him to the boat and with a sign bade him push it out into deeper water. As he obeyed, he found himself standing with one foot on the shore and one foot in the waves, and it was the time-between-times.

"The lady smiled and said, 'Welcome, Prince Bladudd. Would you see a wonder?' At these words, Hafgan forgot his former life; he became Bladudd and joined the lady in the boat. Off they went, gliding across the glass-smooth sea, passing far beyond the ninth wave so swiftly that no sooner had Bladudd settled back than the boat's keel touched the shore of a mist-covered island.

"Bladudd leapt from the boat and turned to help the lady, but she had gone. He climbed a nearby sea cliff, and thought he saw her walking along the grassy path, so he followed, trying to overtake her. He soon found himself approaching a caer more splendid than any he had ever seen. He slipped through the fortress gates and saw a company of Fair Folk hastening toward the great hall.

"Joining the throng, Bladudd entered the hall and hid behind a pillar. Wherever his eye strayed, he saw treasures marvelous to behold; wonders beyond counting filled every corner and cranny of the hall. The least treasure would have been greater by far than any in his own world. At one end of the hall, on a jeweled throne, sat the king; his hair gleamed bright as a flame, and his face shone like the sun.

"Bladudd thought he would not be discovered. But as he peeped from his hiding place, up jumped the king and exclaimed, 'There is a mortal creature among us! Come out from behind that pillar and declare yourself, Little Man!'

"Stepping forth, Bladudd greeted the king and said, 'I am a man of noble birth. Therefore, I claim the same hospitality that you would ask of me if our places were changed: the best of meat and drink, a fair woman to be my companion, harpers to fill my ears with praises, the warmest place by the fire, and a pile of new fleeces for my bed."

"'Here is an arrogant guest,' observed the king. 'What is your purpose in visiting my realm? What do you want from us?'

"'I swear by the gods my people swear by that I mean no harm,' Bladudd answered. 'Ever and in all things I merely seek the truth. Indeed, all my takings will leave you no poorer, for I desire only a measure of your wisdom.'

"When the king heard Bladudd's declaration, he threw back his head and laughed. 'Think you that we part with our wisdom so lightly, Little Man?'

"'I find it never hurts to ask,' replied Bladudd.

"'So be it,' said the king. 'Your wit and fearless tongue have won you a place among us—though not, perhaps, the place you might have hoped. You shall tend my pigs.'

"Thus, Bladudd became swineherd to the King of the Fortunate Isle. These pigs, Bladudd soon learned, were creatures of considerable merit. Their chief virtue was this: as often as they were killed and eaten, they returned to life the next day. Moreover, eating the meat of these pigs preserved the Fair Folk from the ravages of age and death.

"For seven years, Bladudd watched over the wonderful pigs. In all that time he never got the chance so much as to dip the tip of his smallest finger into the juice of a roasting pig, let alone to taste any of the meat.

"Still, every day at midday the king's servants would come and drive away as many pigs as were needed for that night's feasting. And every morning the pigs would be back in Bladudd's care. With his pigs he walked the Fortunate Isle, met the Tylwyth Teg, conversed with them, and observed their ways. At night, he listened to the bards in the great king's hall and began to understand their songs. Ever watchful, he kept his eyes and ears open and learned many charms and enchantments which he practiced in secret.

"Thus, Prince Bladudd grew in wisdom but, alas, remained

discontented, for his low estate chafed him sorely. He decided to leave. On Samhain night, when the hidden ways between the worlds stand open and crossings can easily be made, he found his chance. While everyone else feasted, Bladudd left the fortress, driving nine of the wondrous pigs before him, for he wanted to bring a boon to Ynys Prydain.

"As ill luck would have it, the peerless pigs squealed as they ran. The Fair Folk king heard their piteous cries and gave chase. Bladudd fled, trying various charms to elude the mighty lord. He changed himself into a salmon and the nine pigs into silver scales upon his back, but the king took the form of an otter.

"Then he changed himself into a squirrel, and the pigs to nine nuts in a pine cone, but the king pursued him in the form of a ferret.

"Whereupon Bladudd changed himself into a heron, and the pigs to nine feathers on his neck—but the king became an eagle.

"Lastly, Bladudd changed into a wolf, and the nine pigs to burrs in his fur. But the king overtook him in the form of a hunter on horseback and, shaking his spear over them, Bladudd and the pigs were restored to their own shapes.

"'You stole my pigs!' railed the King of the Fair Folk.

"'Not so, Mighty Lord,' answered the brazen prince. 'In truth, I have undertaken to save the honor of your name by delivering these pigs to my kinsmen as a gift from you. This I have done so that no one could think you mean and miserly.'

"The king's face became black with anger. 'That was ill spoken, thief! You have no idea of the troubles your meddling would have caused if I had not prevented you. A most terrible and wearisome tribulation awaited you if these pigs ever set foot in your own lands. Yet, for the sake of the innocent I will prevent it. You can thank me for my kindness.'

"'Then I thank you for nothing,' snapped the insolent swineherd.

"'You came seeking wisdom—'

"'Yes, and wisdom I received—no thanks to you.'

"'Ah, if you had but given up your selfishness and pride, you would have received a far greater gift than even you could dream of asking.' So saying, the great king raised the butt of his spear and struck Bladudd squarely on the head so hard that he fell down as one asleep.

"When Bladudd opened his eyes he was once more in this world's realm, but the terrible blow had blighted him: his hair fell out, his teeth rotted, his skin became gray and scaly, his muscles withered, and his bones jutted out sharply. His handsome clothes fell from him in filthy rags. He appeared as one whom Lord Death had groomed for his own.

"Bladudd realized his state, and he mourned bitterly. Gathering his ragged clothes around him, he made his woeful way to a cave in the mountains where he dwelt alone in utter misery for seven years. In all that time, no human came near him, until one day a stranger appeared and summoned him from the shadows.

"Creeping forth, he saw an old woman possessed of neither beauty nor bearing: walleyed, gap-toothed, and heavy-lipped, with skin as creased and rough as old leather. Even so, she was beguiling to Bladudd for she came blithely into his presence and did not flinch or retch at the sight of him. Warmly she greeted him, showing neither fear nor disgust at his hideous deformities.

"'Who are you, woman?' inquired Bladudd. 'What errand brings you here?'

"'I come from a place well known to you, and I bring you glad tidings, for I know a way to heal you if healing be a thing you desire.'

"'Desire!' cried the blemished prince. 'The bards themselves have no word for the breadth of my desire to be healed. I will tell you about desire! Indeed, I have not so much as seen a woman in seven years. Seven years! Of course I desire to be healed!'

"'Very well,' replied the hag with a smack of her lips, 'follow me.' The blemished prince followed his grotesque visitor to a barren hill, and beyond the hill to a barren moor, and beyond the moor to a pool of stinking, black, bubbling mud.

"'Throw off your rags and bathe in the pool,' the crone told him, settling herself upon a nearby rock. 'There is healing in the water.'

"Unhappy Bladudd peered doubtfully at the mud which heaved and sighed, exhaling foul fumes. It seemed to him more punishment than cure, but he gathered his courage and into the foul slime he slid.

"The mud was hot. It burned his skin. Tears ran from his eyes in a stream. But Bladudd, who had borne his sorry affliction with great patience, endured the pain for the sake of his desire to be healed. Still, he could not endure forever. When at last the scalding mud bath grew too hot, he pulled himself from the stinking pool to stand before the woman.

"'This is splendid, to be sure,' Bladudd remarked, looking indignantly down the length of his reeking mud-caked form. 'Yet, I had hoped for more.'

"'For that remark I should leave you as I found you,' the crone snapped. 'Nevertheless, your cure is almost finished.' The gap-toothed hag pointed to a willow tree Bladudd had not observed before. 'At the foot of that tree is a vat of water. Wash the mud from yourself and be quick about it.'

"Bladudd climbed into the vat and found the water clear and cool, soothing his mud-blistered skin. He relaxed in the water and forgot his pains. Indeed, he forgot all his former hurts and troubles. When he finally stirred to rise from the vat, he had been renewed in his mind. He looked at his poor, ravaged body and, marvel of marvels, saw that his body, too, had been renewed.

"'I am healed!' he cried, gazing with joy upon his firm straight limbs. 'Indeed, I am better now than when the Lord of the Fortunate Isle smote me with the haft of his spear.'

"When the hag made no reply, the prince looked up and saw that the disagreeable old crone had vanished and in her place was a beautiful maid, lovelier than any he had ever known. Her hair was pale yellow and braided with shimmering gold; her skin was fair and smooth as milk; her eyes were deepest blue and gleamed like gemstones; her teeth were fine and even, and her nose straight; her brow was high and noble; her neck was slender and elegant; her fingers were long, her arms supple, her breasts soft and shapely.

"'Lady,' breathed Bladudd in a small, awestricken voice, 'where is the ugly old woman who conducted me to this place? I must thank her for the mercy she has shown me.'

"The comely maid looked at Bladudd; she looked to the left and to the right also. 'I see no other woman here,' she replied. And, oh, her voice was like melting honey. Or, perhaps you believe that I am old and ugly?' At this she smiled so sweetly that Bladudd's knees trembled and he feared he might fall on his face before her. 'Lady,' he said, 'I detect neither fault nor flaw in you at all.'

"'Nor I in you,' the lady told him. 'But perhaps you would be more at ease if you were clothed.'

"Bladudd blushed but, espying his tatters lying on the ground, replied, 'Alas, I would go without cloak and clothes rather than wear those filthy rags again.'

"'Ah, well,' mused the maid, 'you must be accustomed to very fine clothes indeed if these be rags to you.' So saying, she leaned from her rock and took up the discarded heap. The startled Bladudd saw that his tatters had become handsome garments once more.

"'My clothes?' he wondered aloud, as well he might, for he beheld cloak, siarc, breeches, and buskins more costly, more luxurious than any he had ever known. 'Are they mine indeed?'

"'You cannot think they are mine,' the lady replied, smoothing her soft white silken mantle with slender hands. 'And between the two of us,' she added, 'it seems to me you have the greater need.'

"The astonished Bladudd dressed himself quickly, and when he had finished, he appeared a very nobleman. 'In truth,' he announced, 'I am no stranger to fine attire, but I have never owned clothes of such quality.'

"'Will you forget your sword?' asked the lady.

"The astonished prince saw that the lady held a golden-hilted sword across her palms. 'Is this mine also?' he asked, suspecting a trick. He had never owned such a magnificent weapon.

"'I see no one here but you,' the lady replied. 'And I tell you the truth, I am well pleased with the sight.'

"Delighted, Bladudd strapped the sword to his hip and felt a very king. He gazed lovingly upon the maid. 'Great Lady,' he breathed, his heart swelling with love and gratitude, 'what is your name that I might thank you?'

"The maid returned his gaze from beneath her long lashes. 'Do you not know me at all?' she asked.

"'If I had ever seen you before,' he answered, 'I would never have let you escape my sight. And if I heard your name but once, I would live forever on the sound.'

"The maid rose from her place on the rock. She smiled and lifted her hand to Bladudd. 'My name is Sovereignty,' she replied. 'Long have I sought you, Bladudd.'

"The renewed prince held his head to one side. 'A name like no other,' he said. 'Yet it becomes you nobly well.' Then he took her warm hand and the holding of it filled him with pleasure. 'Lady,' he said, 'will you stay with me? Before you answer, let me say I do not think I could live one more day if you removed yourself from my sight.'

"'I will stay with you, Bladudd,' the maid replied.

"'Will you wed me?' asked Bladudd, his heart beating like a struck drum.

"'I will wed you, Bladudd,' the fair lady vowed. 'Truly, I was born for you, and you for me—if only you knew it.' She pointed to the willow tree where two tethered horses now stood. So, together the maid and the unblemished prince rode to the realm of men, whereupon Bladudd and the beautiful maid were wed that very day.

"The prince's people rejoiced at his fortuitous return and hailed him king. Lady Sovereignty placed the golden torc of kingship around her husband's throat. From that day, Bladudd ruled wisely and well. His keen desire for truth, and his loyal wife, stood by him through all things, and through all things did Bladudd prosper his people.

"Having dreamed this dream, Hafgan awoke, and it was the time-between-times when the morning stars yet linger before the rising sun. From that day, he sang his dream wherever he went. And blessed were those who heard him."

Finished, we both sit in silence for a moment and let the story settle. When she stirs, Aurelia regards me with an expression I have seen many times over my years as a bard: mingled amazement and wonder, tinged with a hint of reverence and, perhaps, a touch of awe. Reaching out, she places a cold hand over mine, "Thank you, Merlin. That was beautiful," she says. "And strange."

From behind us on the road there comes another thump, accompanied by more swearing from the drivers, and the spell of the song is broken. "The town lies just beyond those hills to the south," I observe. "If the carriage cannot be mended, we can send for help, or ride the rest of the way."

Aurelia shakes her head gently. "My riding days are over, my friend," she replies, gently and somewhat allusively. Before I can probe further, she turns an inquisitive gaze on me, and says, "But you, Wise Emrys—you do not age as others do. Why is that?"

I shrug and offer the answer I usually give when anyone asks such a question: "It is merely my Fair Folk inheritance. Those born of Llyn Llyonesse seem to carry their years more lightly. It is nothing more than that."

"Not magic?" she wonders. "That's what people say, you know."

"Perhaps," I allow. "What is magic except something we do not understand? There is so much about this worlds-realm we have yet to discover. And then, there are things that men say about me—and those things I do not understand! Some of them you would not believe."

"I know that only too well!" she hoots. "It is the same with me. Why, the way some tell it, I strangled my best friend so that I could steal her husband and make myself Queen of Armorica." An old fire flares instantly, then subsides just as quickly. "Ah, but that is as far from the truth as the moon from a mushroom."

"Life is often like that," I agree, thinking of my own strange journey to this time and place. "And the truth of a thing is the province of but a blesséd few."

"Yes, well, it is at least true to say that if I had never gone to Deva Vitrix, I would not be here at all," she declares firmly. "Especially, as it was not in my mind to go there in the first place."

"Yet, go you did. What happened to change your mind?"

"My father died."

1

THE FUNERAL OF TULLIUS GAIUS PAULINUS was an occasion of great local importance, and some regional import as well. The tragic and untimely death of a prominent public figure—a long-serving magistrate of good repute and high personal regard—was a genuine sensation for little Venta and beyond. My father was loved by those who knew him personally, and highly respected by most everyone else. Consequently, the countless details and preparations such a significant public event demanded quickly exceeded my young grasp.

Both Augustus and our good priest Tomos came to my rescue. They did their best to protect my feelings and interests, I know; but word spread through the town and countryside on winged feet and preparations soon grew beyond any involvement, much less control, I might have commanded. A grand procession was planned, a carved stone sarcophagus complete with plaque and plinth commissioned, a ceremonial service led by the bishop and burial in the church, followed by a funeral meal with speeches by dignitaries who knew Tullius and, perhaps more importantly, wanted to be recognized as worthy successors or at least bask in the warm glow of his memory.

None of this touched me. What did any of it matter? Devastated, numb with shock, and deep in grief, it was all I could do to rise each day, splash water on my face, and force down a morsel of the vast quantity of food that flowed into the house from neighbors and well-wishers. Dorcas, bless her, took it in hand to manage all the domestic dealings, and did so with a supremely gentle touch. Her kindly

97

ministrations went unremarked by any in those difficult days, but I cherished her for it.

On the day of the funeral, I woke early, washed, gathered my hair into a loose braid held in place by a bone comb, and chose my long white mantle and wide yellow girdle; I brushed and put on my best gray cloak and fastened it with one of my mother's fine silver brooches. Then, after lacing on my soft leather shoes, I squared my shoulders and stepped into the courtyard, determined to conduct myself with fortitude and dignity—neither of which I possessed: my stomach was all in knots over what was to transpire. Dorcas met me, took my hands, and gave me words of encouragement and a little sweetened wine—to settle my nerves, she said—and then priest Tomos arrived, and we sat together with Augustus standing by while he explained the order of events.

Outside, the street sounds increased, growing louder, reaching my ear as a slowly building jumble of confused babble. Finally, there came a loud thump on the door. Augustus answered and returned to announce that it was time to go. Tomos rose and, taking my hand, led me out into the street where most of the townspeople were already gathered and waiting.

As the nearest relation of Tullius, I was to walk at the head of the procession and lead it to the church, but I clung tight to Tomos' hand and insisted that he stay beside me. We were followed by Augustus in his role as adiutor of many years and, behind him, the very somber and upright Bishop Bevyn. Our bishop—severe for no good reason, as it seemed to me—was well-meaning withal and his attendance at this provincial ceremony was appreciated by all. My father had no living relatives that I knew of, so for comfort and succor I had only Tomos and another other cleric, Egan, a young priest who was new to Venta and did not really know my father.

Immediately behind the bishop in the procession came one of Venta's worthies—a fellow named Grifud who, apparently, represented the town in some way or other—given the task of ringing a bell and leading the cart bearing my father's body. The shroud-covered corpse had been placed on the door of the church, removed that morning to serve the purpose. A symbolic gesture, but a nice one: in death, as in life, Tullius would enter God's realm through the wide-open and unobstructed portal of the faith—as expressed by its physical representation on earth, our stone-built church.

Mind, I cannot claim this learned observation as my own. It was Tomos who explained the significance of the church door to me. But I remember it as I remember few other details of what happened that day; so much occurred in such a short time that it all passed in a blur of muddled sound and motion around me. Having never been a member of a funeral party before, I did not know how to act, but I played my part, as best I could, hoping against hope that I would not dishonor the occasion by embarrassing myself or my father in some memorable and unforgivable way.

In the end, I need not have worried. The funeral service was populated with so many other dignitaries and celebrants from near and far that I was almost entirely overlooked. I might as well have been a passerby who, arrested by the crowd, stopped to wonder what was taking place. Indeed, the only time a thought was given to me was when Bishop Bevyn looked down from the altar and beckoned me to bring the token that would be placed in the sarcophagus.

For this, Augustus and I had chosen an object that defined my father from my earliest memory: his well-worn penknife. Not for Tullius a golden bauble or silver trinket, but an item of humble service, one used to sharpen the reeds he used to write his innumerable letters and accounts day on day as a busy magistrate in pursuit of his official duties. Though the bone handle was worn smooth of its carved decoration and the blade whetted thin, Tullius was almost never without it when at his work attending to the affairs of the province.

The bishop offered a kindly smile when I handed him the penknife—he, at least, understood its worth—and then he returned it to me and gestured for me to place it atop the shroud. I accomplished this small task without falling over and Bevyn gave me a kindly nod of gentle dismissal; I returned to my place with Tomos and Augustus, and the service moved on.

Then it was to the church's burial ground—a fine green plot to the south of the church—where my father would be placed in the grave which contained my mother's remains of many years ago. A new stone was to be cut with his name and that of my mother and would be set up when it was ready. As with many other things, I was not consulted—nor did I like to think about it anyway, so was content to allow events to take their course.

Though I could have collapsed into a sodden heap of sadness, I forced myself to stand like a marble statue and watch as my father's body was lowered into a stone box sunk in the earth with little heaps of dirt on either side...

And that's the last thing I remember clearly, for I must have drifted away on clouds of memory: Tullius in his big chair, the tidy piles of messages arrayed before him, scratching away with his reed pen; or hearing his voice as he tromped through the streets hailing constituents; head to head with some local official, deciding the fate of this or that project; wine cup in hand discussing the day's events with Augustus as they sat in the courtyard of a golden evening...

When I returned to the world around me, my father was buried and Bishop Bevyn was singing the 'Amen' to a prayer I had completely missed.

Most of the townsfolk dispersed after that and I was among the last to leave the burial ground. Tomos, good and true friend, stayed by me and accompanied me home where Dorcas and, I do believe, most of Venta's widows had prepared a funeral banquet for our guests. This meal was more of a formal function than anything I might have arranged; still, it was a suitable event. I was heartened to see so many friends and neighbors filling both house and courtyard, and all of them sharing glad stories and fond memories of my father. I could catch but fleeting snatches of what they said, though the spirit animating their faces spoke more clearly than words. Dear hearts, every one.

The wine flowed and the tables were continually replenished, and the talk grew louder. This went on far into the night, but I could not. The constant concentration and attention required to make sense of all the chatter around me, combined with the heavy emotions of the day, eventually overthrew me. I stayed awake as long as I could until, dazed with fatigue and a little muzzy from food and wine, I crept away to my bed.

I slept long and rose the next day to a world now changed and, with it, my life as I had always known it.

2

SOMEONE OF GREATER WIT, someone more canny or worldly wise might have guessed what lay ahead. I confess that I did not. I suppose my own cares loomed so large with me that I could not see beyond them; here I was, standing in the middle of a forest with trees crowding my view in every direction. Should I have at least tried to glance beyond my worries to see the shape of things to come?

Perhaps. But what would that have done?

After all, I attended the conclave in Viroconium, and I was there when Procurator Constantine delivered his urgent call to action to meet the rising threat of invasion in the face of Rome's fecklessness and failure. I was there when Constantine made that fateful proclamation that Britain would no longer look to our Great Mother for nurture and protection; henceforth we would provide these things for ourselves. I should have recognized this for what it was: a cataclysm in the making. But the sorry truth is, I was oblivious to all but my own small concerns.

Certainly, I might be forgiven my blindness. The tempest of waves stirred up by Tullius' death swamped my own miserable little boat and continued to occupy my life following the funeral and for many days thereafter. Where was I to go? What was I to do? What would become of me? These concerns were all my waking world.

One plan after another was conceived, weighed, and, for one reason or another, discarded. The first I realized that the procurator's decree would alter the existence of every citizen on this island—and far beyond, come to that—the very first glimmer of the disaster to come, was when the messenger arrived some days after my father's funeral. Like many another before him, the skinny youth simply appeared in the courtyard bearing a small leather pouch from which he withdrew a scrap of parchment, this one bearing a red seal.

Aware of his arrival, I glanced out into the courtyard and saw Augustus accept the message and dismiss the courier with a coin. He returned to the workroom with the packet in his hand, regarding it as if it were a sleeping snake that might bite if awakened.

"What is it?" I asked upon joining him. He did not reply. I think he already guessed the contents and was trying to think how best to respond. "Augustus?" I asked again. "What's wrong?"

"This is from Glevum," he replied, still looking at the sealed parchment. "From the proconsul."

"Glevum has a new proconsul?" I wondered. "So soon?" Well I might ask. Esico had been slain in the same attack that had wounded and eventually killed my father; and Mona had also been slaughtered by brigands on the way home—a brutal assault I was trying very hard to forget. These were recent events and, as my father insisted, I knew that a replacement would be found, but it still surprised me that the change had come so quickly. I pointed to the parcel. "Open it and see what it says."

Augustus nodded and slid his thumb under the flap and unfolded the stiff parchment. He read a moment, then regarded me with an expression I had never seen before—a look of mild astonishment, or was it dismay? "He's coming."

"Who is coming? The proconsul?"

He shook his head. "The magistrate."

"Which magistrate?" I demanded. "You're not making sense, Augustus. Tell me."

"*Our* new magistrate," he replied in a hollow voice. "The proconsul has appointed a new magistrate for Venta and he is on his way here. He should arrive any day."

"A new magistrate ... here ... but ..."

Well, of course. That is the very nature of things. Life goes on. Old things pass away and new ones replace them. Still, it can be a shock when it happens to you—all the more when it happens so fast.

It seemed to me that the funeral had only just taken place. Sunk so low in grief and mourning, I had paid no attention to the passing of time, or what must come after. Now, the reckoning had arrived. Augustus and I stood in silence for a long moment, each thinking how this change might affect us. Finally, I said, "Can he do that?" At Augustus' blank look, I added, "Can the new proconsul of Glevum simply appoint a new magistrate for Venta just like that? Don't *we* have any say in it at all?"

Augustus looked at the message in his hand once more. "It seems not. Venta is within the provincial boundary and Glevum is the principal *civitas*, so . . ."

"So that is that," I concluded, anger at some perceived injustice springing up within me. "A new magistrate just like that. It isn't fair. We should have been consulted—or at least told."

"I think we just were," replied Augustus with large, sad eyes. He waved the message in the air. "We have just been told."

With the benefit of time, the nature of the situation has become clearer to me. The raiders' attack at the conclave meant that a valuable southern province had suffered not one but two painful losses—that of an able proconsul and an esteemed magistrate—leaving two empty places, essential posts needing to be filled. There was nothing to be gained by leaving those offices vacant; the smooth functioning of government required a swift response. Procurator Constantine had wasted no time in appointing a new proconsul to Glevum, who had appointed a new magistrate to Venta. All right and proper.

Older now, and with many years of life and the judgment of hard-earned hindsight, I realize that these changes were inevitable—of course they were. At the time, however, the arrival of the new magistrate came as a blow I felt down to the soles of my feet. And, though I could not have guessed, it was but the first of many jolts that were to come following my father's death. I was not to know it then, but my feet were already on the path leading to places I had never been and could not have dreamed I would go.

"There it is," Augustus concluded, snapping the parchment with a fingernail. "The new magistrate is coming. We can but hope he is an able, upright, and honest man."

"Thoughtful and kindly would be nice, too," I added, resignation settling over me like dust from a coming storm.

Ah, well. Able and honest Lucanus Marocanti may have been, but thoughtful and kindly he was not. This we were to learn within the first moments of his arrival.

Four days after the message announcing his appointment, Lucanus Marocanti climbed out of a horse-drawn cart and stood in the street outside our door. I cannot now recall what I may have expected, but it was decidedly *not* the sudden appearance of a young man of striking mien: quick, dark eyes, immaculate black beard razored short, hair like curly black fleece. He was arrayed in the old-fashioned Roman style with a long cream-colored tunic, half-sized cloak, and short red trousers, and wore the fine woolen stockings and high-laced sandals favored by those of an archaic aristocratic bent.

Tall and decisive in movement, always giving the impression that he was about to dart away on some errand of import, or ready to take immediate action, he seemed never to rest, and never to have any but the briefest of moments to greet you or deal with you about anything at all. Smiles were rare and fleeting. I never saw him laugh.

Lucanus—or Luc, as he preferred—was young, as I say, but ever strove to appear a much more mature man. I suppose he had risen so swiftly to his position of prominence that he had adopted this guise in order to be more readily accepted by his fellow officials, as well as by those he must govern. Then again, it might have been that as an upward-thrusting official from some distant province, he knew himself foreign and ignorant of local affairs and sought to make up this lack of experience with a show of busy efficiency. Whatever the reason, I am not at all convinced that the pretense served him as well as he imagined.

Our new magistrate also came with a wife. Oh! And such a wife!

If Lucanus imagined himself an elder statesman of lofty mien, then Velvinnia was a princess of vast domain and golden renown. Imperious to an intense and insufferable degree, she was also lazy and endlessly self-besotted. In fact, she was not long in Venta before merchants and townsfolk began calling her Queen Velva. If she had commanded slaves, I do believe they would have strangled her in her bed before the month was out.

The carriage drew up, as I say, and Lucanus stepped out, took in the place of his new appointment, and swept into the courtyard, closely followed by his wife. The new magistrate stopped in the middle of our cozy little enclave and cast his imperious gaze around, a slight frown forming on his face as Augustus, Dorcas, and I assembled to greet him.

His wife took her place beside him and gave the house and courtyard a quick once-over glance. "Shabby," she pronounced.

"No matter," he said. "We can change it."

Augustus moved quickly to introduce us to the new administrator. The magistrate raised his hand in an indifferent greeting. "I am Magistrate Lucanus," he said, "you may call me Luc. And are you the steward for this estate?"

"No, Magistrate," replied Augustus, "I am Magistrate Tullius' *adiutor* and assistant."

"Was."

"Pardon, sir?"

"*Was*, you meant. *I* am magistrate now."

"Yes, I *was* his assistant." Augustus turned to me and Dorcas and put out his hand to continue the introductions.

"I won't be needing an assistant," Lucanus informed him. "Though I shall keep you on a few days to brief me on any outstanding business Tullius left undone."

He made it sound as if my father had been careless and neglectful by dying so inconveniently. His tone rankled instantly; my fists clenched and my spine stiffened.

"And after?" wondered Augustus.

"After what? Do strive to make yourself understood, man."

"You said you would keep me on a few days. I was merely inquiring about your intentions after that."

"We shall see what we shall see." He gave the courtyard and house another glance and said, "The magistrate's chambers—where are they?"

"This way," said Augustus, indicating the separate wing of the house.

"Show me." He turned and started away. Dorcas and I were left standing in the middle of the courtyard with the magistrate's wife.

She regarded us for a long moment. "You two—who are you?" she asked. "Servants?"

"No, we are—" began Dorcas.

"To be sure, I'll be hiring my own household staff in due course. A magistrate must have the best servants obtainable." She turned to me. "What do you do?"

Her voice was low and I did not hear her properly. I stared back, hoping she would repeat the question so I could understand.

She moved closer. "I asked you a question," she snapped. "Are you mute?"

Dorcas made to intervene. "If I might—"

"I am talking to *her*," she said. "I will speak to you directly." She turned back to me. "Well? I am waiting."

"Not mute," I muttered. "Deaf."

"What? Speak up, girl!"

"I am part deaf," I said loudly. "I do not hear very well."

"Oh. I see," she sniffed. "Was that so difficult?" She turned to Dorcas. "And are you the housekeeper, I suppose?"

The elder woman shook her head. "I am ... ah ..." Here she faltered as her role had never been properly defined. "... a friend. I have been helping here while Tullius was ill."

"What is your name?"

"I'm called Dorcas."

"You will call me Domina Velvinnia," she declared, then turned her disapproving gaze on me. "And you?" She remembered what I had said then repeated the question in an exaggerated, overloud voice—as if I were an imbecile who might not understand simple words. "What ... is ... your ... name, girl?"

"I ... am ... Aurelia," I replied, meeting her tone, "daughter ... of ... magistrate ... Tullius."

"Hmph!" she sniffed. "Aurelia, is it? Odd name for a girl such as you. Your father's idea, no doubt. Provincials always attempting to advance themselves by putting on airs."

Well, I heard this plain enough. "No such thing," I replied, speaking up with some force. "It was my grandmother's name. She was a queen of the Silures."

"Was she now?" she snipped dismissively. "Local tribe, I expect." She frowned and regarded us as annoyances to be dispelled; then, with exaggerated care, she said, "So long as you remain here, you will make yourselves useful." Pointing to me, she commanded, "*You* may begin by bringing in our baggage." Turning to Dorcas, she said, "I want to see my rooms. Take me."

This was the commencement of the new regime, and the beginning of my long travail.

3

THE NEW DOMINA DECIDED that *my* room was best for her personal use. Our house was of the old villa style, with rooms in short wings around a central courtyard. Though a small, square chamber—the one I had occupied for as many years as I could remember—it had a narrow lattice that opened onto the courtyard and its door opened onto the main corridor to the interior of the house. Velvinnia took one look and determined that this room would henceforth be hers.

The rest of Magistrate Lucanus' goods and possessions arrived by wagon later in the day and, with it, two servants—one male, Fulvius, for him; and one female, Flavia, for her. After cursory introductions, the two set about unpacking their masters' things and rearranging the interior of the house to suit the domina's fancy. I kept out of sight in the kitchen where I helped Dorcas prepare a welcome meal for the new magistrate's table.

Not until I came into the main dwelling some time later did I see that my few personal belongings—my clothes, cloaks and mantles, my precious books, my little box of pins and brooches, and the like—had all been dumped in a heap in the courtyard. I stormed at once to confront the culprits. "You threw out my things!" I charged. "Why?"

Fulvius and Flavia were shaking out a thick woven cloth to lay on the floor beside my bed. Fulvius replied, "Domina said to take them away. This is her room now."

Uncertain whether I had heard correctly, I said, "*Who* told you?"

"Domina . . ." He pointed vaguely in the direction of the house. "The new lady master . . ."

"Velvinnia?" I asked. "What do you mean 'her' room?"

"That's right," Fulvius replied without a glance at me. "The domina will have it for her private chamber."

"Please, I do not hear very well," I told them. "Are you saying that this is to be *her* chamber from now on?"

Fulvius, without deigning to look at me, said, "You heard right."

"Where am I to go?"

Flavia—a squat, fat-faced young woman with a slight limp—turned to me and, speaking slowly so I would not misunderstand, was slightly more forthcoming, "We were not told anything more. Domina Velvinnia only said to clean out the room and make it ready for her."

I did not care to cross paths with the domina again, so I went straight to the magistrate and entered the official chambers. The workroom was empty; he and Augustus were in my father's chamber. The door was closed, but I gave a loud knock and stepped inside. Augustus stood beside the table on which were spread all the messages and petitions that had accumulated during my father's infirmity. Lucanus glanced up.

"You do not enter the magistrate's chamber uninvited," he declared. "Never do that again."

Augustus made to intervene. "If you please, Magistrate. Aurelia was her father's aide and assistant. She served him—"

Lucanus cut off his explanation with a chop of his hand. "Tullius is dead and I am here now. I do not require the assistance of a former official's family members." He made to wave me away but, seeing as I did not move, he snarled, "Well?"

"They have taken my room and thrown my possessions into the courtyard," I informed him with as much calm as I could command.

"Who has done this?" he wondered blandly.

"Your servants. They say they are acting on the domina's instructions."

"There you are then." He nodded and returned to his survey of the work before him. Augustus, standing off to one side, gave me a sympathetic look.

"What am I to do?" I demanded. "Where am I to go?"

Lucanus looked up sharply. "That is not my concern."

I do not know what I expected, but it was not that. "Where am I to go?"

He dropped the scrap in his hands and regarded me as he might a buzzing insect intent on annoying him. "Am I to understand that you have failed to make suitable provision for yourself?"

"N-no," I stammered. "I didn't know . . . *we* didn't know . . . everything happened so fast, I . . ."

"But, you must have relations—a brother, aunt, uncle . . . someone? Go to them."

I was already shaking my head before he finished. "I have no one," I told him. "No one like that."

Augustus and Tomos, sad to say, were the only ones I could truly count as friends. Augustus bit his lip, but remained silent.

"You cannot expect to stay *here*," said the magistrate with a finality that allowed no argument. "Just because you lived here owing to your deceased father's position does not give you the right to live here indefinitely. You'll have to find someplace to go."

The enormity of my predicament revealed itself to me then. "I have nowhere else," I said, more to myself than anyone else. Whatever fight I had left bled away as a heavy, dark hopelessness descended upon me.

Lucanus stared at me, smug in his superiority. "Are you telling me your father was so reviled and despised in this town that no one is willing to come to the aid of his brat?"

A swift hot surge of anger flooded my being, scattering the despair of moments before. I stared at this jumped-up coxcomb in a rage of disbelief. How could anyone think this of my father—the best man I had ever known? I tried to find words and breath to defy his spiteful accusation, but words failed me. I could hardly breathe, I was so angry. If looks alone could have butchered, that man would have been a heap of flayed flesh, bones, and entrails at my feet.

Yet, there he sat in his oily conceit, his arrogance thick as the stupidity that nourished it. "So, you have nowhere to go."

I did not trust myself to answer, but stared mutely furious at him.

But the man sitting in my father's chair was not finished humiliating me, the orphan before him. "I cannot accept that this is my problem," he said. "You should have been thinking what to do long before this. You knew this day was coming. You should have been making plans for yourself. This, you failed to do, so now you come crying to me. Again, this is not my problem. *You* are not my problem."

He made a flicking motion with his hand to shoo me away. Again,

Augustus plucked up his courage and spoke. "Tullius devoted his whole life to Venta. He was neither reviled nor despised—far from it. He was highly considered and there are many here who owe him a debt of gratitude. Allow me to speak to them and I am certain a place will be found for Aurelia. But it grows late and I do not think—"

"Enough, you two!" Lucanus cried. "Enough." He straightened and, crossing his arms over his narrow chest, glanced from one of us to the other as he considered a solution. Finally, speaking loudly so there would be no mistake, he said, "You can stay here until you find someone who will have you—a few days only. Until then, you will help the servants with their chores. I'm sure there is much to do to make this place livable. Go see Fulvius and he will put you to work."

Thoroughly humiliated, my cheeks burning with shame, I turned without a word and left the chamber.

I did not go directly to Fulvius, but instead returned to the kitchen. Dorcas was peeling onions into a bowl. She saw my face and realized something terrible had happened. "Aurelia, dear—what is it?" I had held my tears until I she spoke, and then the deluge began.

When, after several halting attempts and a sip of sweet wine to calm me, the flood resided enough, I explained to her the awful things the new magistrate had said, and how my room had been taken over by his hag of a wife and my belongings thrown out into the courtyard. We talked awhile after that. Dorcas, good and kind, listened to me and did what she could to comfort me. She was mother to me in those moments. "What will you do?"

"I don't know." I shook my head, desolation once again descending over me in a dark, gray cloud. "My father is dead. I have no other family."

That night, after helping serve the meal Dorcas had prepared, I ate from the leavings—the scraps Lucanus and Velvinnia discarded—and slept on the kitchen floor. It was not the most comfortable or restful sleep I had ever known, but at least it was warm and quiet—and away from the two tyrants.

Over the next few days, Fulvius treated me as his personal slave, giving me the chores he found too odious or tiresome to do himself. And when he was not ordering me to fetch that, or carry this, then it was the domina issuing commands. The female servant, Flavia—for reasons unknown—was released from kitchen duties at night and I was made to serve the meals in the evening. I learned quickly enough to eat from the preparations *before* the dishes were served, so I got more than just the crumbs and leavings. Velvinnia also made me wash her underclothes and empty her chamber pots; but I was not allowed to touch what she considered her finer things since, as she explained, I obviously would not know how to treat them properly.

One morning she went out to, as she said, "delight in the steaming waters of the local baths."

Venta does not have a bathhouse—as I might have told her, if she had deigned to ask me. The town *did* have a public bath once upon a time, but the roof collapsed some years before I was born and, through lack of funds or skill, or both, the damage had never been repaired and the place—like so much else in our little outpost of the empire—was slowly crumbling into ruin, the bricks and stones being carted off for more useful purposes elsewhere.

Domina Velvinnia returned some time later in a red-faced huff. She stormed into the courtyard fuming about the shocking lack of basic necessities and human comforts in this fly-blown turd of a town. She had worked herself into a rage and vented her anger on the first person to cross her path. Unfortunately, that was me. I was carrying a basket of eggs that had just been delivered from the market and she saw me darting into the corridor leading to the kitchen and called to me.

I pretended I had not heard and kept going.

"Girl!" she shouted, angrier and louder. "Come here when I command you!"

I stopped and turned. "Did you speak, Domina?"

"Come here!"

I moved a step or two closer. "Was there something you wanted?"

She glanced around furiously. "Look at this place!" she growled, casting a wayward hand toward the empty courtyard. "Filthy as a pig wallow! Clean it!"

"Clean it?" I looked around. The courtyard had been swept the day before and was just as tidy as it ever was.

"Sweep it!" she screamed. "Sweep it at once!"

"But it was swept last evening," I pointed out. "There is nothing to sweep."

She charged forward and snatched the eggs from my grasp. Raising the basket she hurled it across the stone-paved yard; it spun in the air, spilling eggs along its path until smashing against the ivy-clad wall. Broken eggs marked the flight of the basket, bright yellow yolks and whites oozing into a sticky goo on the pavement.

"There!" she cried, shaking with rage. "Now wash it! I want it to shine! Do you hear? I want everything to shine!"

I stared at her for as long as I dared, then turned away and retrieved the empty basket. I then went to fetch washing cloths and a bucket of water. Queen Velvinnia was gone when I returned and I proceeded to scrape up the broken eggshells and gunk; after that, I washed the entire courtyard just as she ordered. I was still down on my hands and knees, scrubbing the threshold at the street, when she returned. Hands on hips, she gave the courtyard a cursory glance and informed me that it was not good enough. "Do it again!" she said. "Do it right this time."

I knew better than to argue. So, without a word, I refilled my leather bucket and began once more with new washcloths. I did not see her again until evening. But my degradation was not over. Flavia and Fulvius had been freed from their duties for the night, so it fell to Dorcas and me to serve the highly exalted Magistrate of Venta and his consort their evening meal. Yes, Dorcas had been employed as cook until another, perhaps more suitable, kitchen master could be found. My own position remained undefined, but I was content to help Dorcas. I ferried the dishes to and from the table, poured the wine, and such.

This night, Lucanus had invited two of Venta's leading elders to join him—an attempt to curry favor among the town's elite—men I knew, or at least had met once or twice before through business with my father. Both, so far as I knew, were honorable citizens, upright and of good repute, and their wives were respected women. Wine and olives from Iberia had been bought for the occasion and special dishes requested. Dorcas had performed wonders and I was on my best behavior—after what had happened earlier in the day, I did not wish to invite another confrontation or rekindle the domina's wrath.

"Thank you, Aurelia," said one of the visitors as I made to refill his cup. "I am sorry about your father. He was a good man." He smiled sadly. "How are you faring?"

"She serves here," Velvinnia cut in. "For now." As if to emphasize this point, she said, "We'll make a decent servant of her yet."

The guests exchanged awkward glances, but I continued as if I had not heard and the uncomfortable meal continued. Lucanus, however, was not finished. Perhaps he wanted to show himself master over his house, or wished to impress his august visitors, or demonstrate his authority—I don't know. But I had just placed the bowls of olives on the cloth-covered table, and finished pouring the wine into the fine cups, when the magistrate demanded, "Where are the eggs?"

"Magistrate?" I was not certain I had heard him correctly.

"I asked you a question, girl!" he said, raising his voice. "Did you hear? Where... are... my... eggs?" He glanced at his guests and gave a little half smile. "She is deaf, you know."

Turning back to me, he said, with humiliating exaggeration, "I gave specific orders that eggs in spiced wine were to be served tonight—a delicacy for my special guests." He put out a hand to his table companions and bathed them with his benevolent smile. "Good food for good company, am I right?"

I hesitated, deciding how best to answer. The magistrate frowned, his guests looked uneasy, and his harpy wife pursed her lips and gazed in smug satisfaction at me having to answer for this unforgivable infraction.

"Girl, I asked you a question," he declared. "The eggs. Where... are... my eggs?"

"Velvinnia broke them," I blurted. Unable to avoid the looming conflict, I waded in boldly. "Your wife threw them across the courtyard and broke them."

"What?" he challenged.

"The boy brought the basket you ordered from the market," I explained, keeping my tone even, factual. "The domina was angry at not finding a bathhouse in town. She grabbed the basket from me and threw it across the courtyard. All the eggs flew out and they smashed on the pavement."

He gawped at me. His guests, stunned, lowered their cups, uncertain how to react. One of the women gave me a sympathetic look.

"Am I to believe this?" demanded Lucanus.

"It is the truth." I was aware of Velvinnia glaring razors at me. "If you don't believe me, ask your wife."

Slapping her hand flat on the table, Velvinnia reared up out of her chair and shouted, "Lying bitch! Get out of my sight!"

I looked to the magistrate. "There are no spiced eggs tonight," I said—as if I had not heard the insult. "Would you like more olives instead?"

"Go!" he said, flicking his hand at me. "We will speak of this later."

Needless to say, Dorcas served the rest of the meal. I retreated to the kitchen where I spent the night. Then, some little time before dawn, I awoke with a stiff back and a bold new thought: *There is someone I can go to.*

What is more, the invitation had already been given—the voice warm, heartfelt, sincere. As I sat in the silent room, the early morning light creeping in through the open doorway, the very words came back to me. *You can stay as long as you like. Please, do come.*

4

"YOU MUST LISTEN TO REASON," Augustus told me. "This plan is foolhardy and doomed to failure."

"Why? Because it is *my* idea?" I spat. "Or is it because I'm only a weak and foolish girl—is that it?"

Augustus sighed and looked to Dorcas for help. "Aurelia, dear," she offered, "you must listen to him when he says it is simply too dangerous for a young woman to travel all that way alone—with no guide, or friends along the way."

"Think what happened on the road last time," added Augustus. "And even then you traveled with an armed guard..."

"Take that back!" I snapped. The memory of that attack and its aftermath was still too raw.

"I'm sorry, Aurelia, but it's true," he replied. "You would have no legionaries to protect you this time. Your safety... your *life* would be at risk every step of the way."

He was right, of course. And he meant well. I took a moment to compose myself before saying, "What else am I to do?" I looked to Dorcas, who was biting her lip. "Tell me. What am I to do? I have nowhere else to go!"

"You could stay here until we find a better place for you," she answered. "The domina has said—"

"Queen Velva hates me!" I snapped. "She has made it exceedingly clear that I am welcome here only as her household slave. I tell you the truth, both of you, I would rather die than serve that pair of preening magpies."

I saw the hurt in Augustus' eyes and realized I had gone too far.

"*I* have agreed to stay on and serve them," he said quietly.

I reached out and took his hand in both of mine. "I'm sorry." I pressed his hand.

"He said he would value my experience and opinion."

"As did my father," I told him. "And I am certain you will prove your worth a thousand times over. But, can you not see that it is different for me? They look at me and see only a half-deaf scullion—an orphan, a nuisance to be tolerated that they will doubtless cast off at the first opportunity. After last night, they don't need another excuse to do it."

Augustus and Dorcas heard me then at last; they regarded one another in silence for a moment, then Dorcas said, "How do you know this woman—this legate's wife in Deva—will have you?"

I sensed their objection beginning to soften. "She has told me so," I answered quickly. "She invited Tullius and me to sojourn with them in Deva while he healed from his injuries." I lowered my eyes and added, "If only we had accepted her offer, my father would still be alive today."

"Don't say that," Dorcas chided. "Don't even think it."

"Why not? It's true, isn't it?"

"Nothing in life is ever so forthright as that," she countered. "Only our Wise Redeemer knows what the future might bring. We must trust the one who holds our destiny in his hands to know what is best."

"Are we in church now?" I grumbled. "You sound like Bishop Bevyn."

Oh, I knew she meant well, and spoke the simple truth. But I could not admit it. At the time, all I could think was that we had ever trusted the wisdom of God and look where it had gotten us: my father dead, and myself hostage to unfeeling usurpers. Either hostage or homeless—which was it to be?

Homeless, perhaps, but not hopeless. I *would* go to Helena and Aridius, and they *would* take me in. And if not? Well, then at least I would be free of the self-important tyrant and his insufferable despot wife, free to make my own decisions. One way or another, I would begin a new life in a new place.

There was more discussion after that, but in the end the two of them agreed they would help me with what I now thought of as *my escape*. This help was not long in coming. I endured three more days of senseless humiliation at the hands of my tormentors. Then, as the sun was lowering on the fourth day, Augustus burst into the cookhouse, where I was standing at the fire stirring a bubbling pot of pease porridge, trying to keep it from burning.

"Good news! I have just come back from the harbor," he announced, holding a brace of sleek mackerel by a string through the gills, a fine meal for someone's supper—but not mine. "I have spoken to my cousin and he says he has a ship being loaded now and soon ready to sail north."

I looked up, eyebrows raised in surprise. "Your cousin?"

"A trader—a local man, named Drustan. He knew your father. You might have seen him. He came here sometimes for taxes and permits and such." He saw my uncomprehending expression and waved it away. "You'll remember when you see him. Anyway, he is taking some goods to Deva Vitrix. That's were the legate lives, yes?"

I nodded. "Aridius and Helena, yes."

"Well then," Augustus rubbed his hands. "I have begged a place for you to travel with him and he has promised to look after you and deliver you to the legate's door."

"He agreed to this?"

"Happily. Drustan said your father helped him—some difficulty about a license or something a few years ago—and he said he would be delighted to repay the debt." He beamed. "Is that not good news?"

"I am to go on a ship?" I asked, still trying to take in what it meant. "Truly?"

"They hope to depart tomorrow or the next day," he continued, glancing around the cramped cookhouse. "You won't have to be a kitchen slave anymore."

"Tomorrow?"

"Or possibly the day after," he confirmed. "They are waiting for some supplies and then they'll be ready to sail. We'll have to get *you* ready, too."

Beaming broadly and humming to himself, he scurried off to attend to other duties, leaving me with word that he would make all the necessary arrangements and that I would only have to gather the things I wanted to take with me. "Leave all the rest to me," he said as he hurried away. "I'll see you right, never fear."

Long wooden spoon in hand, I stood staring at the green sludge boiling away in the iron pot, and that now-familiar feeling of sudden desolation swept over me once more. It stayed with me most of the day—which is why I crept off to see Tomos at first opportunity.

"Forgive me, Aurelia," he said, his lips pursed in benign confusion, "but I cannot for the life of me see any difficulty here. It is your desire to go, is it not?"

We sat alone on a bench in the yard outside the little church—not far from where my father had been buried. I glanced toward the still-fresh grave. "Maybe," I allowed. "But I won't see you anymore, or Augustus or anyone else again." I moaned as the thought occurred to me. "I'll never see Venta again."

"Why think that?" he asked. "You will. Of course, you will. How not? When you are settled, older maybe, you can come back from time to time to visit us." Tomos, smiling at me and willing me to put off my unhappiness, said, "Little Venta will always be here, Aurelia."

I thought about this for a while, then said, "Will you come to see me away? Please, Tomos, will you?"

"Let anyone try to stop me."

And this is how I came to be standing on the rough timber dock in the tiny harbor on the great Hafren estuary, waiting for a leaky trading ship—bravely named *Epona*—to depart.

5

I LOOKED OUT ACROSS THE FLAT, gray expanse of slow-moving water, gleaming dully in the thin early morning light. I could make out the low hills on the other side of the estuary now shrouded in silvery mist. The sun was rising into a blue, cloud-dappled sky. It would be a good day, but my heart was full of leaving. I bore the full weight of my decision now, and the burden was almost more than I could bear.

After all, Venta Silurum was where I was born and the only home I had ever known. I had never lived anywhere else, and the thought that I would not spend my life within the safe boundaries of its strong walls had rarely, if ever, crossed my mind. It had simply never occurred to me that I might one day be forced to leave my home and make my way in the world—bereft and alone.

I was dressed in my travelling clothes with a thick, dark wool cloak, into which I had sewed a sturdy pocket to contain my clutch of coins I had been able to scrape together. Under the cloak I wore my close-woven green mantle—a hard-wearing garment I used when cleaning the courtyard and kitchen. I also wore the heavy shoes I had bought in Viroconium—yes, I still had them, but had not yet worn them. The wooden box containing clothes and my few possessions—my mother's pins and hair things, my father's brooch, my books, and such like—lay at my feet. Gulls wheeled overhead with their laughing call as if enjoying my agitation. My legs were jittery and the palms of my hands damp with sweat.

Augustus and Tomos had brought me to the wharf and had gone off to speak to the ship's owner and chief, the *capitaneus*, to ensure my safe passage. Augustus' cousin Drustan had appeared to introduce himself and welcome me and two other merchants, both from Isca, who had goods consigned to the cargo. The three of us had joined Drustan's trading party.

A compact, energetic man with a head bald as an upturned bowl and heavy jowls that wobbled when he talked, our trader was all smiles and pleasantries, and gave every impression of being one of nature's jovial souls whose principal work in life consisted of making everyone around him feel better for having seen him. Merely a moment in Drustan's company gave me to know why he was a wealthy and successful merchant. Unassuming in appearance, he neither threatened nor daunted, and his sunny outlook and cheery demeanor were winsome. He insisted on pressing my hands and promised he would look after me and see me safely to my destination as it was the least he could do for the memory of his friend.

"Worry for nothing, daughter of Tullius," he told me. "I will make this journey as comfortable for you as possible . . ." He smiled and cast a hand toward the low-lying vessel. "At least as much as a perch atop barley sacks and oil casks will allow."

I thanked him for his kindness and indulgence in allowing me to travel with him. "It is entirely my pleasure," he declared, bowing his head. "Now, I must see to arrangements on board. The tide is turning, and we will soon be ready to sail."

Standing alone, the future stretching before me . . . Indeed, the future stretches out before *everyone* all the same, does it not? But this journey was an enormous leap—as my father used to say, "a flight across the chasm of the dark and vastly deep"—and I did not know if I would arrive safely on the other side.

Tomos returned from blessing the ship and speaking to our *capitaneus*, a robust, red-faced man named Gubric. The priest gripped my arm and assured me that he had every confidence all would be well.

Augustus also returned from his survey of the ship's quarters to report, "Very small, but room enough for you and a place to keep your things. There is a curtain, at least, around your sleeping place."

Tomos grew serious. "I have given both Drustan and Gubric stern admonitions and placed them under the fear of God."

"You did?"

"I made them swear an oath before God and all the saints to look after you and protect you." He smiled with satisfaction. "They dare not break that oath or Heaven help them—for only Heaven will!"

I accepted this and thanked him for his diligence. Meanwhile, the fellow whose wagon they had hired to bring us the few miles to the harbor was anxious to get on with his day. He called across the loading yard where he waited with his wagon and team. "You should go," I told them. "The wagoner is growing impatient."

"Let him wait," Augustus said. "I promised we would see you safely away, and so we will."

I thanked him and said, "I'll miss you, Augustus. These last few days, I don't know what I would have done without you."

"You'll come back—"

"I will."

"Well, then . . ." Words failed him, but he gave me a sad-eyed smile, swallowed hard, and patted my shoulder.

"And *I* will miss you, too," said Tomos. "But do remember to give my letter to Bishop Idnerth at Deva. He is a good man and will welcome you into his flock." Tomos gave me a firm hug, and there came a call from the deck for everyone to come aboard. Raising his hands over us, he said, "A prayer for leaving." Then, taking both my hands in his he bowed his head and intoned in the speech of prayer song:

May Jesu, ever faithful, savior and healer, redeemer of souls—
Be keeping you at morning,
Be keeping you at midday,
Be keeping you at eventide and night,
On the rough course faring, wherever life takes you,
Ever you helping, ever safeguarding,
Your strength when tired, astray, and stumbling,
Ever shielding you from all hurt, and all harm, and every sin . . .

It seemed he would say more, but there were tears in his voice and he said, "Amen."

I leaned up and gave him a quick kiss on the cheek and then turned away, lest I, too, loose my tears yet again. Augustus, bearing my chest of belongings, indicated the loading ramp. "I'll see you settled aboard."

So, with a prayer and a blessing to see me on my way, I waved one last time, turned, and followed Augustus up the narrow wooden ramp.

I have seen more graceful craft; no one would ever call the *Epona* elegant. But she was broad and sturdy. What she lacked in style, she more than made up in strength—broad of beam, with a wide flat deck and heavy rails, and a short, sturdy mast in the center. Behind the mast stood a low, hut-like structure which, I supposed, passed for shelter. The deck was stacked high with bales and bags of various kinds, and small wooden casks secured in rope netting.

"It is crowded, as I say," Augustus repeated. "But there should be more room once they've made a stop or two and unloaded some goods."

"It is only for a few days anyway," I replied. "I won't mind."

Drustan appeared from the door of the hut and hurried to stow my box of belongings for me. "Say your farewells," he told us. "Gubric says we are about to cast off."

He disappeared into the hut, and Augustus and I stood somewhat awkwardly together. Now that the time of parting had come, neither of us knew how to act or what to say. I had known Augustus almost as long as I had been alive. He was more an uncle, or even a grandfather to me than simply my father's assistant.

"I don't know when I'll see you again," I told him finally.

"No"—he shook his gray head—"but whenever it is, it will be as if you've never been away. Until then, I will look forward to the day." He dug into a fold of his mantle and brought out a leather purse. "Here," he said, pressing it into my hands. "A few coins only, but you may find them useful."

Surprised by the weight of it, I said, "I cannot take your purse, Augustus. I—"

"It's *your* purse now," he said. "Lucanus wanted to be rid of your father's chair and dispatch boxes, so I sold them to Olandus, the taverner. When he heard what it was for, I got a good price." He closed his hands over mine and squeezed. "No traveler should ever be without a few coins in the purse."

"Very kind and thoughtful of you," I muttered, unshed tears closing my throat. I drew a shaky breath. "My good and faithful friend, thank you for . . . for *everything*. I could not have survived these last days without you." I leaned up and kissed him on the cheek. "I'll miss you."

One of the sailor's called that they were casting off. Augustus dabbed at his eye, then turned, climbed over the side and hurried down the ramp. A moment later, there came a low, hollow groan and the ship began to move.

"God with you, Aurelia!" the priest called, raising hands of benediction as the ship drifted out into the tide flow and away.

"Farewell, Tomos!" I called with a final wave. "Farewell, Augustus!"

We stood watching until each was out of sight.

6

THAT FIRST DAY ABOARD THE *EPONA* WAS, for me at least, the most difficult. Passage down the ever widening estuary was swift and smooth enough, the ship floating gently with the tidal stream. I had never been aboard a ship before and soon grew used to the gentle rise and fall and swaying motion. I even began to enjoy the sensation as I stood at the rail, marveling at the grace and speed of the craft as the keel carved through the water.

But then, as soon as we reached a point some little way below Caer Dydd—I could just make out the hazy smudge on the nearer bank that marked the town—the sea flow became more disturbed. I gripped the rail with both hands and watched the land slide further away.

Then, around midday the ship passed into the open sea where the waves were sharper, deeper, more agitated. To keep from toppling over the rail, I backed away and leaned against a stack of boxes, grasping one of the securing ropes, and I began to reassess my former placid opinion.

As the land fell further away, our heavy-laden vessel lunged and lolled as wave after wave slapped against the hull and all sense of balance deserted me. My head swam. I grew dizzy. It was all I could do to stand upright. My stomach heaved with every lurch and surge. The deck pitched like a living creature as the sail alternately flapped and strained, the ropes first slack, then taut in the fickle wind.

The pilot steered for calm water where he could find it, but constantly having to brace myself against the violent toss and roll of the deck drained away my strength as the endless day wore on. I closed my eyes, but that only made things worse, so I stood grimly holding onto the rope and praying that the day would be over.

The sailors went about their various chores with the skill and confidence of long experience. Drustan and his trader friends made themselves comfortable elsewhere so that I was spared having to speak to them. If anyone noticed my stricken state, they gave no sign, and I was happy to be ignored for I did not want to be seen as a feeble female, an object of pity or, worse, derision.

The endless day dragged on. By the time the hazy sun began its downward descent, it was all I could do to hold up my head. On hands and knees, I crawled to the bow of the ship and found a place among the grain sacks to make a little nest. I squirreled myself in tight and prayed the awful surge and sway would cease. Around dusk, we made landfall at a place called Merthyr Mawr, I think—a fishing settlement with a tiny market—where the merchants did very little trade; it was mostly for the sheltered bay that we stopped for the night.

The *Epona* slid into the harbor and moored alongside a handful of other vessels of similar size. The crew made the ship fast, and only then did I begin to feel able to stand and hold my head upright again. I returned to the rail and breathed a long sigh of relief.

"Enjoy it while it lasts," said Drustan. He and Gubric joined me at the rail. "We will not tie up again until we're past the Irish Shore."

"Irish?" I wondered. "Did I hear you say something about the Irish?"

"Aye," muttered Gubric. "The bastards." He spat and walked away without another word.

"He lost a boat and three crewmen to Irish raiders a few years ago," Drustan confided, and explained that the sparsely peopled area along the southwestern coast of Britannia had been settled by fisher folk from Eire, and it was there that, from time to time, raiders from the Green Isle made landfall among their tribesmen who allowed them leave to cause their havoc. Drustan and his merchant friends considered them little better than Saecsens, if not worse, and had no desire to trade with them. All things considered, it was best always to give them a wide berth.

Irish raiders, he said, more often hunted the northern waters and preyed on the unwary. "We'll be keeping close to shore as they rarely risk coming too near land." He gave me an hopeful smile. "Also, the season is turning and it will soon be too late in the year for raiding. We won't worry too much about them."

Despite his optimistic reassurances, I now had something new to fear. Of course, I had long heard various rumors about trouble with Irish incomers—who hasn't?—but I had not thought to add them to the burden of my cares. Until now.

Supper that night was simple—bread and fried fish—but food held no appeal. After a few mouthfuls, I gave up and looked instead to crawling into bed. But even that proved an unexpected ordeal. Eight people retired to the hut: along with our *capitaneus*, Gubric, who was also the pilot of the ship, there were two crewmen—swarthy, active lads with such strong northern accents that what little I heard I could barely understand. Along with them, there was Drustan and his the two merchant friends, one of whom had brought along a servant. Eight bodies for the small hut that served as the vessel's only shelter and sleeping room made it cramped and stuffy, and it smelled of stale sweat and rancid oil from a broken jar that had been stored there on a previous journey. Any semblance of sleep eluded me that first night.

The next day was all but identical to the one before, as was the next after that, for the weather remained good and, save for that first rough day, the sea stayed calm. Slow, heavy-laden *Epona* hugged the coast, rarely venturing too far from the sight of land; we saw few other boats about and made what travel we could so long as the weather held. Despite these peaceable days, nights aboard ship were more an ordeal than a rest.

I slept poorly, if I slept at all. The thin curtain separating me from them was Drustan's thoughtful gesture to modesty, but did nothing to aid repose. What with the stink of unwashed bodies, the snoring and snorting, grunting and farting of my shipmates, I might as well have laid myself down in a cattle pen or hog wallow. I do believe I could have got more sleep among farm animals. My companions seemed not to mind the close confines, but it taxed me sore. Nevertheless, I endured it with firm resolve—what other choice did I have?

After seven or eight days at sea—I had lost count—Gubric announced that at the next stop we would reach Aberdyfi, our halfway point. There, we would take on fresh food and water for the push to our final destination which, he allowed, was also likely to be the most fraught part of the voyage for it meant sailing around a long finger of a peninsula and up through a very narrow straight between a broad island and the mainland.

"But do not worry, young lady," he told me kindly. "I have sailed this many times and know the passage well."

Drustan overheard us talking and added, "And once we have come through the straight, we will have three stops and several good days of trading."

"And then?" I asked.

"And then on to Deva," he said. "That will be . . ." He tapped his chin in thought. "Four days? A week at most, perhaps."

"Allowing for weather," Gubric cautioned. "Always allowing for weather. But we have the strait to navigate first."

Some little time later, we sailed into the harbor of Aberdyfi, tucked into a sheltered cove where the river Dyfi spread out to meet the bay. The town itself was a somewhat haphazard settlement with little stone houses and wattle-and-daub buildings dropped here and there along the seafront and nestled in among the steep hills. On one of the near promontories sat a timber fortress, squatting like a guard dog, keeping watch over the harbor crowded with trading ships and many fishing boats at anchor. There was ample room at the long wooden pier, however; and, while Gubric and his crewmen made the ship secure, the merchants all clambered quickly ashore to search out and bargain for fresh supplies and do what trade they might. Eager to get off the boat and stretch my legs on solid ground for a change, I hurried ashore, too.

The market was located near the harbor, and I saw that it was doing an easy, unhurried business; not overcrowded, but with enough folk around to make it interesting. My own attentions were not taken with the glistening fish and tubs of mussels on offer, but with the town and its people. As usual, I soon found myself wondering what it would be like to live in this place: What about this house? What about that one? What were the people like? What would *I* be if I lived here? A weaver, maybe? Or a baker? Could I do that? Some kind of merchant, maybe? If so, what would I sell? And on and on.

My mind wandered with my steps as I strolled among the rising paths and lanes of the town. I stumbled upon the church a short way up the hill from the market. A simple, square building of gray stone, it had a wide iron-clad wooden door which was flanked either side by two long and very elaborate benches with high backs and carved armrests. The little church was surrounded by a low wall and a green burial ground studded with stones of various sizes and shapes, many with the haloed cross: something I'd seen only once or twice before in churchyards. Several paths led to the gate and all were worn hard and smooth by the feet of worshippers—signs of a fair-sized congregation.

I continued my ramble, past the church and surrounding houses, and reached the top of a low hill. Fields lay in patches hewn out of woodland, and there was grazing land for pigs and cattle tended by boys and younger men. The path turned into a muddy cow trail, and here I stopped and turned to look down on the town and harbor and gleaming silver sea beyond.

In all, it seemed that Aberdyfi was a good and peaceful place— perhaps as good and peaceful as Venta—and it gave me hope for my new home. *Could Deva be like this?* I wondered.

By the time I got back to the boat, the sun was already fading, sinking into a low bank of yellow-gray clouds to the west. The merchants in the marketplace were closing up their booths and the *Epona*'s chief and crew were loading fresh water and bundles of foodstuff aboard. Out on the great expanse of sandy beach to the north of the pier, I spied Drustan and several traders and merchants from the town squatting around a fire. I made my way toward them. Drustan saw me and waved me over. They had bought fish in the market—mackerel and eels and small silver somethings—and they were preparing them on spits for the fire. They also had loaves of fresh bread, new butter, and sealed jars of beer and wine.

"Join us, Aurelia," he invited. "We are making a feast."

Happy not to have to eat aboard the boat, I thanked him and asked, "What are we celebrating?"

"A successful voyage half completed and fresh food in our bellies," he replied expansively. One of the merchants had unstopped a jar and was pouring wine into little wooden cups. He handed one to Drustan and one to me. As soon as we all had a cup, Drustan raised his and said, "Drink, my friends! To fine weather and good trade—may it long continue!"

"To fine weather and good trade!" the merchants chorused.

All drank and I took a sip with them. The stakes were driven into the sand and the spitted fish put to roast slowly around the fire. I found a rock to sit on and took my cup of wine to watch the fire and enjoy the moment, and to consider the unfathomable strangeness of life. When did I set off with my father for Viroconium? When did I stand by Aridius' side and hear the pronouncements of Procurator Constantine? When was my dear father wounded and when did he die? When was his funeral? Could it be only days ago that I had looked my last on the only home I had ever known in this world? Already, even that seemed half a lifetime ago. What is more, I had not thought of Venta at all the last two days—not wondered what Augustus or Dorcas was doing, or what new outrage Velvinnia was perpetrating, or whether anyone missed me . . .

Yet . . . and yet, here I was: sitting on a beach in a pleasant bay, wine cup in hand, watching as the dying sun bled glorious showers of color into the clouds, smelling the enticing smoke of roasting fish, and listening to the happy chatter of the men as they prepared our modest feast. Though I could not make out much of what they were saying, I could sense the joy of their fellowship, and it made me glad, too. My previous cares seemed a world away and of very little consequence next to this.

There is a lesson here for the learning, I could hear Tullius telling me. Indeed, this would be the very time and place he would say such a thing.

Ah, well, if there *was* a lesson to be learned, like most lessons it flew right over my head. I had neither the ability nor the inclination to think what that improving instruction might be. Instead, I sipped my wine and luxuriated in the gentle closing of the day and a voyage half completed.

Gubric and his two crewmen joined us. Everyone sat on the sand around the fire, drinking, talking, laughing, occasionally turning a spit or adding another. When the fish was finished, it was piled onto a bit of flat planking and passed around along with chunks of buttered bread. I took a bit of mackerel and sucked the oily, succulent dark flesh off the bones, savoring the rich, smoky flavor. More wine was poured and more fish served up and we all ate and drank our fill as evening closed around us; a bright spray of stars appeared overhead, and a chill seeped into the air on a light breeze off the sea.

The talk and laughter grew louder, more raucous, the banquet turning into a revel and I thought I saw one of the merchants eyeing me with something like appraisal—a glance I did not like. Also, I was beginning to feel the wine and the chill, and decided to remove myself from the festivity before any of the men got the idea that I might like more intimate male company. I rose from my perch and thanked Drustan and Gubric for a splendid supper and a most enjoyable feast, then started away.

"Not leaving already?" called Drustan loudly. "Stay and tell us tales of old Venta Silurum." To the others he said, "Aurelia here is daughter of the magistrate. Did you know?" He raised his cup. "The finest magistrate I ever met! And I'll fight the man who says otherwise."

I smiled at his well-intentioned compliment. "Some other night, perhaps. I will creep away to bed and leave you to enjoy your celebration." I thanked them again and made my way back to the pier and boarded the ship.

I was asleep when the men returned to the ship, but their clumping and banging around as they settled in our overcrowded hut woke me. They fell asleep quickly, however, and all was quiet once more...and then the snoring and snuffling and grunting began. I was wakened again at once and then remained awake for a long time—until at last I understood there would be no return to sleep while I remained in the hut.

Rising silently, I took up my cloak and lifted the curtain and, quietly, carefully stepped over the sleeping men and tiptoed from the hut. I shut the door and looked for a comfortable place to spend the rest of the night. I thought there might be a bench at the end of the pier, but I was mistaken. And then I remembered the church with its walled yard and the long benches—quiet and secure, no one would disturb me there. That is where I went.

The moon was high overhead, lending light enough to find my way. I reached the market easily enough and the path leading to the church—all calm and bright in the moonlight. I entered by the gate, crossed the grassy yard and lay down on one of the benches. I remember nothing after that save breathing in the cool night air, and looking at the bright spray of stars overhead and thinking what a passing stranger might make of finding me there.

What the locals made of me I was all too soon to find out. For, I came awake at the metallic clang—a white-robed priest standing at the church gate, ringing a bell for morning prayer. I arose with a start and looked around. I had slept deeply and long—at least, longer than I intended. Even so, it was early yet, and I thought that if I hurried I could still make it back to the ship before the men were up and around.

I picked up my cloak and ran to the gate, brushed past the startled priest—mumbling a hasty apology as I fled—and raced down the path leading to the market and harbor. I had taken but a dozen paces when the seafront came into view below. I saw merchants erecting their booths in the market square and the bay beyond. I also saw a low, gray overcast sky and the broad stretch of pooled sand where the harbor used to be: boats lay on their keels, stranded. Of course, the tide was out...

With a sudden horror of comprehension I turned my gaze to the long wooden pier and confirmed my worst fear: the berth was empty. The *Epona* had sailed with the tide.

7

STUNNED BEYOND ALL THOUGHT, I felt a strange sensation of light-headed disbelief. My legs went weak and I collapsed in the lane. I drew up my knees and hugged them to my chest. I wanted to scream: *THE SHIP IS GONE!*

Astonishment turned swiftly to rage: *Those flaming idiots! They left without me!*

Rage melted just as quickly into forlorn self-pity: *How could they? How could they just go away and leave me? Drustan promised to take care of me.* He *promised! How could he do this to me?*

I began rocking back and forth as the enormity of my predicament fell full upon me with the weight of a mountain. I was stranded, lost, without food or water, without money, abandoned in a place where I knew not a single soul and no one knew me. What, Lord help me, was I going to do?

I sensed a presence behind me and started as someone coughed to draw my attention. I whirled around. It was the priest from the church; I had not heard his approach. And now he was bending over me. He spoke quietly and I touched my ear. He repeated, more loudly. "Girl? What's the matter?" he asked, his voice full of concern. "Are you ill?"

"The ship . . ." I flung a hand toward the pier. "It's gone."

"Ship?" he wondered, turning his gaze to the seafront.

"They left without me!"

He offered a puzzled frown. "I don't understand."

132

"The ship!" I jabbed my finger at the waterfront. "*My* ship—it's gone!" I wailed. "They left without me!"

"Who has done this?" he asked.

I started rocking again and the tears began to flow.

"Miss?" he asked. To my surprise he gathered the hem of his long priestly robe and sat down in the dirt road beside me. He drew up his knees, like me, and stared out at the sea-starved bay. "Let me see if I understand this," he said, his voice calming, gentle. "You arrived here aboard a ship and expected to depart with it when it sailed. But this vessel has sailed and you have been left behind."

The way he said it—so simply, directly, without the mind-numbing panic that gripped me—somehow reduced the immensity of my dilemma. It became a difficulty rather than a disaster. Trouble, yes—definitely that—but not utter tragedy.

"Were they people of yours?" he asked.

Not certain I had heard him correctly, I asked him to repeat, and tapped my ear again. "The ones who left you," he said, speaking clearly, "were they people of yours—your relations, perhaps?"

I shook my head. "No," I told him. "No relation at all. They were traders. They were going to Deva and I was travelling with them. They were meant to look after me."

"Ah-h-h ... Deva," he replied as if this explained everything he needed to know. He regarded me for a long moment. I sniffed and dabbed at my tears. "You have people there maybe?"

I nodded. "Friends, yes."

He was silent for a time, content to sit with me in my misery. Finally, I stopped my sniveling and, drawing a deep breath, turned my face to him and asked, "What am I going to do?"

He smiled. "Go on to Deva, I expect."

"How? I don't even know where Deva is, how far it might be, or how I might get there."

"Yet, the way is known," he said simply. "Perhaps not by you, but there are others who know how to get there—and they will also know how far it is. We will ask them."

"But my things—my clothes and possessions ... my books," I complained. "Everything I own is in a box on the ship. I have nothing." Even as I spoke, my hand moved to my purse secure in its deep pocket beneath my cloak. I felt the reassuring weight of coins and my panic receded a little. I was not completely beggared. I still had my money.

"Ah, well," my priestly companion said. "Our Lord Jesu traveled about the land without these things. You can do likewise, I think."

For some reason this made me laugh. "But our Lord could also walk on water when he wished. I don't think I can do likewise at all."

He chuckled, too. "No, maybe not that."

He rose and brushed the dirt off his robe, then reached down a hand for me. "I am Heddwyn, cleric of this cantref."

I accepted his hand and allowed him to help me to my feet. "I am Aurelia," I told him. He invited me to break fast with him in the Priest House where his wife was preparing a meal. The offer was kindly given and, though I was still wildly anxious over my plight, I saw no reason to decline—who knew when I might eat again? Turning away from the seafront, we started back toward the church and he asked me how I had come to be sleeping on the churchyard bench.

"Were the men—ah . . ." He paused, considering how to ask the question. "Abusing you?"

"Abusing me?" Uncertain I had heard correctly, I glanced sharply at him. "You mean . . ."

He made a gesture toward my body and nodded.

"No! Oh, no—nothing like that," I answered quickly. "Drustan and Gubric were looking after me. They are good men. No one so much as touched me."

"Looking after you," he said, nodding slowly and regarding me somewhat doubtfully. "And yet, they abandoned you."

I sighed. "So they did." Haltingly, and with one or two sniffles, I explained how we had all enjoyed a fine evening on the beach with wine and bread and fish roasted on spits around the fire, and how I had gone back to the ship to sleep. "The men came back much later and woke me," I said. "They were very noisy with their snoring, so I got up and went in search of a quiet place to spend the night."

"My churchyard."

I nodded. "I saw it earlier in the day and liked it there. It was peaceful."

Priest Heddwyn nodded again and fell silent. We reached the churchyard where he paused with the gate half open. "Might it be," he said, his hand on the latch, "that your friends did not know you had come ashore in the night?"

"No, I—I..." Fear and anger had so consumed me that any such thought had not yet had time to wangle its way into my thick head. I stared at him. "Do you really think...?"

"It *is* possible, is it not?" Heddwyn suggested. "If they were asleep and you were very quiet..."

The realization shook me like thunder.

"They didn't know!" I gasped. I quickly explained that my sleeping place aboard the ship was separated from that of the men by a curtain at the furthest corner of the hut. If, as Heddwyn suggested, they had awakened and hurried to ready the ship to sail with the outgoing tide, they could very well have thought me asleep and did not wish to wake me. "They might think me still asleep even now," I concluded, then wondered. "But what will they do when they realize what has happened?"

"Will they?"

I did not hear him clearly and asked him to repeat.

"*Will* they realize what has happened to you?" he said simply. "It may be that all they can know is that you were asleep on your mat in the boat's house and now you have vanished."

A heavy load of woe descended fresh upon me. "Not even that," I replied bleakly. "Drustan will not know what has happened to me. How can he? For all he knows I might have fallen overboard and drowned."

We entered the churchyard in silence, allowing all this to sink in. Heddwyn led me across the burial ground to a lane at the end of which stood a small house, half hidden in a little wood. The house had a thatched roof and two tiny wind holes covered with bits of old glass; pale smoke threaded its way into the surrounding trees. He rapped on the door, opened it, and stepped inside, beckoning me to follow.

"Flori," he called. "We have a visitor." To me, he said, "Come in, come in. Be welcome here."

His wife was a busy little sparrow of a woman, with quick, dark eyes and a beaky nose, and she examined me with a bird's keen attention. "God with you, daughter, and welcome," she said. "I am Flori." She looked to her husband for further explanation.

"Oh! And this is Aurelia," he told her. "Come all the way from..." He chuckled and looked at me. "I don't know where you're from—"

"Venta," I said. "It's a small town in the south near the coast. My father was magistrate there—Tullius Paulinus. Maybe you've heard of him?"

"Venta?" the priest mused. "That I have heard of. But I cannot say I know of your father. But you said *was* just now. Is he magistrate no longer?"

"My father died recently," I replied, my voice cracking unexpectedly.

"Ah!" he exclaimed. "And that is why you are going to your friends in Deva Vitrix. I see now—yes, I think I see. And these friends, they are—"

"Heddwyn!" scolded his wife. She stepped close and shooed him away. "Stop pestering the girl with all your prattle. She is hungry, I expect. Go fetch a chair from the church and we will all sit down to our meal."

She led me further into their home—a single room with a hearth at one end and a box bed at the other, and all kinds of dried herbs and vegetables and things hanging from the roof beams. The room was warm and lit with candles in several places. A large table held pride of place in the center of the room and it was piled high with more dried stuff and bits of cloth, and a collection of pots and jars of various shapes and sizes. Two chairs stood at one end of the table where the couple took their meals and did their homely work. My hostess saw me eyeing the assortment of containers and said, "I make unguents and potions for the folk hereabouts," she explained. "They bring me eggs and butter and honey, beeswax and suchlike. In return, I give them medicines for their ailments." She smiled. "I've never had to make butter or cheese since we came here."

I smiled and mumbled something about not hearing very well, adding, "If only there was a medicine for that."

"My husband did not say how you came to be here," she said, speaking loudly and clearly. She moved some of the clutter on the table and pulled out one of the chairs, gesturing for me to sit down. "Aberdyfi is far from Deva."

"It is," I agreed. "But I was travelling on a ship with some merchants who were going there to trade. There was a mistake last night and they sailed this morning without me."

"Oh! You poor poppet. Stranded!" Flori reached over and patted my hand, then went to the hearth and took up a pot that was bubbling away near the fire. "Are you a Christian girl? Is that why you came to the church?"

"I am, yes," I replied, "but that's not why I came to the church." I then tried to explain, without delving too deeply into the debacle, how I had come to be sitting in her house on this dull, dismal day.

Flori poured some of the liquid from the pot into a bowl and set it before me. "A tisane of chamomile," she announced. "Good for calming the heart and soul. We drink it every day."

I thanked her and she poured herself a little bowl of the stuff and we drank together. Heddwyn returned with a chair from the church. He placed it at the table across from me and the two of them began pulling things together to make a meal. Another pot near the hearth contained a thick gruel of oats, flavored with dried berries, and this Flori ladled into bowls. There was heavy dark bread and sweet butter, and a sort of mush made of cherries and apples, I think, and cooked with honey. This she smoothed on thick slices of bread and dolloped over the oat gruel.

The food was warm and comforting in its own right, and I ate as if I were a child who had never swallowed a single bite in my life. The two kept up a light chatter about this and that—not all of which I heard—about local life and the folk round about the cantref. I cleaned my bowl and held up my hands in submission, refusing another offered ladle, and Heddwyn said, "Well, now. What are we going to do for you, eh?" Before I could think what to say to this, he continued. "I have it in mind that we can do no better than to go to Cadwgan Call. He will know what to do."

"Go to Cadwgan?" wondered his wife. A shadow of doubt passed across her kindly face.

"Indeed, yes! If anyone can help, it will be our wise chief and elder." He put his hands flat on the table and pushed back his chair. "Cadwgan the Wise will know what to do for a sailor stranded ashore."

Without waiting for a second opinion, Heddwyn jumped up, kissed his wife on the top of the head, pulled his cloak from a peg by the door, and hurried out, leaving me and Flori gazing at one another over the remains of our meal.

A long moment passed and the woman cocked her head to one side as if satisfying herself that her husband had truly gone. Then, leaning forward, she reached out and took my hand. "You *cannot* go to Cadwgan."

"What?" I was not sure I had heard correctly.

She gripped my hand for emphasis, speaking quickly and in earnest, "We must get you away from here. Quick! Before Heddwyn comes back!"

8

"THIS IS ADDAS, my husband's curate," Florina said, introducing me to the slender fellow before me. Ten years or so older than me, the cleric was lanky, with a heavy pelt of thick black hair, deep dark eyes, and a wide mouth that curved up at the ends, giving him an unfortunate smirk. I regarded my new traveling companion doubtfully. He was dressed in coarse-woven dun-colored short robe, with trousers to cover his bare legs. The robe was cinched by a wide belt of woven leather strands; he had heavy, thick-soled shoes on long feet, a bulging cloth bag over one shoulder, and a cloak folded over the other. "Aurelia," he said, repeating my name in his thick accent. He gave me a little bow. "I am happy to meet you."

"Glad to meet you," I replied, and wondered how we would get along together.

Having leaped up from the table the moment Heddwyn had gone, we had fled up the road a little way to a wooden house where Flori told me to wait in the yard. She disappeared inside and came out a short time later with this brown-robed cleric in tow. While he strapped on his shoes, she explained that we were to leave Aberdyfi at once and not look back.

"Addas will take you as far as Caer Gwyn where you'll meet the road to Deva."

"And then?"

"And then he will see about finding a wagon or carriage from there." She gave her husband's curate a sharp look. "Will you not, Addas?"

"It will be my privilege." The young man beamed as if this was his sole heart's desire.

"There, then," continued Flori. "You two best be on your way before Heddwyn returns or you'll never get away."

"I don't understand," I said, renewing my original complaint. "Why not go to Cadwgan?"

Flori was already shaking her head. "I do not trust our chieftain as much as does my husband. Heddwyn sees only the good in folk—for all, he's a priest. But it makes him over trustful, if you know what I mean."

"Cadwgan Call," said Addas with a sniff. "There are those who call him Cadwgan Cuall."

I glanced sharply at him, struggling to make sense of the words.

"Cadwgan the Wise," he explained, "is more like Cadwgan the Oaf."

Flori gave him another sharp look and wagged a warning finger. "Never let Heddwyn hear you say that—nor anyone else, either, come to that." She turned to me and explained, "There is no help to be had from Cadwgan. God forgive me if I demean the man, but he is only interested in what is best for Cadwgan. I greatly fear you would fall foul of one of his schemes."

"If this Cadwgan is so bad, why does Heddwyn want me to see him?"

"Because our chieftain is liberal to those who honor him and pay him compliments. He gives lavishly and with both hands. He supports clerics in lonely places that would have none otherwise, and he has given lands and money to build churches." She lowered her voice. "Mind, there are plenty around who say for all his preening, it is the *wife* of Cadwgan who inspires this abundant generosity."

She stole a glance behind us on the road. Seeing no one, she continued. "Two summers ago, Cadwgan dusted off the old shipwreck and indigent laws and pledged to enforce them. And he does! Oh, yes, he does—for the benefit of none other than Cadwgan himself."

I had heard of these laws—or at least a rumor of such from my father, but only that. "We don't have shipwreck laws in the south."

"Thank the Good Lord and all your lucky stars," she said, leading me further along the road, leaving Addas to trail a step or two behind. "We are that close to Ireland," she said, waving a hand vaguely in the direction of the sea. "Those rascals come across the Narrow Sea in their coracles to steal sheep and cattle and anything else they can get their filthy hands on. Well, often enough the sea gets the better of them and the rogues wash up on shore—shipwrecked, see. They have no people, no money, starving, half naked, and mostly dead. So, they go around begging and pestering people, stealing when they think no one is looking."

"They're a very plague," Addas confirmed. "I've known one or two."

"We used to try to move them on," Flori said, "take their trouble somewhere else. But folk around here got tired of having their things pilfered and then peddled in the markets. The cry went up and Cadwgan's shipwreck law was the answer. So, now anyone found shipwrecked and without money to support himself, or anyone found begging, come to that, is declared indigent."

I nodded as understanding slowly took shape in me. "I have no money and my ship is gone . . . ," I said. "Am *I* a shipwreck indigent?"

"Oh, you *are* a clever little thing," Flori said. "This is my very fear. If you were to go before Cadwgan he maybe would not see a lorn soul abandoned by her travelling companions. No, our top-lofty chief would see a beggar and would sooner declare you indigent than find you another way to Deva."

"What would happen then?"

"You would be bonded over to someone who paid right handsome for your labor."

"I'd be sold as a slave?"

"You'd be a bondmaid."

Slave, bondmaid—all the same in my mind. "You said this Cadwgan was a Christian!"

"He is a Christian, yes, but he is a *bad* Christian," she retorted. "Only ever thinking about how to pinch a little more wealth or power for himself."

"Would he really sell me into bond?"

Flori shook her head. "I honestly don't know, girl. But if I stood aside and let that happen . . . well, God might forgive me, but I could not. Hard as it will be, this is the better way, believe me."

I did believe her. And, looking at the rutted road stretching over the hills before me, I thought that however hard the journey, it *was* better than being a slave to some Aberdyfi pig farmer, or fish monger. And, with the cleric Addas as my protector on the road, I imagined I would not fare so badly.

"If we had more time I could maybe make a better plan. This is the best I can think to do. Now, off with you while you have a chance. I don't expect they will spend much time looking for you, but you never know." She leaned close and kissed me lightly on the cheek. "Fare you well, child."

"I don't know how to thank you, Flori," I told her. "You and Heddwyn have been most kind. I am in your debt, and I will not forget it."

"Shush, girl. I would do the same for any niece of mine." She gave me a hug and then stepped away. Addas and I put our feet to the road. I looked back and gave her a wave. Kindly Flori waved back and called, "God with you, Aurelia."

MERLIN AND AURELIA

AURELIA PROVED HERSELF master of a storehouse of local knowledge and our talk ranged as wide as the coastal hill country around us. But as we neared Venta, Aurelia grew more reticent and, upon approaching the old *civitas*, she lapsed into silence—contemplating, I suppose, the great collection of memories residing beyond those walls.

The town gates—if you could call them that—were open. Roughly patched, they had been mended as if by chance. I doubted the two huge doors even closed at all. There was a gateman—a straggly youth leaning against a spear—he eyed us without interest and waved us along. The carriage rolled into the little town, and Aurelia stirred herself. "That gate is a disgrace," she tutted. "Such disrepair would never have been tolerated in my father's day."

We passed one street and then another, and stopped, climbing from the carriage to stand a moment in the town square where a gang of boys suddenly appeared. No more than seven or eight summers old, they beseeched us for anything we could give them. I directed Pelleas to dispense a coin or two for them to share, and then sent them off. Aurelia watched them run away. "And *that* would not have been tolerated, either."

She turned her gaze to the houses and buildings around the square. Some of these were occupied; others were little more than ruins: doorways without doors, without shutters, without tiles, and at least one with a staved-in roof. What was once a busy bakery was now mostly rubble around the cracked, hollow shell of a large oven. There was rubbish of one kind and another piled up against the buildings and half-starved dogs skulked around, heads down, looking thoroughly beaten and miserable. Oddly, aside from the begging boys and the sleepy youth at the gate, there was not another soul to be seen.

My companion sighed and I saw her shoulders slump as she took in the waste of the town that occupied a more exalted place in her memory. "Where was your home?" I asked.

Glancing around, she pointed to a street across the square and started toward it. "Just up there," she said.

I directed Pelleas and Mairenn to have a look around to see if they could find refreshment of some kind for the drivers. Then Aurelia and I entered a narrow lane at the north end of the square, passing along a row of houses, most of which were more-or-less better maintained than those fronting the square. Near the end of the lane, we came to a large house with a rusty iron gate. A wide wooden door opened onto the street but, from the look of its warped, dilapidated exterior, that door had not been opened in years. Stepping to the gate beside Aurelia, I could see a courtyard with what must have been a small pool with a stone bench beside it. One pedestal of the bench was broken and the seat lay collapsed on the courtyard flagstones. The pool was empty of everything except weeds.

"Tullius' official chambers were through there," Aurelia said, indicating the unused door. "That's where I spent most of my days." She looked to the house. Many of the old red roof tiles were missing and had been replaced by slate brought up from somewhere on the coast—the same with many of the buildings within sight. "I wonder who lives here now?"

She had but voiced the question when a little woman appeared in the courtyard carrying a bowl covered with a cloth. The woman did not see us watching, so I called out to her. She glanced toward us. I saw fear sweep across her pinched features, and she almost dropped the bowl. "Peace, good woman," I said quickly, and gave her a smile. "We did not mean to startle you."

"What do you want?" she demanded, suddenly angry. "I don't have anything to give you."

"We'll not ask for anything," I told her, "save a little information. And then we'll leave you to your work."

She regarded us warily, but took a few steps closer, clutching her bowl to her breast as if she feared we might try to snatch it away. "What do you want to know?"

"This lady used to live here," I replied, indicating Aurelia, who was studying the woman closely. "She grew up in this house."

"Oh, aye?"

"My father was Magistrate of Venta," Aurelia told her. "His office and workroom were through that door." She nodded toward the weathered door. "I worked for him."

The woman relaxed somewhat and took another step or two closer. "Did you now? I imagine, you must have been quite young. Your father—what was his name?"

"Tullius Paulinus. Did you—"

Before she could finish a man's voice called out across the courtyard. "Woman! Where's that glaze? I'm waiting!"

"Coming!" the woman shouted back over her shoulder. To us, she said, "I never heard of him."

"He was magistrate here for many years, and—"

"Maybe he was," interrupted the woman, "but I never heard of him. I'm sorry, I cannot—"

"Celia!" came the call again. "The glaze!"

"I'm needed. I must go." She turned away just a man in a mud-stained tunic appeared in the courtyard.

"Where've you been, you—!" he began, then saw us. "Oh! Ah, yes." He gave a sheepish smile. "I didn't know we had visitors. Have you come to buy?"

I explained what we had already told the woman, whom I assumed to be his long-suffering wife.

"Magistrate, you say?" He pulled a thoughtful expression and rubbed his neck. "I think I remember something about that. Tullius, you say?"

Aurelia nodded. "I'm his daughter."

"The name wasn't Tullius," said the man, shaking his head. "No, it was something else . . . something Roman . . . Lorca, or Lucas, or . . ."

"Lucanus?" suggested Aurelia.

"Aye! That's it! Lucanus—that's the one." He shook his head again. "I heard of him. But that was a long time ago."

"It would be," Aurelia agreed. "Can you tell me who is magistrate now and where I can find him?"

The man glanced at his wife, shrugged, and said. "There hasn't been a magistrate here for . . . I don't know—maybe twenty years or more." His wife quickly added, "The house was empty when we got it. This is a pottery now. Aled, here, is a potter."

"Aye," said the man; by way of confirmation, he pulled out the hem of his tunic to show us the smudges of drying clay. "I'm a potter. If you want to buy something, I could let you in and show you—"

"Thank you, no," I replied, sensing we'd gleaned all we could from them. "We won't keep you any longer." To Aurelia, I said, "Shall we go?"

Aurelia thanked the two for their help, and we retraced our steps to the square.

"Did you want to go inside and see the house?" I asked, thinking I might have been too hasty.

"No, no," she replied, her voice quietly reflective. "It would have served no purpose." She thought for a moment, then said, "But I'd like to see the church." Turning abruptly, she started off. "It's this way."

She led me along winding streets to a slightly better kept area of the town; there were a few more people about and they marked us instantly as strangers—some smiled, others frowned, but no one made bold to greet us. We reached the church which, despite a few alterations in evidence—a crude little box of a room had been added to one end of the building, and one section of wall patched with what looked like stones gathered from a riverbed—appeared in better repair than most of the other buildings we had seen. The churchyard was tidy enough, but overgrown and hemmed about with brambles. The church itself stood proud and the carved cross atop the roof seemed to offer some hope that Jesu was yet honored in this place. Aurelia clasped her hands beneath her chin when she saw it. "Oh!" she breathed with relief. "It's still here. It's still here..." Her eyes shone with sudden delight. "Let's go in."

I opened the low gate and she moved along the path, pausing now and again to look at some of the tombstones. At the arched door, she halted again, reached up and placed her hand flat against the weather-scarred wood, letting it rest there for a moment as she bowed her head—a prayer? A silent remembrance? The moment passed and she took hold of the latch's iron ring, turned it, pushed, and... nothing. The door was barred. "That is strange," she said, turning to me. "The church was never locked before. Bishop Bevyn insisted that it remain open at all times—and with a candle burning inside."

"You there!" someone called. "May I be of service?"

We turned to see an aging priest in a faded brown robe hobbling toward us across the churchyard. We greeted him as he neared and he joined us saying, "I'm Brother Sebastian, is there something I can do for you?"

"We are visitors only," I replied. "We were merely wanting to see inside the church."

"And you are...?" He smiled as he asked, and I sensed a wariness in his manner; I had seen it before—often enough these days when folk encounter strangers.

"I am called Myrddin," I told him, "and this is Aurelia Paulinus Verica. She grew up here in Venta. Her father was the town magistrate and they belonged to this church."

Brother Sebastian glanced at the woman beside me, his eyebrows raised in mild surprise. "The magistrate you say?"

"Tullius Paulinus," Aurelia offered. Seeing the man's look of incomprehension, she added, "Ah, well, it was many years ago. Those I knew are long gone by now—like so much else, it seems."

"Who was bishop when you lived here?" wondered Sebastian.

"Bevyn was bishop," replied Aurelia. "Tomos was one of the priests—the one I knew and liked best."

"Tomos, you say?" Sebastian put a finger to his lips in thought, then agreed, "Yes, that would make sense."

She leaned close to hear him better. "Do you know him?"

"Oh, indeed I do."

"You mean he is still here?" she asked, her voice rising in expectation. "He never left?"

"In a manner of speaking," said Sebastian. "Tomos was bishop here for some years, but I knew him only briefly. I came to Caerwent just before he died. His grave is here in the churchyard."

"Ah," she sighed, and it was then that the rigors of the journey took their toll and the weight of the past, with its burdens, settled full upon her. She swayed a little, and I moved closer to keep her on her feet with a supporting arm. Accepting it, she nodded gratefully and asked, "When did he die? How long ago?"

Sebastian tapped his jaw. "It must be just shy of fourteen years, I think. That's how long I have served here. I never knew Bishop Bevyn, that was before my time." Reassured by this friendly exchange, he grew more welcoming. "You say you want to see inside the church, yes?"

"Please?" said Aurelia, "It would mean a great deal to me."

"It would be my pleasure," Brother Sebastian declared expansively. "Just you wait here while I unbar the door."

He disappeared around the side of the old stone building and we waited, old memories and blackbird song filling the silence between us. A few moments later, I heard the scrape of a bolt being drawn and a bar being lifted. The door swung open and we stepped into the dim coolness of an unlit church empty as the inside of a discarded shell: no candles, no altar, no cross, nothing. There was not a stick of furniture anywhere to be seen—only dust and cobwebs. There were holes in the roof and a bird's nest up in the eves.

Aurelia looked around, tears misting her eyes. "Where is"—she lifted a hand to take in the decrepit building—"everything?"

"I should have told you, we don't use this building anymore. We have a new church at the other end of town near the wall. It's smaller and easier to keep. There are only two of us priested here now."

"And the tombs?" said Aurelia, gazing around at the darkened, empty space. "Where are they?"

"I'm sorry to say that, along with most everything else, the tombs were desecrated in the attack—dug up, I'm told, by looters. I was not here then, but I assume Bishop Tomos had the remains reburied." He shook his head. "I don't know where."

"An attack you say?" I asked. "What attack was that?"

Sebastian pursed his lips. "Ah, well, I'm told it was during the great Irish raid—a dozen keels or so landed somewhere to the south of here during the night. They came in force and overran the town. Many people were killed and houses burned. The raiders struck at Isca, too. But, as I say, that was some time ago."

Aurelia nodded sadly, turned, and walked out of the church. I thanked Sebastian for showing us, and left him to lock the door again. She stood in the churchyard, her face raised to the sky, eyes full of unshed tears. "I so wanted to see my father's resting place once more," she murmured as I came to stand beside her. "And now I never will." She sighed again.

"Shall we go back?"

She nodded and we started back the way we had come. Upon reaching the gate, however, Aurelia put a hand to her head and swayed on her feet. "Oh...oh!"

Her eyes fluttered in her head. I took her elbow to steady her and keep her from falling over. "Aurelia, are you well?"

Sebastian appeared around the side of the church again and I called to him. "Bring her some water. Hurry!" Supporting Aurelia by the arm, I led her to one of the stone blocks in the yard. "Here, sit down. Rest a little."

Aurelia waved my help aside. "No, no," she coughed. "It is . . . it will pass. I am . . ." Her voice faltered and she was overcome by a sudden fit of coughing, collapsing heavily onto the stone. For the next few moments, her body was wracked by a deep and worrying cough; convulsed by it, she was unable to speak.

Gradually, the coughing subsided. She sat, eyes closed, fanning her face with a hand. When she could at last draw a steady breath, she raised her head and was once more herself. Seeing the expression on my face, she said, "You needn't look so concerned, Merlin. I expect it was just the heat."

She and I both knew it was more than that, but she was determined to make light of the incident. She stood slowly and took in a last view of the church—recalling, no doubt, the many services attended with her father—then turned abruptly and started away. She took but two or three steps and stumbled. Instantly, I was at her side and, taking her arm, led her back to her perch on the stone. "Let's wait for that drink of water," I suggested. "Look, here is Brother Sebastian."

The priest hurried to us with a jar and a small wooden cup. He dashed some water into the cup and handed it to Aurelia. She thanked him and drank it down. Handing back the cup, she declared herself much refreshed.

He filled the cup again and handed it back. "Is there anything else you'd like to see?" he asked. "The new church, perhaps?"

"No, no," replied Aurelia; she drank and returned the cup. "I thank you for the thought—and for the water—but no. I don't think I want to see anything else."

I also thanked Sebastian and gave him a silver coin from the purse at my belt, and we left the churchyard. Aurelia did seem better refreshed, but her sudden dizziness raised a worry. "That was not the heat just now, was it?" I said as we passed through the town once more on our way to the carriage.

"I'm an old woman," she protested. "You know how it is with us.

Not so old as she pretends, I thought. But, there was nothing to be gained in pursuing the matter, so I let it rest. We continued on in silence, each wrapped in separate thoughts and recollections. Upon our return to the town square where the others were waiting with the carriage, Aurelia announced, "I don't think there's anything for me here anymore."

"And your father's property?" I asked, already guessing the answer.\

She sighed. "I don't know how I'd locate it now—if it existed at all. Just another thing carried off by the raid, I suppose."

I thought for a moment. The property was merely a pretext, then—an excuse to put her sons' minds at ease and to come and see her childhood home once more. I allowed her to save face and changed the subject.

"Come with me to Ynys Avallach. I'd like you to meet my family."

That is how we came to be on our way to the Summerlands and the Isle of Apples.

I DO CONFESS THAT CURATE ADDAS would not have been my
first choice as a traveling companion. Older and given much to endless
talk and singing—when he was not talking, he was singing. Oh, how he
loved to talk! More to hear the sound of his own voice, I suspect, than
to engage in any meaningful conversation. I learned fairly quickly that
my constant participation was not strictly required. He would ramble
on regardless of any remark or observation I might make. If this seems
like a complaint, it is not. The sound of his soft burr droning ever on
was more than agreeable to me—I could make out only half of what he
said in any case—I simply liked the comforting presence of a fellow
rambler, someone to share the vagaries of the road. In truth, it was less
a road than a hole-studded dirt path liberally strewn with rocks and
other difficulties too numerous and tedious to describe at length:
everything from mud wallows where run-off streams from the hillside
had washed out the track thereby requiring extended, sometimes
dangerous detours, to toothless beggars lying in wait for passing purses
and prepared to hobble for miles in pursuit of a coin or two to shut them
up. The former we could navigate, the latter we avoided as best we could
since Addas had no coins to spare and, with the way ahead so uncertain,
I did not care to part with any from my hidden purse. If that makes me
a hard-hearted miser, fair enough. I own it.

As I say, Addas was happy to ramble on at the mouth, and had a
ready supply, apparently bottomless, of stories, observations, and local
knowledge. Some, I tried hard to listen to; mostly I allowed it to pass

by like birds winging south overhead. These I also noted with some concern. The season was on the change, and I only hoped that we might reach our nearest destination before bad weather caught us.

"This Caer Gwyn," I remember saying a little after midday. "What is that—Fair Fort?"

"Mmm, more like White Fort," he lightly corrected in his lilting accent. "I think because the walls are made of stone."

Since we traversed a landscape covered in gray stone, I asked, "So why not Gray Fort?"

He laughed. "I think somebody painted it white for some reason."

"Anyway, how far is it?"

"Not far. In good weather with an early start, I can make it in one day—a long day, mind."

"And if the weather turns?"

"There is a shepherd's hut where we can shelter. I use it sometimes." He smiled. "That, or I sleep under the stars." He waved a hand over his head and beamed as if this was the most splendid outing he could imagine. "Shepherds do it all the time."

"Are we shepherds now?" I asked tartly.

He put back his head and guffawed. "I like you, Aurelia. You make me laugh."

"Do I indeed?" Wary that he might be mocking me, I challenged him. "What else do you like about me then?"

He gave me a sideways glance. "Your red hair and your smile."

I was aghast. "I *don't* have red hair!"

"You do," he insisted.

"It is russet."

"And what's that?" He grinned. "Another word for red—that's what."

I stared at him. "And you a curate," I said at last, thinking to repay his insult, mild though it might be. "I wonder how you have survived so long with only half a brain."

"Ha! Ha!" he laughed again. "See what I mean?"

That was Addas—his sunny outlook was proof against many of life's indignities. Well, I had plenty in my life to shadow *my* sunny outlook— not least the journey ahead of me. So, rather than get tangled up in useless argument, I changed the subject to one more pertinent to our predicament. "After Caer Gwyn, how far is that from Deva?" I wondered, resuming my calculations.

Addas shrugged. "I can't say as I ever heard."

"Never heard of Deva?"

"Deva—I've heard of that, to be sure. But I don't know of anyone who has ever been there—save a merchant or two, maybe."

"Most encouraging," I grumbled. "To be sure."

"But I *have* been to Caer Gwyn," he said happily. "There is a church where Heddwyn often offers services and sometimes I go with him to assist. More often I go on my own. The people thereabouts are good folk, and you should hear them sing…"

He was off, but I stopped listening and concentrated on the road as it wound its way up and up into the wild, empty hills—him talking and me pretending to listen. At midday, we ate a few mouthfuls from his bag and moved on. Later, as the sun dipped low in the west and the clouds began rolling in, I began to wish this shepherd's hut of his would come into view sooner rather than later.

What I did see, however—a fair distance from the track—was a good-sized holding of two or three houses, barns, granaries, and even a separate cookhouse. We also saw the dogs: five big rough-coated, ugly brutes with huge, muscled forequarters and narrow haunches. Their wide slavering jaws were filled with wicked sharp teeth—the hounds of Hell could not be any more vicious. The beasts came streaking toward us barking furiously, baying for our blood.

I was for running. Save for Addas' stern and urgent admonition to remain still and calm, I would have taken flight.

The fearsome beasts covered the ground between us in swift leaps and bounds. With Addas' firm hand on my arm, holding me in place, we stood our ground and allowed them to confront us. I think this confused the animals. Likely, they expected us to flee so they could give chase and, inevitably, pull us down and rip us to bloody shreds. But we did not run, so it seemed they did not know what to do.

I can still see Addas—motionless as a rock, staring the baleful creatures down, refusing to be cowed. Every fiber in me screamed for flight but, drawing on that brave man's strength of conviction, I forced myself to remain immobile, hardly daring to breathe, every beat of my heart a hasty prayer.

"That brown brute, there," Addas whispered loudly in my ear. "He's the leader. Look him in the eye and don't look away. Stare at him. Make him feel your courage."

"I don't *have* any courage," I whispered back.

"Do it anyway. Believe—and it will be so."

I did as he asked. What else could I do? We were stuck there until . . . until the creatures grew bored, or frustrated, exhausted their ferocity, or attacked. However it was, the brutes soon gave up their growling and howling and, one by one, simply slunk away.

I watched them go and gazed at the cluster of dwellings in the near distance. All this commotion had failed to raise any interest from the houses or outbuildings. No one came to call off the dogs, nor so much as poked a curious head out the door to see what had roused the beasts to fury. We stood watching as the dogs trotted away, and I said, "Now what?"

"You can let go of my hand if you like."

I glanced down, saw that I was tightly gripping his hand in mine—when had I done that? I instantly released him. "Sorry," I muttered. Then asked, "How did you know what to do?"

"Heddwyn taught me." He smiled. "I've seen them before. They're not usually so feisty."

"*Feisty?*" Well, that was one word for it.

We resumed our journey into an increasingly lonely hill country under an increasingly cloudy sky. Well, that farm holding, unwelcoming as it may have been, was also the last one we were to see in the daylight that remained. We passed no other settlements, houses, or trails leading to any habitation, and the day closed over us.

Indeed, the sun was well down and I was once again searching the hilltops and valleys for that shepherd's hut. As it was, we did not see that small, round dwelling of wattle and daub until the moon was peering over the distant hills. Save for Addas' knowledge, I would have missed it. We made our way to it and, thankfully, found it empty, then quickly set about scraping together a few twigs and branches from the nearby bushes to make a fire. Inside the hut was a small stone hearth and a little dry kindling. There was also a pile of fleeces hung over one of the beams. We dumped our gleanings on the hearth and while I set about spreading the fleeces for sleeping places Addas lit the fire. I heard him say something and turned to see him down on his knees, hunched over a tiny heap of shredded bark, repeatedly striking sparks from the flint and iron he carried in his bag, and singing to his little heap of kindling.

"What are you doing?" I asked, arranging my cloak beside me on the dirt floor.

"Making a fire," he said, without looking up.

"I mean, what is that you're singing?"

"Me? I wasn't singing."

"You were, you know," I insisted. "I may be mostly deaf, but I heard singing just now, and you're the only other one here."

He regarded me shrewdly. "You're not as deaf as you pretend, I think. You hear well enough when it suits you."

"So speaks the great physician, Addas of Aberdyfi."

He laughed and admitted, "Well, I *might* have been singing 'The Kindling'—it's an old song my mother sings when the flames won't catch. She says it helps." He shrugged again. "Who knows?"

"Maybe it does help," I said. "How does the song go? Sing it for me."

He bent forward and struck the flint again . . . and in a moment, his voice filled the hut. He sang:

In Jesu's holy sight, King of Sun and all that shines,
I stretch my hand on high and let it fall,
Swiftly, swiftly, let it fall to strike,
And strike again the kindling spark.
Thou Spirit of Love, hearth's true warmth,
Breath of Life, Lord of Light and all things bright,
Illumine thou our passage through this dark night,
Illumine thou our passage through this dark night.

As he sang, he struck his chip of flint to the iron and sent the sparks into the dry stuff he'd gathered—once and again and again, many times, until at last a red gleam appeared followed by a tenuous thread of smoke. Bending low, he cupped his hands around the pile and, blowing gently, coaxed the fledgling flame to life.

Once he was satisfied that the flame had caught, Addas sat back, beaming and announced, "You see? It worked."

"Your mother taught you well."

We made ourselves as comfortable as possible beside the hearth, feeding twigs and bits into the slowly growing fire. When at last we had a goodly blaze going, we sat back—Addas on one side of the hearth and me on the other—and let the warmth seep into us for the night was growing chill. Addas opened his bag and brought out bread and cheese: hard brown bread, and soft sweet cheese. He also had apples and a bit of fish, smoked and dried and wrapped in oak leaves.

We shared the meal and I began to think that this journey to Deva might yet be saved. True, I had lost my berth aboard the ship and my belongings with it; but if the days ahead continued as well as this one just past, I would reach my destination. With this thought in mind, I stretched out on my rough pallet and pulled my cloak over me, snuggling in to watch the flames and let the night and sleep overtake me. For, it had been a day begun in panic but ended in peace. I sank into to my night's rest content.

10

The rain began just before dawn. I felt the first drops on my face and awoke. Our cozy fire had burned down to embers and we had used all the firewood Addas had collected, and rain was leaking through holes in the roof of the hut. I wormed my way deeper under my cloak, trying to avoid or, failing that, ignore the annoying drip. I tried to sleep a little more, but the rain grew more intense, spattering the remains of our fire and removing any chance of lighting it again.

Addas, feeling the rain now, too, woke up and looked around. Seeing me, he smiled and said, "Wet day ahead, I think."

"I expect."

"We best be on our way." He climbed to his feet, shook out his cloak and wrapped himself in it head to heel like a true traveler. I did likewise. He kicked the hissing embers around to make sure they were well and truly extinguished and we opened the door and peered out into a gray, wet, and unwelcoming day.

"How much further?" I asked.

He frowned and looked at the sky as if reading the answer there. "In this? We'll be fortunate to reach Caer Gwyn before dusk," he decided. "But, sooner there, sooner dry," He added with a smile.

I grimaced and started off.

Dry? I was drenched to the bone the moment we left the spinney and long before we reached the road—which was already a trickling stream of running water by the time we started up the long slope leading to the next rise. These streams would become muddy torrents as the day wore on.

Whether the rain did or did not dampen Addas' spirits, I could not tell—but the noise of the pattering drops, the squelching of our feet, and having to hide so deeply in our hoods, did, at least, quiet his mouth. We slopped our way up the steep trackways, stepping from stone to stone or slogging through water to our ankles. Tedious and tiring work it was, and cold. My good wool cloak offered what little warmth there was to be had on the windy heights, but that was little enough—heavy with rain it felt as if I were carrying a dead sheep over my shoulders.

By the time the last valley came into view, with the settlement of Caer Gwyn nestled in the crux where two main roads met, my feet were numb twice over, my toes no longer worked, my jaw hurt from clenching my teeth, and I could no longer feel my fingers.

Across the way, on a near hilltop overlooking the little town and guarding the crossroads, stood the old stone fort. Whatever whitening it had once enjoyed had long ago worn away, for it looked as gray and cold and bleak as the fast-fading day. Addas, despite his best efforts to keep his cheery inner flame aglow, appeared just as drearily wretched as I—like some drowned half-human creature cast up from the sea by a tempest. He put forth a hand and declared, "Behold! Our destination shines glorious before us!" I could not help but notice that hand was shivering.

Stumbling stiff-legged down the hillside track, we slithered into the town. There were few folk about and those few could not be persuaded to pause and talk to strangers in the street. Who could blame them?

We continued further down the single main street. "The church is just there," he told me, pointing some way along the muddy track. It, like many another of the town's dwellings, was built outside the protecting walls of the old garrison—though close enough that folk could flee to the safety of those strong walls in times of trouble. And like the church at Aberdyfi, it was a small, square building of uncut local stone with a single low doorway and high-pitched roof. A priest's house had been attached to the south end and, after trying the door of the church—which was locked—we went around the back where Addas pulled the bolt and lifted the latch. He turned to me, his hair in snaking tendrils—each one a rivulet—rain dripping off his nose. "After—" He sneezed. "—you."

Just like the shepherd's hut we had left that morning, the priest's house was a single room, spare of any furniture save a three-legged table, a chair, and a stool. Dark, with only a small slit wind hole high in the wall, it was at least blessedly dry. And, Lord be praised, there in one corner was a hearth with a full box of firewood and a bundle of kindling waiting beside it. I suppose that Heddwyn, or whatever itinerant cleric came to serve the church was, like us, often cold and wet, so the local congregation made certain he could at least warm himself on arrival. And this is exactly what we did.

Before I had even removed my sopping cloak and hung it on a peg on the wall, Addas was on his knees arranging kindling and twigs into a little pyre. Much as the night before, he soon had a red spark glowing in the raw wool provided, and we spent the next few moments willing the flames to catch and thrive. As soon as the fire was properly alight, the young curate sat back on his heels and offered a prayer of thanks for our safe arrival and the gift of fire to warm and cheer us, to which I offered my heartfelt "Amen."

That done, I began stripping off my mantle, girdle, and tunic.

Addas, taken aback by my brazen immodesty, tried to cover his embarrassment, saying, "Not one to spare a fellow's tender feelings, I see."

"Perhaps you'd be more comfortable sharing the room with my frozen gray corpse," I told him. "I've got to get out of these wet things while I can still move. You should, too."

"But I'm a curate. I cannot—" His argument died before he could find words to speak it.

"You needn't fear for your honor or position," I told him. "I will remain in my under shift until my cloak is dry. So, go on—get out of your wet things."

He looked down, ashamed. "I have not under clothes," he confessed.

Ah, well that was a problem easily solved. I made light of it, saying, "Whatever have I done to make you think I care about so trivial a thing as that? But if you would spare a maiden her blushes, then wear your cloak until your clothes dry out. No one will know."

Ruefully, he agreed that would serve; I turned my back while he removed his short robe and trousers and wrapped himself in his damp cloak. Placing the lone chair close to the fire, we draped our wet things over it and settled down to warm ourselves as best we could and let the flames do their work.

So, there we sat, shivering in our damp things, feeding the fire and waiting for the hut to warm. Suddenly ravenous, I dreaded the thought of venturing back out into the rain again to see what might be had in the town. I said as much to Addas, who told me that there was a tavern where we could get something to eat. We were discussing this when a knock came on the door and the door opened to admit a woman carrying a bowl covered with a wooden platter.

"Brother Bellinus, I have brought you—" She took a step into the room and then stopped, her mouth open as she took in the sight of two strangers crouched over the fire burning brightly on the hearth.

"Addas!" she gasped. "What are you doing here? I thought Brother Bellinus was coming this week." She glanced around. "Is Heddwyn here?"

"No," he said. "Only me"—he put out a hand to me—"and my friend Aurelia."

I stood up in my shift and gave her what I hoped was a winsome smile. "I'm going to Deva," I told her, quite without thinking.

"Deva is it?" She seemed doubtful that anyone would want to go there. "That's a long way for a girl on her own. Are you a runaway?"

I suppose she meant a runaway slave or bondmaid who has fled her master. "I'm looking after her," Addas explained. Then, perhaps sensing from the woman's dubious expression that more explanation might be in order if he continued down this path, he adroitly changed the subject. "We've come for the market—"

"The market is two days away," she said, and cast a glance over me.

"We came in to get out of the rain," I said. "I'm Aurelia, and your name is . . . ?"

"Oh, I am Docilla," she said. "I saw the smoke earlier and thought Brother Bellinus must have arrived early."

"And you brought food for him? How very thoughtful. But, here— that looks heavy." Addas, ever the helpful cleric, reached for the bowl. "Let me take it for you." She gave up the bowl and he placed it on the table. "It smells wonderful."

"Is Heddwyn coming, then?" the woman asked, handing him the bag that was hanging on her arm.

"Not this time, no," Addas said, shaking his head. "No doubt Brother Bellinus will arrive shortly. I expect the weather has delayed him." As if to lend credence to his words, the door rattled in a gust of wind just then.

Standing there in my thin shift and bare feet, I shivered and glanced back at the warming fire. The movement caught Docilla's attention. "You poor thing!" she exclaimed. "Look at you—cold to the bone. You must come home with me. Both of you. It's warmer and you can wait for the market there."

"But you said the market is not until day after tomorrow."

"Well, then," replied Docilla decidedly, "you'll stay until then. There's just my husband and me now, but he won't be of a mind to disagree." She was already making plans in her head. "You'll have to sleep on the floor, but we'll make do. Gather your wet things and bring them along. We'll get you dried out proper." Glancing at the bowl and bag on the table, she told Addas, "Bring that, too. I'll put it back in the pot and heat it again and we'll all sit down together."

I pulled on my half-dry mantle and threw my cloak over my shoulders, and slipped back into wet shoes. Addas grabbed up his clothes and the bowl on the table—not easy when trying to hold all his various garments together and keep the cloak from sliding off him.

"Come along now," said Docilla, firmly in control once more. "It isn't far, but it's slippery under foot so watch your step."

Out into the storm we went—drenched again in less time than it takes to tell. The woman lived just down the way a bit and across the lane. How she ever saw the smoke from our fire, I'll never know; but I was heartily grateful that she did. Not only did we have a warm place by the fire, dry cloaks to wrap up in while ours were drying, and a fine hot meal of mutton stew, but there was a jar of beer as well. Docilla's husband Julius—or Julian, I never did hear correctly—insisted on pouring out his dark brown brew once he learned that he was hosting uninvited guests for the night.

Later, after our meal and having diverted our gracious hosts with news of the wider world—if only as far as Venta and Aberdyfi—Addas took it upon himself to explain my need to visit the market in hopes of finding merchants who would be travelling to Deva. Our hosts accepted this naturally enough and, as night closed over this chill, rainy day, we prepared our beds: goatskins spread on the floor by the hearth where our clothes were almost dry. Well tired by the day's events, I lay down on one side of the hearth, and Addas on the other.

I sank into sleep content and grateful for the kindness extended and the comfort of a warm place to lay my head—somewhere not under a bush in the cold wind and rain to spend a hungry night freezing under some storm-wracked tree and waking up dead in the morning.

Docilla, bless her, having encountered strangers needing a bit of care, did not hesitate to do what she could to help us. Christians are like this as often as not, I find. The good ones, I mean.

11

THE NEXT MORNING Addas and I went to the crossroads hoping to see anyone passing on the Deva road. The plan was to simply waylay likely travelers and induce them, one way or another, to take me with them. Thankfully, the rain had moved on and the day, though overcast, remained dry. We watched and waited through the morning—taking it in turns to sit on the stone waymarker—few travelers appeared at all and none going to Deva. Later, as the day wore on, traffic on the road increased and our hopes rose. In groups and gaggles they trooped by— some coming to the market, others moving on to local places—all of them going the wrong way.

Dispirited, we dragged ourselves back to Docilla and Julian's house. Though the good woman had insisted I could not go on my way alone and refused to let me leave until I had a suitable escort, I was feeling ever more guilty for imposing on her generosity and on Addas, who must have had duties he was neglecting. Nevertheless, I was glad to sit down at her supper table once more. She tried to cheer me up, saying, "Well, the market is tomorrow, so there will be plenty of folk around. You'll find someone travelling on to Deva, never fear."

So, the next morning, we hied ourselves once more to the crossroads to find the market already in full cry. Like markets everywhere, people had come from miles around with something trade or barter: cream, butter, eggs, hard and soft cheese of various kinds; smoked and dried meat and fish; grain and beans; raw wool and woven goods, metal utensils, pottery, wooden objects, tools, and such

163

things. In all, it was a goodly market, much as one would find anywhere in the south.

We moved here and there, searching among the various merchants, asking if any would be heading toward Deva or returning there when the day was over.

Though we spoke to nearly every merchant and traveler, we found no one either going to, or from, Deva. Weary of all the asking, I treated Addas to a midday meal of apple beer, flat bread, and little spiced sausages from one of the vendors and we sat down to eat and devise another plan. "I'll take you there myself," he declared, stuffing a sausage into his mouth. "I got you here and I can take you the rest of the way."

"What?" Did I hear that correctly? "No. You have duties, responsibilities—"

"None so important as this," he countered.

"What about Heddwyn and Flori?" I asked. "They'll worry what has happened to you."

"I'll explain when I get home," he said lightly. "They'll understand."

I stared at him doubtfully. "You are kind to offer, Addas, but you cannot possibly take me to Deva. We'll just have to find another way."

He would not be put off. Convinced that he had undertaken this charge, he would see it through to the end. The more he talked about it, the more I warmed to the idea. I hit upon a possible solution. "Could we hire a wagon do you think?"

He shrugged. "If we had money enough."

"I have money," I told him, and explained about Augustus giving me his purse. "But where could we find a wagon and driver?"

"We can ask at the fortress," he suggested. "They'll know—and maybe we can beg a soldier to go with us."

The more we talked, the more it seemed like a good and practical solution. We were still discussing this when Addas nudged me with an elbow and directed my attention to three wagons just then passing by. These were covered wagons: two with leather stretched over hoops, and one with a sort of raised flat roof that slanted from front to back. The arrival of these vehicles caused an immediate sensation among the market goers and many went flocking to the wagons before they had even rolled to a stop beside the road just beyond the market.

"Merchants from the south," Addas said with a nod of recognition.

"Do you know them?"

"Not these ones, but others like them come through Aberdyfi often enough."

"Are they going to Deva, do you think?"

"There's one quick way to find out." He jumped up and headed off. "We'll ask them."

"What about our plan?" I called after him, but got no reply.

We sidled up and Addas made conversation. We learned that, as he surmised, they were indeed traders from the south—from Durovernum, they said, wherever that is—and there were four of them with five servants, all men. They were on their way to the far northern reaches, making one last trip before winter rendered travel impossible in the snowbound fastness of the high hills and mountains. There were few enough outposts up there, but good business to be done for any bold enough to accept the perils and risk. And, more to the point, they would be passing through Deva before returning by way of Mamucium and Eboracum.

These merchants, I decided, *were* bold enough for the risks of the road and more: rough men for rough trade in rougher places. In attitude and appearance they were a far cry from the affable Drustan and his shipboard friends. They wore their hair long and tightly braided, and two of them had blue tribal markings etched into the skin of their faces and hands. They were dressed in heavy tunics and short trousers with tall leather boots and overlarge cloaks woven in distinctive stripes and checks. They each carried weapons. Three wore the short-bladed *gladius* of the legion strapped to their hips, but one had the long, thin blade of old-fashioned Celtic design. In all, they looked like the clan chieftains who sometimes ventured into town from whatever godforsaken hinterland they ruled.

The leader of the group was a man named Gnaeus. When asked, he told us that he made this particular journey twice a year, sometimes more if demand was strong; mostly, he traveled in the company of the same three merchants of his group. They called themselves the *Triumvirate*—although there were four of them. I don't think they knew what the word really meant at all. They spoke little and most often tersely, their Latin crude and mixed with various local words and phrases picked up, no doubt, in the different provinces they traveled through.

Not the friendliest fellow I'd ever met, but perhaps that brutish exterior was the greater part of their protection on the road: a thorny shell to ward off any unwanted interest or intrusion. Then again, I considered, maybe they were every bit as uncouth and uncultured as they looked.

However it was, Addas made bold to present the appeal on my behalf. Though I did not catch all of it, I gathered he explained about my father's death and my ill-fortuned abandonment in Aberdyfi— though, strictly speaking, I was not deserted, merely misplaced, but his telling made the tale better and it amounted to much the same thing in the end: I was stranded. In any event, I let him have his say and stood there, looking lost and confused, I expect—feeling like it, anyway—and Gnaeus passed a critical eye over me from head to toe as if being asked to buy a stray sheep.

"Deva, you say?" He gave a knowing nod. "Aye, that's one of ours."

"And she could travel with you?" he asked. "You'd take her along and see her safely to her friends?"

Gnaeus made a face which I imagined was him considering the proposition as presented. "No," he said with gruff finality. "Not interested."

I'd seen enough. I tugged on Addas' sleeve and backed away. He thanked the trader for his time and we returned to the waymarker to wait for another opportunity to present itself.

None did. So, as the day drew to a close and the market began to thin out, we decided to go back to Docilla and discuss how best to hire a wagon. We started back and as I passed a vendor selling candles and herbs, I decided to buy a little gift for our hostess to repay her kindness. Addas thought this a good idea and said he would go to the tavern and buy a jar of beer to take back. We agreed that I would meet him there. I chose a fine new candle of yellow beeswax and a hank of fragrant lavender woven into a tidy braid to hang above a door.

I withdrew my purse and counted out the coins and thanked the merchant. I was just turning away with my purchase when my arm was seized in a tight grip and I was yanked roughly, an arm thrown around my neck. "You're coming with me," growled a harsh voice in my ear, and the purse was snatched from my hands.

The force and ferocity of his assault rendered it useless to resist, and I was quickly marched back to the rough traders we had spoken to earlier. Gnaeus was waiting, gave his partner a nod, and I was swept bodily off my feet and shoved into one of the leather-covered wagons, bales of furs and bundles of goods heaped on top of me—so many and so heavy that it was all I could do to draw breath, let along cry for help.

Half suffocated, I heard a muffled shout from somewhere outside. The wagon lurched off with a jolt, leaving Caer Gwyn, Addas, and my best-laid plans behind.

12

MY HEART BROKE. Thrust into that wagon against my will, stuffed in like a bundle of rags with sacks and barrels and baggage heaped over me, I cried. Despair drew its black wings over me like a preying bird, and the tears ran freely. I thought about my father and that hideous attack that cost him his life . . . about Augustus and Tomos, good and faithful friends that I would never see again . . . about Dunstan, Justina, and Docilla who had helped me on my way and, yes, even Addas—who was probably looking for me and wondering what had happened. I thought about all that had brought me to this place—only to end my life smothered under a weight of cargo in the wagon of a malicious, devious merchant.

I cried, each breath depleting my strength. But I ceased to care. *Let me die,* I thought, *and be done with it.*

It occurred to me to say my prayers and confess my sins so that I might be carried away to paradise where I would see my mother whom I had never known, and my dear father who had loved me as much as any two parents. I closed my eyes and, with shaky breath, passed out of consciousness.

At some point, I became aware of a sharp pain in my chest and awoke in the land of the living, still angry, still hurting, and still in that hateful wagon. My next thought was that the wagon was no longer moving and there were voices outside—muddled and indistinct, but someone was talking. Then the weight on me began to lessen as bags and bundles were pulled off me and I was dragged back into the world of men. Bad men, yes, but alive all the same.

The thug who had stolen me dragged me from my rude nest and stood me on my feet outside the wagon. He leered at me and Gnaeus appeared and mumbled something. The man walked off and, Gnaeus spoke to me. I touched my ear and said, "I don't hear well."

"How old are you?" he asked, raising his voice and speaking with exaggerated care.

"Fourteen summers," I admitted.

He looked me up and down, then grunted as if this somehow confirmed some private speculation. "Can you cook?"

"I can," I replied, and looked around. We had stopped for the night in a hollow—little more than a wide spot beside the road with a spinney of rowan trees and a stream nearby. Clearly, the place had been used before. The grass was matted down by wheel tracks, and a ring of stones and damp ash marked the place of previous campfires. Three servants were pulling things from one of the other wagons and setting up camp, and the other two were making a fire while the other traders tended the horses.

After a moment's deliberation, Gnaeus turned and, pointing toward the two at the fire, said, "Over there. Get busy."

He made a flicking motion with his hand to dismiss me. I swallowed my indignation and joined the two menials who had been tasked with preparing food. Neither of these appeared to speak any language that I could recognize, so we communicated through grunts and signs and gestures and got along with our work. Easy enough: chopping up root vegetables and gobbets of meat and chucking them into an iron pot with a little water. I was given a knife and a board and did most of the chopping while the others gathered bowls and ladles and other bits of this and that. Meanwhile, the three remaining servants prepared sleeping places around a second fire their masters would recline beside.

It soon became apparent that, aside from boiling up stuff, the two I was with knew next to nothing about cooking. Possibly they had been abducted, too, and, like myself, forced to work. However it was, I shortly found myself ordering them around and took control of the chore: adding salt to the water for the onions and turnips, and instead of boiling the pork, threaded the chopped gobbets onto long forks to act as skewers. It would be nice to have some garlic, I thought, so went in search of it. I wandered only a few paces and came upon a clump growing beside the road—planted by the soldiers in earlier times as they marched from garrison to garrison across Britannia. As Tullius had once explained, at each place a legion made camp the soldiers would push a thumb in the soil and plant a clove of garlic; that way, they would have it should they pass that way again. From one end of this island realm to the other, travelers could find little pungent bulbs. I pulled up a few, thinking: Rome might have left Britain, but the garlic was still here.

I returned to the cooking pot where the vegetables were boiled and soft, I put them in a bowl and mashed them up together with salt, dried parsley, and a knob of butter—all of which I found in the store of provisions. My two helpers were more than glad to be spared these tasks, leaving me to get on with it and the work took my mind off my plight—if only for a little while.

The merchants kept to themselves. They had bought jars in the market, and these they brought out and all four sat around the fire and shared out their beer while awaiting the meal. They talked together, their voices low; I could not make out what they said, but the occasional gusts of laughter gave me to know that if they did not enjoy one another's company, at least they had learned to tolerate one another.

Night had fallen full dark when the meal was finally ready. I spooned the mash into a wooden bowl and piled the fire-roasted meat onto a platter, sprinkling salt over it. I took a stack of bowls and a clutch of wooden spoons to the campfire and passed them out, then ladled the mash into the bowls along with cubes of roast pork and a thick slice of buttered bread. The men received their bowls and began to eat, mostly in silence. I retreated to the cooking fire and shared a little of the meal with my fellow slaves. When the merchants finished, I set about collecting up the spoons and empty bowls.

"That was good," Gnaeus told me when I picked up his bowl. "What's your name?"

"Aurelia," I said.

"Eh?" He did not understand the word.

"That's my name—Aurelia."

His eyebrows lowered in thought. "Where are you from? Your people—who are they? Demetae?" he asked. I touched my ear and he repeated.

"Silures," I told him. "My people were Silures."

"Ah." He nodded thoughtfully. "I knew it was one or the other. Ever been to Maridunum?"

I shook my head. Of course, I'd heard of the place from the time I was able to walk, and I knew that it was said to have been an important place somewhere down along the coast from Venta. Not all that far, I think, but who ever had reason to go there? Anyway, it was in Demetae territory.

Gnaeus thumped himself on the chest proudly. "Maridunum— that's where I grew up."

I forced a smile, and nodded as if this was the most fascinating fact I'd learned all day. "Venta," I told him. "That's where I grew up."

He considered this and appeared to think that this made us somehow friends. "Well, cook like that," he concluded, "and we'll get on."

"Get on?" I said, anger igniting once more and flaring up. "You stole me! And you stole my purse!"

If my rash outburst was meant to provoke him, it failed. Instead, he regarded me with that shrewd, thoughtful look. "You wanted to go to Deva. I'm going to Deva."

"And you'll take me there?" I said, a faint hope stirring in my breast.

He nodded and said, "You agree to cook for us until we get there and I'll take you to Deva."

"And you'll give me back my purse?" I said, making this a condition of my servitude.

"I'll give you back your purse," he agreed. "But not until we get there."

I accepted his terms. What other choice did I have? If I yet held any hope at all of reaching my friends, this was my only chance. "Done," I told him. "I'll be your cook."

Gnaeus gave me his fishy smile. "We'll get on."

The camp settled down for the night. After everyone had tended to nature's necessities, we made our own beds where we could and went to sleep—the four members of the so-called Triumvirate around the campfire and the rest of us hugging the cooking fire. I lay a long time awake, unable to rest for distressing thoughts of all that could befall a girl on her own amongst a gang of brutish men. Sometime during the night, sleep overtook me and I knew no more until I awakened the next morning, cold and aching and miserable, to begin my bondage as a cook.

The day dawned fair and bright with no hint of rain. We did not pause to break fast, but made to push on as soon as camp was struck and everything packed away. While the horses were watered and put to harness, I climbed back into the wagon, the main cargo of which was made up of bundles wrapped in skins and leather; there were also a goodly number of small wooden casks and chests. In amongst these were tight-bound rolls of cloth that looked to me like some of the stuff produced from somewhere far beyond the shores of Britannia. There were grain sacks, too—mostly oats meant for the horses—and these served me as a nesting place. My roost was lumpy, but nowhere near as uncomfortable as the day before, and with a little arrangement I was able to gain enough vantage to allow myself to see the road ahead and some of the passing countryside. We paused briefly at midday to eat and water the horses, then traveled on without stopping again until dusk. It seemed the traders were intent on covering as much ground as possible each leg of the journey—which was all very well by me.

The travel the next day was the same as the day before, but I noticed that the land had begun to rise: the hills were higher, more rugged, the trails narrower, rockier. We reached a well beside the road at the bottom of some nameless valley, and here we paused. All the water vessels were emptied and refilled, the horses watered, and I made a cold meal of cheese and brown bread smeared with honey before moving on.

That night was more or less the same as those before, and the next day—aside from the sharpening wind and low, menacing clouds— much the same again: plodding through empty hills over bare, broken trails, passing lonely settlements and holdings and occasional flocks of sheep, cattle, or goats. Upon reaching one such settlement, we were met on the road by the farmers who sold us fresh meat and vegetables to replenish our stocks, and sealed jars of mead. That done, we moved on.

I cooked a good and hearty supper that night such as we had not had since starting out. I was even able to make a batch of sweet honey cakes which the traders wolfed down with childlike delight, and drew praise from Gnaeus who, a little woozy from the mead, gave me a smile and a wink when I fetched his empty bowl.

The sun was already down behind the western hills when we reached a fair-sized holding the next day. Larger than any we'd seen since leaving Caer Gwyn, it lay at the far end of a very long, slender lake called—if I caught it right—something like Llyn Tegid. The lake was pleasant enough in its way, with blue misty hills rising in the distance and green meadows all around, but it was the settlement that impressed: a proper villa in the old Roman style surrounded by numerous dwellings, barns, granaries, store houses, and sheds. The central complex was constructed mostly in dressed stone with timber outbuildings. The main compound was bounded on three sides by a stone wall, and the land outside the wall given to pens for animals and, beyond those, cultivated fields. A nearby stream supplied fresh water, and a substantial forest lay no great distance to the north and east, providing ready access timber.

It was easily the most prosperous steading I had seen since Viroconium, no mistake. Home to perhaps fifty or so—including wives and children—and I did not wonder but that the man who owned it exulted in his wealth and the power it gave him. He even wore a chieftain's golden torc—an ornament often spoken of in the old tales, but one I had never seen. Head to toe, the man styled himself a king. Perhaps, among his kind, he was just that.

Ederyn Longknife he was called, and tokens of his authority were everywhere—most obviously in the number of well-armed men he kept: young, for the most part, muscular, agile, and bristling with the telltale swagger that suggested aggression barely under control. Warriors all, and just as assertive were the dogs ranged around them; great, shaggy, long-legged beasts—big as the boars they hunted—the creatures roamed about the place, scrappy, ill-tempered, and loud.

We had seen some of these—both men and dogs—when a greeting party rode out to meet us on the road. I suppose very little passed in the region that the residents of the villa did not regard, and the approach of wagons in that wild hill country was certain to draw attention. Among those who stopped us to enquire after our business were two or three who recognized the merchants, so the implied challenge turned into a genial welcome and we were escorted to the villa where, it soon transpired, we were to spend the night.

With much hailing and backslapping and gripping of arms, the traders were welcomed into the king's villa. Mind, I don't know if this

Ederyn, or Eternus as others knew him, possessed any genuine royalty at all, but in that wilderness country such niceties tend to matter less than they do in more civilized regions. Be that as it may, from what I saw around me, Ederyn did possess wealth and, no doubt, the strongest arm in the province to go with it. Backed up by his private army—a warband, it was called—this chieftain took it on himself to rule and I could not imagine another in that remote province to challenge him. This, I thought even then, was the way the world was going: a return to the old ways of tribalism and constant aggression.

In any case, the traders were invited in to accept the welcome cup. The servants, myself included, were left outside to tend the wagons and ready the goods for whatever trade was to be done. I did not think it likely much business was to be had in this place, but this notion was wholly mistaken. Our presumed king, it turned out, was one of Gnaeus' better clients.

I soon learned why—and in doing so, discovered the true purpose of our little trading company and their dark secret.

13

I WAS AT WORK helping the servants unload some of the trade goods. Standing at the rear of the flat-roofed wagon one of the traders passed me a leather-wrapped bundle, far heavier than I might have expected for its size. Staggering a little, I delivered my burden to the courtyard where it was added to the others ranged along the outer wall of the villa. A good few of the young warriors gathered to watch. They stood around talking and nudging each other, but none offered to help. That they should stand idle and allow a reedy girl to struggle with an unwieldy burden told me everything I needed to know about their character.

On my third return to the villa, with another leather bundle, I approached the gate and I was halted by one of the other servants. He shouted something to his fellows in the wagon and then turned me around, directing me back to the wagon. I saw then that the parcel I carried was bound in a red leather strap different from the others. This bundle was quickly exchanged for another and then Gnaeus called to those in the wagon and the unpacking of goods concluded.

Having delivered this last load to the courtyard, it was placed in line with the others. Then, since no one told me otherwise, I retreated a few steps to watch as an undeniable sense of anticipation mounted among those gathered to watch the unloading. Clearly, everyone was waiting for something important, or at least diverting, to happen, and while we waited the warband talked and laughed, their spirits high. But all the chatter and laughter ceased when King Ederyn and some of his subjects emerged and I got my first close glimpse of the great man himself.

He was taller than his fellows, with heavy, broad-shoulders and a slightly thickening waist; his legs, however, were peculiarly thin—a certain sign, I've heard folk say, of spending too much time in the saddle. I don't know, but it seems you see it often among horsemen: the strong upper torso, and the scrawny lower half. The build gives many an unmounted horseman an odd appearance—like puffed-up roosters strutting about the yard on their thin spindle shanks. His face was full and unlined, his eyes clear and deep set; his hair was dark, long, curled; he wore no beard, but kept a luxurious moustache the ends of which wreathed his mouth.

Ederyn took his place before the neat row of bundled goods lined up against the wall, and Gnaeus and the other traders followed, ranging themselves either side of him. At Gnaeus' direction, one of his fellows selected a bundle, brought it forth, and offered it to the chieftain. With a solemnity I thought excessive as it was unnecessary, Ederyn raised it and offered it to those looking on before slowly untying the leather binding strap. Laying the bundle at his feet, he bent and lifted the wrap and opened the package to reveal a collection of long, slender shafts of gleaming, razored steel: swords.

From the collection, Ederyn selected one, fit his hand to the hilt, and hefted it once or twice. Then he raised the blade high as if he would strike down an enemy and, with a swift, sweeping motion, brought it down. The sharp point struck the paving at his feet. Powdered rock made a little puff of smoke, accompanied by a clear, distinct note like that of a tuned bell. The blade neither shattered nor bent. Lifting the blade, Ederyn examined the tip. He brushed his thumb along the edge and a smile spread across his lips.

He then showed his thumb, which displayed a single ruby drop of blood, to gasps and cheers from those looking on. The excited warriors crowded around as more bundles were opened and more of these wondrous blades passed among them. Their delight and the noisy acclaim of the onlookers filled the courtyard—so much so that a mere passerby would have been forgiven thinking that a realm had been delivered from a major calamity or a marvelous victory achieved.

That this kinglet required such weapons, I could well understand. Had weapons like this been available to the legionaries protecting

Esico and the others, my father might still be alive. Then again, maybe it was such a blade that killed them. Lawlessness, I thought ruefully, was everywhere descending over Britannia and men sought any advantage they could gain in the fight for survival.

Many of the warband already owned swords of one kind or another. This fact did not stop them making much over the weapons, however. Chattering like excited children over a new toy, they examined each and every one, practicing lethal thrusts and feints, and testing the blades against each other. I wonder that no one was stabbed.

Some of the villa's serving folk appeared after awhile and set up a vat on a stanchion which they filled from leather buckets. The drink was beer dipped out in cups and bowls to be passed about and, since no one appeared to notice, I accepted a bowl, too—and why not? I had earned my share.

After a time, the regal host and his esteemed guests retired to the dining hall while the rest of us remained in the courtyard to enjoy the revel. Well, the sun had already passed midday when we arrived at the lake settlement, and by now it was lowering in the west, and smoke from the cooking fires began wafting through the courtyard. At the first whiff of roasting meat, I remembered I had not eaten since that morning and was now ravenous, and slightly light-headed from the sweet brown beer. I had no part in the revelry, so rather than sit on a bench in the corner, I went in search of the cookhouse to satisfy my curiosity about what kind of kitchens a place like this would keep.

I followed my nose and the thin smoke trail to an outbuilding set off a few paces from the main dwelling. Cut stone, like the villa, it was a squat, low-roofed affair, the door a simple ox-hide covering; there were two very narrow slit wind holes covered with reed matting on either side of the entrance. A large fire pit had been built directly in front of the cookhouse where two male servants stood tending an iron spit on which the carcass of an entire pig roasted over a low flame of charcoal embers. The aroma was so delicious I almost swooned with hunger. Other servants, both male and female, busied themselves about the place, preparing what amounted to a feast in celebration of the arrival of the traders with their valuable cargo of weapons.

While I stood with watering mouth, watching the pig roast, a gray-haired fellow with a stick came out of the cookhouse and called orders to a couple of other servants. He saw me standing there, gave me a quick look and, recognizing a servant when he saw one, approached me, saying, "If you have come for the spiced wine, you'll have to come back. It is not ready yet."

He spoke good Latin loudly enough and with a lilting inflection. This took me aback somewhat. I had not expected to hear such learned tones in this remote place.

Before I could reply, he said, "Are you not the new bondmaid?"

"No." I shook my head. "I am travelling with Gnaeus."

He regarded me more closely. "That is very brave."

"*Brave*—did you say?"

He nodded. "By all accounts, the land north of the Wall is fraught with enemies of all stripes, and Celyddon a most dangerous place." He gave me a dismissive shrug and made to turn away. "At least, that is what they say."

North of the wall? Did he mean the Wall of Hadrian? *No one* went beyond Britain's northern boundary—at least no one with any good intent.

"I'm only going as far as Deva," I called after him.

He looked me up and down, then said, "Was there something you wanted? No? Then I must return to my duties."

He disappeared into the cookhouse and I sauntered back to the courtyard, pondering what he had said. The easy assumption that if I was with Gnaeus I must be travelling into enemy-infested northern territories was at the very least troubling. Yet, he had so effortlessly made that leap. All I could think was: *Why? What did he know?*

I arrived back in the courtyard to find that long boards were being erected. Other servants were carting all manner of jars and drinking vessels and platters and bowls of various sizes into the dining hall. I followed them in to see a huge, barnlike room of whitewashed walls and long boards on trestles arranged to form a hollow square with low benches being placed all around. The floor in the center of this square was a mosaic—made not of tesserae, but of smooth river pebbles of gray, black, and white. The designs were simple patterns with none of the images or symbols found, say, in a church or old basilica. At the far end of this hall, there was another, smaller fire pit and above it, a hole in the roof to carry away the smoke.

King Ederyn was hosting his guests in chairs around the fire pit. With him and the trading Triumvirate were three other warriors, and three more stood around the perimeter. All were in jovial high spirits, making the hall echo with a gabble of voices. One of the young warriors at the fire pit saw me and beckoned me over. When I did not immediately heed his summons, he repeated it with a call of command. A finely dressed, handsome fellow with long dark hair and a short-trimmed beard, I went to where he sat, approaching somewhat cautiously, as I did not know what he wanted of me and, with the din, unlikely to hear him in any case.

But, as I came near, he held out his mead bowl to me. I took this wordless gesture to mean that I was to refill the bowl for him. Glancing around quickly for another servant, I did not see any close by. Nor did I see a mead jar ready to hand. The fellow shoved the bowl at me again and mumbled something I did not catch. I looked back at him and shrugged.

The warrior tipped the bowl to show me it was empty and then thrust it at me once more. He pointed at the door and repeated what he'd said. I snatched the vessel from his hands and hurried back to the courtyard to find a mead jar. But could I find one? No, I could not. There were plenty of jars around, to be sure. Many were empty, and those that still had something in them contained beer. I went to one of the serving maids and asked for mead, but she just looked at me with a blank expression and went on pouring beer into the offered cups.

I turned to continue my search elsewhere and I felt a hard tap on my shoulder. The same haughty warrior stood behind me with a frown on his face. I guess he thought I was taking too long and had come looking for his bowl. I returned the empty vessel to him, and explained, "I think the mead is finished. I couldn't find any more jars."

He regarded me more closely. "You speak Latin."

I did not catch this so I simply returned his gaze.

"Answer me, girl. I said you speak Latin."

"I do, yes. Though, I am surprised you would understand it." My reply was needlessly waspish, I admit, but his arrogance rankled and I was in no mood to exchange pleasantries with such a boorish lout.

Rather than be put off, however, a broad smile spread across his handsome face. "Do you know who I am?"

"No." I gave my head a quick shake. "Should I?"

"I am King Ederyn's son," he said, "Cunomor." He smiled. "They call me Cuno."

"A fit name," I suggested. "For a hearth hound."

I should *not* have said this. His name, so far as I could work out, meant something like Big Dog; and I guess I thought to taunt him with it. He might well have given me a slap, and the blame would have been all mine. Instead, he put back his head and hooted. "'Hearth hound,' she says!" He ambled away in search of a mead jar, still laughing. "I like that!"

I hurried from the hall and joined the three servants guarding the merchandise at the wagons. Their company was far more preferable to me than any to be found inside the villa. We idled and talked, listening to the occasional gusts of laughter or jeering—which reached me as bursts of confused sound—and the day slowly closed around us. When at last the meal was ready, we trooped back into the courtyard to get a little food for ourselves. The so-called celebration had of course become an unruly revel, and everyone was deep into their cups—slaves and servants included. As for myself, I intended to keep my wits about me and saw no reason to join in this tedious debauchery. If this putative lord wanted to extol the purchase of some weapons, what was that to me? It was none of my affair.

Oh, but it should have been. It *should* have been.

After I had eaten my fill of succulent roast pork served with a sort of mush made of honey-sweetened cabbage and apples—and, yes, enjoyed a small cup of beer—I retired to my place in the wagon where I curled up in my cloak and went to sleep. I rose early the next morning and, with the other servants, went down to the stream that ran along the back of the villa and took care of our necessaries. On my return, we waited for the Triumvirate to emerge from sleeping off last night's excesses and set about rearranging the cargo in the wagons for the next leg of the journey.

The sun was well up by the time the traders appeared at the gate along with Ederyn and some few of his men who had come to see us on our way. Gnaeus and the king exchanged parting words, and the traders and warriors likewise. I recognized the dark young warrior I had spoken to the previous evening and caught him eyeing me, a sly smile curling his lips.

The lord of the villa and the traders made their farewells and Gnaeus gestured for us to depart. I went to the wagon and, as I started to climb up, I felt a firm hand grab my arm.

That is when my troubles began.

14

I MADE TO SHRUG FREE OF THE GRASP, but the iron grip held firm. I glanced around to see the pompous smirk of the young warrior I had encountered the night before: Cuno, the king's son.

Gnaeus turned from exchanging a few last words with King Ederyn and moved to his wagon—pausing when he saw the warrior holding me firmly in place. He raised his eyebrows in question. Before he could ask what was happening, Cuno spoke up. "How much for the girl?"

Gnaeus glanced at Ederyn who only gazed benignly on. "I don't follow."

"The girl," Cuno repeated, giving me a little shake. "I'll take her. How much do you want for her?"

I expected Gnaeus to laugh off the suggestion as the mistake it surely was, but his response should not have shocked me as it did. He was a trader, after all. "Well," he said, rubbing his stubbly jaw as he regarded me with casual calculation, "she's young and able. A good cook. A virgin, I suppose. What's she worth to you?"

By way of reply Cuno put his free hand into the pouch at his belt, fished around in it and brought out a narrow gold bracelet. I recognized this as a form of currency sometimes used in the remote rural regions where minted coin does not flow so readily. He hefted the thin gold band in his hand, judging the weight, then broke it in two and handed half to Gnaeus, who took it and examined it closely.

Gnaeus nodded and, eyeing the other half made a beckoning gesture indicating he wanted that portion, too. Cuno shook his head. Gnaeus, blast him, shrugged, accepted the trade. He looked at the half bracelet and then at me and nodded once. "Take her. She's yours."

Did I *hear* that aright? Did he just say what I thought I heard him say?

My mind spun. Suddenly dizzy, I nearly swooned. My mind shrieked: *He sold me! The filthy, lying bastard sold me!*

If I could not believe what I had heard, I did believe my eyes—for Gnaeus merely stuffed the gold into his belt and, without so much as a guilty glance in my direction, turned and climbed up into the wagon.

Dazed, I stared in stunned silence as the other traders, leering and chuckling, clambered into the wagons and, with a flick of the reins, one after another started off.

"Wait!" I shouted, darting forth. "You can't—"

Strong hands seized my arms and pulled me back. "Stay!" The word came hot in my ear. "I bought you. You're mine."

"Gnaeus!" I shouted. "Wait!" Again and again, I called after him. But he did not so much as look my way. "Devil take you!" I spat.

Some of the warriors standing nearby laughed and one or two slapped Cuno on the back in rude appreciation of his audacity. Servants appeared just then, leading five horses. Ederyn said a few words to his son and then went to his horse and mounted to the saddle. Four other warriors joined him, and they prepared to ride away.

"You serve *me* now, girl." Cunomor snarled; he turned and pulled me roughly with him. "Hearth hound I may be, but I am your lord and master. Don't you forget that."

Almost yanked off my feet as I was pulled away, I glanced around at the wagons with their warrior escort trundling slowly away, taking my freedom with them. Then I was marched back into the villa to begin my servitude.

Inside the walls, I was thrust into the hands the chief steward—the old gray hair with the stick. He took me aside to explain the workings of Ederyn's household, the duties of the various servants and what would be expected of me. I tried to pay heed. Truly, I did. But inside I was so enraged and raging against my unjust fate, that I could nowise take in anything he said.

Gnaeus sold me! How could he do that? How could anyone do that? He promised to watch over me. He stole my purse and then sold me—and not even two gold bands! Traitor! The Devil take him! May he rot in Hell forever!

Such were my thoughts. If I could have set fire to Gnaeus and all the goods in his wagon right then, I would have. I would happily have struck the flame and sent him to face the judgement he so richly deserved.

"I am Nonus," the old servant was saying. "What is your name, eh? Do you have one?"

I came to myself and had to think what he was asking.

"If not," he shrugged. "It doesn't matter . . ."

"What?" I touched my ear and shook my head. "I do not hear well. You will need to speak up and let me see your lips when you address me."

"Did your former master—" he began.

"I am neither slave nor bondmaid," I declared, my temper flaring up once more. "I am the daughter of Tullius Paulinus, Magistrate of Venta Silurum. My name is Aurelia and what happened out on the road just now is an injustice that will not stand."

This put old Nonus back on his heels. He looked around as if expecting aid to come to him from some unseen quarter. But there was none to be found—for either of us, it seemed. He knit his old, gnarled hands together and pursed his wrinkled lips while giving me a slightly wary gaze of appraisal. Finally, he said, "I do not know what happened out there . . ." He flapped a hand vaguely in the direction of the front gate. "But I *do* know that if a mistake has been made as you say, then the mistake, however unfortunate, will stand. I have served this family long enough to know that nothing good will come of trying to change it now."

"How can that be so?" I demanded. "I must speak to your lord at once."

"Ederyn has departed."

"Departed . . ." My heart sank. That, at least, was true. I had seen him ride off in escort of Gnaeus and the other merchants.

". . . going to Mamucium, I believe," the chief steward was saying. "He will not return for some days and has left his son to rule in his stead. If you would speak to someone, it must be Cunomor."

"He's the one who bought me!" I snapped, my voice rising. "Cunomor is a low, scheming rogue."

The elderly servant gave me a sympathetic look, then shrugged. "There is no one else."

In that moment, I realized just how gullible I had been—accepting the lies of Gnaeus. That pig-muck merchant probably never had any attention of making good on his promises to return my money and set me free. He sold me at first opportunity and never looked back. My one great fear had come to pass: I had fallen into a nest of vipers.

Ignoring my tears, Nonus endeavored to move me past this awful truth. "Come, I will take you to the kitchen where you can get something to eat," he said—though, still shocked and fuming, I only half heard. "Then I'll have Lydia give you something to do."

He led me away and, attempting distraction, told me a little about his life. A sympathetic fellow, as it turned out, Nonus explained that he had joined the service of Ederyn's father, the illustrious Padarn Beisrudd—old Red Robe himself. The faithful servant had remained with the family after his term of service had been repaid and, since the life of a servant was the only life he had ever known, he served them still as chief steward of the house. "Worry not," he told me kindly. "You will learn to live with them in time."

I was not worried in the least, because I did not intend to *live* with them any length of time whatsoever. I would not stay in that place so much as a single day. This I vowed and swore an oath on my father's life: Before the sun rose again, I would be gone.

Nonus delivered me to the kitchen and told those working there that I was a new bondmaid, purchased by Cunomor to join them, and he suggested that I might begin by serving in the cookhouse and at table until other work could be found. Of course, it infuriated me no end to stand there and pretend to be what I was not, but it was no use protesting to the other servants. What was the point? At best, any moaning or complaining on my part would only annoy them, and at worst turn them against me.

No, I decided, my best course would be to accept whatever I could get by way of food and drink and calmly bide my time until nightfall. If I could but hold my peace until then, I would count that a victory.

Thus, I was put to work in the cookhouse doing various little chores: chopping things, stirring things, carrying things from place to place. The other servants—two older women and two younger—showed but little interest or curiosity in me and I was happy with that.

Since I did not plan to see any of them again after tonight, it was all the same to me.

Cunomor and most of his men had been out hunting all day and they returned hungry and, of course, thirsty. Their efforts had been successful: two large boars were hauled to the yard behind the cookhouse and left there to be hung and skinned for roasting in a few days' time. The dogs were rewarded with the viscera and entrails of the kill which they rolled in, fought over, and snaffled down in the most abhorrent display imaginable. Like their masters, they were uncouth beasts.

The triumphant hunters herded into the hall, clamoring for beer as they replaced their weapons on the wall and took their places at the board. The older servants rushed to fetch the drink and vessels; myself and one of the other servants—a young woman with the long, fair braids of the Saecsen folk—were given the task of serving at table.

While not an onerous chore, it might even have been somewhat pleasant—if not for the boorish men. True, they were all young fellows in robust good health and full of the high spirits following a good hunt. Even so, I find it hard to believe that this gave them full warrant to indulge what our blessed Tomos so often called "the baser animal instincts"—those low, crude, vulgar behaviors some folk so readily embrace in the mistaken belief that it makes them somehow appealing. And, judging from those loutish lads gathered around the long table, those baser instincts were low, crude, and vulgar indeed!

It is not my place to judge them, I know. There is a righteous judge on high who marks well enough their failings; he does not need me to point them out. Nevertheless, it seems I failed to keep my innate disgust sufficiently disguised. I expect my efforts might have been more strenuous in this regard, but my disdain must have shown plainly on my face, for I had but made one circuit of the board with my jar of mead when a hand snaked out from one I had just served and snagged me by the arm as I turned away. I glanced down as a leering mouth inquired, "Who are you?"

With the chatter and clatter of voices in the lively room, I was not certain I had heard. I gazed at the dark-haired young warrior on the bench before me and waited for him to repeat the question. He declined, and shouted, "I asked you a question, bitch!"

I looked around innocently. "Are you talking to me?"

"I don't see anyone else."

"As you used the word *bitch* just now, I assumed you were speaking to one of the dogs."

The fellow sitting next to him heard what had passed and laughed out loud, giving his companion a nudge. "Ha! She's got you there, Turon!" Across the table, another piped up, "Bettered by a bondmaid." And he nudged the one next to him and repeated the exchange, and soon others were laughing, too. "What do you say to that, Turon?"

This merriment at his expense beggared churlish Turon's slender means of composure. His face grew red and his neck bulged. He tightened his grip on my arm and squeezed hard. I tried to pull free, but he held tight and came up out of his seat.

"Bitch!" he sneered, raising his other hand to strike. I cringed away from the coming blow and the mead jar slipped from my hands and shattered on the stone floor. "Now look what you've done!" he raged.

He let fly with an open hand. I flinched and he caught me a glancing blow on the jaw below my cheek. This angered him more, so he reared back to strike again—a fist this time.

His fist swung down and . . . stopped. Hanging there in midair. Cunomor, standing behind him, gripped the offending arm in his fist. "Sit down, Turon," he said, his voice tight. "You've made your point."

"Did you hear what that slut said to me?" whined Turon.

"I heard enough," Cunomor said. "Sit down and drink your mead."

Turon fell into his chair. "She has to be put in her place."

"She is *mine* to deal with as *I* see fit," Cunomor declared. To those looking on, he said, "Did you hear? The girl is mine to deal with. Touch her and you answer to me." Turning to me, he pointed at the broken jar and spilled mead on the floor. "Go and fetch another jar, and clean up the mess."

I lowered my eyes and hurried from the room, burning with rage, indignity, and anger, my cheek throbbing from the blow. Back in the cookhouse I paused to catch my breath and scrape together what little dignity I had left, if any.

Another jar was poured and put into my hands. With a nod and a gesture, I was pushed back into the hall to resume my duties. Though I did my best to pretend that nothing had happened, I could sense the snickers, the sideways glances and sly nudges as I moved around the board filling cups and bowls. No one spoke to me again. I expect no one dared make another remark.

When the food was ready my fellow serving maid and I put out the platters and saw to it that they remained filled. Gradually, the board emptied as the warriors quit the table and, hunger satisfied, went in search of other amusements. Cunomor was among the last to leave and when he finally rose, those with him rose, too, and started for the door. Cunomor came to where we were clearing the remains and said, "You gave good service tonight." He gave me a wolfish grin and said, "Let's see what other services you can perform, girl. Come to my chamber when you finish. You will spend the night with me."

I stiffened, a platter halfway off the table.

"Did you hear?" he said, and repeated the command more loudly. "You sleep with me tonight."

There came a call from the doorway and Cunomor turned and followed his men out. I stood motionless, my heart pounding. I knew what lay before me and I did not see any way to escape. My serving companion saw how stricken I was and, reaching out, put a warm hand on my arm. "Sometimes they give you presents," she said, trying to soften the blow. "It isn't so bad."

"To me it is," I replied, my voice cracking. "To me it is."

15

THE SERVANTS ATE IN HALL, huddled around the fire's embers, picking morsels from the detritus of the lavish meal and from bits and bowls that had been saved in the cookhouse. The others ate well, but any appetite I had fled the moment Cuno's hot breath touched my neck. All thoughts of food—and future, come to that—utterly vanished as I contemplated the night before me. I had never been with any man, and it was not with Cunomor that I would ever contemplate ending my virginity. The lout was not anyone I would remotely consider an acceptable bedmate, much less a lifemate. I know many may not set much store by such things, but I do. Perhaps priest Tomos' beliefs and teaching have persuaded me in this; that, or the virtuous example of my mother and father. However it may be, there it was.

Now that it came to the time of trial, I was bereft, with neither friend nor champion to defend my honor. I was to be abused, despoiled, and violated—and there was nothing I could do about it. A more forlorn and pathetic wretch within those walls could not have been found that night.

So wretched and pitiful, in fact, I was not thinking clearly. I don't believe I was even thinking at all. My firm resolve to be gone by morning might as well have been smoke on the wind, a candle snuffed out, the flame extinguished as if it had never been.

If the other servants noticed my distress—and at least one or another of them must have—they did little to relieve it. Beyond admonitions to "Eat, it's good..." and "You'll be hungry later..." there was no comfort to be had from them. It was only later, as the night drew on and I could avoid my fate no longer, and I began preparing myself for the ordeal ahead, holding it at bay as long as I could, that a faint gleam of hope appeared.

I was standing over a heap of dirty bowls, staring at them in glum despair, unmoving when one of the Saecsen girls noticed my vacant stare, and asked what was wrong. Bless her. In truth, I don't honestly know if she was Saecsen or Angli, but she nevertheless displayed something of the shrewd nature alleged of those tribes.

She had to ask again before I realized she was speaking to me.

"What is wrong?" I repeated. Then moaned, "*Everything. Everything is wrong.*"

At her sweetly sympathetic look, I quickly explained about Cunomor's carnal plans for our night together.

She listened, nodding. I still see her kindly features soft in the rushlight. When I finished, she simply shrugged and, picking up a stack of dirty platters, replied, "Well, there is always pig's blood."

Pig blood?

Is that what she said? I could not be certain, so assumed I had misheard as I so often do. But it was also the *way* she said it that spoke to me. I repeated the words and followed her out to the trough where she began scouring the platters with wet sand. I came to stand beside her and told her I didn't hear very well but that I thought she had said something about pig blood. She glanced at me, nodded, and went on with her work. "I don't understand," I said. "I don't know what that means."

The girl gave a little half smile and finished the platter she had been cleaning by dipping it in a basin of water. She put it aside, upright against the trough to dry, and then, wiping her hands on a scrap of cloth hanging from her girdle, led me around behind the cookhouse and into the yard where the two boars had been bled that day. Beside the wall sat a basin filled with a dark liquid which she pointed to and said, "Pig blood."

I stared at the basin in the dim light from the cookhouse, but nothing came to me.

She noticed my confusion and, taking the drying cloth from her girdle, she tore a strip from it, rolled it neatly, and dipped the edge of it into the basin. The blood was thick and sticky. She handed the dripping roll to me, and I began to catch her meaning. When she pointed to my groin all doubt fled. "Am I to put this between my legs?"

Again, she gave me that sly smile and nodded. "It has been known to work."

She offered to help me with it, but I told her I knew what to do and, taking the cloth roll, I cast aside whatever modesty I might have had left, hiked up my mantle, and wedged the bloody cloth high up between my legs. The moist scrap felt cold and slimy, and my stomach lurched. But the thing was done.

"Thank you...ah—I don't know your name."

She held her head to one side and regarded me curiously. "Aedita," she said.

"Thank you, Aedita. I pray this works."

She smiled, warmly, gratefully, and her eyes glistened. I imagine it had been that long since anyone had called her by name; longer still when anyone had last thanked her for anything, God only knows. She put her hand on my arm, squeezed it, and said, "Your luck with you, sister."

There was nothing to be gained by delay. Aedita pointed me in the direction of Cunomor's private chamber, my heart pounding as I fumbled along the darkened corridor. I stood for a moment before the door, then gave it a rap with my knuckles—I didn't know if this politeness was observed in this part of the world, but it was in the house where I grew up, so I did it here. I heard a grunt from inside which I took to mean that I should enter.

A single rushlight burned near the sleeping place where Cunomor sat on a pallet piled with sheepskins. He stood and beckoned me nearer. I drew a deep breath and went to stand before him while he examined me—much as one would examine a cow or sheep for the chop.

Seizing my hand in a firm grip, he pulled me closer. He must have noticed my quivering, for he placed a hand on my back as if to steady me, and then passed that same hand over my breasts. I looked down at his groping fingers and restrained myself from biting them.

"Take off your clothes."

Steadying myself, I untied my girdle and shoes. I drew my mantle over my head and stood there shaking in my thin undershift. He kicked it aside. "Everything," he said, this voice thick with lust.

Slowly, I lifted my shift and pulled the blood-dipped rag from my legs and he saw it. Some of the pig blood had, of course, smeared the inside of my thighs leaving an unsightly stain and a little of the gunk had dripped down the inside of my leg. "It is my time," I told him simply. I held out the bloody cloth to him and he recoiled in disgust.

"Get that filthy thing away from me," he growled.

I stood holding the rag for a moment and made as if throw it aside. But he put a hand to my chest and shoved me away. "No! Not here! Get out," he snarled, stepping back. "Leave me!"

Scooping up my clothes, I fled to the door. He called something as I left—something about meeting again in a few days' time—but I did not stop running until I was once more in the darkened courtyard.

Look for me in a few days' time, I thought, *and good luck to you. For you will not be finding me here.*

16

I HAD BUT LITTLE TIME TO ACT. The villa was dark and quiet. There seemed to be no one about. Little wonder that—after the night's revelry the men would be deep in their mead-soaked dreams. Back to the cookhouse I went. I took a little care to wash the dried blood from my legs and clean myself as well as I could, then set about gathering a few bits of things to see me on my way: a few small crusts of black bread, some of the dried meat of the kind the hunters took with them when they rode, a few apples, and some cheese. I wrapped everything carefully in one of the shifts the servants wore over their mantles when cooking. I considered taking some beer or wine for drink, but I had nothing to carry it in; anyway, water is not difficult to find in the hill country. That done I retraced my steps, taking care to remain in the shadows.

The courtyard was still. Deserted. Even so, I decided to simply sit and wait just to make sure. I perched on one of the stone benches against the wall and remained still and silent. Neither echo of voice, nor gleam of light disturbed the peace of the place, so after I was certain I was alone, I gathered my cloak around me, picked up my bundle of provisions, and stole to the gate.

I paused, cast a look behind me—there was no one to see—and then lifted the beam as carefully as I could. It was heavy but came free easily enough. I put it aside and, pushing open the door just a crack, slipped out. Once beyond the walls of the villa, I put my feet to the trail and walked—quickly, not running so as to tire me, but with urgent purpose—to get as far away as possible before dawn. My aim was to rejoin the road and continue my journey north to Deva.

True, I did not know how many days it might take, but I reckoned that providing I walked steadily, and the weather did not delay me overmuch, I would reach it before many days had passed. That was my hope and it burned in me like the flame of a candle, lighting my way in the dark.

In fact, I did not make it to the end of the track leading to the road before I sensed, rather than heard, a surge of motion behind me. Then came the barking.

The dogs!

Until that instant, I had not spared a thought for them. Stupid girl! In all my scheming I had not considered that they would be let out at night to guard the villa, and now the pack came snarling and yapping after me—seven of those rangy, sharp-toothed, shaggy dogs the size of ponies—called deer hounds, or wolf hounds, I think—effortlessly bounding over the track on their absurdly long legs.

The biggest one raced up and nipped me on the heel when I tried to run. Suddenly, I saw myself as a mauled and bloody carcass beside the road. But, even as panic welled up inside me, I recalled what Addas had said—that running would only make them chase and they would pull me down and tear me apart like a deer or errant sheep. Thanking the Good Lord once more for Addas and his sage advice, I plucked up my courage, stopped, and slowly turned to them. They stopped, too. I thought it might be best to try calming them with soothing words and a gentle voice.

It was no use. It only made them bark and howl all the more. Likely, they would have gone on yapping and snapping if the noise had not wakened the old servant who was keeper of the kennel. He came limping up the trail, shouting and waving a stick.

"Coch, down!" he called. "Orm, down!" He smacked the biggest dog with his stick and grabbed the iron-studded leather collar. "Ursa, down!" In no time at all, he quieted the dogs and then confronted me.

"What are you doing out here?" he demanded.

I had nothing to say to that, but I suppose he already guessed. He took one look at the bundle clutched to my chest and said, "Running away, eh? They'll whip you raw for that, you know." I must have appeared such a pitiful sight just then that he softened somewhat and added, "*If* they ever found out."

"Please," I said, "don't tell them. Don't tell anyone."

He frowned and looked me over. "If I do that for you," he said, "what will you do for me?"

A cold finger descended down the length of my spine. Give him money? I had none. My virtue? I was fleeing to protect it. Food? He was fed from the table. I had nothing. I waited for his reply, fearing it.

But his answer surprised me. "You work in the cookhouse, yes?"

I nodded warily.

"You can get me beer," he said.

"I can," I told him. I would find a way.

"Then this is how it will be," he decided, and told me that if I would bring him beer of an evening, he would not tell anyone that I had tried to run away.

This simple bargain would gain him a small pleasure and save me a fearsome beating. I accepted at once. "Done," I said. "You have my word and I'll take yours."

He led me back to the villa then, the dogs trailing behind, still snuffling and crowding, but no longer raising an unholy racket. He made to push me through the door, but pausing, put his face close to mine and said, "I'll see you tomorrow with a fresh jar. And I mean *fresh*, girl—I don't want last night's dregs, and I don't want it sittin' around half a day. You understand?"

"I understand."

He pushed me through the door and closed it; I lifted the beam back into place and dragged myself to the cookhouse in a welter of emotions: devastated, appalled that my escape was so easily thwarted, relief that I had escaped a mauling or worse, deeply fearful that my failure meant I would face Cunomor again, yet immensely grateful for the mercy shown me by the kennel keeper. In this raddled state, I crept into the empty room—where else was I to go? No one had shown me where to find another bed—and curled up in a warm corner near the oven.

Sleep was a long time coming, but as my eyes closed on the day, I glimpsed the form of my next escape and knew exactly how I would do it.

I was still asleep when Lydia, mistress of the kitchen, found me in my corner the next morning when she came in to kindle the oven and cooking fires. I came awake with a start and sat up. "Did you spend the night here, girl?" she asked.

"My name is Aurelia," I told her, stifling a yawn. "And, yes—I slept here. I did not know where else to go."

She regarded me as if trying to decide how to pluck a grouse. "I'll find you a place," she said at last. "Now, get you up and fetch me some water from the well." She handed me a big copper basin and pointed out the back door. "We'll make porridge for any who show themselves in the light of day."

I stood, pulling my cloak around me, and she fumbled with the fire. I took the basin and went out into the yard behind the cookhouse to the well in the far corner near the wall. The day was bright, but brisk, and I imagined what it would be like on the road had I made good my escape. The season was on the change and the days were already growing shorter; they would not be getting any warmer. If I was to flee, it would have to be soon.

This was in my mind as I lowered the leather bucket, pulled it up, and tipped water into the basin, then staggered back to the cookhouse trying not to spill it all on the way. Lydia took the basin from me and poured most of it into a large iron pot that she put on the fire; while she mixed the milled oats and barley and herbs, she gave me a knife and set me to the task of cutting up little cubes of salt pork. "They like the meaty porridge best," she told me, trying to be friendly.

Her back was turned and I replied to what I thought she'd said. "I suppose most everyone likes eating porridge."

Lydia stopped stirring and turned to me. "You didn't hear what I said, did you?" It was not a question, but a statement of fact.

I shook my head and tapped my right ear. "I'm part deaf."

She merely nodded and went back to her work. "Did your master beat you?" She raised her voice this time in recognition of my defect. "Is that why?"

Who knows the why of anything? I wondered—but merely replied, "No, I was born with it."

"Never mind," she said with some measure of motherly kindness. "These things happen. It can't be helped. I'll try to remember to speak so you can hear me."

I thanked her and continued with my chore—cutting the slab of pork belly into cubes—and every now and then I took one of the cubes and dropped it into an empty jar I placed under the board. Before the morning porridge was boiling in the pot, my new escape plan was already in motion.

17

BIDING MY TIME and trying my best to stay out of sight, I spent most of the day in and around the cookhouse, helping Lydia and learning the names of the other servants who came and went on chores of their own. We had a little rest after the midday meal was done and before we began preparing the evening meal. Although Lydia tried to make good her promise to find me a sleeping place, it seemed there was none to be found—at least by her. Apparently, Cunomor's rash impulse to buy me did not stretch to considering how I might be housed, or where.

"I think you must sleep in the kitchen for now," Lydia told me. "I will speak to Ederyn when he returns. He will find you a better place."

I thanked her for her efforts and said that I did not mind sleeping in the kitchen as I had done it before. I did *not* tell her that it mattered not a whit to me where I slept, as I did not plan to remain in that house any longer than necessary and, in any case, the kitchen was much to be preferred as it kept me warm at night, safe, and free to creep about more or less unnoticed.

As the sun touched the low western hills, I stole quietly to the brewhouse with a good-sized jar and, as the place was empty for the moment, I drew off a jarful of the brown, frothy liquid, carried it back to the cookhouse and put it behind some others on the board. I stood by and watched as the folk of the villa clumped into the hall for their evening meal—mostly men, as the women and children most often took their meals apart—and helped serve up the platters and bowls.

That finished, I ran back to the cookhouse and fetched my jars of beer and pork belly, then flitted to the hound keeper's hut. He lived next to his dogs in a squat hovel next to the kennel. As he took his meals with the other slaves and servants after the king and his household had eaten, he was idling on a stool outside his hut, playing with a brown puppy.

I greeted him nicely, and presented the jar of beer in the same way I would if he had been King Ederyn himself. He took it, sniffed it, and then gulped down a healthy swallow and wiped his mouth on his sleeve and gave me a gap-toothed smile. "Good," he said, remembering my deafness, he added clearly, "We'll get on, girl."

"My name is Aurelia," I told him. "What is yours?"

"My name?" The question seemed to catch him off guard. He had to think a moment. "Mab," he said at last. "Just call me Mab."

"I'm happy to know you, Mab." I smiled, but felt sad for him. The name simply meant *boy*. I suppose no one had ever given him another, or ever called him anything else. "And I'm glad you like the beer. I brought something for the dogs, too."

He eyed me warily. "Eh? What is it?"

Producing the second jar, I shook into my hand a few of the little cubes of pork belly I had filched. "Just a little something I thought they might like. May I give it to them?"

"Aye." He nodded and went back to his beer. "Mind they don't bite your fingers—especially that big black bitch. She'll have your throat out before you can swallow."

"Which one is that?" I asked.

"Ursa—pack leader. Stay away from her, hear me?"

"I'll be careful." I proceeded around the side of the hut to the kennel where the dogs were kept—a good-sized area fenced in by a sort of slatted wooden screen made of hazel stakes and woven willow, and secured with a chain. There were nine dogs in all—not including a litter of pups that waddled out of the kennel shelter—and they all started barking as soon as they saw me and the more aggressive of them flew to the screen, slavering and snapping. Feral beasts, these, if I needed any reminder. I began to mistrust my plan, but I had come this far so I carried on. Speaking gently and calmly, I put one of the fatty bits of meat on my palm and held it up to the wickerwork. "I brought something for you," I told them softly. "Would you like a taste?"

Pressing my palm against the screen—making sure to keep my fingers out of reach—I put the meat through. The first dog sniffed it and then gobbled it up and yapped for more. Success! The big black dog, the leader, stepped up; the members of her pack moved aside to let her through. Speaking gently, I plucked out a big, juicy cube, and called her by name, "Ursa, come. I have something for you."

The enormous dark beast regarded me with her deep brown eyes, but made no move. Pressing the gobbet of meat to the screen, I said. "This is for you." The other dogs crowded in, but I pulled it back. "No, this is for Ursa."

Holding the morsel to the wickerwork once more, I said, "Ursa, come. For you. Take it."

The canny creature padded over and sniffed the offering. I praised her, telling her what a beautiful creature she was and how wise and brave. She snaffled down the tidbit and then looked me in the eye again. Strange to say, but something quickened in her dark eyes—perception? Some sort of animal intuition? Understanding? I don't know, but in that moment I felt something pass between us.

She turned away, allowing the others to crowd in once more. I fed out my little treats one by one until the jar was empty. The hounds yapped for more but, errand finished, I hurried back to the cookhouse. I told Mab that I would come again tomorrow to collect his jar. "Don't worry, I'll bring a fresh one when I come."

Mercifully, I was able to avoid Cunomor while serving at the board that night. Then again, he might have been just as eager to avoid me—for the next day or so at least. A day or two more that's all, before he called me to his bed again ...

I did not like to think what would happen then, nor did I imagine that two short days would be time enough to see my furtive plan to fruition, but what else could I do? I could but hope for the best and pray that a day or two would be enough.

Next evening as the sun dropped down to meet the horizon, I found another excuse to go out to the kennel to visit Mab and the dogs. Again, I brought a jar of beer for him and a small bundle of morsels for the beasts in his care. Mab professed himself well satisfied with this arrangement, and the animals appeared to anticipate my arrival. I delivered the fresh jar to Mab and went around to the kennel. The puppies eagerly welcomed me and the little scraps of meat I brought.

They wobbled out of the shelter on their little fat legs and, seeing me, came tumbling and stumbling to the screen where they yipped and hopped to be fed.

The others crowded in and, as before, I spoke to them gently, praising their fine appearance, intelligence, and strength. Ursa stood watching a little apart. I called her by name and offered my gift. She approached and I looked into her big dark eyes and assured her I was her friend and meant her no harm. Once again, that curious connection passed between us and I came away feeling there was something about her that I had never seen in any creature before, more than animal intelligence, more than her dominating physical strength and appearance. True, she was undoubtedly the leader of the pack—I could have seen that from the way the others submitted to her—but it was as if she was assessing me, judging me.

I fed the others then, making sure to include them all, often refusing one already fed to allow another dog a turn which, when it came, the hungry hound was eager to snaffle down the morsel I offered. When I was finished, I retrieved the empty jar and, with the promise to return the next night, I hurried back to the courtyard.

Happily, everyone was still at the board, so my sly visit to Mab and the hounds that night, and the next, went unseen and unremarked by the other servants; that is, if anyone *did* notice, they neither questioned nor mentioned it. I suppose the appearance of a servant bearing a jar or two was a thing so ordinary as to be beneath comment. Even so, I knew Cunomor's summons to his bedchamber would not be long in coming. Like the fall of the headsman's axe, I feared and dreaded my fate and went about my chores hoping that by staying out of sight, I would stay out of mind.

I managed to achieve this modest aim, until the next morning when I was awakened—along with nearly everyone else in the villa— by shouting. "Cuno! Hurry! You are needed!" Aedita and Lydia had just come into the cookhouse. They put aside the vessels they were carrying and flew to the courtyard to see what was happening, arriving just in time to see Cunomor emerge from the hall after another night's debauch. They shouted again and Cuno moved quickly to meet them. They conferred quickly and then all dashed away again with more shouting and waving and cries for warriors to assemble. Warriors boiled from the hall, groggy and unsteady on their legs, trailing after their chief of battle, and we standing by were left staring after them.

"What is it?" I asked Aedita, standing next to me. "What's happening?"

"I cannot say for certain," she replied. "But I think Irish raiders have been seen in the south."

"Aye," Lydia confirmed. "A rider has come from Selwyn at Penllyn," she explained. "Lord Selwyn thinks they may be massing for an attack. He has sent out a call for warriors to come drive them away."

"Penllyn?"

"That was the place the rider mentioned." Lydia shrugged, and added, "It's a caer in the south somewhere. One of Lord Ederyn's client chiefs and his tribe live there."

"This place . . . this Penllyn—is it far?"

"Far enough," Lydia replied, starting back to the kitchen. "They will be gone a day at least, maybe more if there is a battle."

A day, she said, maybe two . . . Hallelujah! Merciful God be thanked! I had at least one day more to pursue my escape plan without hindrance—a day free of Cunomor and his odious bedchamber. That night I visited the kennel with Mab's promised beer and while he settled on his stool to slake his thirst, I took my bundle of treats to the wicker screen to feed the dogs and praise their many fine qualities. By now, I was even able to work my arm between the staves to stroke the more agreeable ones. I was happy with my progress, but there was only one sure way to judge it: go into the kennel with the beasts. That, I decided, would take courage—and Mab's help, to be sure. This, I considered, was next evening's chore.

It was not to be.

18

NEXT DAY DAWNED BRIGHT and breezy. I spent the morning helping wash clothes and other things in the nearby stream. The villa had a washroom, yes, but it was moldy, cramped, and damp most of the time. The women much preferred washing in the clear running water, airing the heavy cloaks, mantles, tunics, and trousers in the sunlight whenever they could. Nonus had sent me along to help. Not at all an onerous chore, I enjoyed the idle banter among the women. Though I caught only part of what they were saying, the sound of their twittering laughter lifted the clinging gloom and cheered me.

We had been at the river for some time and the day was beginning to dwindle as we finished and made our way back up to the villa. Walking with the others, a bundle of still-damp clothes in my arms, we came around the corner of the wall and saw the lathered horses in the yard outside the gate. Some of the grooms and bondmen were tending to them, but the riders were nowhere to be seen.

"The warband has returned," called one of the women, "and the king is with them." Another said, "I wonder if there was a battle..." Or something like, and everyone began chattering about that, eager to rush back to find out what had happened. Everyone except me, that is. I wanted nothing more than to keep out of Cunomor's sight.

The moment we entered the villa courtyard, I handed my still-damp bundle to one of the other girls, saying that the warriors would be hungry and I must go to the cookhouse to help prepare meat and drink for them. This I did, busying myself with such tasks as Lydia gave me. I allowed myself to hope I might yet evade the hateful encounter, but that half-formed hope was quickly dashed. Cunomor came striding into the kitchen—which he never did—and announced in a booming voice that he and his warband were dying of thirst and demanded jars of beer be brought to the hall at once and without delay.

At first glimpse of his sweaty features, I hastily turned away and hid my face. *He was back! And so soon! Don't let him see me...please, don't let him see me....*

And then came the loathsome tap on my shoulder and a hot breath in my good ear. "Tonight, girl." He gripped me hard. I froze. "Do you understand? *Tonight!*"

He departed, leaving the servants to their work—and all of us, myself included, trying to make as if nothing unsettling had happened. Aedita had heard and put a reassuring hand on my arm and gave me a look of such sympathy I drew her to me in a hug. Then, she and I ferried beer to the hall and, when the meat was ready, platters of roast beef, great steaming bowls of pottage, and piles of black bread, and blackberries sweetened with honeyed cream to fill the bellies of hungry warriors.

In the hall, the talk was high and rowdy, loud with boasting and laughter. So far as I could tell, the warrior's great good spirits were the result of what they considered a victory in that a mob of Irish raiders had been halted and engaged before any attack could be formed; a brief chase had ensued, and the raiders fled. Blades had hardly been lifted and, aside from the horses, it seemed no one had been anything more than inconvenienced by the encounter.

Though they boasted and crowed as if they had defeated an entire Saecsen horde rather than a mob of Irish marauders, I suppose we must thank the Good Lord for *any* triumph no matter how small. At the very least, a few would-be thieves had been shown that the hills and valleys had eyes and little passed that was not marked.

As usual, the men roistered far into the night, celebrating what they considered an estimable success in preventing a ruinous raid on one of King Ederyn's client chieftains. I watched and waited, filling each cup as soon as it became empty, hoping to keep the merriment going so that I might hold off my odious reunion with Cuno as long as possible. In this, I was mostly successful—not that it required much effort, mind, for they were young men, exulting in their strength, and only too ready to enjoy themselves beyond any restraint whatever. Accordingly, more than one head was resting on the board before King Ederyn rose and thereby ended the feast.

Jar in hand, I was standing at the far end of the table when Cunomor staggered to his feet. He gazed blearily around, saw me, and pointed his finger. "I'll be waiting," he slurred and then stumbled from the hall, followed by those of his men who could still stand up on their hind legs and walk.

The moment had come, and now that it loomed stark before me, I was filled with calm determination. While the board was cleared and scoured, I returned to the kitchen and retrieved a bundle I had stashed there earlier in the evening. I gathered up my cloak, the small bag of food I had collected, and, spying a small kitchen knife someone had left on the board, I slipped it under my belt. After making sure there was no eye to see me, I stole across the courtyard, opened the gate, and slipped out into the night.

The wind was up and the darkness now seemed darker to me than ever it was, the moon wan and cold, small and distant. With as much resolve as I could muster, I set my feet to the track, walking quickly and with purpose. I did not run. I made it beyond the furthest edge of the outer wall when the dogs came after me.

I had expected this, prepared for it, but the sound of their barking and the sight of their dark forms bounding toward me at such alarming speed still set my heart racing. This time, instead of trying to flee, I stopped and turned, and called them to me. Their pursuit faltered at the sound of my voice. They still came on, but now became something of a greeting.

I called again, this time, summoning them to me with the command Mab had used. I told them how brave and strong they were, and how good they were to protect the villa at night when everyone was safe asleep. I brought out the parcel of meat scraps I had filched from the night's feast.

"To me!" I called, using the same tone I normally used when speaking to them. "To me, lads. See what I have for you?" I unwrapped the parcel. "I brought you something nice tonight."

The creatures lowered their ears and approached at a trot. They knew me now and were eager to see what I had for them. The first dog reached me—the big gray shaggy brute named Orm—and he leaped up on me, almost knocking me over. "Down!" I said sternly. "Orm, down!"

To my relief, the excitable beast obeyed my command. I praised his obedience and tossed him a scrap. He caught it out of the air and swallowed it in two bites. He begged for more, and I tossed him another. The other hounds came trotting up and also begged. "Sit!" I told them, and they likewise obeyed. I tossed them their treats and soon had the entire pack sitting on the ground around me, begging for the morsels I had brought.

Ursa appeared out of nowhere, and came padding up. She made no sound but paused a little way off and stood looking on with her head cocked to one side. As always when I was around, she watched me with particular intent—as if evaluating a fellow creature she found of particular interest. "Ursa, come," I called. "I saved the best for you."

I did not have to call her twice; she obeyed at once. I held out the morsel of meat on my palm. She sniffed it and, like the others, took it and gulped it down. "Good girl," I said, and stroked her head, which she allowed. "We're friends, you and I."

"You want to be careful there."

I gasped and looked up.

Mab stepped out of the night and stood in the road with a stick in his hands.

"How long have you been watching?" I asked, my voice quivering.

"Long enough," he said. He took in my little bag of provisions, my cloak and heavy shoes, and nodded. "Long enough to know." With that he simply raised a hand, turned, and faded back into the night the way he had come.

Turning my attention to the dogs once more, I ordered them back to the kennel. At first they looked at me, but I told them again to go back and—God be praised!—they obeyed. First one, and then the others. Ursa was the last to go and when she turned to follow the pack, I resumed my escape.

I had almost reached the main road, intent on making as much distance between myself and the villa as possible and feeling very proud of myself, imagining that all was falling out just as I had planned—when I felt a cold, wet, something pressed against my palm. I gave a little yelp and, jerking my hand away, I glanced around to see who or what had assaulted me.

There was Ursa. Again. The rest of the pack had followed her, too, and stood a little way off, watching us—waiting, I suppose, to follow Ursa's lead.

"Go back!" I told her sternly and, in my most imposing manner, ordered the animal away. Instead, she came closer. "You heard me, girl. Go back."

The stubborn beast refused.

The night was speeding on and the longer I tarried with this recalcitrant creature, the more likely it would be that someone would notice my absence and come looking for me. I turned around and started walking quickly, glancing back to see if she had obeyed. But the big hound remained in place. And then, two things happened I will never forget: she came to me and licked my hand, then returned to her pack where she stood before Orm, the huge black male, and licked him on the face. Orm lowered his head and she put her foot on his neck, then released him and came trotting back to me.

In utter disbelief, I could but marvel at what I had just witnessed. Ursa took her place by my side. Orm and the pack remained where they stood, watching silently, but making no attempt to follow.

"Well, old girl," I told her, starting once more for the road, "if you are determined to come with me, so be it. You can be my shadow."

Ursa would be all that and, God knows, so much more.

BOOK THREE

DEVA VITRIX

"I FEEL LIKE SUCH A FOOL," Aurelia sighs with a forlorn shake of her head. "What was I thinking—that the tidy little Venta of my youth would remain unchanged through the years? That I could walk through the streets and see the folk I once knew, and have them hail me and welcome me back?" She turns mournful eyes on me. "The place I knew changed the moment I left, of course it did." She gives her head a weary shake again. "*Before* I left it, even. What else could I expect?"

We have resumed our journey and are now almost within hailing distance of Ynys Avallach. The carriage rattles along the rutted road. Pelleas and Mairenn are asleep, Brother Ruan is sitting with the drivers, and Aurelia is gazing wistfully out at the green-clothed hills and mist-heavy mountains the road reveals as we travel ever southward. Her experience in the deserted church at Venta has put her in a thoughtful, melancholy mood.

"So much change . . . so very much," she murmurs, her voice so low I do not know if she is speaking to me, or to herself. "So much of the old world has gone—never to return."

"It is the way of things," I say, knowing full well the cold comfort of those words.

"Well, I have only myself to blame," she snaps, a little of her customary vigor returning to her tone. "I knew it would be like this. I should have prepared myself better." She turns her gray eyes to me. "What is it? Nostalgia—is that the word? Thinking the place where you were born and raised would somehow remain the way you still see it in you mind?"

"It is the same for everyone, I expect," I tell her. "Did you never go back?"

"No." She is blunt. "I never did." She takes in her surroundings. "I think I was happy to allow myself to hope that somehow the place would still hold a trace of the town as I remember it, that there might be a welcome for me there. You'd think I'd have lived long enough in this world to know better."

Oh, how well I knew that feeling: the insistent longing, the needing to see, to know, followed by the cruel heartache of finding out, of realizing that all your memories are dust and ashes. We were old friends—painful memory and I—with a companionship to span the age.

As anyone with a sliver of sense can see, the world is ever changing, never remaining still for a season, for a day. "Every moment is a fleeting moment," I tell her. "Everything alive is either coming or going, growing or dying. Nothing ever stays the same. Every change is a change forever. Ah, but nothing is forever changed that will not change again."

Aurelia regards me curiously, and smiles, "The bard in you is coming out," she says. "And so it is—only in our memories does the world remain just as we will have it."

"Yes," I agree. "So it is."

In the hallowed glow of memory the world resides just as we will have it, untouched by time or circumstance. Can it also be altered? Yes, but only if we choose to change it; we are the agents of that alteration; neither time nor circumstance have power there.

Ruminating on these things, I see that I had made the self-same mistake when, after my long sojourn in the wild forested hills, I returned once more to Ynys Avallach. In my desire to see Charis and Avallach again, I had also expected them to be as I always see them in my mind, had I not? While it is true that the Fair Folk partake of a singular life, the world did change—more slowly in the Summerlands, to be sure, but even in that half-enchanted place the events of the outer world could, and often did, intrude. I had seen it myself in the change wrought in that time-hallowed realm.

As it happened, on that occasion I had been pleasantly surprised. And even now, I feel something of that encouragement once more as our carriage rolls over the causeway across the marsh and pauses at the foot of the tor. As before, as on every visit to the Isle of Apples, I seem to enter a waking dream where the more mundane concerns of life fall away, or shrink to irrelevance, amidst the calm and peace of a tranquility this worlds-realm would envy. I draw a deep breath and savor this still, sacred moment. Great Light, may Your grace abound!

Out on the lake, I spy Avallach's fishing boat and, as the day is good, the Fisher King himself at his favored occupation. At the sight of the carriage, Avallach puts down his willow pole and begins rowing to shore to meet us. Pelleas sees him, too, and jumps down from his bench and, as the boat draws nearer, he splashes out to meet the boat and pulls it ashore.

"Pelleas!" Avallach shouts, his voice resounding across the lake. "Pelleas! Good to see you, my friend." He stands up, almost capsizing his little craft, climbs over the side and into the water where he grabs Pelleas in a hearty embrace, pounding him on the back as if to reassure himself that it is a being flesh-and-blood he is greeting and not a ghost. "I had not hoped to see you so soon. Is Merlin with you?"

Before Pelleas can reply, Avallach's eyes fix on the carriage where Aurelia and I are just disembarking. "My boy!" he cries, making the very hills ring with his shout of delight. "There you are! You're here!" Sloshing up out of the shallows, he stands before me, joy lighting his entire face. "Wait until Charis learns you are here. I hope you can stay a little." He spreads his arms and gathers me to him—just as he did when I was a lad. In his eyes, perhaps I still am.

"And who is this with you?" he asks, turning to Aurelia first, and then glancing at the others waiting beside the carriage.

"Grandfather, meet my friend Aurelia," I tell him; I put my hand to her shoulder and feel the thinness there. "A woman of noble lineage and, with the help of Heaven, mother of the next High King of Britain."

My pronouncement is mostly hope, I admit. Yes, I have glimpsed the shape of things to come, and will work to make it so. That labor is now before me.

"Good lady, it is a pleasure to meet you," says Avallach, bestowing a regal bow. "May your sojourn here well become you. Any friend of Merlin's is a friend to me and my house. I would be honored if you would share with me the welcome cup."

Aurelia, flattered by his effusive greeting, smiles her most radiant smile and, just for a moment, her entire face is transformed: the years fall away and I glimpse something of the young woman she must have been. I see something else, too: a trace of Aurelius' unaffected ease and friendliness—the winsome qualities his brother Uther would do well to emulate.

"I am honored, Lord Avallach," replies Aurelia nicely. She then introduces her handmaid, Mairenn, and Brother Ruan to the Fisher King.

I watch my grandfather move from one to the other and now I think my first thought that nothing had changed was perhaps mistaken. Though outwardly the same in most every respect, the Fisher King himself wears a different face and displays a fresh demeanor: more effusive, more personable, more open in a way I have not seen before. It is as if he has somehow come fully into himself, or at least is more lighthearted. I will gently probe this change when the time is right and see if I might discover its source.

Just now, he is greeting our awestricken drivers and the soft-spoken Mairenn, whose eyes will soon be wide with absolute astonishment as we are bundled once more into the carriage and proceed to the Fisher King's palatial stronghold: a sprawling edifice built on the lower slopes of the hill with towers and terraces and outbuildings—all encircled by high walls. In this, I imagine, it echoes something of the great houses of Atlantis and a time long past. The carriage wheels sound hollow as we cross a narrow bridge and roll through the iron gates and onto the stone flagging of a spacious courtyard. I look around, filling my gaze with the familiar glories of my former home. Despite all we have said about the ever-changing world, the Fisher King's palace is exactly as I recall. The years find no purchase here and I am oddly gratified—as if something much in doubt has been confirmed. This reaction surprises me. Why? I cannot say. Perhaps it is because here, at least, I am reminded that my life is measured differently from that of my fellow creatures. Have I lived so long in the world of mortals whose lives and concerns are so fleeting and insubstantial that I have forgotten my own heritage, my own nature and being?

This I think I would do well to keep in mind when dealing with headstrong lords and their stubborn ilk. They are such temporary hindrances and feeble impediments, their time so limited. True as that may be, the damage they can do can live long after them. This, too, should be remembered.

"Where is Charis?" I ask as we climb from the carriage. I glance around, thinking to see her running out to meet us. "I'll go surprise her."

"Ah!" says Avallach, as if just remembering something important. "Yes, well, Charis is not here—gone to the abbey to help the good brothers there."

This, as I suspected, has become my mother's chief occupation—helping the priests there look after the sick and injured brought to them for prayer and healing. The abbey, in truth, is little more than a church and a rustic cluster of wattled huts and wooden outbuildings at the foot of the ancient tor that folk are now calling Shrine Hill.

"She has been gone most of the day. I think she may return soon. How long can you stay?"

"Not long, unfortunately. A day or so, perhaps." Even as I say this, I feel the tide pull of events that will shape this worlds-realm for years, generations, to come. I am needed elsewhere now—or soon will be. "I would like nothing better than to sojourn here awhile, but—"

Before I can explain, Avallach nods knowingly, "It was ever thus."

"Too true."

"Oh, well, never mind, eh? You're here now and, little or long, we will enjoy the time we have." He spreads his hands wide in invitation to include the entire travelling party, "Be at home in the Summerlands, my friends. Worry for nothing while you are here."

We start toward the palace, and as the Fisher King gathers Pelleas to him for a private word, I feel Aurelia tug on my arm. "This . . . this place . . . it is . . ." Words fail her. Her amazement warms my heart. I know exactly how she feels. I was born and raised here—on what many regard as a holy isle. Such is the power of the place, it can still work its magic on those who enter its domain. There can be few places like it anywhere.

"I've heard about the Summerlands, you know," Aurelia says. "Like everyone else, I heard the stories about the Fair Folk when I was young. And like everyone else, I only half believed them—if that—like the tales they told about the Land of the Everliving." She shook her head in amazement. "To think it was this close to Venta all the while . . . and yet . . . I never knew it."

"Come along, let us go in. There is more I want to show you."

Later, when the welcome cups have been poured and the guests settled in their chairs and on the bench in the king's great hall, servants appear with the tokens of welcome. The platter comes to me and I take a bit of bread and dip it in the salt and thank the servant; only then do I glance up to see who it is that serves me: none other than the Lady of the Lake herself. Wearing a simple mantle of creamy white with a belt edged in silver, a slim silver torc gleaming at her throat, her nobility shines through the simplicity and restraint of her dress. More and more she is adopting the dress and style of those she serves. In all other respects, however, age has touched her lightly—if it has touched her at all.

"Mother!" I leap up from my chair.

Charis laughs at my surprised expression. "Forgive me, my son. I did not mean to startle you, but I could not resist." And, oh, her voice takes me back to the earliest days my childhood when that sound filled all my world. She passes the silver tray along and I am pulled into her warm embrace. I feel her arms around me and time stands still. When she releases me, she holds me at arm's length to examine me more closely—as if inspecting a length of cloth for imperfection. She herself displays nothing of the sort nor, I expect, ever will.

"What has got into you?" she laughs. Before I can frame a reply, she turns to Aurelia, and asks, "And who is this you have brought with you?"

"Mother, this is my friend Aurelia," I say and, with a glance at her, proclaim, "God willing she is the mother of the next High King of Britain."

"He's not High King yet!" Aurelia protests, waving away the designation, but is flattered nonetheless.

"She is just returned from Armorica to join her sons and is in need of a place to stay until the kingship has been won."

"Then she must stay here, of course," Charis replied nicely. Leaning close, she takes Aurelia's hand in hers and says, "It will be my very great pleasure. Indeed, having another woman under this roof will be a blessing." They exchange a few words and she moves on with her tray . to greet the others around the board.

"Please, sit with us awhile," I say, when she returns. "I would hear how Ynys Avallach has fared since I was last here."

"But that you already know," she replies lightly, and give me a sideways look. "You were only just here."

"I would hear it all the same."

"Well, there is little enough to tell. The work at the abbey keeps me well occupied and there are plans to improve and enlarge the holdings there—though Avallach can tell you more about that," she replies. "But, you, Merlin—you have thrown yourself into the struggle once more. What news of events beyond these walls?"

We talk awhile of the ongoing trials and tribulations to secure the high kingship, the plans to rebuild Britain's defenses and how, at last, that is beginning to be possible. And I explain how Aurelia's sons are the prime reason for my optimism. Charis listens to all this attentively, and then remarks, "This sits well with you, my son. It cheers me to see you this . . . this buoyant."

"How so?"

She regards me with a knowing, motherly, look. "You seem lighter, more cheerful—as if you no longer carry the cares of the world like a sack of stones on your back."

I laugh at her depiction of me. "It is called *hope*," I tell her. "And it is that which buoys me up." Turning to Aurelia, who has followed our talk with bemused attention, I add, "For that hope, I have this remarkable woman to thank—for raising two sons worthy of their rank and station. For the first time in a long time, I have solid grounds for thinking our dreams of a just and true sovereignty can soon become reality."

Later—after a meal of fish and greens at the Fisher King's table, and our bedazzled traveling companions have been shown to their lodgings, and Pelleas and Avallach have gone off to talk—Aurelia and I are alone in one of the many chambers provided for the rare visitor to the palace, where we have a chance to speak again. "I am so glad I was able to meet your mother," Aurelia tells me. "To think of all she has seen in this life."

"It was an honor to introduce you. And I am pleased that you will have the chance to get to know one another better in the days ahead. Both Avallach and Charis assure me that you are more than welcome to stay here as long as you like."

Aurelia smiles, but I sense her hesitation. She looks away slightly, and says, "That may prove the briefest of stays."

Thinking she is referring to the struggle for the High Kingship, I hasten to put her mind at ease. "If you will allow me, dear lady, I would heartily advise you to abide here until Aurelius has secured the High Kingship. There will be upheaval in the land for some time to come and both he and Uther will rest easier knowing you are safe and well cared for here." I reach out and press her hand, urging her to accept the offer. "There is no safer or more comfortable place in all the land."

She offers a vague smile. "You are kind to intercede on my behalf, but that was not in my mind just now."

"No?" Then it comes to me: this illness she alludes to but does not name—the reason she has ventured to see her sons, to visit her homeland one last time.

Then, as if realizing what she is saying, she waves aside the comment, gathers her composure and adds, "You are kind to put up with my grumbling. I should be more grateful—and in all honesty I *am* grateful. Indeed I am. I will not reject the sanctuary I have been offered, and I will bless those who provide it." She squeezes my hand. "Thank you, Merlin."

"If I indulge you it is as much out of self-interest as kindness," I tell her. "I want to know more about the upbringing of the man who will rule Britain." Oh, yes, I do indeed want to know more about the future king and his headstrong brother, true enough; but, as I am beginning to fear our time may be more limited than I might have guessed, I am even more eager than ever to know about the remarkable woman who raised them.

"Luck and pluck," she replies. "Things worked out for the best, that's all."

"Even so," I allow. "I recall you saying that you walked all the way from Ederyn Longknife's stronghold through the wilds of Gwynedd entirely alone," I mused. "That, I think, took *more* than a little pluck."

"Oh, I was never alone," she quickly corrects. "I had Ursa with me, remember. And there were ever guides and companions along the way—my friends for the journey, I call them."

"Tell me," I invite, seeing as we are both in a mood now to remember. "Who else did you meet?"

✠ ✠ ✠

1

ONCE BEYOND SIGHT of Longknife's villa, I stepped up my pace and Ursa loped along easily at my side. Anxious, almost sick with dread, and ruing the coming daylight, I ran. By then, a gray dawn had lightened the track making it easier to find my way. I soon came to the old Deva crossroads where the traders had turned aside to the villa; there I paused to catch my breath and risk yet another backward glance along the trail. In my worst fears, I imagined warriors spilling from the villa in fevered pursuit, but all was dark and quiet. Then again, what made me think that the disappearance of a low scullion—bought cheaply for a broken band of gold—would merit raising the warband to give chase?

Without another backward glance I hurried on. All too soon, the first rays of morning touched the eastern hills, already beginning to burn through the night mist; it was light enough to see both ways along the road: there was not a single soul to be seen in any direction.

As I moved along, my thoughts turned to the new and troublesome prospect of what I would do when meeting someone on the road. My last encounter with traders taught me the folly of trusting too much to strangers. Naturally, I was in nowise eager to repeat my recent mischance with the rat-faced kidnapper Gnaeus and his rat-faced rogue friends, much less with that lecherous lout Cuno. The misadventure at the villa might easily have ended far worse for me, as I am only too happy to concede. But even misfortune can sometimes carry a benefit for, all things considered, I had at least gained a little

217

something during my sojourn in King Ederyn's villa. I left with a modicum of confidence—what my father called *pluck*—and I had learned a few new kitchen skills to add to my modest store of knowledge. Compensation, of a sort, for the fear, dread, humiliation, and degradation I had felt as an unwilling bondmaid and potential harlot.

With that in mind, I decided the best course would be not to take chances with any more strangers. At first glimpse of another traveler, I would quit the road and find a hiding place, hunker down, and wait until the they had moved on. I also considered that it might be best to travel only at night. I did not relish the latter prospect. Nights out in the wild hills would be cold and if the weather was foul, it would go bad with me. Even so, the thought of being captured again by Cunomor, or anyone else, filled me with such dismay that facing a dark night on the road seemed the more reasonable choice. In any event, I had Ursa with me now, and with her beside me I could endure most anything, could I not?

The first test of my new-minted resolve came a little before midday when I saw two mounted figures on the road ahead. They were still far off, so I abandoned the trail and dived into a spread of heavy bracken at the base of a nearby hill. I wriggled into the stiff foliage with Ursa following willingly at my heels, and the two of us settled down in our hidden nook. I whispered to my furry companion that we must keep quiet and let the riders pass. Thus, we waited, not sorry for a chance to rest...

When I awoke some time later, the clouds had come in and the sun was well down and sinking below the western hills. I shook myself from my nest in the bracken, rose, and looked out to the road: no one to be seen in either direction. So, we set forth again and I was beginning to wish I had been able to squirrel away a little more food for the journey. I was thirsty, too, but this was soon remedied at the next fresh-water trickle we came across; the hills were seamed with silver threads—each one a small freshet of clear, running water. We each drank our fill and moved on.

The miles went by and, save for the wind, we had the road to ourselves. Eventually, what little was left of the day subsided into a dull, misty twilight and we walked—my self-appointed escort and me—in an increasingly easy companionship. To pass the time and keep my mind off the hunger beginning to gnaw more fiercely at me, I told Ursa about my former home in Venta. I told her about the marketplace, and about my father the magistrate. "Never heard of a magistrate?" I queried. "Well, let me tell you . . ." I told her about Tullius and the duties of an official, and more. I told her how I had come to be traveling to Deva and what I hoped to find there.

"You'll like Helena," I told her. "She is very kind and also very beautiful—not that this is the most important thing, mind, but many people seem to set great store by this. I don't know why. Beauty is only skin deep, but God judges a person's true worth by what is in the heart. At least that's what my father says." I looked down at Ursa and she looked up at me. "What does *your* father say?" I wondered. "The same thing? Well, there you are, you see, it must be true."

We chatted like this for a long time and it was a comfort as the night closed around us. Fortunately, the old road through the hills was high and reasonably straight; we encountered no streams to ford, no bogs to slog through, no mud wallows. These roads were well-built and I had no doubt they would last forever. Though the dark was deep around us, the sky was light enough to allow me to make out the path without too much difficulty. From time to time, Ursa would stop; she would bark and some creature we had disturbed would bolt into the night.

In this way, we passed our first night on the road.

Yawning, weary, staggering in my steps, I must have been half asleep when I noticed that I could see more of the hills and further over the vales. Raising my eyes, I looked up to see the dawn lightening the sky in the east. Inexplicably, the sight warmed me and I suddenly felt a small portion of vigor return. "Look at that, Ursa," I said. "Sunrise! I think we'd best start looking for a place to sleep."

Ursa agreed with me, and I began searching for a suitable roost—and this I found when, cresting the next hill, I spied a sheltered dell at the bottom of the valley not far from the road. Closer, I saw a little rill and bank of brambles lay to the far side of the bowl, and the whole rimmed with rocks and, in one corner, a sort of wide crevice protected by an overhanging ledge. Not the most comfortable place, but at least it was somewhat protected from the wind and, more importantly, out of sight from the road. Even though the sun had not fully risen, I thought I would not find a better place any time soon and decided to put up there until nightfall.

"Come, Ursa, we'll take our rest here," I told my silent friend as we abandoned the road and picked our way down the slope into the dell.

As expected, the brambles were well supplied with big, ripe bulging berries, and I picked and ate them by the handful until my fingers were stained deep blue and dripping with juice. Ursa watched me with intense canine interest. "Would you like some of these?"

I offered her a handful of the shiny, black berries. She sniffed them and licked one, ate it, and then turned away. "Sorry," I told her, "I don't have anything else to give you." She seemed to understand. Lifting her head, she scented the air, and then trotted off into the brush along the rill. I marked where she went, but did not follow—intent as I was on gorging as much fruit as I could cram into my belly.

When at last I could guzzle no more, I wiped my sticky hands on some dry grass and washed them in the trickle of water in the rill before slurping up water from my cupped palms. Then, drying my hands on the hem of my mantle, I went to see about making a nest in the rocky hollow and found the space beneath the overhang shallow and lumpy. I removed my cloak and spread it over a bed of dry leaves and bracken, making it as snug as I could, then sat down. Fatigue seemed to come oozing out of the rocks around me; heavy headed, I leaned back; my eyes were just closing when I heard a single, sharp bark.

Ursa!

I sat up and looked around. The bark did not come again. In a moment, I saw her big, dark form emerge from the brush along the rill. As she came trotting closer, I saw she had the body of a rabbit in her jaws. She came to where I sat and dropped the blood-spattered carcass at my feet and then stood proudly over it as if waiting for me to praise her prowess. This I was only too happy to do.

"What a mighty huntress you are, Ursa. You are a canny thing, are you not? Yes, you are."

She regarded me with placid brown eyes and nudged her kill closer to me. "Thank you, girl," I told her, "but I've eaten. You can have it. You can have it all."

As if that was all the approval she needed, the big dog snatched up her kill and carried it into the brush and proceeded to tear it apart. I could not watch her poor victim being turned into a messy meal, so I lay back and closed my eyes once more—secure in the knowledge that

I need not fret about finding food for my furry friend; she could fend for herself.

Somehow, during our night on the road, the dog had grown more understanding of me, more attached. Perhaps it was that without her pack to look after, I was all she had. Or, maybe, I fancied, she had felt herself a captive, too, and yearned for freedom from the confines of the kennel and its masters. However it was, whatever loyalty or affection or duty she felt in her canine soul, she now conferred on me.

As I was thinking these things, sleep overtook me and I let myself drift off. Sometime later, I felt Ursa curl up beside me; I was aware of this, but did not wake. Indeed, I did not come fully awake until sometime later—much later, it must have been, for when I finally shook off my grogginess, the sky was cast over with low gray clouds and the sun, the little left of it, was lost behind the western hills. I rose, stretched, and went to the brooklet to splash water on my face and attend my necessities; Ursa joined me and we both took a last drink before starting off on our long-night's ramble.

It was over almost before it started.

I climbed the slope back up to the road, turned north, and had taken only a few dozen paces when Ursa stopped. I glanced around and saw her staring straight ahead: two riders were coming toward us, close enough to see us clearly, too close for me to hide. Because of the bend in the road, I had not seen them—and, of course, I had not heard them, either—and now it was too late. Like it or not, I would have to brazen it out and hope beyond hope that they left me in peace.

I waited until the two were within hailing distance and raised a hand. One of the riders—thick-necked fellows, both, with dark beards and long dark braids at the side of their heads; one in brown tunic and breeches, one in green—raised his hand in greeting. They reined up and waited for me to come closer. For one awful moment I thought they might be Irish, but then the one on the left spoke and it was the lilting tongue of the Gwynedd hill country. "God with you, girl," he said. "You shouldn't be out here all on your own."

"I'm not alone," I lied. "My brothers are coming along behind."

Both men glanced over me down the road, then at back one another. A sign of some sort passed between them. "I don't see anyone," the second one said. "Are you sure?"

"They stopped to water the horses." I glanced back, too, as if expecting to see them riding into sight. "They'll be here soon enough."

"It isn't right—them letting you go off on your own." He looked around at the darkening land around us and then back at me. "These hills aren't safe at night. What say you, Cletus? Maybe we'd best keep her company until those brothers of hers appear."

"No need to concern yourselves," I said. "My brothers will be here any moment."

"Will they now?" said the first one. He glanced once more down the road behind me and then made to dismount. I suddenly wished I had thought to bring a better weapon than a kitchen knife. "Maybe we'll just wait and see."

He threw a leg over the neck of his horse and slid to the ground. A greasy smile played over his face, but his eyes narrowed. "What shall we do while we wait, eh?"

He took a step toward me and Ursa growled, low in her throat. The rider seemed to notice her for the first time and halted. He pointed at her. "That dog safe?"

"Mild as milk," I said. "To *me*, that is."

He took another step nearer and Ursa growled again, louder this time. The horses, uneasy now, nickered nervously and jigged in place.

"Call off your dog, girl." The burly fellow jabbed a finger at her.

Ursa gave a fulsome bark that caused all three of us to start. She took a sidestep and pressed herself against me.

"I said to call her off!" His hand went to the sword at his side.

Ursa, ears flattened and teeth bared, snarled. She lowered her head and stared at the man with baleful, unblinking eyes.

Speaking very slowly, and in a calm, even tone, I looked the rogue in the eye and said, "Draw that blade and she'll have your throat out before you can take another step."

"There's two of us, girl." He glanced back at his friend who sat looking on, a worried expression on his face. "You can't take us both."

"I only see *one* standing here," I replied. Pointing to the rogue before me, I said, "You can be first."

"Leave her, Jago," said the second rider from his safe perch on the back of the horse. "Look at her—scrag of a thing. She's not worth the trouble."

Ursa chose that moment to loose a ferocious, guttural growl that ended in another savage bark. She took a slow step closer to the man, hackles raised like knives along her back, eyes narrowed and fixed.

This settled the fellow's mind. His hand came away from the sword hilt, and he moved back a step with hands raised in surrender. "Call her off."

"I will," I told him. "As soon as you're back on your horse and on your way."

"We're going," said the second rider. "We don't want any trouble."

"Then you should not have stopped," I told him, speaking much more forcefully than I felt. Where had this mettle come from? Was it Ursa's presence that somehow lent me the mettle, the audacity?

The rider remounted his horse. "Stupid cow! We could have made it worth your while."

"Oh, it has been worthwhile," I assured him. Lord help me, I could not resist. "I think we've *all* learned something this day."

With a flick of the reins, the two started away. The one called Jago hurled one final pathetic insult. "Slut!" he sneered as he passed.

Ursa, calmer now, started barking and took a few steps as if she would follow. The horses picked up their speed.

"Oh, you brave, gorgeous girl," I told her and ruffled her ears and stroked her head. "Let them go, and we'll be on our way."

2

WE WALKED THROUGH THE NIGHT, my furry companion and I, meeting no one—save a few hares we scared up from the brush and, once, a small herd of roe deer. Ursa gave chase but caught nothing, and we walked on. Just before dawn, we came to a valley with a pool at the base of the hill opposite the road. A beechy copse grew at one end and, all but staggering in my steps, I decided we'd gone about as far as we could for one night. It was time to stop and rest.

"I'm tired, Ursa. Let's have a sleep, shall we?" We left the road and picked our way down the slope and into the glen, making our way over the marshy reed-grown ground toward the stand of slender beech trees. It was dry enough, and somewhat protected; the brambles I found along the way were thinner here and the birds had taken most of them, but I ate enough to take the edge off my hunger. Having seen rabbit droppings and a burrow or two since starting down, I knew Ursa would find the food she needed. Deep in the copse, I found a small cup-shaped depression lined with dry leaves—perhaps used by a deer or some other creature—and curled up in it. Ursa sniffed around the area a few time, then came and looked at me. "I'm just going to close my eyes a little," I said, and patted the ground beside me. "You can share my bed."

The big dog did lie down—but only for a moment—then jumped up again and ran off. She was gone some time, and when she did return it was with a muzzle dripping water and flecked with blood. "Found something to eat?" I said sleepily. "Good for you. I wish I could fend as well."

The day passed quickly—all too quickly—and I was still tired when I woke, groggy, my mouth dry as the leaves beneath me. At some time while I was dreaming, Ursa had come and nestled in beside me, warming me with her body. She was still there when I woke, her head resting on my hip—protecting me, even in our sleep. This, I marked, was Ursa's way of letting me know that I was hers and she was mine; we belonged to each other and she would allow nothing to come between us.

Reluctantly, I rose and looked around. The sun was low in a gray sky, and a chill was creeping into the air. It would be a cold night, but I had no way to make a fire and, anyway, it was time to be moving on. Wrapped in my good cloak and with Ursa beside me, I started off again.

Sometime around midnight, the cloud cover began to thin and break up. A pale moon shed a thin light over the land. Mist rose in the valleys and glowed with a silvery sheen in the moonlight. I marveled at how still it was, and how empty the land. To keep myself company, I talked to Ursa and sang her some songs I knew—a few of my favorites and Psalms I knew by heart—and told her more about Venta, and about my friends: Augustus and Dorcas and Tomos and some of the other people I knew. However, remembering began to make me sad and homesick, so I quit thinking about that and turned instead to imagining what I might find in Deva and what life might be like for me there. It was no use, I knew nothing of Deva or the welcome I might receive.

I must have dozed while I was walking—if such a thing is possible—because it seemed that we had just climbed up one hill and down another and the sky began to lighten in the east. From somewhere nearby a blackbird called, spilling its liquid song into the early-morning mist. Everything was so peaceful, so serene, the melancholy I had labored under vanished at once and I was overwhelmed by a feeling of joy; an almost sublime happiness stole over me. And I thought: *What if the world could always be this way?*

Hard on this notion came the realization that I had been walking for some time and watching a thin pillar of smoke rising into the stillness of the early morning sky. It appeared to be coming from just over the next hill. Weary as I was and longing to rest, curiosity drew me on; I decided to see what the smoke signified. This was easily done. I gained the top of the hill and looked down into the next valley to see a single small steading—merely a few houses and outbuildings surrounded by fields, with a pasture along the stream that ran along the valley floor.

I paused a moment to observe the place and hunger, awakened by the dawn, closed its hand on me in such a fearsome grip that before I knew it my feet were already starting down the narrow beaten path leading to the settlement. Indeed, I was halfway down before a thought about what I would do there beyond beggar myself for a meal and a quiet place to rest.

"What say you, Ursa?" I said as we drew closer. "Will they have us do you think?"

Three houses sat clustered together; oversized dwellings of timber roofed in the flat gray stone of the hill country. Two barns or cattle sheds stood nearby and other sheds or granaries close about. I did not see a cookhouse or brewhouse. Closer, I had just gained the valley floor and was entering the wide foreyard when the door of the central house opened and out stepped a fellow in a pale yellow tunic and shapeless breeches. He wore a length of green cloth wound round his head in a peculiar fashion, and in his slender hands, he carried a large wooden bowl.

As he started for one of the outbuildings, I gave out a call. The fellow glanced around, saw us, and stopped to stare—at Ursa as much as me. I raised my hand and he responded with a slight nod, and allowed me to approach. As I neared, I called a greeting and he replied in a soft, pleasant voice which somewhat confused me. Then I took in the shape of his body and the softness of his face and realized it was *not* a man I hailed; it was a woman in a man's clothing.

Though dressed as a man, I could now see that she was trim and comely; indeed, she reminded me somewhat of a slightly younger Dorcas—with her heart-shaped face and smooth dark brows. She regarded me warily, and waited for me to approach.

"God's blessing on you this day," I said, using the greeting Tomos so often employed. "I hope I find you well."

"Good day to you, traveler." The cast of her speech was so odd I could hardly make out what she said. Eying Ursa with some concern, she added, "And to your dark friend." Glancing to the path leading up to the road—as if expecting to see someone else there—she said, "A little young to be traveling alone, are you not?"

Touching my ear, I explained that I did not hear too well and so she repeated her question a bit more loudly. I caught the import of her words and replied, "It is not at all as I had planned, believe me. And I could heartily wish it otherwise."

She nodded. "Is that the southland I'm hearing in your voice?"

Not certain I had heard her correctly, I asked her to repeat and then answered, "It is that, yes. I am from Venta. Do you know it?"

She shook her head. The name meant nothing to her. I tried again. "My people are Silures and Demetae on the south coast."

"I've heard tell of them," she allowed. "We're mostly Ordovici up here, and some Deceangli scattered about." She looked me over again. "You're far from home, then."

"Far enough." I glanced around at what I took to be a substantial holding. "What place is this?"

"This is Tŷ Bryn," she said, the north-country lilt coloring the words. "What about you? Do you have a name?" Her question was blunt as her manner.

I smiled and put out a hand to her. "My name is Aurelia."

She merely nodded. "That sounds like a southland name." Putting a hand to her chest, she said, "I am called Catia." She glanced again to the road winding through the hills above the valley. "I expect you are hungry." Without waiting for me to answer, she said, "I was just going to the dovecote to get some eggs. Come along with me."

Behind the house stood a tall, thin wooden structure with dozens of tiny square openings in the sides. Catia slipped into the building while Ursa and I waited outside—a dovecote is no place for a dog—as the sun began to warm my shoulders and back. Catia returned with a few small white eggs in the bowl and then led me back to the house. Pausing at the door, she looked at Ursa and said, "Tell your beast to stay here. I will fetch water and a bone for her."

I did as she asked and when she returned she placed the bowl of water on the ground with the meaty bone beside it; leaving Ursa to her meal, I followed Catia inside. The room was dark and it took me a moment to see that an old woman sat on a stool beside the hearth, tending the fire and stirring a big black iron pot of porridge.

"Mother," announced the woman in a loud voice. "This is Aurelia. She is a traveler come to beg a meal."

I felt my face redden. Was my purpose so nakedly obvious?

Perhaps it was. No doubt the hunger showed on my face. Then again, perhaps living so close to the road the steading saw more than its share of travelers stopping by for a drink or a meal—so many that this was merely assumed. However it was, though I had not so much as hinted at a meal, I readily agreed. The old woman merely nodded and went back to stirring the pot.

"That's Mara. She's mostly deaf, too," Catia confided. "Come sit down and rest." She pointed to the bench at the board which was piled high with fresh-picked herbs, some already bound into bundles to be hung and dried. She picked up a bunch and put them aside to clear a space. She then busied herself pulling bits of this and that from little nooks and crannies in the wall alongside the board. "Have you walked all night then?"

"I have," I told her. "I think it is much the safer way."

"I don't know about that," she said. "I don't know about that at all."

Just then, there was a shout outside and Ursa started barking. I heard what sounded like a muffled curse. I leapt up and ran outside to find my loyal protector holding a bearded man at bay. "Ursa! Quiet!" I shouted and took hold of her collar. "Be still," I told her and to my immense gratification, she obeyed, stopped growling, and sat down.

"Keep that killer away from me!" cried the man. He was dressed in a loose, mantle-like garment and carried a thick hazel stick, waving it before him. He glanced around, gave me a frightened look, and said, "Who are *you*?"

"This is Aurelia," the woman told him, stepping quickly between us. "She's a traveler."

"Oh? Is that so?" he regarded me with a doubtful expression. "Where are you going?"

Again, that same blunt manner. Were *all* folk up there so uncivil?

"To Deva Vitrix," I answered. "I have friends there."

"And you alone on the road?"

His accent, like Catia's, was so heavy I had to work to make sense of what he was asking. "I am alone, true enough—though not of my own choosing." I explained that I had been abandoned by my companions in Aberdyfi and was forced to travel the rest of the way on foot. "I was hoping to reach Deva before too long. Is it far?"

"Far enough," replied the man unhelpfully.

"She's been walking all night," put in Catia. Then, as an afterthought, she said, "This is Seisyll, my husband." Turning to him, she said, "You should not be out on your leg. You should be at your rest."

He waved aside her complaint, muttering, "I had to tend to the calf."

"Your father and the boys can do that. They don't need you poking your finger in the pie."

"*They* aren't here, are they!" he snapped. "They're not coming back!"

I saw anger in his face, yes, and something else: fear and pain—a great deal of pain—pinching his expression, giving him a tense and desperate look. He turned away and hobbled to the door, leaning heavily on his stick. Catia reached out to help him, but he shook off her hand. "Leave me be, woman!"

Seisyll heaved himself inside, moving with such difficulty, I could not help but ask, "Forgive me, but what is wrong with his leg that he walks so?"

"He should not be walking at all!" Catia replied sharply. She gave out a growl of frustration and said, "He was chopping wood on Creddin Hill—by himself, alone he was—and a boar attacked him."

I gasped.

"Oh, the creature must have been sick or crazed. Seisyll hit it with the axe and the wicked thing ran away, but not before it gashed his leg bad."

I was beginning to get a better grasp of their speech and understanding came a little easier. "I'm sorry to hear it."

Catia shook her head. "That was seven, eight, days ago. I've done all I know to do and the man's leg is no better." She paused and turned worried eyes to me. "Between you and me, I think it is getting worse." She shook her head as if coming back to herself. "I don't know why I'm telling you all this."

It came to me then *why* she was telling me: the Good Lord was sending me a sign.

"Maybe I can help," I said.

3

I WILL BE THE FIRST TO CONFESS my lack of knowledge—in healing, certainly, and in most everything else, truth be told—but I *had* learned a few things about wounds recently. What is more, I had learned from excellent teachers. My offer hung in the air for a moment as Catia considered. Finally, she said, "What would you do?"

"First I would clean the wound with vinegar," I told her, and explained what I had seen Lucius do for my father. "Then make a poultice and bind it to the wound with clean cloths. Then, if we could get some willow scrapings, I would make a tisane to ease the pain and help him sleep."

She gazed at me with something like wonder in her eyes. "How do you know these things—one so young?"

"I helped my father," I said simply, to avoid a lengthy, possibly painful explanation.

"Your father," she repeated. "Was he a physician?"

"No, he was a magistrate," I confessed. "But he was badly injured in a raid and I helped tend him. The little I know I learned from a physician in Viroconium and a healer named Agnese."

The farm woman's brow creased with uncertainty.

"And I know this," I continued, confidence making me bold, "if Lucius and Agnese were here, they would do the same." Still, she hesitated, looking toward the house.

"Do you truly think it will help?"

"I do. But, whatever happens, it will not make matters worse by trying."

She agreed and led me back into the house. Seisyll had taken to his sleeping pallet on the ledge in a far corner of the house. Catia and I settled at the table and discussed what would be needed for the poultice and tisane. And she said she would get these things for me. Then she went to her injured husband and explained what I had offered to do. I watched from a distance as Catia bent over her husband, her hand on his arm, speaking urgently and low. Fortunately—or perhaps, providentially—he agreed, but only after some resistance to the idea of a stranger tending his wound.

Catia returned from speaking to him and told me, "He will allow it. I'll fetch your things."

As she busied herself elsewhere in the big house, the old woman at the hearth, Mara, rose from her stool and brought a shallow wooden bowl to the board and put it down in front of me. With a toothless smile, she handed me a large ashwood spoon and gestured for me to eat. Under her watery gaze, I took up the spoon and sampled a bite. "Mm-mm," I said, nodding enthusiastically.

Indeed, I would have eaten a bowl of live crickets just then; but the simple porridge was just as good as any I had ever tasted. Mara, looking on, gave me a gentle pat on the head to smooth my hair and shuffled back to her stool beside the fire. As I spooned up the warm food, the fatigue of the previous night's journey came over me all at once. I yawned and might well have put my face in the porridge if Catia had not returned from her herb store just then to announce, "I think I have everything—except the willow. And that, I can easily get." She placed a jar on the board before me, saying, "I only have a little vinegar left. I'm making more, but it isn't ready yet."

"This should be enough," I replied, hefting the jar. "And the herbs?"

She placed two wooden bowls of withered leaves before me. "The comfrey and thyme," she said. "I have more—as much as you need."

Unable to help myself, I yawned again, and shook my head to clear it.

"Aurelia, girl, you are fair exhausted," Catia said, watching me. "You should sleep. We will tend Seisyll when you are rested."

A low moan came from the bed niche along the wall just then. I suspected that Seisyll's latest exertion had taxed him heavily and he was paying for it now. "It has been eight days as you said," I pointed

out. "I don't think he can wait any longer." So saying, I put off my
fatigue and formed the plan by which I would proceed, then sent up a
prayer asking for a little skill and much wisdom to help me ease his
pain and make him better. "We'll make a start."

Catia gave me an uncertain look, but said, "Do you need anything
else?"

"Only some honey and a few clean cloths."

She turned and called to the old mother to bring her the honey;
then went to fetch a few rags of raw linen cloth. I rubbed the dried
herbs into dust and mixed them in a bowl. Catia returned holding a
pile of folded cloth. "These scraps were leftover from tunics I made
last spring," she said. "Is it enough?"

I shook out some of the cloths. "Perfect," I told her. "I couldn't ask
for better."

We spent the next little while preparing the poultice and ointment.
Catia watched me closely, marking all I did and how I did it, asking
questions from time to time. Old Mara, from her place by the hearth,
watched, too, keeping her own counsel. When I finished, I announced
that we were ready to proceed.

Catia led me to the sleeping nook where her husband lay. She shook
him gently awake and told him I would tend his wound now. Though
he opened his eyes, he said nothing and I noticed his face was pale and
his eyes bright. Indeed, he appeared worse now than when he had
ventured outside.

Mara brought me her stool and then stood back with Catia to
watch. Pulling the stool close, I sat down and, balancing the bowl of
warm vinegar water on my knees, I spoke to Seisyll, telling him what
I planned to do. "It might hurt a little," I explained, "but I do think it
will be for the best."

Receiving only a grunt in reply, I lifted the hem of his mantle,
exposing his injured leg to view. What I saw took my breath away: a
long gash that ripped the skin and flesh of his lower leg, tearing into
the raw, red muscle. Dried blood and yellow pus crusted around the
wound and the edges were red and inflamed; the flesh around the
wound was swollen, discolored, hot to the touch, and weeping an ooze
of watery blood.

I suffered a rush of serious doubt. So far, I had been certain of my
competence and understanding. Now that the deed was before me, I

realized what I imagined as ability was likely arrogance in disguise. *What was I thinking?*

Well, as my father used to say: "Being is mostly doing." In *doing* the work of a healer, I would *become* the healer—for Seisyll, at least. Trusting that this was so, I marshalled my resolve and dropped one of the linen cloths into the warm solution, wrung it out, and gently, gently dabbed at the crusty matter that had formed around the gash. Despite my utmost care, Seisyll winced and tensed his leg. I whispered that I was sorry to hurt him, but it had to be done. He grunted and I carried on. The cleaning took some time, and my back and neck grew stiff for hunching over him. In the end, however, I could but admire my handiwork: the ugly gash, though still raw and oozing matter, was clean.

I imagined the old physician Lucius would approve of my effort, and his words came back to me so clearly it was almost as if he stood beside me: *It is the corruption that kills.* With this in mind, I took up the bowl and began applying the poultice of honey and mixed herbs that Catia and I had prepared. I did not know how much to use, but on the reckoning that too much would be better than too little, I lavished it on the wound until I'd used all we'd made. Then, while Catia lifted her husband's leg, I wrapped the injury with strips of clean linen Mara provided, wrapping them around his leg and tying them tight to hold the poultice.

"All neat and tidy," I pronounced, and sat back to admire my handiwork. If I had possessed one of Lucius' slender needles and a length of that fine catgut, I might even have been tempted to try sewing the gaping flesh together. But a fledgling bird can fly too high, they say, so I set aside the empty bowl and contented myself with having done what I could do.

Seisyll moaned and mumbled something and I looked to Catia. "He says it tingles—like nettles," she repeated.

"I think that is a good thing," I offered—hope speaking rather than experience. "The medicine is meant to draw out the poison that inflames the wound."

She regarded me with something approaching wonder. "We will make more of this medicine, I think."

I agreed. "That would be best, but now we will do all to keep the wound clean and let the medicine do its work."

Seisyll muttered something I did not catch, and closed his eyes. He was soon asleep—his small store of strength drained, the jar empty.

Catia drew a covering over him and we retreated to let him rest, joining Mara at the hearth. I blushed to hear Catia praise my skill and wisdom; the old woman smiled and nodded, and patted my hand.

"Your father must be very proud of you," Catia said, taking up a poker to arrange the fire.

"Well, you would have to ask him about that," I said. I had not the heart to tell her that my father was cold in his grave.

"I wonder that he has allowed you to travel alone—and so far from home."

"Oh, but I *wasn't* alone when I started out," I replied. "I was with friends who were meant to look after me. But accidents happen." I shrugged, as if this was only to be expected. "I had no choice but to come on alone. And anyway, I've got Ursa to watch over me."

"Ursa? Is that your dog?" Catia's eyes grew wide. "I would be more afraid of *her* than any rogue on the road. A fierce beast, I'm thinking."

"She is that," I agreed. "And that much more besides."

We talked a little more; Mara watched us the while, mumbling now and again, but not entering in much—until she said something about cows, I think.

"Yes, well . . ." Catia rose, saying, "I have to go and tend the calf."

I stood, too. "I'll go with you."

"You must be exhausted, travelling all night and all." She put her hand on my shoulder as if to push me back down. "Sit here and rest a little."

I thanked her, but said, "If I sit here any longer, I'll fall asleep in the fire. Better that I should keep moving. And, anyway, I should tend to Ursa. She's probably wondering what has happened to me."

"Come then, we'll find something more for her to eat," Catia told me. I could tell she was glad for the company.

Ursa was sleeping just outside the door, but awoke the instant we stepped into the yard. I greeted her with a gentle pat on the head and told her what a good and obedient dog she was. I introduced her to Catia, and explained that we were going to get her some food and water. Ursa, intelligent thing, seemed to accept this and wagged her tail; I do think she was happy to see me and even nuzzled my hand as I stroked her ears.

Catia fetched another hefty meat bone from the little smoke shed and brought a bowl of clean water which I placed before Ursa; the big, shaggy creature fell upon it and lapped so greedily I felt guilty for not attending to her sooner. "I'm sorry, Ursa," I told her. "Just you finish that and I'll get you some more."

After refilling the dog's bowl, we walked across the yard behind the house to the larger of the two barns where a good-sized spotted calf was penned. The amiable creature stood gazing at us with its big, liquid eyes. "Two were birthed this spring," Catia told me. "But one died along with the mother." She picked up a leather bucket. "There is fodder in that box there." She pointed to a large wooden box beside the door. "Put some in the trough for it, and I'll fetch the water."

Gathering an armful of the fragrant fodder from the box, I carried it to the fence rail, dropped it into the long, stone trough and spread it around. The calf watched, uncertain whether to approach or not. By the time Catia returned with the water, it was happily nose down in the trough. We watched it for awhile, and then started back to the house. "You have sons, I think?" I asked. "You said Seisyll's father and sons could tend the cows, and I wondered—"

"Why they're not here?" Catia guessed. "Well, they've taken hogs and a few of the yearling sheep to the market at Bryncadlys."

"Is it far—the market?"

"Not so far that a good day's journey couldn't get you there. Though, with pigs to herd it would take longer." She paused to calculate. "Even so, they should have returned by now." She turned worried eyes on the door as if expecting them to enter. "I worry about those boys and the old man with them."

On entering the house, we heard Seisyll call. He was awake again and Catia went to him. They spoke together in voices too low for me to hear. Then Catia summoned me to her and said, "Seisyll wanted me to thank you, and . . ." She hesitated, knotting her mantle in her hands.

"What is it? What else did he say?"

"He wanted me to ask if you would stay to help butcher a hog."

"But I thought you said your sons had taken the hogs to market."

"Aye, so I did. Some hogs and sheep we sell and some we keep. Winter will be on us soon enough, so it's time to slaughter and get the meat smoked." She gave a little laugh. "I guess you *are* a magistrate's daughter."

I understood then why Catia was wearing men's clothes: She was doing all the work of the menfolk while they were away, so dressed like one of them.

She saw my hesitation and guessed the reason. "I would rather wait for the menfolk to return. That would be best, but we do it by the moon, you see, and tomorrow is the day. The butchering must be done and," she put out a hand to indicate her injured husband and aged mother, "I cannot do it on my own."

I understood the problem now, but the idea of delaying my journey by even another day or two was disheartening.

"If you stay," Catia continued, "we'll feed you and give you a roof over your head and a warm place to sleep. You can't be traveling on tonight, anyway. You haven't had a moment's rest since you arrived."

I was considering, how best to refuse her without offending, when she reached out and put her hand on my arm. "Please, stay," she said. "I cannot do it alone." She glanced back to where her ailing husband lay with his arm over his face, and lowered her voice. "I fear Seisyll would kill himself trying to help me." She offered a forlorn smile. "Please?"

How could I refuse this sister in her time of need? Swallowing my disappointment, I gave the only answer I could. "I would be happy to do what I can—little as that may be. Whatever you need, I'll do it."

Catia gathered me in a heartfelt embrace; she pressed me to her bosom and thanked me.

"You must show me what to do. Truly, I don't know the first thing about butchering hogs. I've never killed anything."

"I'll guide you. But first, you must rest," she told me firmly. "It is heavy work and you will need all your strength." She looked me up and down. "I'll find you something to wear so you don't foul your nice clothes."

This was an over-generous description of the clothing I had worn continuously—rain and shine, day and night—since Dunstan and his crew sailed away with all my worldly goods and left me stranded. I was more than aware that everything I wore was travel stained by my nights in the wilds, and smelled of sweat and fear and exhaustion. Even a moment away from their grubby company would be bliss. How could I resist?

Catia went away fairly humming with happiness. I looked at Ursa, lying at my feet. "Well, old girl, I think Deva must wait to greet us. But at least we won't be hungry the while." I shrugged. "Is that a fair trade, do you think?"

Ursa, regarding me closely, gave out a short, sharp bark.

"Yes," I told her. "I think so, too."

4

I WOKE FROM MY SLEEP to find the sun well down on the day. Catia and Mara were preparing the evening meal and Seisyll was sitting up in his bed. Though still very pale and haggard looking, he seemed no worse to me and, perhaps, even somewhat better—though that might have been my imagining. He smiled wanly when he saw me, then closed his eyes again. *Pain is wearing him away,* I thought, and I wondered how long it had been since he had eaten.

I shared this concern with Catia at the hearth. "Mara is making some bone broth for him," she told me. "We'll add some bread to it and if Mara can't get him to eat, no one can." She then observed that we must eat heartily, too, for we would begin the butchering first thing in the morning when we had a whole day ahead of us.

I went out and refilled Ursa's water bowl and saw the remains of some meat scraps that Catia had provided for her. She had eaten well and was happy to see me. I sat down and put my arm around my faithful friend and we watched the farm sink into the stillness of a radiant twilight. When Catia stepped out a short time later, I went with her to the barn to tend the calf and settle it for the night.

Back at the house, we found Mara sitting with Seisyll while he spooned up the bread broth she had made. When he finished, we examined his wound, and he professed to feeling better—though, I think he just said that to make *us* feel better. We made him as comfortable as we could and left him to Mara's care.

After our own meal, we sat talking by the fire. Catia told me about her family and what it was like growing up on a hillfarm; and I told her what it was like to live in a *civitas*. We talked long into the night, and I was yawning again by the time she snuffed out the candles and we went to our beds.

The next morning, I pulled on the tunic and breeches Catia had found for me, and we broke our night's fast on some bacon, bread, and fresh cheese. Catia had told me how we were to go about it and I recoiled from all thoughts of what lay before us. Nevertheless, I had agreed to help and meant to keep my part of the bargain as best I could.

Catia gave me a very large, very sharp knife and a bucket to catch blood, and we went out into a bright, crisp morning. Ursa greeted me with a wagging tail and I marked how much friendlier the dog was growing by the day; maybe she was getting used to other people. Then again, maybe I was just getting used to how canny she could be: she seemed always to know who to trust and who was best avoided. Catia and I walked across the yard and around the back of the bigger barn to the pen where the sows waited, watching us with their tiny eyes.

I steeled myself to begin our grisly work as Catia stepped into the pen containing three pigs—two young ones, skinny things for the fattening, and one large well-grown sow with big, floppy ears and a high, sloping back. "That's the one we take," she said, pointing to the sow. "I will chase it into the killing gate and we will begin."

This killing gate was nothing more than a narrow place between two doors, with gaps in the fence through which a butchering knife might be thrust. And this is what we did: Using a herder's staff, Catia coaxed and chivvied the pig into the enclosure and I closed the door behind it. Stepping to the side, Catia took up the knife and, with a deft, decisive thrust, ended the creature's life. I learned right away that one had to be quick with the bucket to catch the blood—that was my job— for the hot crimson gush spewed out in pulsing torrents that went everywhere. And that was bad enough. Worse was the squealing! An infernal wail like that of a tortured wraith taking flight filled the air. The poor animal struggled, but could not run and so quickly succumbed to its fate.

"It's all in knowing where to put the knife," Catia explained.

Together, we lugged the blood bucket to the barn and emptied it into a clean barrel—for use, I was told, to mix with oats and herbs to make black sausage.

"Now comes the hard part," Catia said as we returned to the pen. "The carcass must be hung and gutted." She pointed to a nearby pole to which a rope and chain had been attached. Taking a trotter each, we dragged the beast from the killing gate to the pole and secured the hind legs with the chain, and we began pulling with all our strength. At last, I understood Seisyll's insistence that I should help his wife: this took all the strength two lone women possessed—and then some.

Slowly, and with many halts and pauses, we inched that heavy carcass up the pole and off the ground so that the belly could be slit and the edible organs retrieved. This was to be my job: to pick out the liver, kidneys, and heart, separating them from the rest of the intestines and muck.

The long body stretched out and when we could lift it no higher, Catia tied the rope and took up her knife. "Stand back," she warned, "this will splatter, and you won't want it on you."

Using both hands, Catia plunged the blade into the soft underbelly and began to carve through the skin and muscle. The flesh parted neatly, revealing a glistening pink interior. I stood by with my big wooden bowl to begin picking through the viscera for the organ meat and separating it from the rest.

Catia sawed away. The slit opened and the guts spilled out. The stink was not to be believed! I moved another step back.

When she finished, we sorted through the mess on the ground, saving the useable parts and bunging them into the bowl. Most all of a pig is useable, of course, so this occupied us for some little while. By the time we were done, the bowl was heaped to overflowing and we set to stripping out the intestines to be emptied and cleaned. That done, Catia said, "Now we skin it."

Standing there—sticky, reeking—I formed a lasting appreciation for those who ply the butcher's trade. Such work should be lauded and richly rewarded by all.

We went to the well to wash and have a drink before beginning the long, onerous process of removing the tough, hairy hide. Catia was in the midst of explaining how this was to be done when there arose a furious barking and shouts from the yard.

"Ursa!" I gasped.

"They're back!" cried Catia, dropping the bucket. We hurried around the barn in time to see three young men and an elder white-haired fellow—her much-delayed sons and father—entering the yard beside a small mule cart. Ursa, hackles raised, was holding them at bay.

The boys were close versions of one another: thick, dark hair like ill-kempt thatch; big, dark eyes like their father's; deep-clefted, smooth-shaven chins; long legs. Some might call them handsome. Two of Catia's sons carried long spears and one had a rust-spotted iron sword that must have been a generation or two older than the one toting it. The white-haired fellow was also tall and slender but, from the droop of his shoulders, appeared tired and worn—exhausted, no doubt, from the journey and trying to keep up with the younger men.

Ursa, alarmed at their arrival, was tensed and ready to launch herself at them. I called out and ran to her, grabbing hold of her collar and speaking soft words of assurance that all was well. "Thank you for warning us," I whispered into her ear. "But these men are friends. So, no more growling. We will greet them nicely." She calmed for me at once and ceased barking, but kept a wary watch all the same.

Catia fell to hugging her sons and soon everyone was chattering all at once. The tallest among the boys—the one I took to be the eldest of the three lads—gestured toward me and said something like, "And who is this?"

The one standing next to him, leaning on his spear, said to his mother, "You didn't say we had a comely guest."

"No more of that." Catia gave him an affectionate cuff on the chin. "And when did I have chance to say anything at all?" She pulled me into the group. "This is Aurelia. She is travelling to Deva and has kindly stayed on to help me with the chores while you were away."

She then introduced the others. Pointing first to the old man, she said, "This is my father, Ruarc." He gave me a little nod. "And this is Garan," she indicated the tallest of her boys then moved down the line "and Dyfan, and Orrin."

I greeted them each in turn and repeated my own name and that of my dog. They all eyed the fearsome creature with some suspicion and not a little unease. "Never fear," I told them lightly. "She won't hurt you if you don't hurt me." I meant it in jest, but they all glanced uneasily at one another.

"Well, now," said Catia, gazing happily the home-comers, "you're home and no sooner than you should be. We were just now getting ready to skin the hog. What has taken you so long, anyway? I expected you back days ago," she said, a motherly reprimand in her tone.

"Ask Orri," said the one called Dyfan. "It's all his fault."

"Not so!" protested the youngest son. "It was an accident!"

"I saw what happened, and you—"

"Enough!" snapped Catia. "You're only just back and already bickering."

"Where's Seisyll?" said Ruarc, looking around—eager, I expect, to change the subject.

"He's in his bed—resting." Catia explained briefly that his injury was no better, and the men trooped into the house to see their father and take a little food. Catia followed, leaving me and Ursa in the yard.

I fetched water and gave Ursa to drink, then went to tend the remaining pigs. I was still at this when the eldest son, the one called Garan, found me talking to the beasts. "Mam says you saved our Da," he announced happily. "Is this true?"

I asked him to repeat this, and then replied, "It is true that I made a poultice for his injury. If this has helped him, I am glad. What else did your Mam tell you?"

"She says you are half deaf and that I am to take you to Bryncadlys and put you on the way to Deva by way of the hill path." Though he spoke evenly enough, I sensed resignation in his tone.

"I suppose that is the last thing you want to do—having just come from there and all—but this half-deaf girl would be most grateful for your help," I told him.

"Aye," he agreed. "Mam said you were abandoned by your friends and have been making your way alone."

"Abandoned, yes—but not on purpose. It was more a misunderstanding," I countered. "It seems I was not where I was supposed to be."

"Neither was Orri!" he hooted. "That cost us three whole days!"

He did not offer any further explanation and I did not ask, but he seemed to wear the inconvenience easily enough. He regarded me, his look lingering so long I grew uncomfortable under his gaze. "What is it?" I asked at last, touching a hand to my hair.

"Is that Dyfan's tunic you've got on?" he said. A grin appeared and spread across his broad face. "It is!"

"We were slaughtering the hog. Your mother gave me these clothes to wear so I wouldn't ruin mine." I brushed a hand down the garment and tugged at the breeches. "I didn't know these were Dyfan's."

He laughed. "The look on your face just now." He laughed again—happy, carefree—and I liked the sound. "It doesn't matter," he said. Turning away from the pigs, we started for the door of the barn to see to the calf. "Besides, you won't have to worry about ruining anything."

"No?"

He shook his shaggy head. "Now that we're home, my brothers and I will finish the butchering." He smiled again. "Though we wouldn't mind an extra pair of hands to help with the skinning."

"I've never skinned a hog," I told him. "I've never skinned anything."

"Don't worry. I'll show you all you need to know."

True to his word, Garan and the others got down to it and were soon elbow deep in gore. They took turns guiding me through the awful process. Before that long day had run, I had skinned, beheaded, and quartered my first hog—and, I dearly hope, the last. A more grisly, gruesome work I cannot contemplate, and never wish to repeat—despite the fact that, if allowed, I would happily eat my weight in ham.

It was almost dark by the time we finished and we all went down to the stream at the bottom of the valley to wash off all the filth and stink. We went into the water in our clothes to wash them, too; and then shucked them off to soap ourselves. Catia and I went some way apart from the others, of course, and as we bathed she told me how all the meat we had butchered that day would be preserved. "Winter is hard in these hills," she said. "But we will have plenty of good meat and sausage to see us through—and the grain and flour the boys brought home from the market."

Her mention of winter rekindled the urgency of my journey. Already long when I began, the way grew longer by the day! It seemed that the further I went, the further I still had to go. Well, I would leave the next day with a guide and, with luck on my side, I would reach Deva with no further hazards or delays.

As if to mock my resolve, the weather changed during the night. I awoke to a cold drizzle, driven on stiff north winds. That, combined with Garan's reluctance to repeat the trip he had completed only the day before, cooled my ardor enough to see the sense of remaining at Tŷ Bryn yet a little longer.

In fact, it would be many more days before the dark skies lifted and the rain ceased its lashing and thrashing. I bided my time, helping out around the farm as needed until, at last, a day dawned fair. We ate a solid meal and I made my last preparations. Then, Garan took up his spear and tucked a knife into his belt and we stepped out into the yard beneath a high blue, cloud-flecked sky with a crisp breeze at our backs to speed us on our way. Seisyll even rose from his bed and, though wan and yet pained by his injury, he hobbled out into the yard to wish me well. Holding to Catia for support, he told me that he believed my poultice had been the saving of him and for that he would be forever grateful.

And then Catia embraced me warmly and gave me a motherly kiss, smoothed my hair and, tears starting to her eyes, bade me farewell, inviting me to return any time for a visit. "Worry for nothing, Garan will see you right," she said, and then addressed her son: "Now, Garan, don't dawdle—and mind take her all the way to Bryncadlys." He nodded his understanding, and she said to me, "Once you're there, he'll show you the quicker way to Deva."

"The *quicker* way?" I pulled back in surprise. "Did I hear that right? There is a quicker way to Deva?"

"Aye," she replied easily. "There is a trail through the hills and it is much the swiftest way—and safer, too, I'm sure. Once on it, you're soon there."

I pressed her hands and thanked them all for their kindness and friendship and, with a final wave, I turned my face to Deva and to my precarious future.

5

"**YOUR FRIENDS IN DEVA**—are they anyone?"

Uncertain that I had heard Garan correctly, I asked him to repeat the question. He did, but I was none the wiser. "Anyone?" I wondered. "Of course, they are. *Everyone* is *someone*."

He only shook his head and laughed.

"I don't understand," I confessed.

"Anyone important, I mean..." His voice trailed off as he considered what he was about to say.

"Say it," I told him. "What are you asking?"

"I want to join the legion," he said, as if this was some kind of secret. "And they say the Valeria Vitrix is the best. I need to find somebody important to put in a good word for me, so I can join. I'm old enough."

"You want to be a soldier?" His assertion seemed odd to me. For all I knew—and as everyone kept reminding me—the legions were not at all what they had been when at full strength and Britannia a valued province. I regarded him more closely: square-jawed, trim, well muscled, a goodly height—at least he was head and shoulders taller than me—with long, strong legs and a broad, sturdy back, he would not be out of place in a cohort. Still, I could not picture him in a helmet and lorica; he was not like any of the soldiers I had met.

"Don't they need you here on the farm?"

"There's always the farm," he allowed, a note of resentment shading his tone. He jabbed at the path with the butt of his spear. "With my Da and uncle and brothers, we have more than enough hands to do the work. But the pay a soldier earns—we could use that, too. Especially now."

"Why now—especially?"

"Not so long ago we could count on good trade and any number of markets to choose from. Now there's only one market—"

"The one at Bryncadlys."

"Aye," he nodded, "and that one is piss poor. It used to be a right fair place, and folk came from all over to trade. But not anymore. Da says that he remembers a time when the legion at Deva patrolled as far as Bryncadlys and even further. I've never seen a legion on patrol. Folk do say there's a garrison at Deva, so I know they're still around. God knows, we could use them up here."

"You're not wrong," I said, and told him about the rogues I'd met on the road. "They'd have taken me—if not for Ursa."

"That brute dog of yours?" He cast a worried glance at my furry guardian padding faithfully by my side.

"Yes, Ursa," I said. "But she's no brute!"

"She's killer mean," he allowed. "She snarled at me when I came out this morning."

"She's trained to watch over her own, and that's me," I said. "She's not mean—just protective."

He nodded, thoughtfully. "We could use a dog like that on the farm. Thieves tried to steal our pigs a month or so ago." He laughed. "Middle of the night, it was—and the squealing woke us up and we chased 'em off."

"Ursa would have had them on the ground before they knew what hit them," I said.

Garan chuckled. "I'd like to see that!"

"No," I told him, remembering the fright Lord Ederyn's guard dogs had given me—not to mention the mess they'd made of the wild pig guts they cavorted in following the hunt. "No, believe me, you really wouldn't."

We talked like this awhile, growing easy in one another's company. The sun rose higher and the miles receded behind us. Once or twice I glimpsed a lone hilltop settlement or steading tucked into a cleft in a valley, but mostly, I saw a land forlorn of folk—unlike the well-peopled southlands where a traveler would find not only farms and settlements, but villas and towns and *civitas*; where the roads were not disused and decrepit trails and beaten footpaths, but busy high ways of cobbled stone. Compared to the northern wastes and wilds, the south was heaving with humanity and roaring with life.

Out on the lonely track through the empty hills lay a region rich with timber in forests and groves, and seamed through with streams flowing with clean water along valley meadows grown thick with sweet, green grass: everything any settlement would need . . . except people. Blessed with the folk to work it, I had no doubt the land would repay the effort a hundredfold or more. Little wonder barbarians of every stripe coveted this fair isle for themselves, and would kill to get it.

As the day slowly faded into a yellow-white haze around us, I wondered aloud where we might make our camp for the night. We had not met many travelers along the way—a farmer or two hurrying home from the field and one returning from Deva. Mounted on a mule, he was in a rush and, after exchanging a few words, rode on and soon disappeared from view. Aside from those, we seemed to have the entire province to ourselves.

"There is a place we stop sometimes," Garan told me. He pointed to an outcrop of broken stone near where the trail passed some way ahead. "See there? Just under the shelter of those rocks."

"That's miles from here," I complained. My feet were already aching and my legs growing weary.

"It's not that far," he insisted. "If we hurry we will be there before dark."

At that, we stepped up our pace and arrived at the place he had indicated from the path: a clearing formed by a hollow beneath a towering stone overhang. Signs of previous camps were obvious: dried horse dung and the sodden ashes of fires, shards of broken jars, poles on which to stretch a cloth or skin for a roof, and a few bits of leftover firewood. Ursa ran around sniffing here and there, and then raced off into the bush on the trail of something she might catch for her supper.

Garan watched her go and I laughed to see the look on his face. "Ursa can look after herself, don't worry. She'll return when she's caught a rabbit. Who knows? She might even bring back a deer."

"Really?"

"No!" I hooted with a laugh. "What do you think?"

He shrugged, an embarrassed smile spreading across his open face. "It wouldn't surprise me at all if that dog fetched back a whole cow."

That thought made me hungry. Besides a handful of seeds and berries gleaned from brambles, we had not stopped to eat all day. I was famished and told Garan I could eat that cow right now, hooves, horns, and hide. He said we did not have any beef. "But we have some salt pork and black bread. And Mam always puts in a little honey for the bread. We won't be starving."

We set about making a little camp for the night. After scraping together enough dry wood for a fire and spreading our cloaks, we hunkered down to warm ourselves by the fire, eat our simple meal, and watch the stars come out. Hungry as I was, I struggled to stay awake long enough to eat and I all but fell asleep with a crust of bread halfway to my mouth. Garan advised me to go lie down before I slumped into the fire. While he set about stoking up the blaze, I bade him a good night and crawled further under the overhanging ledge of rock where it was dry, and there was enough dried moss to make a pillow for my head. Wrapped in my cloak, I slept the deep and dreamless sleep of the righteous.

Our journey resumed as soon as we had washed in the brook and refilled the water jars. In the early light, the hills and valleys round about seemed new made—fairly gleaming with last night's dew and the fast-fading mist. Everything looked clean and fresh and . . . oh, so empty. Garan and I might have been the only two people in the world, and that world was ours to make of it what we would.

The feeling, exhilarating as it was, did not last. Around midmorning, we saw traders returning from the market—four of them with pack mules piled with goods; three of the group carried spears and all wore brimless head coverings that looked more like woolsacks than hats. Upon seeing these fellow travelers, I was wary—not without good reason—but Garan thought they looked familiar. "I think I've seen them at Bryncadlys before. We should go meet them."

Garan strode out, quickening his pace. "You go on ahead," I called after him. "I'll stay back with Ursa and join you later."

With a hand to Ursa's collar, I watched as Garan hurried to catch the traders; he hailed them and they paused, I suppose to exchange greetings, and then continued on. They passed me going back the way we had come but, aside from a nod of acknowledgment did not deign to notice me at all. I glanced up the road to see Garan walking back, brow lowered, his mouth bent in a frown.

"What's wrong?" I called as soon as he joined me.

"Bad news," he said, his frown deepening to a scowl. "There's been a raid at Bryncadlys. It was bad—eight, maybe ten people killed and several more injured."

"Who did it?"

"They didn't know." He shook his head. "But the market is all smashed up. Burned. People are leaving town because it isn't safe—at least until they can get soldiers to protect it."

A pit formed in my stomach as I took this in. "So, what do we do now?"

"What do you want to do?" He waved a hand in the direction of the traders just then disappearing around a curve in the road. "Do you want to go back?"

I considered for a moment, then said, "No. I want to press on."

"Then I'm going with you."

"Garan, you can't. What about—"

He cut off my protest. "Listen, I've been thinking about this. We were meant to find someone you could travel with to Deva," he said. "But if there's no market, I'll go with you." He smiled and added, "It's the only way."

"No." I held up a hand as if to dismiss the very notion. "I cannot allow it."

Garan, bless him, actually laughed out loud. "*Allow* me?" He laughed again. "I don't see how you can prevent me!"

"You'll be missed at home. When you don't return, your family will fear the worst."

"I said I would take you there, not that I would *stay* there." He paused, then added, "At least, not yet."

This last part was said under his breath, and he had to repeat it for me. "What do you mean *not yet*? What are you saying?"

"If I take you to Deva, then I can go to the garrison and speak to the commander there—"

"About joining the legion!" So, that was in his mind, and likely had been from the start.

"Aye," he confirmed. "I can ask him myself and see if he will accept me."

His plan, such as it was, became clear to me then. "You asked if my friends were anybody..." I said, recalling what he had said before. "I did not tell you then, but . . . well, as it happens, my friend's husband is the Legate of Deva."

"Legate!" he cried, and stopped walking to give me an openmouthed gape. "Now *that* is somebody! The Legate of Deva! With a recommendation from him, I would surely be accepted. A legate—that's almost an emperor! Why didn't you tell me?"

"I don't know," I replied lamely. "I didn't think it mattered."

Garan, shaking his head in amazement, could not contain his surprise. "If your friend is the Legate of Deva, what are you doing out here?" He flapped a hand at the empty hills around us. "You should be travelling with an armed escort—at the very least!"

"You make more of it than it is," I told him flatly. "My father was a magistrate and knew him. That's all."

"What!" Garan stopped walking again. "Your father was a *magistrate*? How so? If my father was a magistrate, I would travel in a carriage and have servants to run after me. You wouldn't catch me wandering around in the lonely hills with only a dog for company. What happened? Did you run away?"

"My father died."

That shut him up—but only for as long as it took him to put the pieces together. "Oh," he said, after a moment. "So, you're on your own. And that's why you're going to Deva."

"Yes, that is why I'm going to Deva," I confessed. I could not bring myself to say more than that. We walked in silence for some time after that, each in a cloud of our own private thoughts, until our destination came into view.

I suppose I had imagined that Bryncadlys would be something like Caer Gwyn, but that was a stretch. Although the settlement was nicely situated on a wide, flat place in a generous valley with a fair stand of trees and a nearby lake, it boasted but few houses, a single street, a church—and that was it. There were a few farms huddled close about, but not many and not large. The market itself was merely a few pens for livestock, a food stall or two, a storehouse, and several large leather tents. The recent raid had taken two more substantial timber buildings; they had been burned and were now nothing but charred posts and rooftrees on foundations of rubble stone.

The rough timber palisade that ringed a nearby hilltop to guard the road and travelers passing through the town, having failed to prevent the raid, still gave the place a modest air of security. There were still folk lingering about, some of them travelers who, like Garan and myself, were now having to make other plans. Ursa saw the people and, as we passed further into the town, she pressed against the side of my leg as if to reassure me with her presence.

Garan made for a place at the far end of the town where several wagons had drawn up. Once again, I stayed with Ursa and watched and, while the men were in a tight group, head-to-head in deep discussion, I passed my gaze around the town. Other than the burned buildings, no other sign of the raid was visible; the barbarians had struck, killed, looted, and disappeared, leaving only the smell of stale smoke and a much subdued atmosphere behind. When I looked around again, Garan was hastening back to say that, like us, the traders had planned on attending the market. But, inasmuch as it would be some time before any meaningful trade would resume in this place, these disappointed merchants were considering whether to go on or go back to Deva instead.

"It makes good sense," he said. "Though trading in the town is more controlled and there is a heavy tax, Deva is bigger and closer than any other market in the region—less than half a day from here."

The words were hardly uttered when one of the men turned and raised an arm to summon Garan back; he hurried to rejoin the group, exchanged a word, and returned grinning. "It's decided! They're going on to Deva and we can go with them. They say they're leaving tomorrow morning."

"No," I shook my head. "I want to go now." It was approaching midday, and though it meant we would have to hurry if we were to reach Deva by nightfall, I had to try.

"If you're sure . . ." Garan said.

"I am."

"Then we should eat before we go." Garan lifted his head and sniffed the air, then looked toward the food stall. "I wonder what they have over there?"

We soon found out; and, after a shared loaf and wedge of fresh soft cheese flavored with green herbs, a jar of small beer, and a few scrag ends of gristly meat begged for Ursa, we struck out on the road to begin the last leg of our journey.

Just knowing that by day's end I would be standing in Deva made the journey pass the quicker. As it was, once Bryncadlys was behind us, the clouds came down and the wind kicked up in fits and gusts, and the day closed over us in a dull mist. We walked through the night, holding our cloaks around us to keep out the chill. Once, Garan suggested we stop for the night, but the thought of sleeping in some damp wayside dell held no appeal—even if we could have found such a place in the dark.

The hill path was well traveled and easy underfoot, so we kept going. Garan, bless him, tried to keep our spirits up by telling stories about the silly things he and his brothers got up to on the farm: from riding pigs to making beards out of wool at sheep-shearing time. I caught most of what he said, but mostly it was just the sound of his voice that kept my feet moving.

The night wore on. And then, just when I thought I would fall over from exhaustion, the sky began to lighten in the east, announcing the beginning of another day—and yet another hill before us. Drooping, numb with fatigue, I looked at that long rising slope and my heart quailed. "We should stop and rest," said Garan, his voice a little croaky.

I shook my head. "If I stop now, I'll never get up again," I told him.

We kept going, more slowly now. It was all I could do to keep putting one foot in front of the other. The sky continued to lighten and the bright disk of the sun peeped above the horizon as we reached the top of the hill and paused to look down. And there it was: Deva Vitrix!

6

NESTLED IN THE SWEEPING CURVE of the wide estuary, I saw a large *civitas* of brick and stone and ordered streets. There were houses and villas and churches and markets stuffed with goods, and a harbor boasting a wharf and timber docks with ample mooring places for all the ships and boats anchored there. The lower slopes of the surrounding hills were dotted with clusters of dwellings and . . . more than I could readily take in at once. Indeed, everything I had imagined—and over the many miles and daily trials of my long journey, I had unknowingly allowed myself to imagine very much indeed—it all was there, sprawling before my eyes on a shining river. Deva lived up to my dreams and surpassed them in ways I could not have conceived.

Admittedly, looking back now, much of my flattering assessment of the place was yet to come: all in good time, unfolding like a roll of fine-spun cloth, over the course of many days. The more I came to know this almost perfect harbor town, the more wonders it revealed.

In those first heady moments as we crested that last long hill and paused to gaze down upon our destination, I was glad beyond words to see the end of the road at last. Truth to tell, with my sore feet and tired legs, and the thirst clawing at my throat, the sight of *any* haven of rest would have cheered me just as much at that moment, I'm sure.

"Well, there it is," Garan said, indicating the *civitas* with a wide seep of his arm—as if he had conjured the town solely for my pleasure. "It is grand, is it not?"

"And big!"

"Aye, grand and big."

I stood there filling my gaze with this wonderful sight when I realized that Garan was already starting down. I stirred myself to follow, but Ursa hesitated; she made two steps and then stopped, still looking down at the town.

"Ursa, come!" I commanded, putting some force to the words and patting the side of my leg. The dog looked at me with her large dark eyes, shook herself, but refused to budge.

"What's wrong?" I asked her. I went to her and put my arms around her neck. "What is troubling you?"

"It's the town," suggested Garan. "She doesn't like it."

"Nonsense," I told him. "She's been in towns before."

He shrugged. "Not one this big."

I put my arms around her and whispered. "Come on, girl. We're almost there." Cocking her head to one side, she searched me with her big, dark eyes, and I felt again that curious bond we shared. "It's going to be all right," I told her. I stood and patted my leg again and held out my hand. "Come, let's go find something to eat."

Ursa nuzzled my extended hand, licking it both sides, then took her place beside me. We joined Garan and he said, "Well? Shall we go down and see if Deva Vitrix will have us?"

Setting my sights on the road ahead, I nodded. "We shall."

Down the hill, morning light strengthening as we went, and we soon approached the town gates with soldiers standing guard either side. They paid us no attention as we passed through and into the town. Full to overflowing with a welter of emotion—joy, relief, exultation, triumph, and thankfulness—my eyes welled up with tears so that everything seemed a dazzling blur.

"Where to now?" Garan asked as we paused in a busy square to rest. Just reaching Deva had been my sole ambition, my all-consuming desire for so long that it was only as I sat on a mounting block in the corner of the square that my thoughts turned to how I might find Helena and what she might say when she saw me.

Shoes off, I sat rubbing my feet, looking around as if I might see her or Aridius strolling through the square in amongst the townsfolk hurrying around us.

"Where are your friends?"

I shook my head. "I don't know. I've never been here before."

He shrugged. "Well, your friend is the legate, is he not? He won't be difficult to find. I expect we can just ask anybody..."

With that, he hurried across the square to accost a man selling bread from a sort of table on wheels. I watched while I laced up my shoes, and saw Garan move on to one of the stalls lining the perimeter of the square. There, he spoke to a man in a leather apron; I saw the man point across the square; they exchanged a few words, and then Garan was back to report: "The Civitas House is at the end of that street—" He pointed in the direction indicated by the man in the apron. "We can ask there." Without waiting for a reply he started off.

I finished tying my shoe and gave Ursa a pat on the head. "I could not have got this far without you, my friend. Come, just a little farther." Her ears pricked up. Clearly, she did not like the noise and commotion of the town—ever alert to every sound and movement, it put her on edge. I tried to reassure her now even as she had sought to protect me on our way.

"Coming?" called Garan a few paces away.

I stood, adjusted my cloak, and, with a guiding hand to Ursa's collar, said, "I'm ready."

Crossing the square, we entered a narrow lane—walled on one side, and lined on the other with shops including a butcher, with the dressed carcass of a wild boar hanging on a hook, its head on the ground beneath it. At the end of the street a large whitewashed building rose behind an iron gate. Before the gate stood a young soldier in a helm and hardened-leather breastplate, and leaning on his spear. At our approach, he straightened himself and made a halfhearted challenge.

"We've come to see the legate," Garan announced, trying to make himself sound important.

"Then you have wasted your time," the soldier informed us, his voice full of the lilting speech of the hills 'round about. "The legate is in council today. He sees no one." He cast his eyes over us from head to toe and back again. Apparently unimpressed by what he saw, he made a gesture with his spear. "Move along."

Garan made to leave, but I stood my ground. I had not come this far, endured so much and risked even more, simply to be turned away by some pimple-spotted youth with a shiny helmet.

"We will go," I said, speaking loud and slow so there would be no misunderstanding. "But you must think carefully what you will tell the legate when he asks you why you turned Domina Helena's cousin away from his door."

I turned on my heel and walked away, and had taken but a few paces when the guard called, "Wait!"

I glanced back at the young fellow's anxious face. "Her cousin?"

"That is what I said," I replied. Garan, silent beside me, stared, but held his tongue. "If I were you, I would be thinking of a very good explanation. I'm sure the legate will want to hear it as soon as you tell him you refused me."

"Wait there." The suddenly solicitous soldier slipped through the gate and ran to the entrance of the big white house.

Garan bent close and said, "You told him you were his wife's cousin?"

"No, I didn't," I replied. "I merely advised him to think what he would do if she should appear. Best to be prepared if such a thing were to happen, don't you think?"

Garan laughed and shook his head. "I would never have—"

Before he could finish, the soldier reappeared on the run. "Enter, please," he said, pulling open the gate for us. "Follow me. The legate will see you."

The young guardsman led us up a paved walk to the Civitas House door. As we stepped beneath the shelter of the portico a tall, dark-haired man in a spotless white tunic and dark leggings appeared. One look at me and a look of astonished amazement washed over his handsome face. "Aurelia?" he cried. "Is it Aurelia?"

I halted as relief and joy flooded through me. He remembered me! Only slightly less relieved, I suspect, was the young soldier who thought himself to have avoided an imagined scolding.

Spreading his hands wide in welcome, Aridius rushed to gather me into his embrace. "Aurelia! Do I believe my eyes? My dear, dear girl," he said, speaking mostly to the top of my head, "what are you doing here?"

I could not speak for the sudden tears. He hugged me and then, holding me at arm's length, glanced around quickly, and said, "Does Helena know you are here? No, of course not. Come, we will go to her at once."

He stepped away and summoned one of the aides who followed

him from the house and now stood looking on. "Bring my carriage!" he commanded, and the man darted off. To the second aide, he said, "Run ahead to my villa and tell my wife that Aurelia of Venta is to be our guest."

Aridius then looked down at Ursa, standing stoically by my side. "And who have we here?"

"This is Ursa," I told him proudly, "my most loyal companion and protector." The dog regarded Aridius with such an air of watchful intelligence that it brought a smile to his face.

Looking up, he saw Garan standing in mute amazement at the reunion. "You, there," he called, "are you with her?"

"This is Garan," I said, speaking up. "He's been my guide through the hills."

"Then you must come along, too. I would hear more of your journey."

"I am at your command, Legate," replied Garan, adopting a formal tone I had not heard before. Clearly, he wanted to make a good impression on the man who might secure him a place in the legion.

The next thing I knew I was bundled into a large, well-made carriage and we were rolling through the streets of the town. Aridius sat next to me; restraining his curiosity for my sake, he said, so that I would not have to repeat everything all over again for Helena. Meanwhile, he interrogated Garan about how we had come to be there. "Am I to understand you have walked all that way? Alone?"

As far as I could make out, Garan told him how I had turned up at the family steading where it was agreed that he would accompany me to the market at Bryncadlys. "But the market was overrun in a raid some few days ago," I heard him say. "Barbarians..." He said some more and then ended saying, "...for her safety..."

"I know about what happened at Bryncadlys. God knows, you were lucky to get here alive." Aridius said, and gave my hand a little squeeze. "You are both to be commended for your bravery in undertaking such a journey."

Commended, he said. Perhaps he was right and praise was in some way fitting; but I remember thinking: *Ah, but you don't even know the half of it.*

He lapsed into a thoughtful silence that lasted until we reached a small square lined with ash trees. The carriage drew to a halt and Aridius declared, "We're here! Helena will be so pleased!"

We emerged from the carriage to stand before a large, walled villa which, like the Civitas House, featured an iron gate and a soldier to guard it. At a gesture from the legate, the guard opened the gate and Aridius led us inside, shouting for his wife to come and greet their guests. Before I could take in much more than the spacious courtyard and the red-tiled roof of the central wing of the villa, a cry rang out from a darkened doorway; there was a sudden rush and Helena stood before me. She snatched me to her and hugged me as a lost sister returned from long exile. "Aurelia! Oh, Aurelia! I have so often thought of you and yearned to see you again. And here you are!" She kissed me on the cheek and smoothed my hair and hugged me again, before asking, "And who is this with you? Hello," she said to Garan, "I don't think I know you."

"I'm Garan," he said simply. "Aurelia's friend."

"He's been travelling with me." I started to explain but, confounded by the length and complexity of all that had happened, ended in a sigh instead, saying, "It's a long story."

"Never mind, we'll have plenty of time to talk later."

"They've come all the way from Tŷ Bryn," Aridius announced. To Garan he said, "Have you eaten? No? And what of this magnificent animal?" He gave Ursa a pat on the rump and then clapped his hands and called for a servant. A pale, slender youth appeared and Aridius told him to hurry with water and meat scraps for the dog, and cakes and sweet wine for the rest of us. Then he turned to shepherd everyone into the house. "Come in! Come in! Let us sit down and you can tell us everything th—"

"Ari!" snapped Helena. "Aren't you forgetting something?"

"Forgetting?" He looked around, surprised. "What am I forgetting?"

"Tullius," she replied. She reached out and took my hand. "Aurelia, where is your father? Something tells me he would never have sent you off on your own. What's happened?"

A lump formed in my throat and I could not speak.

"Where is your father?" The softness of her voice told me she already suspected the worst, and the look of sympathy on her comely face sent fresh tears to my eyes. Instantly, I was awash in grief renewed. "Where is Tullius?"

Tears stared to my eyes as I struggled to force out the words. "My father is . . . gone."

"Gone? You mean—"

"He died," I choked out. "The wound worsened and the poison spread. Tullius is dead."

"Ohhh, Aurelia." Helena gathered me to her once more. "Dearest heart, I am so, so sorry. This is terrible news . . . simply terrible." She looked to her husband. "Did you know about this, Ari? Oh, Aurelia, you poor thing. I am so very sorry."

Bless them, they did not require any further explanation than that. They both glimpsed the shape and meaning of my predicament in that instant and did not press me then for more. After a moment, Aridius said, "Well, come inside. Sit down. We'll eat something and when you are ready, you can tell us all about it."

"Take all the time you need," Helena told me. "You are here now and you are safe. Consider this your home—for as long as you care to stay."

7

AFTER ONE OF THE MOST RESTFUL NIGHTS of recent memory, I rose to a new day and a new life in a new home. Helena would have it no other way but that I was to stay with them and become part of their household. Her welcome, so warm and effusive, was a healing balm to my bruised heart. To know that I had a place to live, friends to look after me, the protection of a man of authority and influence was beyond gratifying—it was more than anything I dared hope.

Just after breaking fast, the legate had spoken to Garan and the two of them had trooped off to the garrison to see the commander, returning later to announce that Garan was assured a place in the next round of training for new recruits. Garan, delight shining through his grin, took me aside to share his joy. "Legate Verica spoke well for me. It is thanks to him I have a place."

"It's what you wanted," I told him. "I'm happy for you, Garan. Truly, I am."

"But it is thanks to you I'm even here at all." On sudden impulse, he seized me and pressed me to his chest. "And if not for you and your friendship with the legate, I would not have a place with the legion."

"You've been a good friend to me, Garan, and I won't forget it." I could see I was embarrassing him, so I said, "What will you do now?"

"I'm to return home and winter there," he said. "I will join the new recruits in the spring to begin my training at the garrison. After that..." He shrugged. "Who knows?"

"You'll come see me when you come back, won't you?"

"I will. I promise."

"Good."

"I've got to go now," he said.

"Now?" I wondered. It seemed so abrupt.

"I want to share the news with everyone at home as soon as possible. The garrison commander is sending a cohort to Bryncadlys to bolster the troops at the caer. They are marching out soon, and the legate has arranged for me to go with them—that far, at least."

"Your triumph is complete!" Reaching up, I gave him a quick kiss and pressed his hand. "I shall miss you, Garan. And I'll hold you to your promise to come see me first thing you return in the spring."

"Farewell, Aurelia." Unable to think of anything else to say, he turned to go.

"Oh! Be sure to give Catia and Seisyll my thanks for...for everything."

He nodded and assured me my greetings would be conveyed, then hurried across the courtyard and out the gate, giving me a last, cheerful smile and a wave before disappearing into the street.

I stood a long moment after he was gone, offering a prayer of thanks for his kindliness and care of me, his friendship and that of his family, and for strong protection for him and a safe return home. Aridius joined me then, and said, "Has he gone so soon? I meant to say farewell."

I nodded. In that moment, I accepted that I would never see Garan again. His feet were on a different path now, as were mine.

Aridius saw the look on my face and said, "Take heart, Aurelia. The garrison commander is a good man, and Garan will make a good soldier. God knows we need them."

I gave him what must have been a forlorn smile. "Thank you for helping him. It was his dream to serve in the legion."

"Anyone who cares for one of mine is friend to me." He started for the gate. "Now, I will beg your pardon, but I must go and tend to my affairs. The life of a legate is never dull. Tell Helena I will try to be home before dark."

With that, he was gone, leaving Helena and me alone to talk and renew our friendship. We sat a small table in her bedchamber with a bowl of black berries between us and Ursa curled on a mat at our feet.

"I meant to come to you the day you left Viroconium," Helena was saying. Bless her, she remembered my deafness and took care to speak so I could hear her well. "I wanted to see you again. I thought I might make one last appeal to your father to come to us for his recovery."

"He would never have done it," I told her. "The death of Proconsul Esico made his return to Venta all the more urgent—in his mind, at least. I wanted to see you, too. I would like to have said farewell."

She pressed my hand. "I'm so sorry. I meant to come, as I say, but it was not to be."

"I understand. Things happen. Plans change."

Helena nodded. "Things *do* happen..." Her hands brushed the front of her mantle and I saw, for the first time the slight swell of her stomach. She noticed my glance, smiled, and nodded.

"You're with child!" I gasped.

"I am," she confirmed smoothing her hands across her belly. "And having a beastly time of it. Sick every morning and every night. I hope the child I carry is worth all the trouble it's causing me."

We quickly fell to discussing that and the disastrous conclave in Viroconium that had ended up costing my father his life—beginning with the day we all departed the *civitas*.

"That morning," Helena continued, shaking her head. "As fate would have it, *that* was the morning my suspicions were confirmed. I was pregnant—and with a vengeance! I woke dizzy and sick to my stomach and sweating through my clothes, my head pounding. I couldn't stand up for falling down. Couldn't eat—couldn't even *look* at food without throwing up." She groaned at the memory. "I spent most of the day in bed sucking on a wet cloth."

"Oh, Helena, if I'd known I would have come to you."

"I did send a boy with a message," she said, "but he was too late. You had already gone. A few days after we returned to Deva, I sent you a letter at Venta." She looked at me wistfully. "I guess you never received it."

"No, I didn't," I said, thinking that maybe the self-serving Lucanus intercepted it and neglected to pass it on to me. "But how are you feeling now? Has the sickness passed?"

"God be thanked, I think the worst is over—for the most part, at least. I still have a bad day now and then, but I am much better. Aridius has engaged a midwife and she looks in on me every—" She stopped.

"Listen to me! Braying on and on. My pitiful inconveniences are nothing." She dismissed them with a wave of her hand. "I want to hear about *you*, Aurelia. What happened after Tullius' funeral?"

Well, this would be the shape of the next few days. We would rise and break fast together, Helena and I, and talk awhile before she apportioned the duties required for maintaining the busy house of a legate. She had three young serving women: Junia, the daughter of a veteran and his wife who lived in the town; Deidre, a lithe young thing from a nearby hill tribe; and Tatiana, who was born in some remote corner of the eastern empire I'd never heard of. The three of them lived in the servant's wing of the villa. There was also a young man only a few years older than myself; Jason was his name, an obliging lad who readily took on any chore asked of him without complaint, as he clearly hoped to advance his fortunes by working in the legate's household. Then there was Nona, an older woman who served as both cook and substitute mother for the others. Nona lived in the town and usually arrived midmorning with provisions needed to prepare the meals she had in mind; she assigned the chores to the others as need arose and, just as importantly, dealt with the never-ending stream of tradesmen who appeared at the gate with one or another item required by the kitchen.

For his part, Aridius was seen only fleetingly. He would have already disappeared by the time Helena, Ursa, and I sat down together each morning. Most days, he hurried off to Civitas House for the first of his innumerable meetings and consultations with officials of various stripes—including some from other provinces. He would return at dusk, or sometimes after dark, and often with a guest or two—a visiting dignitary or a local worthy—someone he felt duty bound to entertain, or cajole into agreeing with some plan or other.

As the days passed, I began to conceive the notion that events of great import were taking shape in the region and beyond. Though, to be sure, it would be some time before I learned the nature of these actions and the tremendous impact they would have on my life and those who were growing ever more dear to me.

All that was yet to be. For now, it was enough to know that I had found a safe haven and a welcome among friends. I felt as one who had survived a terrible storm and could look upon a world cleansed anew by the ordeal. And Deva, it seemed to me, was just the kind of place to begin a new life: larger, busier, cultured, the life there more rich and varied than any I had encountered. The grandeur of the place—to my eye, at least—was enough to impress a girl from a small coastal town, enough to make me think that instead of a provincial *civitas*, I was living in the heart of Rome itself and that it was the Tiber flowing nearby, not the river Dee.

As I had no official duties or chores for the household, yet, I was free to roam where I would and made the most of my freedom, strolling wide streets lined with trees and gawking at the villas and houses—any one of which might have served a governor or procurator. I visited the port and saw boats and ships from places I had never heard of. I found busy markets with stalls and traders of all kinds: cheese from Gaul and the mountains of Lusitania and Baetica in Hispania; cloth from Arcadia, Massilia, and Mauritania; wine and oil and olives from Macedonia, Sicilia, Sardinia, and Gaul—places that all sounded strange and colorful and impossibly remote. Just wandering among the vendors and their exotic wares and cries to come and buy made me feel the utter immensity and complexity of an empire beyond my comprehension. It would, I imagined, take a lifetime to understand it, and then perhaps leave much undiscovered.

My wanderings were not without their share of mishaps. Much about the place defied easy understanding. The names of streets and places, the local speech and accent, the way the port intermingled with the town— one could turn a corner and see a ship at the end of the street!—made no sense at all. I expect the local folk, if they noticed me at all, saw a girl and a big furry dog wandering the town in a state of confusion.

"Don't worry, Aurelia," Helena told me one day after I got lost coming back from a simple errand, "it was the same with me when I first came here."

Had I heard that right? "Did you say when you *first* came here?" Her words came as a surprise to me. "But I thought you were born in Deva."

"Born in Deva?" She laughed lightly. "Far from it! I was not even born in Britannia."

She then went on to relate that her father was a Goth of the Suevi folk in Iberia. "I was born in Gallaecia." She shrugged lightly. "At least, that is what I was told."

"You don't know?"

She shook her head. "Truly, I don't." She leaned forward and confided, "I was pledged as a hostage to my father's overlord before I could talk. I was raised a fosterling."

I stared at her, unable to believe what I was hearing. "That is horrible, Helena." Then, to make sure I had heard her properly, "You did say 'hostage,' didn't you?'"

"Oh, it wasn't as bad as you might imagine," she continued happily. "Giving and taking hostages is a common enough practice—a good way to ensure peace and goodwill among rival tribes. It's what you do when you need powerful friends and can't marry someone into the tribe. My father was a prince of the Suevi and owed fealty to King Hermeric. And, anyway, what was one small girl more or less?"

"But, your name..."

She put her head to one side. "What about it?"

"With a name like Helena, I thought..." Unable to say what I thought, I spread my hands.

"And no doubt you would be right in thinking whatever it was you thought." She laughed again, shaking her head. "But no, no—life as we know is not always the straightest of paths. It *could* have been very hard for me—of course, it could. Things could have turned out very badly. I know that. But, God is good, and He was looking out for me. King Hermeric had a kingdom to rule, so he gave me in fosterage to a priest and his wife who lived in a nearby town. A loving pair, they were. And, as the wife was barren, she doted on me. They taught me to read and write, and schooled me in proper behavior and manners for a true Roman citizen. Helena is my foster name." She shrugged. "I don't even remember my birth name. When word came that my father had been killed in some battle or other—I must have been eight or ten at the time—Petronius and Lavinia adopted me."

Overwhelmed by the wonderful strangeness of it, I could scarce make sense of what she was telling me. My aristocratic friend—the most cultured and refined woman I had ever met—born a barbarian! If anyone had told me that my best friend would be a barbarian fosterling elevated to the station of legate's wife, I would not have believed it. Truly, the path of life was crooked indeed.

Only such a circuitous route could have led us to this place, I remember thinking. Where it would lead next, neither of us knew. For, other paths were about to converge with ours. The joining of these ways would bring changes no one could have foreseen.

8

A NOBLEMAN NAMED VALENTINIAN, who was related to one of the emperors in Rome, also called Valentinian, had taken power at that time. It was told officially that he was given power by his predecessor. But there were other, darker rumors as well—that the old emperor had been killed in battle without ever having met the new pretender, or that he had been murdered by his servants, or generals, or rivals . . . there was no way to know what really happened, not from as far away as we were, not with the Empire in such a constant churn of turmoil as it was then. But as day follows night, a new emperor would have taken the throne still warm from that last occupant. Perilous times for the ruling elite, to be sure; no less perilous for us all.

I might be forgiven my ignorance. I came by it honestly, after all. Until arriving in Deva, I had no idea the Empire was in such a tenuous state. I realized this was by design of my father, whether deliberately or otherwise. Tullius was not among the aristocrats and their kind. Tullius was of an older order: that of the simple civil servant, a man who administered his post and position with due diligence—the fellow with the rag mop and bucket of goose fat who greased the skids, so to speak—in order to ensure the smooth function of government for the benefit of Venta's citizens. I do not think it ever crossed his honest mind that the Empire he had so faithfully served would fall, in his lifetime, or mine.

Those men whose desires and whims swayed nations, whose ambitions tugged whole armies in their wake, were of a different and, some considered, a far higher order than he. Deva, as I came to know it, seemed to have more than its share of such men—and scheming women, too.

I do not mean to impugn Aridius or Helena in saying this. God knows they were not given to such prideful striving. Even so, their elevated status within what I came to view as the governing hierarchy meant that they were swept along in the surging currents surrounding the mighty men that made the waves. And such waves!

So it was that this Valentinian was emperor, as I say, but his base of power lay in the eastern half of the empire, which had effectively been split in two—the East ruled from Constantinople, wherever that was, and the West ruled from Rome, from which we drew our aid and support. However, this Valentinian's authority was never wholly recognized in the western half of the empire. It seems the legions much favored men of their own rank: battle-hardened leaders who knew how to fight barbarians of which there was an endless supply. Thus, the western empire still looked to Rome and followed the dictates of the Western Emperor and his officials. Naturally, this fueled factions, and caused plots and conspiracies and to spring up like weeds as men vied for power.

And another such quake, I came to understand, was shaking the marbled porticos of Rome now, and the tremors were being felt as far away as Britannia. I had been some weeks in the legate's house and busily helping run the household and looking after Helena, whose pregnancy proceeded its slow, steady course. The poor woman was growing heavily pregnant and finding the days increasingly difficult. Winter was upon us now, the nights long and winter cold with frost most mornings. Though Deva did not suffer the worst of the persistent storms, the weather was not often as mild as what I was used to in the southlands. I took to going about wrapped in my heaviest mantle with a cloak around me both day and night.

On one such brisk morning, a fellow of some elevated rank appeared. A general of the Western legions, his name was Ruitimus or Riothamus—if I heard at all correctly, which is ever uncertain—and by all accounts he was an intimate of the Western court. Why he should have chosen Deva for his festal observances was a mystery to me, but no doubt due to the large garrison.

The first I heard of the general's arrival was also the first I learned of the general; at the time, I merely took him for what he appeared to be: a soldier of high rank and considerable prominence. He arrived with a cohort of legionaries and mounted *alá*—bursting into town like a storm of thunder from an already worried sky.

His arrival set tongues wagging and I noticed the way people talked about him: in hushed, almost reverent, tones and with rare deference— such as one might use when speaking of a long-awaited deliverer, a savior even. I expect that such a man is what folk everywhere throughout the empire craved: one who could save not only Britannia from the ravages of barbarian invasion but the rest of the empire as well. Such tenacious foes, it was thought, could not be cowed by anything save a demonstration of overwhelming lethal force. A forceful argument, to be sure. Who could disagree?

Well, Emperor Valentinian for one. Though I knew nothing of the man, I expect that in his better moments he probably cared about the protection of his people. Yet, like most of those whose grip on the reins of power are tenuous at best, his chief concern lay in preserving his own fortunes above all. And, lamentably, even a weak, self-serving leader can still inspire the devotion of many—those jealous of their own advantage and advancement—and these faithful begrudge the ascendency of anyone who thought to challenge their chosen leader. To preserve his throne, Emperor Valentinian had been bleeding troops and resources from the West to defend his interest in the East—a situation which could not be allowed to continue.

This, as Aridius explained a night or two after the arrival of the general, was the very reason Riothamus had chosen this moment to visit Deva. "He has vowed to return the garrisons of Britannia to full manpower and strengthen the provinces of the West."

"How does he mean to do that?" I wondered, hardly knowing what I asked.

"Riothamus is here raising support for a most-distinguished commander named Aetius who has lately been promoted to *Magister Millitum*." At my blank expression he added, "It is a very high rank if not the highest." He went on to say that this commander, owing to his many victories in Gaul and elsewhere, he had gained much favor with the legions throughout the provinces.

I still did not see what this had to do with Deva, and I said so.

"Ah," said Aridius, leaning forward as if to offer a confidence,

"Riothamus and Aetius have pledged loyalty to a rival claimant to the purple robe. Majorian is his name."

Striving to keep all this straight in my mind, I repeated the name. "Majorian." Aridius nodded. "And this man is the right man to deliver us from the barbarians?"

The legate nodded and leaned back. "This was what their supporters believe."

I attempted to think this through and Aridius must have thought my expression confused, for he continued by saying, "Such a man will always have his supporters—just as he will always have his doubters. And even among those two camps he will have rivals besides. That is the way it always is, I find. In any case, I have no intention of one faction over another unless they can satisfy one question."

"And what question is that?" I asked.

"Can this man, this leader, actually do it? Can he deliver all that he promises?"

I nodded slowly. "And can he?"

Aridius laughs. "If only there was a way to know for certain, eh? It would all be so much easier. But the man with the best chance of success will have my support, for the good of the nation."

Of course, this is what believers always say. Even I knew that. The doubters, of course, would have their doubts as doubters always do. Thus, for every soul in one camp, there was a soul in the camp of another—and there seemed to be no end of either camps or rivals. Be that as it may, whichever camp you belonged to—whether a reverent believer or a sincere doubter—all true Britons wanted the same thing: to be free of the barbaric destruction and mindless bloodshed that was draining the life from us all.

"So this is why Riothamus and Aetius are making a circuit of the various legions," I said. "To rally support for . . . for Majorian, did you say?"

"Precisely," Aridius confirmed. "But they will need to work hard and work fast . . . people with power are easily distracted and are apt to wander after other interests."

Reports to Deva bore out the truth of Aridius' words. Everywhere they went, Riothamus and Aetius declared the same message: We must unite behind a single ruler under whose command the legions could be increased and strengthened to defeat the barbarian menace—Irish and Saecsen alike. This alone was paramount, they said. This alone would make the struggle and sacrifice worthwhile. Anything less would be...

"Catastrophe!" declared Aridius on returning home the evening following our discussion. He had spent a long day attending a sort of council of local worthies summoned by Riothamus to make the case for Majorian.

Helena had heard her husband arrive and we went to the courtyard to meet him; and there we found him slumped on a bench with his head in his hands. At our approach, he raised tired eyes and said, "We were in council, trying to have a meaningful discussion with the general and suddenly thugs charged in and lay rout to the whole thing." He raised his head, "Valentinian's men are responsible."

Helena regarded him sympathetically and handed him a cup of spiced wine. "I can't believe the emperor would send men just to break up your private discussion."

Aridius took a long draught of his wine. "Maybe not," he allowed. "But there are more than a few Valentinian zealots about. Upon my life, I do not trust any of them. Not anymore." He took another drink. "See here, Majorian has achieved great victories over the Saecsen and Goths, strengthened the borders, and renewed trade. People like him—the legions love him. We should at least listen to what Riothamus has to say."

"I'm sure it wasn't that bad," Helena suggested mildly, trying to sooth her husband's sour mood. She settled on the bench beside him and put a hand to his cheek.

"Ha! You weren't there," he snapped, jerking away. "Anything we said, they shouted us down. We couldn't make a single word heard. We were forced to vacate the basilica and went to the Civitas Square and those howling dogs followed us! There was a fight. It was chaos! Catastrophe!"

Aridius looked up and saw me standing there with the jar in my hands. "Oh, hello, Aurelia," he said, thrusting out his cup to me to be refilled. "Please—"

"I understand completely," I told him, pouring the wine.

"You do?" Aridius looked hopeful.

"Well, maybe not *completely*. My father was only a magistrate, but Tullius had his share of chaos and calamity, I can assure you."

"I'm sure he did," Aridius agreed. "Believe me, there are times I wish *I* was a magistrate again. Things were much simpler then."

"This Riothamus—or whatever he's called," said Helena, "who is he? I know nothing of him. I'm sure I've never heard the name before he arrived."

"Ah, yes, well." Aridius sipped his wine and settled back, somewhat less bothered now. "You won't have heard much of him unless you lived in Armorica. He is the Dux Bellorum and leads the legions there and in the north of Gaul. A fine soldier, he has had many triumphs over the barbarians and stands ready to take command in Britain, too, if enough support can be secured to make him Dux Britanniarum. We were about discussing this when Valentinian's men destroyed the proceedings."

"*Destroyed the proceedings,*" chided Helena. "How you talk, Ari! Did anyone get killed? Hurt? Anything damaged? No? Your discussion got interrupted by a group of disagreeable men—so have another discussion. Go to the church this time. These zealots—thugs as you call them—will mind themselves in church, or Bishop Gosselyn will deal with them."

"Perhaps," grumped Aridius, pushing himself upright on the bench. "This isn't the first time it's happened, and it won't be the last. Valentinian is ever jealous of his emperor's robes. I do believe he will stop at nothing to keep the power he has been hoarding."

"You mentioned another man," I ventured. "This Aetius—is he a good man?"

"By all accounts," Aridius said. "And I like Riothamus, too. More than canny commanders, they are true men of the empire. But Riothamus won't put up with being harried and scorned by his own people. If he cannot win enough support here, he will return to Armorica and any hope we have of defeating the Saecsens in Britannia will go with him."

Helena regarded her husband thoughtfully. "You are certain of this?"

"That he will return to Gaul?"

"That he is the one to become the high commander, the Dux Britanniarum," she replied. "That he can lead Britain to victory."

"He has a better chance than most. Certainly better than anyone else I can think of—and far better than any in Valentinian's camp, for that matter." He paused, became thoughtful. "Here is the nut of it: Riothamus has been tested in battle many times over. He knows how to fight the barbarians and, more importantly, he knows how to win. People like him. He is a most capable war leader, and if such a man has pledged support to Aetius, that should tell you all you need to know." He shook his head, contemplating the day's disaster. "Hear me," he intoned, "if we do not support Aetius and Riothamus, and men like them, then we will be battling barbarians for the next fifty years...a hundred!"

Helena nodded to me to refill her husband's cup and levered herself slowly to her feet. "We will leave you to think and determine what you intend to do about all this. When you come to the table, I want to see a light in those handsome dark eyes of yours." She bent down and gave him a kiss on the forehead. We withdrew to allow him to finish his drink and soak up the peace of the courtyard.

"I worry about him," she confided as soon as we entered the dining room. "It hurts to see him distraught like this." She gazed back toward the courtyard. "He cares so much—too much, I sometimes think."

We then went to oversee the table for the evening meal. I pondered what I had just heard, convinced more than ever that the threat to Britain was genuine and growing—worse, at any rate, than my somewhat sheltered life in Venta had lulled me into believing. Well, the attack on Tullius and all the tumult and travail of my recent journey through the land had given ample evidence that the world I had known was fast disappearing—what was to come remained to be seen.

The next day, Helena and I went to the central marketplace to find something nice for the evening meal—something Aridius would particularly enjoy. We were standing near a vegetable stall when we heard shouting—angry, loud, and growing louder and more heated. Across the square, I saw a group of soldiers and they were being harassed by a gang of men.

The two forces had drawn up, the soldiers in a tight knot, the men standing before them, belligerent, taunting, shouting abuse and trying to provoke a confrontation. The legionaries had not drawn weapons, but some of the men carried sticks and club. Other townsfolk were gathering around—most to watch, some to participate. Tempers were running high and mounting higher.

"Troublemakers," Helena observed. Taking my arm, she pulled me away. "Come, Aurelia. We can't stay."

"What is it? Who are they?"

"Those thugs Ari was talking about—probably hired by the Valentinian zealots," she said. "We shouldn't be seen here. We can't be involved."

We made a hasty retreat back to the villa.

It was near sunset when Aridius returned home to report that there had been a near riot in the town square when some of the emperor's devotees clashed with Deva's soldiers. Clubs were used and weapons drawn but, thankfully, no one was killed—although several bystanders had been injured in the uproar. I noticed that Helena did not tell him that *we* had been there when the ruckus began. I suspect she did not wish to add to his worries—God knows he was anxious enough—but I did wonder at her silence.

No more was said that night. But, the next morning, a messenger appeared as the legate was preparing to go out; the two exchanged a hurried word and then Aridius announced that Bishop Gosselyn was convening a council of officials and noblemen to discuss the recent unrest and determine what measures might be taken to alleviate the problem.

"I can tell him how to alleviate the problem," Aridius declared as he prepared to leave. Helena and I were watching from the door and had seen the messenger and guessed that some sort of confrontation was looming. "Give Valentinian's thugs the sharp end of a spear."

Helena rolled her eyes. "I hope you do not plan on speaking like that in the council," she said. "From what you say, the emperor has some very powerful men on his side, and they seem to be a foul-tempered lot."

Aridius frowned. "He may not *be* the emperor for long if I can do anything about it."

"Just be careful," she advised. "That's all I'm going to say."

Aridius went to her, embraced her, and gave her stomach an affectionate pat, pausing briefly at the door. "When have I ever been less than careful, dear wife?"

However careful the legate had been in the past, that proved to be of small value to him now. Word of the good bishop's unofficial council meeting reached Valentinian's faction with consequences for one and all. Not only had the previous council been prevented from completing its deliberations, but the names of those attending the bishop's summons had been noted and marked for certain retribution. Such was the fervor of Valentinian's fanatics that any who opposed them were branded traitor. Reason and rational thought vanished, sanity disappeared—replaced by the kind of willful ignorance and blind obedience of a benighted cult of idol worshippers and bootlickers.

All this was told to us when the legate returned to the villa that night, much dispirited over the exchange that had taken place within the sacred precinct of the church.

"They *will not* listen," he lamented. "Their minds are made up and they will not hear a word anyone says to the contrary. They mean to placate Valentinian and keep his fat rump on the emperor's throne. They will allow nothing to prevent them from acceding to his every whim lest they incite his wrath." He collapsed into his chair at the bare table. "I fear the worst."

It was early yet, and the table had yet to be laid for our supper. Helena had heard him enter the villa and hurried to him to find out what had taken place. I followed. Although I could not make out all that was said, I followed most of what passed between them; and the lines of his face told me the rest.

"But you're the legate," Helena pointed out. "There must be something you can do."

Aridius rubbed his hands over his face and shook his head. "Legate? Ha! That counts for nothing. These men—some I used to call friends—are no respecters of rank, or even the rule of law. Contantine himself has declared for Valentinian and many fear going against the procurator." Aridius shook his head in dismay. "They want what they want and they will have it! No one has ever denied them anything in this life and they are not to let that happen now."

"Is it possible that Emperor Valentinian can achieve what they believe?" I asked.

"Might he rise to the challenge before him? Might Valentinian show himself to be capable and competent?" said Aridius. "Is it possible? Anything is possible, but is it likely?"

"Well? Is it?" demanded Helena.

He shook his head again—sadly this time. "No. I fear not."

Our meal that night was taken in a gloom-laden silence—a mood that persisted the next morning when the legate departed for the Civitas House. After I had risen, washed, and dressed, I found Helena sitting alone on the bench in the courtyard. She gave me a wan smile when she saw me, and said, "I'm glad at least someone slept well last night."

Uncertain if I had heard her correctly, I regarded her expression and the bitter edge to her tone. "Slept well?" I asked. "Did you not?"

"Between the child I'm carrying and the one I'm married to—one kicking and the other thrashing about all night—I did not enjoy a moment's peace the whole night through." She yawned suddenly, holding the back of her hand to her open mouth. She shut her eyes and put her head back as if asleep—but only for an instant before struggling upright again. "I can't sit here. There is so much to do!"

"I can do it," I told her, and I meant it.

Helena hesitated, then gave in and said, "Then I will let you." Sighing, she closed her eyes for a moment as she gathered her strength and stood. Pressing a hand to her bulging belly and another to her back, she steadied herself and then waddled to her room. "You can be mistress of the house." She yawned again. "I'll be mistress of the pillow."

It was in this way that I became the third member of the family—in the servant's eyes, at least—taking on some of Helena's authority and command of the daily functions of the legate's household. As the days passed and time for Helena's delivery drew ever nearer, the servants—and sometimes even the legate himself—looked to me for advice or consent. Do believe me when I say it was never my intention to usurp Helena's place as domina. Her troubled pregnancy demanded all of her strength and attention, so increasingly it fell to me to make the small day-to-day decisions. Rather than disturb Helena, who had largely taken to her bed as the time of her delivery approached, I suppose it was easier just to ask *me* all the little things they were accustomed to asking her.

Nor did I mind the steady accretion of duties and care. My previous life as helpmate to my father in the magistrate's house—and even the modest skills I'd acquired in healing and cooking—stood me in good stead and my competence and assurance grew. For the first time in a very long time, I was content.

 **9**

AS THE DAYS DREW DOWN toward the birth in the legate's house, so too did the conflict between the rival factions increase in the streets outside: those vowing loyalty to Majorian were ever more staunch, while those favoring Valentinian grew ever more stubborn and unyielding.

Violence between the two camps sparked and flared. Assemblies were disrupted and gatherings dispersed by opposing gangs; opinions were more often expressed with fists, and fealty with sticks and clubs; rocks thrown, dung was hurled. People were getting hurt, and citizens were calling for an end to the conflict. Unfortunately for Aridius and his cohorts, Valentinian's faithful were beyond reason or persuasion, their support of the inconstant emperor unbending and—thanks to the roving gangs of hired ruffians—they were largely successful in shouting down any dissenting voice. Though Majorian had many friends in the eastern court at Constantinople, the reality was that we lived in the western half of the empire; Britannia was far removed from what increasingly seemed like another world altogether. Thus, Emperor Valentinian, for all his faults, was able to maintain his shaky grasp on power in the west. Steadily, inexorably, through fair means and foul, the emperor's laurel crown remained on Valentinian's head. The man himself was somehow able to hold himself above and apart from the excesses of his frenzied supporters.

"I don't understand it," complained Aridius wearily, not for the first time. "He *lies* to them and they clamor for more. His latest lie? He has promised to burn all barbarian settlements in Gaul and Britannia and drive the invaders into the sea by Easter Tide. Can you believe it? As if no one has ever thought of that before! As if our legions have not been fighting them along the Saecsen Shore for years!"

He rubbed his hands over his face and leaned back in his chair. "If *I* stood in the basilica and made such a claim, I would be stripped and whipped and run naked out of Deva by a baying mob. And they'd be right to do it!"

I motioned to one of the young female servants and whispered for her to bring the legate some wine and tell the others to help Nona prepare the table for the evening meal. "We will sit down as soon as the legate is ready."

"We cannot go on like this," he continued. "The proconsul is calling for a truce over the Christ Mass Tide to let tempers cool and restore the peace." Aridius shook his head. "But that won't be the end of it. I'm told Londinium in the south and some of the garrisons on the Wall have joined Valentinian's camp. From here, Riothamus goes to Viroconium to secure the blessing of Procurator Constantine and his people. That might help. But I'm even hearing rumors that the procurator himself will seek the High Kingship of Britain if Valentinian remains in power—and who could stop him?" Aridius made a sour face. "But listen to me, dragging all this into my home. How is Helena? I should go to her."

"She has slept most of the day, but she'll want to see you," I told him. "Go in to her and I will see to supper. We can all sit down together whenever you're ready."

Thanking me, he rose and moved off, giving my arm a light squeeze as he passed.

Our supper that night was a glum affair. Though Helena made an effort to lighten her husband's mood, she could not muster strength enough to succeed and tired quickly, pushing aside her bowl as soon as she had taken a few bites. "You must eat more," Aridius chided. "For the baby."

"Don't tell *me* about the baby!" she snapped. Helena shoved back from the table and rose laboriously to her feet, throwing aside her hand cloth. "Your baby lies in the lap of luxury. It is your wife who is suffering!"

Aridius, stricken, regarded her in alarm and put down his bowl.

Helena instantly regretted her angry outburst. "Forgive me, my love," she relented. "I am just so sick and tired of dragging around like a bloated brood mare. I cannot wait until this is over."

"It will be—and soon," Aridius reassured her. "Cornelia tells me it could be any day now."

Cornelia, the midwife, had been coming to the house daily for the last week or so to sit with Helena and perform her little duties. She had assured me of the same "any day now" for some time. No one doubted the truth of that assertion, but the vagueness that made it true also rendered it useless information. "Nature finds her own way, Aurelia," Cornelia had told me. "When it comes to birthing a child, she will not be hurried."

"But when?"

"It takes as long as it takes, dear," she replied. A robust elder woman with short gray hair, strong hands, and years of experience, Cornelia was inured to any anxiety or impatience behind such questions. "And that is how long it takes."

A few days later, was the Christ Mass. Aridius had invited several local worthies to a small, quiet celebration on the evening before. We would enjoy a modest feast and good wine and at midnight wend our way along to the church for the first of two special rites. Helena rallied and, I must say, looked radiant and lovely in a flowing blue robe, her hair freshly braided, coiled, and pinned with tiny gold pins. We enjoyed the candlelit meal and, at the church bell's chime, the household and guests dutifully flocked to an already overcrowded church where we stood in the crush at the back to observe the mass—which was mercifully short, for Helena was feeling slightly queasy.

A happy party, we departed the church and made our way through the dark streets by torchlight, warmed by the thought of angel hosts proclaiming the good news of Christ's birth and salvation for all. We had reached the iron gate outside the villa when the birth pangs began. Helena suddenly stopped in her tracks as the first of the spasms doubled her over. She grasped the ironwork of the gate and held on until the convulsion had passed. "Oh!" she gasped, taking hold of Aridius' arm for support. "That was sharp."

"Is it time to summon Cornelia?" he asked, concern creasing his brow.

"I think it would be best."

"I'll go at once," I offered.

"No," said Aridius. "I'll go. You stay and help Helena."

"Your place is with your wife," I countered. "I will go—"

"Listen to the two of you," chided Helena lightly. "Send Jason." She nodded to the young servant standing by. "He will go more quickly, and you both can stay here with me."

Aridius sent the servant away on his errand and hastened us inside. While the others hustled around making small arrangements, I helped Helena change into her birthing clothes—a loose-fitting, voluminous gown handed down from her own mother—and arranged the couch and bedding for her.

"I expect Cornelia will bring her birthing chair," she said. "I don't know if I should—" She did not finish her thought as another pang seized her. She clasped her bulging belly and stooped over as water spilled down her legs to pool on the floor at her feet. She looked up, aghast, then gave me a weak, embarrassed smile. "Oh! This child is impatient. I think I might just lie down a little before Cornelia gets here."

"Don't worry," I told her as I helped her onto the couch, "I'll see the birth water cleaned up." I went to fetch Tatiana and then fussed around doing little things to make Helena more comfortable—a cup of water, a damp cloth, some candles—unnecessary things perhaps, but it kept us both busy until the midwife arrived. When she did, she brought her daughter, Coeli, along with her—a young woman who had born two children of her own and knew her mother's ways. They worked well together and knew what to do without having to chatter about it. As Helena predicted, they had brought along a sort of low wooden chair, or stool, on which the birthing mother could squat to allow an easier passage of the infant. Fascinated as I was to see how this process might be effected, it would be some time before my curiosity could be satisfied: the child would not be born for another day and a half.

Despite the midwife's repeated assurances to both Helena and Aridius, each was wracked with worry, anxious that the birth was taking much too long. "That is sometimes the way of it," Cornelia explained gently. "When it is time to worry, I will let you know."

In the end, however, it was Cornelia and Coeli—women well acquainted with every mishap and danger and the myriad things that can go wrong in childbirth—who became most worried. I saw them head-to-head more than once through the night and next day, and though I could not hear what they were saying in their whispered tones, their drawn expressions told me their unease was mounting.

Helena endured her ordeal with a warrior's fortitude and valor, but in the end her strength began to wane. She had long since sweated through several changes of clothing and was keeping Nona busy washing and drying her gowns and coverings. Unable to keep away, I haunted the corridor and doorway throughout the day and as evening approached, I risked their disapproval and went in. I was shocked by what I saw: Helena, her flesh waxy, her hair wet and matted, her eyes sunken, staring wildly as the birth paroxysms seized her. I caught Coeli's attention and motioned for her to follow me from the room.

"This cannot be right," I said. "She looks terrible."

Coeli agreed.

"Can't you do something? I don't think she can take much more."

The young woman nodded gravely. "Mother and I have been discussing this very thing."

"And?"

"There is a herb we can try," she said, pursing her lips uncertainly. "We have refrained until now because it is very strong and is to be used only in the most extreme cases."

I did not hear Aridius coming up behind me, but he overheard us. "This is just such a case, is it not?" he said. He looked to me, saw my fraught expression, and said, "Do what you must."

The young woman nodded and retreated into the birthing chamber. She and her mother held a quick consultation and Coeli returned to say, "We will need some hot water to make a tincture. It won't take long. We'll give it to her right away." She glanced at the legate uncertainly. "I must warn you—"

"It is very strong. So you have said," he replied. He looked at his stricken wife moaning and restless in her bed. "I grant you permission and you have my full support—come what may."

Coeli mouthed her thanks and went back to relay the legate's consent to her mother, and I fetched hot water for the tincture. I cannot say for certain what was in that potion they gave her but, as the eastern sky began to lighten, Helena gave out a cry and a short time later the baby was born.

I had been slumped asleep in a chair outside the door of her chamber and woke when I heard Helena's half-defiant, half-agonized scream. I rushed into the room in time to see a slick head of black wet hair attached to a tiny red body shaking with the outrage of being so rudely pulled from the cozy warmth of his home and thrust into this cold, indifferent world. The little squished face clenched and the round mouth opened to emit a cry at once plaintive and a joy to all who heard it.

Cornelia saw me standing in the doorway and said, "Fetch Aridius. Tell him it's a boy."

10

THE FIRST FEW WEEKS of little Victor's life were nothing but peace, happiness, and bliss—at least for those of us inside the villa. Outside the walls, however, the storm clouds of intrigue and violence continued to build and boil, unleashing mighty waves that would sweep over our island realm.

When the tempest finally broke, the inundation caught many poor folk unawares, swamping some and stranding others. Even those who saw it coming were swept away in the flood of conflicting events. Alas, one of these was the Legate of Deva. As a prominent supporter of Majorian, the emperor's rival, his position was well known. Those stalwarts of Valentinian's faction had the audacity to call it *treason*, and claimed that any support shown a rival should be punished. Aridius, and all those who agreed with him were castigated for their dissent. As the cries for retribution grew louder, some of those so accused chose the discretion of retreat.

"I have it that Riothamus has removed himself from the fight," Aridius told me one evening on his return from a long day at the Civitas House. I had just left Helena in her chamber where she and the infant were dozing after a feeding.

"Removed himself?" I wondered, uncertain what he meant by that. "Why?"

"He is sickened by the slander and lies, sickened by Emperor Valentinian's low, dishonest tactics—and who can blame him?" He huffed, puffing out his cheeks in disgust. "Riothamus is returning to Gaul to protect his rank and authority while he still has any to protect."

"Is that the end of it?" I asked. "The confrontation is over?"

Aridius nodded sadly and I saw how tired he was, how much all this was weighing on him. "It is. Even if Majorian somehow gained the throne, he would have half the western legions against him. The best generals will tell you a commander cannot fight a war on two separate fronts."

I took this in as best I could. At the end of the day, the legate had taken to discussing his political affairs with whoever was willing to listen. Tonight it was my turn—though I admit it all seemed far from my immediate concern, or interest. Other matters pressed for more urgent concern; helping Helena regain her strength and looking after the infant were more important to me. Only insofar as it mattered to Aridius, it mattered to me. "What will you do now?" I asked.

Aridius replied, "Riothamus has asked me to come with him."

"To Gaul?"

"To Armorica, yes," Aridius corrected. "I would become commander of the garrison there. *Legatus Legionis*—that is the official title." His expression told me he was not enthusiastic for such a dramatic change.

"But...what?"

"But I cannot think of leaving Deva just now," he confessed. "This is our home. We have Victor to look after, and Helena needs time to heal. I am needed here—perhaps now more than ever."

With the turning of the year, however, it became increasingly clear that the decision whether to stay or go would be taken from him. Or, rather, the decision was reduced to terms that rendered the choice very easy to make: leave Deva, or be stripped of title, duties, and rank.

I cannot say I begin to understand all that lay behind this stark ultimatum—animosity? Revenge? Jealous ambition? I do not know, but I strongly suspect Valentinian devotees—with the help of power-hungry aristocrats—succeeded in maintaining enough support among the people to keep him on the throne.

Not that any of that would have mattered. Valentinian had the laurel crown in his grasp, and no one would pry it from his hand. Delegations were dispatched to Viroconium, Eboracum, Londinium, and elsewhere to solidify his support and strengthen his claim. After Aetius and Riothamus' departure, no meaningful challenge emerged. Valentinian would be Emperor of the West and that was that.

Meanwhile, Aridius' position as legate continued to deteriorate, his future growing ever more fraught and uncertain. The rancor released by that distant imperial contest was not to be believed—or understood. The same men Aridius had served among for years—men he knew and who knew him well, men he trusted—turned against him, shunned him, denounced him in the streets. It came down to this: certain loud voices, the big dogs of local power, wanted Aridius gone and did not greatly care where he went or what happened to him.

Thus, while the legate still had the use of his staff and aides in the Civitas House, he sent to Riothamus and accepted the offer to become the commander of the garrison in Armorica. The speed with which the reply came back astonished us every bit as much as the reading of it delighted. *"God be praised! My prayers for a good man beside me have been answered. Do come, please, in all haste. R."*

Aridius greeted this outcome with both relief and regret. "I will be sorry to leave Deva," he said, gazing on his wife and the infant at her breast. "It has been our home these many years. But we must make the best of what is given us in the time we have."

"There is nothing for us here anymore, my love." She cuddled the baby in her arms. "And now we must think about making the best future possible for our son."

Aridius leaned down and kissed his wife. "Thank you for that," he said. "It makes the leaving easier." With that decided, he was suddenly all business. "Now, then! There are a thousand things to do and the day is speeding forth." With that, he breezed from the room and was gone.

Once we were alone, Helena looked to me. "Will you come with us Aurelia?"

The question struck me oddly. Until that moment, I had not given it much thought one way or the other; that is, apart from a perhaps naive notion that I was naturally part of the household to be moved. It now occurred to me that this assumption was nothing but a fantasy of my own imagining. I blinked and hesitated; I didn't know what to say. I looked to Helena, who regarded me with what I took to be hopeful encouragement. "If you will have me...," I replied.

Helena exhaled sharply and I realized she had been holding her breath waiting for my decision. "Wonderful!" she sighed happily. "For I am certain I would be lost without you, Aurelia. You're my dearest friend and companion. More! You are the sister I never had."

Gratified beyond measure by this effusive reply, this outburst of affection, the swell of emotion tightened my throat and my eyes grew moist. I could not speak, so I embraced her instead and we clung to each other for a long moment—before the baby objected with a loud cry. "I'm not certain little Victor agrees," I said, cradling my hand to his head.

"No, he doesn't," agreed Helena, "and think I know why." Rising up, she called for a servant and Jason appeared in the doorway. "Fetch Aridius, tell him I want to speak to him at once."

The youth bit his lip. "Legate Aridius left the villa, lady."

"Then run after him—catch him! Tell him to come back." Jason stood uncertainly. Helena shooed him away. "Go!"

The moments passed, and we soon heard the rapid footsteps in the corridor and Aridius burst into the room—alarm sharpening his expression. "What! What is it? What has happened?"

"Calm yourself, dear husband. There is nothing to be troubled about. I merely wanted to catch you before you spoke to the *actuarius* to register our son's birth."

"Is that all?" Aridius sighed with relief. "Yes, yes, I mean to see him as soon as I can find the time—" His voice trailed off as he sensed a change in his wife. "Why? What is so important?"

Cradling her son to her breast, she looked down into his little pink face and said, "His name is to be *Aurelius*—the golden one—" She glanced at me and smiled. "—after his adopted aunt."

"Is that so?" Aridius glanced at me, then back at his wife with concern. "But I thought we agreed his name would be Victor."

Helena was already shaking her head. "No," she said. "From now on his name is Aurelius. You will see to it."

Aridius paused and then his furrowed brow smoothed as a wide grin broke across his face. "*Aurelius* . . . my little golden one." The legate held out a hand to me and clasped it tightly. "A fine and handsome name it is. Anyone can see it suits him better."

Helena gave my other hand a squeeze. "We are in your debt, dear sister. I honestly do not know how I would have fared without you these past months."

So, it has come to this, I thought, *another beginning*: a new life with a new name in a new home. The world was changing, it seemed, and we must change with it. Like travelers clinging to a runaway carriage, we must endure the ride or be left in the dust beside the road. Aridius was never one to be left behind, so the decision was easily made.

We would go. It was as simple as that. Oh, but in life, I've long since discovered, those same simple decisions are so very often the most life-changing as well.

BOOK FOUR

CONSTANTIA

THE PEACE OF AVALLACH'S ISLAND realm is all-pervading and, as always, I am loath to leave it. To leave the Fisher King's realm is to enter a world of turmoil and conflict, a world where peace finds little purchase. But, Pelleas has returned from his errand with news that the upheaval resulting from Fox Vortigern's overthrow is now effectively quelled. Word of the traitor Morcant's swift and certain removal from the field of claimants to the High Kingship has spread sufficiently and with such speed that none of his ilk among the northern lordship has been willing or able to mount a serious challenge to Aurelius' path to the throne. Lords Coledac and Gorlas might possess a portion of Morcant's ambition, but lack his wealth and might; also, they are at least canny enough to know when to retreat. Others, like King Dunaut, only ever had one solitary hope: ally with other more able lords, keep his head down, and emerge as the sole survivor of any ensuing battles. Such weakness of character, such cowardice. I pity the people who must live beneath his reign.

I might have found the will to call down a curse upon all their ignorant heads, but for the fact that, whatever else they may be, they are battlechiefs and we will need them strong and able to aid Aurelius in the war against Hengist and Horsa's Saecsen hordes—a war that cannot be held off much longer. As ever and always, there is much work to do, and I must be about it. Rallying stiff-necked kings to support someone they view as inferior to themselves is not the easiest chore I can think of, nor the most pleasant. The western lords and chieftains, to their credit, are somewhat easier to persuade. With men of Tewdrig's stamp on our side, others will surely follow—would that we had ten more like him.

But wrangling contrary kings is a task for another day. Now that I am here, short as my errand may be, I will savor the tranquility of this sacred land. I feel that peace as I go in search of my mother.

"Ah, there you are, Merlin," says Avallach when I meet him on the path leading down to the reed-fringed lake. "I've been looking for you. How long has it been since you caught a fish?"

Unprepared for this question, I laugh. Not for nothing is he called the Fisher King. "Too long," I tell him. "So long ago I cannot remember."

"Then come along," he invites. "We will do what we can to put that right."

"I was on my way to find my mother," I say. "Have you seen her?"

"She is at the abbey just now. She goes there most days. You'll likely find her there." He indicates the lake, blue beneath the cloud-dotted sky, a light breeze riffling the surface of the water. "It is a good day to be paddling about in a boat. Are you sure you won't join me?"

"I would like nothing better, believe me," I tell him. "We'll go fishing once again when all this throne chasing is over. That is a promise."

"And I will hold you to it, my son." He turns toward the little wooden dock where his boat is waiting. "The fish are calling," he says—and I hear again the voice from my childhood.

"Yes, Grandfather," I say and finish the thought, "you go and liberate a few of them."

With a smile and a wave, he hurries off and I watch as he climbs into the boat and pushes away from the dock. Then, I make my way to the abbey that sits on the other side of the lake beneath the rising tor. Always small as such places go, the abbey has nevertheless grown somewhat since its earliest years. Over time the church has been enlarged and a collection of tiny monk's cells have been added, along with a small, barnlike building to shelter the sick and injured who find their way there for healing. I make my way to the path leading up to what has become a compound to stand to observe the latest change: a square stone foundation has been laid and walls are being raised—another chapel? A house of healing? A scriptorium, perhaps?

I find her, as I expected, at the healing house as she emerges from tending a patient. We greet one another with a kiss and she hands me the bowl she was carrying—the remains of some broth-soaked bread she has been feeding to one of her charges. We talk a little about the building work at the abbey as we make our way to the cookhouse to return the bowl and spoon. Then she stops on the path and says, "Something is troubling you, son of mine. I can see it on your face. What is it?"

At first I think to offer a dismissive answer, but at the look of motherly concern in her eyes, I reply, "So much has changed since I was..." I falter on the hateful words. "Since my return from the hills, and so much to be done. I hardly know where to start, much less where or when that work will end—or how."

She smiles knowingly. "This is my boy—taking the whole world in his arms and wondering why his load is so heavy."

Her answer falls somewhat short of cheering me. "Not the *whole* world," I allow, "only this one island realm—and that is weighty enough."

"We are mortals, Merlin," she chides gently. "We tend to forget that this is not our work alone—we have a Heavenly helpmate standing ready to aid our labors. It is His work, too. Let him help."

She was right, I concede—how easily we forget this simple truth. I thank her for reminding me, and we continue to the church where we are greeted by the current incumbent. "Abbot Elfodd," Charis calls, "I want you to meet my son. This is Merlin."

Her introduction takes him by surprise. "Merlin? Myrddin Emrys?" he gasps. "I have heard about you since I was a barelegged brat in Brefi! Can it be?"

"None other," I assure him. "I hope that at least some of what you heard was true."

He thrusts out a hand to me and I take it. "Any of my misconceptions were cleared up by your mother long ago," he continues. "I hope we will have your company for a goodly while. There is much I would ask you."

At his words, I remember why I have come seeking Charis. "Ah, well, I cannot stay long—not as long as I would like, that is. A day or two, perhaps, nothing more. Duties elsewhere call me away."

"Well, you're here now," the abbot tells me. "Come, let me show you all that we are doing."

Elfodd is a true Briton through and through, and he shows it: dark brown hair and eyes in a well-shaped head atop a stout frame with sturdy limbs, neither slim nor fat, but made to thrive in fair weather or foul. I had met his like countless times before among blue hills and green valleys of the Cymry.

I find one of those sober, competent, joyful churchmen who give themselves happily to their work. And, as a gentle reprimand, I am chastened by his example and think, it was right to come to here, to bring Aurelia—if only to be reminded why I have taken on the role of kingmaker.

The day passes as Charis and I spend an enjoyable respite at the abbey, and return to the palace as the sun sinks low toward the western hills. I thank my mother for introducing me to Abbot Elfodd and, leaving her to go to see to preparations in the kitchen and cookhouse,

I go in search of the mother of the man I hope to see crowned the next High King of Britain.

I find Aurelia dozing in a chair drawn up to the low breastwork of the terrace atop a wall at the rear of the fortress. The day holds a little warmth yet, but I notice the robe across her lap. She does not hear my approach, so I have a moment to observe her. Of the illness she has attempted to conceal, I perceive a general fatigue in the slump of her shoulders, and there is a sort of fragility about her that is not due to age—despite appearances, she is not that old. I do not know the nature of her ailment but, surely, in this place if nowhere else, given rest and care, she can recover.

That is heartily to be hoped. After all, here is a woman who witnessed Aurelius' first breath and herself gave birth to Uther. There are things she can tell me that may well smooth the rough path before me. Her experience is a resource to be treasured, and it would well reward me to hear as much of it as she cares to tell.

At my approach, she turns her head and smiles and lifts a hand to smooth her hair—a womanly gesture as old as time.

"I'm sorry to disturb you," I say, "but, I—"

"You're not disturbing me. I was just thinking..."

"About?"

She looks down at her hands, clasped in her lap. "Well, if you must know, I was thinking how very tangled the road of life can be—all the different paths, and how a person can never know which one to choose, much less what waits beyond the next bend." She glances up at me and the light rekindles in her eyes. "Believe me when I tell you it is a hard thing to know if you've chosen well. A very hard thing."

"*Tangled* is a good word for it," I agree and perch myself on the low wall facing her. "You would know this as well as anyone, I would think."

"You couldn't guess the half of it!" She laughs. "To think that I was once the wife of a legate, the commander of a frontier garrison. A thousand soldiers would have leapt to fulfil my least request. Seven servants, two young boys, and a busy husband lived beneath my roof. My table served bishops, lords, and chieftains."

"You mentioned the garrison just now," I say. "Which garrison was that?"

"Don't you know? It was the Flavia Gallicana at Constantia in

Armorica—near the western coast," she replies. "It was home to the First Legion."

"I know of the place, but I have never been there. Tell me about it—about your life there."

Aurelia's glance becomes skeptical. "You really want to hear about all that?"

"It is of some interest to me." Indeed, I have long regretted the slow and steady migration of Britons to lands across the Narrow Sea to escape the barbarian predation, but I had never spoken to anyone with more intimate knowledge than the one who sat before me now. "And it may help me know your sons better."

She puffed out her cheeks. "Well, there is so much. I hardly know where to begin."

"Let's start with Aridius' decision to leave Deva," I suggested. "You said that it was following Valentinian's effort to secure his throne in the west that Aridius decided to follow—Riothamus, was it?—to follow the dux to Armorica and take up the position offered to him there." I regard this remarkable woman whose iron-clad spirit still shone bright and undimmed. "That must have been a difficult move for everyone."

"Difficult!" she scoffs. "You might well say that. From Deva in the north, all the way to Armorica—each so very different from the other—the problems we faced . . ." She shakes her head in disbelief. "I don't know how we survived."

I consider my mother, Charis, who survived and thrived in two very different worlds. "I can well imagine," I tell her.

"I think I was happiest in Deva—at least, as happy as I have ever been," she says, a hint of wistfulness in her tone. "I would have given anything to have stayed there." Aurelia shakes her head and her eyes seem to look through me and beyond to the memories taking shape in her mind. "But, like all forlorn hopes, that was not to be."

She looks at me and I see again something of the young woman who left the known comforts of Deva for the unknown trials of Constantia. "Those first days in Armorica were difficult, as you might guess. But there were some good times, too. Yes, there were." She smiles to remember, then quickly amends, "True, those times were few and far between—at least at the beginning when we were settling in. The garrison! It was enormous—over a thousand legionaries in those days, with upward of five hundred horses, and then all the aides and servants and officials of one sort or another, it was two thousand if not more. Finding my feet in a place so big was hard enough. And what with all the men and shouting and horses and everyone marching everywhere all the time, and forays and sorties and patrols coming and going, it did take some getting used to, I can tell you. But, God is good, and as the years passed and we grew accustomed to this new life, I came to appreciate the rightness of it. There is happiness of a sort in that, too, I think."

She nods at the memory, falling silent as she gazes into a past only she can see. The moment passes, she sighs, and continues. "Ah, but happiness always comes at a price, does it not? For me, that price was nothing less than the life of my dearest friend."

I hear in her gently quavering voice an ache that pains her still. "You haven't spoken of that before," I suggest lightly.

Her gaze grows a little misty. "I mostly avoid speaking of that time—"

"Helena's death must have been a terrible blow."

She nods sadly. "I suppose because the hurt was so great I could not bear it. I don't know how I carried on without her. She had been my sister, my soul mate, and more; she had been my heart's truest friend. And I was bereft—*more* than bereft. I was lost."

She looks to me for understanding, and I assure her I know such sorrow. My own loss drove me to insanity. How well I know the burden of grief.

"How did Helena die?" I ask.

Aurelia gives her head a simple shake. "I don't think I'll ever know. That is the way of it sometimes. The birth of Aurelius was difficult, as I say, but afterward she did recover something of her old vigor. She was thriving, the baby was hale. It seemed her health had returned."

"But it hadn't."

"No." Aurelia shakes her head gently. "You know how, as autumn fades, you might enjoy a last, bright blaze of summer just before the gales of winter arrive? Well, that was the way of it. Helena shined with health and fine spirits for a season, and then came the hard, cold winter. At first it was only the odd complaint—strange pains, headaches, cramps, tingling sensations in her arms and legs. Then nausea and dizziness. The garrison had an impressive young physician, a Gaul—Setonius, was his name—and he had an able assistant called Marius, and another called Linus.

"Medicines, potions, healing waters, prayers...they tried everything...absolutely everything. If there was an herb or unction of promise, we tried it."

"But nothing helped?"

"Nothing helped." Her voice falls on a note of defeat as Aurelia relives those dark, unhappy days. "Oh, Helena railed against her illness, fought it. She was so brave! But nothing helped." Aurelia shakes her head sadly. "It nearly killed me, too, just to see her diminished day by day, her ferocity, her strength, her spirit—ebbing slowly away.

"Eventually, Helena took to her bed. She began sleeping most of the day, and then, at the last, refused food—complained she had no appetite. I used to try to feed her. I'd sit with her, sometimes far into the night, wheedling, insisting, spooning broth into her mouth until she refused to even try. And just as often as not she vomited up anything she had managed to swallow. Then, we'd start all over again.

"Aridius, bless him, summoned the priests from the nearby church and arranged for prayers to be said throughout the day and night. There was someone with her every moment, and I stayed by her bed as much as I might—what with a house and infant to care for, it was always a struggle...I was always torn and the pieces scattered...."

She falls silent and, in a moment, I see her lips moving as she whispers, "The end drew near, as we all knew it would, when she would not wake at all—nor could we rouse her save for as long as it takes to drink a few sips of water." Aurelia lifts an imploring hand and lets it fall. "She lingered long in that state. Too long."

She lapses into silence again, her eyes closed, remembering. Then, with a little shake, she straightens, clears her throat, and continues. "One morning just as the sun was rising, I bundled up tiny Aurelius to bring to her, which I often did first thing of a morning. When I came into the sickroom—heavy with incense, as I recall—I was surprised to see Helena awake at last and listening to the priest as he prayed over her. She smiled when she saw me and I saw a glimmer of a spark in her eyes. I held out the baby to her.

"By then she was too weak to sit up or hold the child, but she lifted a hand to her son's head and placed it there, feeling the softness of his hair. She gazed long into that tiny face and then looked to me and whispered. I could not make out what she said, so I put my ear right up next to her mouth..."

Aurelia swallows hard, but forces herself to go on. "Helena whispered her last words to me: 'He is yours now, dear heart,' she told me in a voice as thin as spider thread. 'Take care of him and let him remember me.'"

Aurelia sniffs back a tear and shakes her head. "Then my friend, my best and truest friend, my sister closed her eyes. She was asleep again before I left the room.

"I ran at once to wake Aridius. Ari threw on a robe and flew to her side. He sat with Helena, holding her hand while she slept. I waited on a bench outside until Ari came into the courtyard a little while later and told me Helena was gone."

Aurelia bows her head and we share a silent reverie. After a moment, she continues, her voice stronger, "I was bereft. But poor Ari was devastated—any loving husband would be. He mourned Helena— yes, he did—but there was little Aurelius to think of and an entire garrison to command. I was the obvious one to care for the baby—and I did. Gladly. The little mite was pure joy, I tell you—but the *work!*

"There were times I swear I could have slept on my feet." She smiles lightly at the memory. "Ari threw himself into his command, and I threw myself into keeping the house and caring for little Aurelius. This, I think, proved a saving grace for both of us. Together we slowly moved on from Helena's sad, sad death. We three became a family then," she concludes. "Ari and I were married three years later."

"And then?" I ask.

I think she has not heard me, but she is gathering the memories of that time, reviving it all in her mind. Finally, she glances up at me and says, "And then? Well, all this time the tide of imperial unrest was rising around us until we feared we would be swept away. But, God be praised, the tide did what tides always do—it rose and receded, We outlasted Rome's relentless intrigues. Emperor Valentinian did hold the throne he fought so hard to keep—no surprise that—and, fortunately for Aridius, the province of Armorica suffered no further entanglement in political intrigues and schemes. I expect the emperor had more pressing concerns elsewhere. We heard constantly about clashes with the Goths and Huns and people I never heard of before— barbarians, all of them."

"Yet, it did not end there, did it," I say.

"No." She shakes her head. "It did not end there—not by a Roman mile. Small mercies—at least the legions of Armorica were left to their own devices. This, I think, is what preserved us. Ari considered it likely that the emperor, weak as he was, realized his rule would meet nothing but resistance from the likes of Riothamus and his commanders so was content to let this particular sleeping hound lie. Armorica kept its own counsel and was left alone for the most part. Oh, every now and then one commander or another would pull men from the western armies to help battle the barbarians tormenting the empire in the north and east. Thankfully, our garrison was never more involved than that. And life in Constantia enjoyed a few years stability and even peace. Aurelius grew strong and healthy, and Ari and I settled into a good marriage—not like Aridius and Helena had been, of course. Good in a different way. We had a fine life together, the three of us. But, like all good things, it didn't last long."

"Why? What happened next?"

"Uther was born!" she beams. "My little warrior was born, and my life changed yet again."

"I can well imagine."

"Oh! You have no idea," she laughs. "You should have seen them together—Aurelius and Uther, each as headstrong and boisterous as the other. There were never two like them for striking terror in the heart of a mother. Growing up in a frontier fortress—the things they found to get into you would not believe."

1

"UTHER!" I shouted from the doorway. "Stop chasing your brother with that knife!"

Always Uther, forever Uther! I stood there with my hands on my hips and my heart in my mouth as the little lad glanced back over his shoulder, laughed at my fraught expression, and continued the pursuit. Aurelius—older, faster, easily outdistanced his little brother—was never in any real danger. Even so, I did not think it prudent for a child of four summers to be wielding a dagger as long as his arm and running with it. So unruly, these two! *If either of them live to see ten summers it will be a marvel*, I thought, dashing out the door.

Joining the chase, I sent up a quick prayer for their protecting angels to be at the ready and the Good Lord to keep them safe in the palm of his hand—at least until I could get the knife away from Uther's tight little fist. That boy! Where he got the knife, I could only guess—but since our home lay within the protecting walls of Constantia, a large and active military garrison, my guesses did not have far to travel to find a home.

"A flame-haired firebrand" is what Centurion Vitus called Uther, and he was not wrong. Though three years younger than his brother, Uther was, ounce for ounce, as strong and thought himself just as clever and capable of doing everything Aurelius did. He was headstrong as a mule and quick as a ferret, and there was no stopping him. Even as a barefoot toddler, once he set his mind to a thing he could not be diverted.

Vitus, watching from the yard, thought the mad chase hilarious; he often took a mild view of such japes. After Helena's death, this Armorican soldier had adopted both boys as a sort of guardian angel and advocate. One of the younger of the garrison's centurions, he had already suffered the grief of losing his wife and daughter in childbirth, and this experience bound him to Aridius and Aridius' two young sons. But he had a special place in his heart for Uther. "A real little soldier," Vitus would say, and named him "the Littlest Legionary" although he knew it rankled my more tender maternal feelings to have either of my sons spoken of in this warlike way.

But what could I do? We were living in the center of a veritable military city, and the boys were surrounded by soldiers and all things soldierly every day: swords, shields, pikes, spears, armor, horses, and more: vexillum, and ballista, and galea, and buccina, and things I knew not what. But Aurelius and Uther knew. They knew all this and more because whatever they asked, Vitus would tell them. Those two followed him around like small shadows.

Indeed, in time I learned that if ever I wanted to find them, I only had to locate Vitus and the boys would not be far away. If he was not teaching them some new skill or maneuver, he was watching over their play and practice. The patience of the man was heroic! More than once through those early years—those difficult years—I had cause to bless the man and pray thanks to the Good Lord for Vitus and his tireless care. All the more so because, as one of the senior commanders of Legio Flavia Gallicana, he also had his daily duties to perform.

"You need to let them risk their necks from time to time, Aurelia," Vitus would tell me. "It's the making of them as men."

"If these horrid games go wrong they won't live long enough to *be* men!"

As they got older, the two young scamps would disappear in the morning, and I would not catch sight of any of them again until they came dragging back at sunset: hair matted with sweat, thirsty, covered in mud and muck from nape to sole, too tired to wash, too tired to eat. More than once they fell asleep over their bowls—spoon in hand, head on table—and had to be carried to bed. Everything they saw the soldiers doing, they did, imitating the moves and feints of training with their ashwood swords and hazel spears, and marshalling the sons and daughters of the garrison's soldiery into their own cohort of children.

My cardinal principle, the only rule I was able to enforce with any regularity, was that they must stay within the walls of the garrison, where everyone knew them. I also insisted that the sons of a legate should spend at least half as much time with their slates and stylus as they did with their sword and shield. I made sure they kept at it until they could read and write a passable letter. All the same, learning sums and writing Latin never captured their imaginations the way soldiering did. So far as Aurelius and Uther were concerned, time spent with Brother Theodorus—the priest who oversaw Bishop Gosselyn's school for the garrison's younger children—was merely time away from practice in the yard, where all their interests lay.

And it only got worse after they learned to ride.

That could not be prevented, even if I had tried. The garrison stables were full of some of the finest horses in Gaul and, thanks to the stable master, the legate's sons had full and ready access to a mount whenever they wished. When the boys were first learning to ride, Matteo, our Master of Horse, would steer them to the older, gentler, more indulgent of the animals in his keep—those too docile to fight, that were now more used to pull carts and wagons. Later, when they had grown sufficiently skilled and practised, the boys could take whichever horse they fancied and so, inevitably, chose the fastest, most high-spirited beasts in the garrison. So long as the animals were not required for official service, Matteo was happy to allow them to ride since it exercised the horses for him and he knew his commander approved. Aridius always looked on his sons' achievements with glowing fatherly pride. His encouragement was boundless as his love for them.

I did not begrudge the lads their father's affection and attention, nor did I yearn for more from my husband than I received. Aridius did love me, I know. That I was not his first love, I knew that, too. Helena would always have primacy in his heart. But because I also loved her, I never felt the slightest twinge of jealousy. If I wanted for myself the bond the two of them had once shared, I would never have agreed to marry Aridius. I knew that her place in his life was never his to give away.

Helena, at the last when she knew she was dying, did what she could to release him from his deep attachment. Even so, there would never be a complete release for Aridius; nor did I expect that there should be. I accepted what I was offered and that offer was genuine. I was content—more than content: I was happy. Even though I was pulled in every direction at once, run to blisters, and harried from dawn to dusk just keeping up with my two young warriors, I was ever mindful of the great, good Providence that made my life so rich. The Gifting Giver, as Tomos used to say, had bestowed on his servant all that she could bear and more! Often, I sat in the little oratory a stone's throw outside the garrison wall—eyes full of tears—overwhelmed by joy and gratitude for the life I had and the blessings showered upon me. I was happier than a deaf girl from Venta had any right to be, and well I knew it.

The first great test of that boundless Providence arrived when, one day, a trumpet sounded at the gates.

2

RIOTHAMUS HAD ARRIVED on one of his many circuits of the region. He came to Constantia at intervals for various reasons which usually amounted to conferring with the legate and replenishing his forever needy stock of men and supplies. This time, however, he wanted something more than extra grain or a few more soldiers.

It had been a fraught summer with many enemy incursions; barbarian encroachment along Armorica's far northeast border had got out of hand—too many raids, too many clashes. Our valiant dux was anxious to demonstrate that these skirmishes were not to be tolerated and that our long-established borders would be defended— by the full might of Armorica's armies if necessary. For this, Riothamus needed men, weapons, horses, and supplies from garrisons throughout the province. So, he came to his legate to ratify the request to unite the garrisons to march under his command to the border.

"By making a show of force," Aridius declared after a long day of discussions with the dux and the legion commanders, "there is a good chance we can not only recover land lost to the barbarians, but break their will for years to come. Armorica could enjoy the blessings of real peace."

I nodded. Who was I to disagree? I glanced at Riothamus, sitting with his cup in his hand, his features drawn, his eyes hooded and unreadable. What he thought about Aridius' explanation of his plan was impossible to tell. I had met Riothamus, of course, and he often visited our home when he came on his rounds. I always found him an imposing fellow: tall and spare, rawboned, as some would say: his hands were huge, and he had two deep-set blue eyes either side of a hawk nose—a Roman nose; he wore the common legionary's tonsure, giving him the look of a new-shorn sheep. Never did I doubt his courage; that had been proven often enough to pass beyond all doubt and on its way to becoming legend.

At the same time, I suspected I knew why Emperor Valentinian was wary of him and his principal patron, Aetius. Both men looked like what they were: commanders of the Roman Empire. Valentinian, on the other hand, appeared to many like a schemer and conniver—in other words, a politician. For all his faults, and they were many, God knows, the face Valentinian displayed to the world was that of a nobleman born to the purple and luxuriating in his power, while his rivals all too often seemed ill at ease in anything but the hardened leather breastplate of a soldier. This, I think, was Riothamus, Aetius, and their champion Majorian's chief failing—along with the fact that they were likely not duplicitous enough for the intrigues of the royal court.

That evening, Aridius and his esteemed guest were sitting in the half-light of a fading sunset, sipping spiced Gaulish wine and eating roasted almonds as they reviewed matters of state elsewhere, and the means that might be used to rally the commanders of neighboring provinces to join Armorica's cause. Clearly, the day's discussions had not proven as simple and forthright as either of them had expected. Feathers had been ruffled, I guess, and toes trod on. By dint of rank and force of reason, however, they had carried the day. Legio Gallicana would march with Riothamus at its head. That much I gathered from the snatches of conversation I could make out—typical military talk, and I was used to it. But then, I happened to catch something that *did* bring me up short.

"What was that?" I asked Aridius, taking the jar from Dyfrig, the servant in attendance, and pouring more wine into the cups. "Did I hear you say *you* would be riding with them?"

"I'm joining the troops, too," he said loud and clear—as if my deafness was the source of my concern.

"Joining the troops?" I could not believe what he was saying. To my knowledge, my husband had never engaged in so much as a street brawl in his entire life. He did not even own a sword. What *was* he thinking? "You mean to fight?"

My alarm brought Aridius up out of his chair. He thrust out his hands in a gesture of calm and conciliation. "No, no, not to fight," he said quickly. "Most assuredly *not* to fight. If all goes well there will be no battle. In any event, I'm merely going along to observe. As *Legatus Legionis*, it would be good for me to be seen personally accompanying the troops under the banner of my office as we travel to the other garrisons and settlements. My presence would let the kings and battlechiefs know that this action has my full confidence and sanction and will induce many of the lords and their men to join us as well. My authority will be recognized and respected." He said this with a pride that did not sit naturally with him.

I looked to Riothamus, who had suddenly discovered a new fascination for the bottom of his cup. "Is this true?" I demanded of him. "This is *your* idea?"

He glanced up gathering his courage to face an irate woman, and finally looked me in the eye. "It is that," he admitted. "I can think of no better way to embolden the border tribes than to have our legate riding with me at the head of our army. Rest assured, good lady, I will be at his side all the way. And if our campaign is successful, there will be no fighting." He looked to Aridius and added, "He will take no part in any battle."

"I'll be an observer," Aridius affirmed again. "Only that. Nothing more."

Later, after an awkward meal and an early end to Riothamus' visit, I went to the kitchen to speak to the servants of the next day's duties, after which I returned to the hall where I found Ari sitting in his chair—eyes downcast, his face half in shadow. I thought he might be asleep, but when he heard my footsteps, he looked up and gave me a weak smile.

"That man," he said, exhaling heavily. I knew well which man he meant. "He is tireless, but I am not. I am exhausted.

I gave my good husband a sympathetic smile and settled into the chair beside him. "Then why do you always allow him full rein?"

Aridius gave a hollow laugh. "Because he is right! He knows what is needed to keep our borders from being overrun—that, and the ability to do it."

I regarded Aridius in silence for a moment, trying to discern what it was that troubled him. "But you do not relish going on this—this operation with him. Is that it?"

He glanced up quickly. "No, no, I am not worried about that—at least not my part in it. Our dux is right about the need, and it is time I was seen riding with the army to demonstrate my support. And he is right that it may well help rally the support of the tribal lords. This campaign is to be a demonstration of power—to prove to the barbarians that we possess the weapons of war, and we haven't lost the will to fight."

"But then ... what is it that is bothering you?"

Aridius picked up his wine cup, looked in it to find it empty, and put it back on the table. "It is nothing to do with any of that." His tone grew darker. "It is the news he brought with him."

"News—is that what you said? What news is that?"

"News from the court of Valentinian."

"Oh, him." I sank into a chair. "What this time?"

"This General Felix, do you remember him? Felix has it in *his* head to try for a chance at the throne. Now, of all times! Valentinian has hardly been more popular after the finish of the Southern campaign. What can Felix possibly hope to gain? The hubris of the man! It's madness—!"

I settled in for what was certain to be a lengthy diatribe of men and their machinations. Ari needed this—someone safe to share his inner thoughts, who would not use his views against him. My role was not to challenge him, but to hear him out as he sought the better course. After he had ranted awhile, I broke in. "Why does this concern us?" I wondered.

"Oh!" exclaimed Aridius. He reached for the near-empty wine jar and dashed the remains into his cup, swallowed it down, and slammed the cup onto the board. "I'll tell you why! Because Felix, this would-be usurper, cannot possibly make a credible challenge without the western legions—Armorica's and those of Britannia as well."

I recalled a scrap of history my father had taught me about our great hero Macsen Wledig. "Is that not precisely how Macsen—I mean Magnus—achieved the throne all those years ago?"

"Yes," agreed Ari, "but Magnus Maximus was successful. This upstart Felix is bent on repeating Emperor Magnus' triumph. He will start by marshalling the legions of Gaul, and Armorica will be first among them. He is already pressing Riothamus to support him and, as legate to the legion here, *I* will be pulled into his blasted plans, too!"

"Would this Felix be a worse ruler than Valentinian?"

Ari looked once more into his empty cup, muttering, "Who can say?"

"But you backed Valentinian's rivals in the past," I point out. "Why not now?"

Frowning, Ari shook his head. "It's not the man I oppose so much as the timing of it all. We have our hands full trying to keep Saecsens at bay." Glancing up, he added in a more forceful tone. "Hear me, Aurelia, I have no appetite to further the imperial ambitions of Felix or anyone else until we have stability in the West."

"Can't you refuse?"

"I don't know," Aridius grunted. "That is what I am contemplating. But if I do, I'll have to find a way to refuse without giving cause for reprisals later on."

Covering Ari's hand with mine, I gave it a squeeze and said, "I'm sure you'll come to the right decision."

"If only it were that easy," he said. Aridius rubbed his hands over his face. "Have Dyfrig bring me some more wine," he said. "I want to sit up awhile and think this through."

"No," I said. "It has been a long day. You are tired, and you have had enough wine for one night. Come to bed and sleep. In the morning things will not appear so dark as they do now."

Grumbling, he rose reluctantly and pushed back his chair. I took his arm and gentled him along to his chamber where I left him to put on his nightclothes and lie down.

"Aren't you coming to bed?" he asked, pulling off his tunic.

"Soon," I told him, taking the tunic and folding it neatly. "Your day is ended, but I still have a few chores to finish before I sleep." I kissed him goodnight and went to ensure that the kitchen fire was banked, the larder secured, the servants had retired, and so on. Lastly, I made certain that the courtyard gate was closed and locked for the night—an old habit from my childhood in Venta. Silly, I know. I lived within the walls of a fortress surrounded by soldiers—one of the safest places in all Armorica. But it was not out of necessity that I performed my routine; it was, I suspect, more a way of keeping alive a past I still valued in a world changing so fast I sometimes had trouble finding a place to stand. That night, I went about my chores breathing a simple prayer: *Lord, save us from the infernal schemes of ambitious men!*

Well, despite my hopeful words about a good night's sleep, I was only partly right about the morning bringing wisdom and clarity. Dawn broke on a hopeful, sun-bright day, right enough, but brought with it a whole new disaster.

3

ARIDIUS LEFT THE HOUSE before I had risen and I did not see him through the morning, nor did I expect I would see him again until evening shadows crept across our courtyard. He often dashed away early on some chore or other and worked through the day—taking meals, or not—with the soldiers and commanders. More and more often, I noticed the boys behaving the same way. While they still lingered long enough of a morning to snatch a bit of something to break their fasts, they would run to what they called their "centurion school" as soon as they could find the shoes they had unlaced the night before.

This morning was no different. I caught sight of them fleeing through the courtyard and called after. Uther waved farewell with a rusk in his hand, and Aurelius shouted a greeting before both of them were out the gate and gone. Well, I went about my duties like any other day, reflecting from time to time about Dux Riothamus' visit and what it might portend—refusing to worry about any of the most obvious calamities that Aridius had suggested the night before. What I did not anticipate was only too soon revealed.

Around midday, Uther burst into the kitchen ravenous and thirsty. I was taking a bowl of apples to the board in case someone appeared wanting something to eat, and collided with him, spilling apples to the floor.

"How many times must I tell you this house is not a stable!" I scolded. "You're too old and too big to be charging around like a bull in a barn! You'll break something next time—maybe your neck."

He mumbled an insincere "sorry" and kept going.

"What is so urgent?" I called after him.

Aurelius appeared just then, following at a slightly more prudent pace. "We need to eat something now," he announced, pausing long enough to give me a fleeting hug.

Something about the way he said it made me question the need. "Or what?" I asked.

"Or they'll leave without us," he replied, disappearing once more.

"Who?" I shouted. No reply.

Handing the bowl to Beatrix, one of my young servants, and leaving her to pick up the apples, I hurried to the cookhouse where Aurelius and Uther were standing over cook's worktable spooning tonight's lamb stew into bowls while cook clucked around them, scolding like a mother hen whose nest has been invaded by foxes. Clearly, both boys were overly excited about something; their faces were glowing with it and they were talking so fast I could not make out what they said.

"Now, then," I declared, stepping to the table to confront them. "What is all this rush and fuss? Who is leaving?"

"Riothamus is marching out and half the garrison legion is going with him." Uther informed me, wiping his mouth on the sleeve of his tunic.

"Yes, your father told me last night," I said, dread waking and slowly raising its fearful head. "And don't *do* that! You'll stain your sleeves."

"That's not all," said Aurelius. "Father is riding with him, too!"

"And *we're* going with them!" crowed Uther, unable to contain himself.

"Da said we could go if we were ready by the time the trumpet sounded the midday call," Aurelius told me.

Speechless, I stared from one to the other of them. Their exuberance filled the room. They were aflame with it. Only the most forceful blow could extinguish that level of exhilaration. They would be disappointed, yes, utterly so. Yet, they would be alive to feel disappointed.

Well, I could not allow this to happen. There was only one way to stop it. Turning on my heel, I left the room, saying, "Slow down—you'll choke yourselves. And don't go anywhere before I get back."

Leaving the villa on the run, I flew directly to the stable yard where

I knew I would find my husband preparing his mount for the journey. "A question, my love," I said in my sweetest tone.

He glanced around from straightening the saddle cloth, saw me, and smiled. "Yes?" he said. "What question is that?"

"Have you lost your mind?"

His hands paused in midmotion. "I don't understand."

"You told the boys they could go on this...this *campaign* with you?" I said. "Is that so?"

Suddenly contrite, he nodded. "I said that, yes."

"What under God's bluest heaven are you thinking?"

"It is the dux's idea," he hedged, "and I agreed."

"Two fools in agreement does not make the judgement any wiser. It is impossible!" I shouted. "Impossible! You must know that."

One of the grooms approached, carrying a warrior's heavy saddle; one look at my expression and he turned around and scurried back into the tack room. The legate adopted his best negotiating demeanor. "I can see you're worried," he said, the very voice of calm and reason. "But, I can assure you there is nothing to worry about."

"I *am* worried, dearest heart of my heart, because there is a very great multitude of things to worry about. They are *children*! They have no place on the battlefield or anywhere near it! They can only bring harm to themselves and anyone who must watch over them."

"*I'll* watch over them," Aridius said. "They will stay with me the whole time and we will be observers only. Remember? The aim is to negotiate peace, and if all goes well there will not be any fighting."

"It doesn't matter," I declared, unconvinced. "I'll not allow it."

"Listen, my love." Aridius stepped close and gripped my upper arms. "You're upset, I know. And I admit I should have consulted you before I promised the boys. But what is done is done, and Riothamus has given me his word that no harm will come to any of us."

"Fine and good for Riothamus," I snapped. "It is not *his* safety I'm worried about!"

"You call them boys, but they are young men now," declared Aridius, losing patience at last.

"They are nine and twelve summers only!"

"Be that as it may, it is time they began seeing the land they will one day inherit—and learn the cost of keeping it. I have given my word. They are going with me, and that is the end of it."

I stared at him with cold fury. "No. They are not going."

"I note your opposition," intoned Aridius, as if calming an indignant citizen. He summoned the groom who was waiting in the doorway of the stable and resumed saddling his mount. I watched for a moment, then retreated leaving a doomful silence behind me. On my way back to the villa, I met Centurion Vitus entering with three mounts in tow. He took notice of my grimly furious expression and guessed its source. "I will look after them," he told me. "On my life, I swear it."

"You had better look after them," I muttered, "because if they come back with so much as a scratch, my friend, what is left of your life won't be worth living. I'll make sure of it."

Aurelius and Uther were still in the cookhouse, sopping up the last of the stew in their bowls with chunks of bread. "Well, I've spoken to your father," I said. Both of them looked up with expectation, their mouths too full to speak. "He is determined that you should ride with the legion—"

"Yes!" cried Uther.

"—as *observers* only," I continued, trying to keep my tone level. "Do you understand? You will *not* take part in any operations whatsoever, and you *will* remain within sight of your father and Vitus at all times."

Uther threw down his bread sop, shouted his thanks, and rushed from the room; Aurelius likewise, pausing only long enough to give me a quick hug.

You never saw two happier boys as they rode from the garrison beside their father at the head of the troops. To see them, anyone would think they were emperors out to conquer the world. I stood with some of the other soldiers' women beside the road just outside the gates and watched as row upon row marched along beneath the legion banner and standard with trumpets sounding and drums beating out the cadence. Some soldiers waved farewell to their wives and children as they passed; others gazed resolutely ahead. *They are going and that is the end of it,* Aridius had said.

Well, they went, but that was not the end of it.

4

ARIDIUS AND THE TROOPS were to be gone eight or ten days, roughly half that time spent travelling to the northeastern frontier and the troubled borderlands. I tried telling myself that at least the boys would learn something of how an army moves and how tedious and exhausting travel could be. I also tried telling myself that perhaps Aridius was right after all—that Aurelius and Uther did need to learn something of the land and the people they lived amongst and would, perhaps, one day lead. I tried telling myself that they would return crowing with triumph, expecting the hero's welcome as if they had conquered the entire eastern empire. I assured myself that I was not much older than Aurelius when I made the hard journey from Vente to Deva—and I succeeded without an entire legion at my back.

In truth, I tried telling myself no end of things to ease the tight knot of fear in my gut. Some of the things I conjured to help calm my troubled mind and spirit did help—but never for long. At night, when alone in my chamber, my imaginings turned lurid and terrible, and shadows of gloom lingered long after sunrise. I grew more fearful with every day that passed. On the eighth day—the first that could have seen the legion's return—I yearned to run to the front gate in order to get the first glimpse of the long column approaching on the road. Dreading the inevitable disappointment, I forced myself to stay away. The dull sun heaved its weary way across the heavens, eventually giving way to a cheerless evening. Even so, against all odds, I rose from my rest filled with the certainty that my boys would return soon.

The ninth day passed without sign or word.

Likewise, the tenth day. On the eleventh day I made so many trips to the gate that I lost count. The twelfth day I spent in and out of the little chapel with a worried Theodorus looking over me trying, with little success, to soothe me with words of comfort and hope and admonitions to take courage.

Finally, sixteen days after the troops set out, the sound of the marching drums came floating over the wall. As it happened, I was already on my way to the gate for yet another futile look down the road—otherwise, I'm sure I would not have heard it: a distant, rhythmic rumble and the blaring notes of the buccina sounding in even, measured blasts. By the time I reached the gatehouse, the doors were being opened to receive the weary travelers. Already, the column was closer than I guessed. The first ranks had almost reached the wall: dusty, tired, care-worn, and few weary smiles among them.

They were led by one of the younger centurions. Neither Riothamus nor Aridius were anywhere to be seen. And if I had imagined Aurelius and Uther would be first to burst through the gate—galloping and whooping as they came—then I was cruelly disappointed. I cannot adequately describe what I felt as I watched and waited to see my men amongst those who made their way, row on row, through the gates of the garrison. I gazed at each face as it passed before me, my soul writhing with worry. *Great God, where are they? Where are my boys?*

Other women and children joined me to watch the parade. Some of these voiced shouts of welcome to their menfolk and received smiles and nods of greeting in return. But there were no such greetings for me. I searched among the mounted soldiers and those on foot, and finally caught sight of Vitus—stumping along heavily like all the rest.

"Vitus!" I shouted, shoving nearer. "Over here!"

He left the ranks to join me and reached out a gloved hand; I took it and squeezed it tight. "Aurelius and Uther—where are they? What's happened?"

"The legate is close behind," he told me. "He will tell you."

"Not so!" I hissed. "*You* tell me! Now!"

He shook his head, unwilling to be drawn, and I saw pity in his eyes. "Aridius is soon here. Talk to him. I'm sorry." He pulled his hand away and strode on. It was then I saw that he wore a stained bandage on his upper left arm.

I could in nowise stand by and wait for Aridius to come to me. I started to run down the length of the parade—past the foot soldiers and then the supply wagons, until finally I saw my husband. "Aridius!" I shouted. "Here!"

He rode from the line, pulled up, and threw himself from the saddle. An instant later, I was in his arms and he buried his face in my neck. I held him and he clasped his arms around me so tightly I could hardly breathe. His shoulders began to shake, and I felt the neck of my mantle grow damp as the tears flowed from him. "I'm so sorry. I'm so sorry," he moaned over and over.

I pulled away from his embrace and stared at my husband, this father, this legate and leader of men. He stank of smoke and horses, and looked as if he had not eaten in days. The damp eyes peering back at me were black coals in his ashen face. He opened his mouth to speak but no words came out.

"Aridius!" God help me, I slapped him. "Where are the boys? Tell me!"

"I . . . I don't know," he stammered. Unable to face my fury, he looked down at the dust in defeat. "They were taken."

"Taken!" I gasped, unable to comprehend what he was saying. "What do you mean—*taken*?"

"At the camp when we were at negotiations," he said. "Barbarians took them—they took our boys. Aurelius and Uther were captured."

It was as if my heart had been carved, whole and beating from my chest. How I survived the crushing weight of those words I cannot now recall. I must have screamed. I must have shouted and ranted and cursed my poor broken husband—all that seems likely. After all, I knew only too well what it was to be 'taken,' and I knew what my boys would be feeling. But the only thing I remember is the numb, hollow feeling that dominated every waking moment. Brother Theo, with his gentle presence, stood by, willingly doing any practical task and constantly praying for the safe return of my boys. That dear, humble man was a rock of strength in a raging sea of bitterness, reproach, and regret. But when I heard him assuring Aridius that "all things remain in the Good Lord's hands, who never ceases bending all ends to his wise and loving purpose," I could not listen. Those words meant nothing to me. I turned away.

The story finally emerged little by little, piecemeal. From the collected fragments, the story as I understood it came to this:

One day when Aridius was at the parlay with the commanders and the Saecsen kings and overlords, Vitus was called away to bring some needed item or something and the boys were left in the care of one of the camp guards. The boys had slipped their overseer and wandered off and by the time Vitus and Aridius returned, they could not be found.

The camp was quickly scoured from top to bottom, to no avail. The area around the camp was searched—including the stream where they might have gone to play. There, signs of horses' hooves and boot prints were found—and a wooden sword on the ground: Aurelius and Uther had been taken.

This information set in motion a chain of events: Aridius informed Riothamus who challenged the Saecsens who denied any knowledge of the abduction. The parlay was over. Riothamus ordered up troops and, rather than face a superior force, the Saecsens decamped and fled to safety deep behind their borders. Meanwhile, Aridius and Vitus organized a party to enlarge the search for the boys—a dozen mounted soldiers—and off they went.

The search continued for ten days and by then it became clear that the legion must return to the garrison. "We came back to get fresh horses and provisions," Aridius explained. "We ride out again as soon as we are ready. This time we will take more men. We will not stop searching until my sons are found."

"But who is searching now?" I demanded. "You said you would not stop, but here you are!"

"One of the local chieftains—King Budic. He and his men have taken over the search. They know the region better than anyone else. They will keep searching—*we* will not give up searching until we find them." He promised.

I had no reply to this.

Ari reached out in a gesture meant to reassure. "On my life, Aurelia, they will be found."

5

THE ENTIRE GARRISON was marshalled—some to aid Riothamus and his border force, and others to ride with Aridius and Vitus to further the search. It took most of the day for all the men, equipment, horses, and supplies to be assembled. While all this was taking place, Aridius would snatch a night's rest before he and Vitus led out the troops the following morning, leaving behind a small contingent to guard the garrison.

If my husband's place was leading the search party, then my place was by his side. Brother Theodorus tried to talk me out of it when I went to light a prayer candle in the church, but I was determined. So, he said he would keep vigil until the boys were found. I arranged for a horse to be readied and then went back to the villa to gather a few things. At one point I must have dozed a little because I awoke with a start having heard the distant call of a trumpet. I thought I must have imagined it, or dreamed it. I waited, holding my breath, and the blaring call sounded again.

I jumped up and ran from the villa, hurrying along the shadowed streets to the garrison's main gate. A westering sun lit the tinted sky with a brilliant ruddy hue. I arrived just as the gates were swinging open, I pushed past the gate guards standing in the road. I heard someone shout behind me, but I did not hear what they said, nor did I care. For I had already glimpsed all I needed to see: a small clutch of riders on dark horses, trotting toward the fortress. Though their faces were still too far away to make out clearly, there were two I would have known anywhere. My sons had returned.

I ran down the road to meet them, calling their names, "Aurelius! Uther!" They saw me and put speed to their mounts. A moment or two later, I was caught up in Uther's strong embrace. He was filthy and smelled of stale sweat, grime, and horse dung, but he was grinning, overjoyed to be home...and he was unharmed. Then Aurelius was beside me, his arms around the both of us—each talking over the other so that I could not understand a word they said. That could not have mattered less. They were home and safe, and that was all the world to me in that moment.

And then I was aware that another had joined us. Like me, Aridius had come running at the buccina's summons; he must also have harbored the secret hope that the trumpet declared their return. Here they were! Aridius, dressed in riding gear ready to depart, greeted his sons with kisses to match my own, and they endured this effusive show of affection with good grace without making too much complaint against it. The boys were old enough to know what their absence meant to us—as well as its implications for the garrison—so allowed themselves to be pawed and pummeled by one and another of the commanders and soldiers who turned out to greet their return with the enthusiasm of men whose lives had just become a little easier.

Even as we stood in the road outside the gate hailing our lost sons' return, I became aware of the other riders in the little party—foremost among them a young, dark-haired man sitting on a pale horse, watching the proceedings with a smile on his broad, open face. He looked to be a lord, or at least a warrior of some status, for he was arrayed as a British prince with a striped cloak over his shoulder pinned by a silver brooch, a long sword at his side, and an elongated wooden shield; a silver torc gleamed at his neck.

I regarded him and nudged Aridius who took one glance at him and shouted, "Prince Hoel!" The legate left our group and ran to meet this newcomer—a stranger to me, though others seemed to know him.

I watched as Aridius and the chieftain embraced each other and, as they spoke together, I pulled Uther aside and asked, "Who is that? Did he come with you?"

"That is King Budic's son. He brought us here."

Aurelius, standing nearby, overheard us and added, "The king and his men took part in the search and they were the ones who found us. Budic sent the prince with us to make sure we got home safe." He looked up at the young man with an expression of admiration and added, "Hoel is a champion warrior."

"Then I think we owe your friend Hoel and his father a great debt of gratitude," I concluded. To Aurelius, I said, "Go and invite him to our home for a feast to celebrate your safe return." He glanced at me, smiled, and I pushed him forward. "Go on. Make certain he accepts."

The homecoming of the captives would be all the talk of the next few days, to be sure; and the tale of how the dauntless boys had gained their freedom would be told and retold. Word spread like wind-whipped fire throughout the province and soon there was not a hamlet or holding that had not heard about the daring escape of Aurelius and Uther, the legate's valiant sons. Their fame was ensured and, I strongly suspect, their fate as well.

Bathed, their hair combed and dressed, and wearing clothes that did not stink of the pigsty, our wayward sons greeted a host of friends and well-wishers in the courtyard the next day. The sun was well down and after a hectic day's preparation our overjoyed cook and servants had assembled a passable feast. Aridius, in his official robes, addressed the guests with a fine speech in honor of the returned prodigals—paying special tribute to Prince Hoel and his men. Then all trooped into the villa's large reception hall—the one used mainly for grand occasions or to host visiting dignitaries of one kind or another—among boards spread with the finest fare that could be secured at a morning's notice: from toasted almonds and meatballs wrapped in vine leaves to a whole roast pig stuffed with apples. There were brined olives, and parsnips and carrots boiled and served in olive oil, and chickpeas with cheese. One platter held a brace of braised partridges, and rabbits roasted and stuffed with prunes. For fish there was mackerel—grilled, or boiled and swimming in a wine sauce, and herring strips pickled with sliced onions. One of the boards offered a haunch of roast venison and one of beef—sliced and arrayed on platters. There were dried dates and figs—from some southern province or other—as well as sweet pastry made of flour, honey, and ground walnuts; peaches halved and lightly boiled, and served in sweet cream. There was wine, of course, the best we could find, in jars scattered about, as well as beer and mead.

The great room was lit with a multitude of candles and rush lights on stands along the walls and torches in sconces. There was not room, or chairs enough, to seat our guests so everyone helped themselves from the platters and tureens, filling their bowls and cups as they pleased with servants standing by to assist, filling the cups and replenishing the platters.

In attendance were several garrison officials, one or two who had taken part in the failed peace talks, and three clerics from the church with Brother Theodorus. Among those of special honor at the legate's table was Prince Hoel, son of King Budic—an affable, well-made lad of sunny demeanor and, I soon discovered, already the master of the assured and easy authority of a true leader. Although I expect he had heard the story once or twice already, he smiled and nodded with genuine interest as the story was related over and again among the guests at the hall, and between the boys who stood with Ari and me and some others to describe what had happened.

"It was all Uther's idea," Aurelius said, slapping his brother on the back. "We wouldn't be here now if not for his sly ways."

"It wasn't only me," Uther countered, pushing back a little from his brother's praise. "It was Auri who deceived them." He grinned in admiration, adding, "Even *I* thought he was dying!"

"Oh, but *I* never would have thought of it," Aurelius continued with the tale. "It was all down to Uther and his quick thinking."

"Will no one say what happened?" exclaimed Aridius. "Tell us!"

"Yes!" I cried. "Before all the food is gone. And do start at the beginning."

Aurelius wet his tongue with a sip of watered wine and took up the tale. "Well, Uther and I were back at the camp with some of the soldiers—all of us waiting for all the talking to finish—"

"There was so *much* talking—" huffed Uther. "Three days! It went on forever..."

"We wearied of sitting on our rumps, so Uther and I decided to go practice with our swords—"

"Da made us stay in camp all day," complained Uther. "There was nothing for us to *do*."

"I warned you it would be that way," objected Aridius, raising a defense. "I told you both before we left—"

I stamped my foot and cried, "Will everyone just *stop*!" I looked to each of them in turn. "You know I cannot understand you when you all talk at once." There were murmurs of apology. I flicked a threatening glance to Uther and Aridius, then looked to Aurelius and urged him, "Go on."

Aurelius began again. "We were tired of waiting in camp. Vitus was with us but got called away—up to the talks or something. Anyway, we couldn't find him. There was a stream near the camp so Utha and me went down with our swords to practice. And that is where the Saecsens found us. We didn't hear them come up. They just suddenly burst out from the bushes and fell upon us. This big hairy one— Cynric, I think his name was, seized our weapons—"

"They tied us up!" exclaimed Uther, excitement lighting his face. "They used horsehide rope." He thrust out his hands as if red rings would still be visible around his wrists. "Then they put us on horses and we were taken away."

"North, I think," continued Aurelius. "We were taken north to somewhere across the border to this old villa. It was mostly ruins, but there were people living there. It was made into a kind of stronghold behind a timber wall and there were all these little hovels and houses and cattle pens. The place stank to heaven."

"Stink! It was worse than that!" cried Uther, laughing. "Cynric put us in a pig shed—with the *pigs*! We were there two days. That first night we got some stew in a bowl and a jar of water, so we didn't get too hungry. We tried to talk to the woman who brought it, but it was no good. She couldn't understand a word of Briton, or Latin, either."

"The next day," resumed Aurelius, "it was the same. Cynric sent one of his men to look on us. He said something we couldn't understand, and we asked for water, making a drinking motion with our hands. A little while later the same woman came with food and a fresh jar.

"And we're all the time wondering *what are they going to do with us?*" said Uther.

"Probably they had plans to ransom us," Aurelius continued. "Anyway, Uther said that no one knows where we are. We've got to break out of here. So, we started making plans."

"We talked it through most all night," Uther said, taking over the telling. "By morning, we were ready. We waited all day, but then we heard people stirring outside the pig hut, and I gave Aurelius the nod." He nodded, and pointed at his brother. "And Auri starts in moaning and groaning. I watch the yard through a crack in the wattle and signaled for him to get louder every time someone came near. It wasn't long before one of them heard us and went to fetch someone. That same woman—Cynric's wife, maybe—came again and looked in—and here was Auri rolling around in the dirt, doubled up, clutching his gut, and moaning and groaning like he'd swallowed a snake."

Aurelius pointed back at his brother. "And Utha starts in shouting that I'm sick and to run fetch help." Aurelius laughs, and I notice how easily he has made a glad memory of his still-fresh misfortune. "This woman takes one look at me and hies back to the hall and all of a sudden Cynric comes running to see what is the matter."

"Oh, Auri put on like he was dying," said Uther. "I keep shouting, 'Help! Help!' And Cynric is looking so worried. He doesn't know what to do. Off he runs and comes back with another woman, an old one with a wrinkled face—one of their healers, I think. She looks at Auri and I make a motion like eating and then point to him rolling around in all that pig shit and rolling his eyes. I do this a few times before she finally understands. She takes over then and the first thing she does is order Cynric to take Auri out of the pig hut and carry him to her house."

"She lived in this little hovel of mud and sticks outside the villa," said Aurelius, "but it was clean and smelled of lavender. So, a couple of Saecsens pick me up and carry me out to the yard and clean me up as best they can. Then they take me and lay me in her house and she starts in making potions and such, and talking to me all the while, but I don't understand a single word she's saying."

"But I'm left alone the pig hut," grumped Uther. "That wasn't part of our plan, but there's nothing I can do about it. Now I'm all alone and wishing I was the one to get carried out."

Aurelius nodded, and resumed his side of the story. "The healer woman gave me a potion that tasted like rotten eggs and it made me throw up. My God—but it was devilish stuff." Shaking his head, he glanced at the priest, and said, "I'm sorry, Brother, but that is the truth. Then the old healer burned some dry leaves and bark, and waved the smoke over me. Then she told me to rest. 'Þu slæpeþ,' she says. So I pretend to doze off. She sits awhile and watches me and when she thinks I'm asleep, off she goes to the king's hall to give him a report maybe, I don't know—anyway, I'm left alone."

"By now its getting dark," said Uther. "And I'm almost asleep myself, but I hear a hiss outside and the door cracks open and there's Auri saying, 'Wake up! We've got to fly!' So off we go."

"We don't know where we're going, but we start down the road, and—" Aurelius stopped and turned a knowing smile on Uther, and said, "And here is where Utha shows his cunning. We only just get beyond sight of the holding and Utha stops in the middle of the road and says, 'We can't go this way. They'll find us sure and certain. We've got to go there.' And he points to this field. 'That's the wrong direction!' I tell him. And Utha says, 'That's why they won't look there first. We'll circle around and then head south.' So, we get ourselves across a barley field and into the woods as fast as we can go—not easy in the dark, but we did it!" he crowed. "We're free!"

"We weren't free *yet*," amended Uther, shaking his head. "Not until we could get help or horses and somehow find our way back. I only hoped we could get as far as we could before they discovered we'd escaped and came after us."

"We ran so hard," said Aurelius, taking up the tale again. "And all the time we're listening for them. We made a wide circle around and then headed off south and west. We came to a stream and walked down it a fair way before climbing out and running on. Well, this goes on until at last we can't run any more, and we stopped to rest..."

"We were laying there, panting like spent hounds," said Uther, "and by then it was getting near dawn and we were tired. So, we hide in a ditch and go to sleep."

"I slept first," said Aurelius, "while Utha kept watch."

Uther laughed. "But I fell asleep, too, after a while."

"When we woke up again, it was near midday. So, we waited until the sun started going down and then moved on. We were so hungry, but we can't find anything so we just keep walking, hoping to get somewhere safe. We didn't stop again until morning. We rested again through the day—except for trying to find some berries and water. By then we were both starving, so when we came upon a track, we decided to risk it. We'd been staying off the road and trails up to then. We hadn't gone far when we heard someone coming through the wood. We left the track and hunkered down behind the biggest tree we could find and prayed they wouldn't see us..."

"We held our breath and hoped for the best..."

Here both boys turned to Hoel, who stood looking on with arms folded, beaming.

"That was where Hoel and his men found us," said Aurelius.

Aridius, standing next to the prince, turned and gripped the young man's shoulder. I could see my husband struggling to contain his feelings in that moment, as I was struggling myself.

"God be praised!" cried Theodorus, raising his hands.

"Budic took part in the talks," Aridius explained. "He and his men rode out when we learned that the boys were gone."

"My father dispatched some of his warriors to the border to keep watch and take account of any movement," Hoel said. "I led some men to search to the north. We found them on the road, just as Aurelius said." He offered a modest shrug. "The escape was all their own doing, we just found them and brought them back.

"And for that we are grateful," said Aridius. Raising his wine cup, he called, "Please, everyone, we drink to Hoel and King Budic, with hearty thanks for their loyalty and service."

"A blessing on you and on your father's house!" added one of the garrison officials, slightly in his cups.

"A blessing!" we echoed as we all lifted our cups to a slightly embarrassed young man. He accepted our tribute with good grace as we drank and then Hoel rose and lifted *his* cup. "Let us also drink to friendship among all Britons, and peace among the peoples."

And so we did.

The meal resumed and there was more talk and wine followed by more food and sweet things. Night was drawing on by the time we quit the hall, made our farewells, and went our separate ways. In bed, I lay a long time thinking about all that had happened and how very resourceful and brave my boys had been. What danger might have befallen them did not bear thinking about. Even so, I went to my sleep with the thought that perhaps what had happened had turned out for the best.

After all, my boys had learned a valuable lesson in courage and self-reliance. God knows, they would have need of both in years to come.

6

ARIDIUS, LIKE ME, was more than relieved and grateful that his sons were safe. Most of the soldiers had returned to barracks and the rest followed a few days later, having engaged in a few skirmishes while helping Riothamus in his efforts to secure the provincial borders of the north and east. Despite the dux's best efforts, the threat was, as always, still very much with us. So, the legate's attention was drawn once more to the administration of a busy garrison.

For my part, I mulled over the abduction, what it meant, and what must come next for my sons. Out of my ferment an idea gradually formed which seemed both undeniable and necessary.

I proposed my plan to Aridius as we dressed for bed one night. He heard me out, but was not wholly convinced. "Dear heart, you are making more of this than is necessary. I made a grave mistake and I own it, but thanks to the Good Lord, no harm was done. For that I am more than grateful, believe me."

"I do believe you," I told him. "Of course, I do. All the more reason that we should do more than walk around with smiles on our faces, patting ourselves on the back."

"Is that what we're doing?" he said. "Not at all. But, see here, it is clear that the boys are more than ready to begin training in earnest. Moreover, they are—"

"No." I stiffened my back against his forthcoming argument. "You and your soldiers have had them on your practice fields long enough. Now it is *my* turn. And I mean to show them other fields and other weapons."

A day or so later, when we were all gathered for the evening meal, I chose my moment to address my sons. "No one is happier than I am that you returned from your adventure among the Saecsens whole and unharmed. Your cunning and daring are a credit to you both." The two of them beamed with pleasure to hear me laud their bravery and resourcefulness.

"You know as well as any legionary in the yard what is required to march against an enemy. You have been training in soldiery since you could walk. You've been taught all the weapons and how best to employ them. You know how to dress for battle. In this, you've become masters. Yes, you have."

This was true, both knew it and took pride in it, and they had nothing to say against my assessment. "But not every enemy you will meet in life is to be found on the battlefield or in a barbarian camp. Not every enemy can be routed with a sword. It is time—and well past time—you also learned how to put on the armor of God and wield the weapons of heaven." This last came from something Brother Theo had once said, but I took it as my own.

My two young legionaries looked at each other, at their father, and then at me. Uther was first to open his mouth in protest, but Aridius cut him off.

"Your mother's right," he said, surprising me somewhat. "It is time you were schooled in higher things. I will arrange for you to take spiritual instruction from Brother Theo. Every day," Aridius informed them.

"We can already read and write Latin," Aurelius pointed out.

"And we can add sums, Da!" huffed Uther.

"This is different," I told them. "This will be instruction in the ways of faith. You will learn the meaning of the Mass, and the prayer of our Lord Jesu—"

"I know it already!" whined Aurelius.

"—and the Psalms, and creeds, and the Good Lord's parables and their meaning." On a sudden inspiration, I added, "I will also have him instruct you in the history of Britannia and its various tribes and peoples. These, too, are things you should know." I said no more. Seeing their stunned and stricken faces, one would have thought I'd taken away their horses and banned them from the practice yard. Their shock was absolute.

And that was the end of it. The boys finished their supper in silence and went to bed with no further discussion.

Thus, at the beginning of each day, when the church bells rang to summon the monks to prayers, Aurelius and Uther would rise and break fast with their father, then grab up the little leather satchels Theo had given them for their tablet and stylus and, snatching a handful of rusks from the plate, run out the gate and to the school Theo had made for them in a cleared-out storehouse near the church—the "higher school" as he called it. There they sat with Brother Klerwi, Theo, or one of the others, to spend the morning learning the ways of God and His Word, of the Blesséd Jesu and His church, and the stories of our faith. Sometimes, I went along, too, and listened in. More and more, I grew in the conviction that in these lessons my two young warriors should learn something of humility and grace and, above all, the need of constant repentance and forgiveness—lessons that would stand them in good stead for the rest of their lives.

In much of this, I think my insistence was vindicated. Both boys eventually accepted, if not enjoyed, our good priest's gentle teaching as he coaxed and prodded, challenged and disputed with them through their daily sessions, and both took up the trials of the course set before them. I like to think that they imbibed as much as they were able: Aurelius to a greater extent, and Uther, admittedly, to a lesser—but he was younger, after all. I expect it could not be otherwise for just as the capacity of one jar might exceed that of another, so too my sons' ability to contain all the grace and goodness poured out upon them.

Touching that, it was brought to my attention one day that Uther was forsaking his attendance at the daily school. I went in search of the truant and found him making himself scarce in the little yard behind the stables, practicing swords with a young friend. Well, I hauled *both* of them back to the schoolroom—whereupon Brother Theo not only welcomed the newcomer, but hit on the notion of offering instruction to five other youngsters of the garrison. In this way, the clever priest renewed interest in his teaching and introduced both companionship and a nominal competition into their day, thereby brightening what they considered a dull chore. Enlarging the higher school in this way did increase the boys' interest in it, and they all went from strength to strength—such that it was not unusual to hear them challenging one another as they tussled in the stable yard: "Psalm 23!" one of them might shout, and the others would chant the answer at the top of their voices even as they lunged with their wooden swords. I saw them at this several times and it warmed my soul to see it.

A season of relative peace settled on us. The ever-upsetting events of the wider world stood off for a time. Indeed, there were only two raids the rest of that year. The entire garrison accounted that a victory and maintained it was the result of the advances the British commanders had made with the Saecsen king Wulfstan and his lords. All laud and honor to the generals, there were many who supported this judgment—mostly those lords with lands and settlements of the borderlands who had suffered the constant incursions and raids that cost men and grain and cattle.

As always, others took a very different view. Some folk who had lost lands, holdings, settlements, farms, or beloved kinsmen—lost to the predations of barbarian raids—wanted revenge.

I had my own opinion. I, too, suffered such loss. I could count the cost. Even so, I wanted to believe in my husband and do my utmost to support him and his efforts to administer a realm that grew ever more unruly. Increasingly, it seemed to me the small kings and lords were losing faith, or at least patience, with the old order and its diminishing ability to preserve a vestige of stability in the region and in the empire at large.

More and more, the lords and chieftains of the province trusted to the edge of their own swords and the spearpoints of their men to protect and defend their interests—even at the cost of their neighbors and those around them. More and more, they turned from the virtue of working together to solve a common problem, or defeat a common foe. More and more, they placed grievance above reason, or even simple logic—even when it went against their own best interests. More and more, every lord did what was right in his own eyes, for his own benefit and those of his immediate kinship. And the invaders chipped away at us bit by bit.

"Look to your own defenses," Emperor Honorius had decreed. Well, this is what it looked like. It tore at my heart to see all that Rome had built, all that it had cultivated and inspired, fade before my very eyes. And it grieved me to the marrow that this was the worlds-realm where Aurelius and Uther came of age and that they would one day inherit. I would have given my life to allow them to know a different world where Roman law and ways were practised and respected by dutiful citizens. But that world was becoming a fast-receding memory. Soon, it would not even be that.

In the early years of our sojourn in Armorica, the garrison received regular dispatches from other garrisons in the province and Britannia—from Verulamium, Silurum, and even as far away as Eboracum. But as time went on and the barbarian predations increased, those dispatches became more irregular, sporadic, and finally stopped altogether. Official communication was replaced by rumor and word of mouth; nothing new there, of course, the more remote regions of Britannia had always depended on traders and other travelers for the latest reports of the wider world. Only now there was little else.

As time went on, we heard of battles in the far north and east, of great victories and crushing defeats, of lands gained and lost, of kings and lords waxing and waning. It was the same in Britannia. Chaos, destruction, and war everywhere. Then, one day we learned of the rise of one known as Vortigern. By all accounts he was a shrewd, up-thrusting, young war leader from Britannia's western hill country, a ruthless chieftain—aren't they all?—with vaunting ambitions, intent on driving the heathen hordes into the sea, or at least confining them to the Saecsen Shore hemmed about with a strong wall of sharp steel.

From time to time, we would hear how this young warlord was winning battles in the north against the Picti, the Scotti, as well as various Jutland invaders. Next, word reached us of his ruthless struggle to gain the throne, and how he was taking other older, seasoned lords into his service. Then came the day when we learned that Vortigern had proclaimed himself High King of Britannia.

This news was received with mixed reactions. On one hand, his achievements—if true—were laudable: Anyone who could rally the tribes and bind them into a single fighting force, regain lands, and curb barbarian incursions deserved to be praised and supported. On the other hand, anyone who had the audacity and arrogance to crown himself High King was not one wholly to be trusted. Armorica's Britons adopted a cautious, not to say skeptical, view. In Aridius' words, "So long as this fellow keeps the barbarians from burning our settlements and slaughtering our people, let him call himself whatever he likes. As for everything else? I'll wait and see."

So, we waited.

News from the homeland did improve. Against all odds, it appeared that Vortigern had found a way to thwart the worst incursions of the hostile Saecsens and their scrappy client tribes. We heard no end of rumors, of course, of dire tidings from one end of the greater empire to the other. And though these storms of war and waste raged in the wider world, our little corner of the empire remained relatively secure—in spite of the occasional confrontation along Armorica's always volatile eastern border.

As Brother Theo is fond of reminding everyone, "God is good, and his love and mercy endure forever." Owing to this milder season of peace, my boys were allowed to grow up far removed from the intrigues and treacheries that stole the lives, and substance, and souls of so many in the arenas of power elsewhere. They grew strong beneath the watch-care of good men like Aridius, and Vitus and, of course, priests like Brother Theo and Brother Klerwi. They learned the craft of soldiery and the mastery of themselves. At their father's insistence, they learned the art of command; at mine they learned the ways of God, the love of his fair Son, and respect for the ways of His Church. I watched them grow into the men they would become and guided them however I could—especially Uther. For him, I had a special care.

Uther had not his older brother's engaging demeanor or winning way with people; he also lacked Aurelius' innate discernment and patience. When younger, he was often frustrated when confronted with a dilemma that did not yield to physical strength—and later, to a spearpoint or the edge of his sword. The things that his brother seemed to accomplish so effortlessly when dealing with a thorny dilemma, often became for Uther almost insurmountable difficulties requiring exertion and extraordinary effort to resolve. He simply did not possess Aurelius' aptitude, and this lack chafed him raw sometimes. Thus, it fell to me to calm and comfort him—a task that only grew more demanding as he grew older.

Despite this—despite all—I was blessed. The solace I received from the support of good men like Theo, and Vitus—lately elevated to the rank of *praefecti*, or prefect—and many of the legionaries, too, cannot be reckoned. God knows I was grateful for every single day these young ones were at their studies in the "priest school" as they called it. How long this might have continued, I'll never know.

For the world is ever on the turn. The fragile peace we had enjoyed those last good years could not last. Like the sound of wolves on the winter wind, people heard the distant howl of chaos and withdrew behind strong gates and high walls, fearing the imminent collapse. Only a few dared dream of rescue. Most would settle for bare survival.

Our little garrison schools came to an end, like so much else, one especially cold winter when, without a hint of warning, a vile pestilence, a death-dealing plague swept through Armorica. Constantia sank, like everywhere else, in the grim torrent of sickness and death.

7

IT WAS A DAY like any other in the thriving garrison and surrounding town. Troops were marshalled in the morning and a patrol rode out, taking over from the one just returned from a circuit of the regions settlements, farms, and holdings—as usual. Happenings so ordinary in the life of the legion, no one marked this changing of patrols in any way. Why would they? Soldiers were always coming and going, and only those marching off to battle—or returning from one—would warrant any undue attention.

That evening, the first of the returned soldiers took to his sickbed. Again, nothing unusual in that. After all, like every other garrison, Flavia Gallicana maintained a good *infirmarium* for the benefit of the soldiers who made frequent use of it for one ailment or another. A single large room with several beds and a large cabinet to store herbs and oils and potions of various kinds, this sick house was presided over by Setonius, with his aides Marius and Linus.

This first illness went unremarked. Yet, over the next few days seven legionaries were stricken down with the same malady—and all of them had been riding the circuit on patrol. This, of course, *was* noticed and remarked on—first by Setonius and several commanders, and then by nearly everyone else. Our good healer and his two aides were kept busy flitting from one bedside to another those first days. The *infirmarium* was soon overtaken as the disease began its spread through the ranks. Setonius quickly rallied aid to have all the afflicted moved to a single wing of one of the barracks, and everyone else moved out. On the sixth morning after the first man was stricken, he died. By then, there were twenty men under the physician's care. Two died by nightfall, and five more the day after that.

On the seventh day, a runner appeared with word that folk in the surrounding town were falling ill—and all with the same dread signs: raging fever and nausea, followed by sudden weakness and throbbing pain in the head and chest and, lastly, extended fits of coughing and a severe shortness of breath. Often the coughing brought up blood; the vomitus, green with bile, was also spotted with blood, as was the sticky black feces that leaked into their clothing. Those so stricken might linger for days in this fevered, painful state, fighting for breath. In the end, however, nearly all those so afflicted surrendered to the ravages of the disease and death bore them away. A few, but only a few, rose shakily from their beds and showed some signs of recovery.

Very soon, more than half of those who had ridden out on patrol had sickened—close to thirty men in all, I think. And half of those died within the first three days. The reports we had from the town told the same sad tale: people fell ill and succumbed to this odious death. Often, it was those who had cared for their sick friends and family who were next to fall victim to the dread illness. Setonius determined that it was the plague—but unlike any he knew. He informed Aridius and they summoned all the garrison commanders to our villa and gave them the awful news. I lingered as near to the long table in the dining room as I dared, and caught the pith of it.

"The disease is in the town and the settlements round about. It is swift and it is deadly," Aridius began bluntly. "Setonius says it is plague, and I fear he is right. If so, we are not going to outrun it."

They all agreed. But what could they do?

"We may not outrun it," he continued, "but we may outlast it. I have it that it may be possible to evade the illness by avoiding those who have already been taken ill."

"How are we to do that?" wondered one of the centurions. "This demon strikes where it will."

The commanders voiced their agreement. Aridius turned to the physician. "Not so," Setonius informed them. "I have seen that this disease strikes first those who have been near to the sick and dying, tending them."

"You've been with the sick and dying since the beginning," Vitus pointed out. "If it is as you say, why haven't *you* been stricken down?"

Setonius shook his head. "I don't know. It may be that it eludes some even as it takes others—just as an arrow will miss one man only to fell the one behind him." He shook his head. "The problem is we cannot always tell who will fall ill and who will not."

This set the commanders grumbling.

Aridius called for quiet to allow the physician to continue.

"Listen," Setonius said, "this is very like what happened in Rome in the time of the Caesars. In that day, when plague would come, those who had relations or homes in the country went there and stayed until the cloud of plague had passed. I am thinking we could do the same."

"What? Have we estates in the country with great houses to go to?" scoffed one. "Or, would you have us go out into the forest?" wondered another commander, looking to his fellows with a smirk.

"To the forest, yes!" cried Setonius. "And to the farms, the wilderness, the empty places. Go wherever the plague has not yet found purchase." He looked at the ring of grim faces. "I think it is the only way."

The idea was discussed but, as Aridius related later, the commanders were wary of removing so many men from the garrison. "If the Saecsens got word that the fortress was undefended, they would surely attack," complained General Comenius, the senior of the commanders, explaining the main objection. "The garrison would be lost before we could get back to defend it."

"Stay here and the garrison will be lost to the plague," the physician insisted. "There is no stopping it."

Aridius backed his assertion. "It comes down to this," he declared. "Stay and lose the garrison, or leave and have a hope of keeping it."

Though the commanders did not relish the idea of leaving the garrison unmanned in this way, they could not find a way around it.

Addressing Comenius, Aridius asked, "How soon can you have the cohorts ready to march as if to battle?"

"By midday," the general replied confidently, and others concurred.

"Then do it," Aridius ordered. "Go out, and then separate into small platoons. Find places in the wood and fields to make camp. Take whatever you need for provisions—"

"For how long?" one centurion wanted to know.

"For as long as must be," Aridius told him. "Until the plague has passed on and it is safe to come back."

So it was. The first cohorts left the garrison; others followed, marching out in groups of fifty or sixty soldiers with enough supplies to sustain them for ten days. The last of those to leave took Aurelius and Uther with them. I was relieved and happy they went—all the more so because friend Vitus went with them and vowed to watch over them. Come good or ill, at least they would be in safe hands.

The boys, frightened, heartsick—yet struggling manfully to hide it—stood uncertainly at the gate of the villa with their satchels slung over their shoulders, gazing at their father and me as if for the last time. I pressed one of Brother Theo's missal books into Aurelius' hands, saying, "Look here for strength and fortitude when you need it." He swallowed hard, then embraced me and his father, his eyes damp at the moment of parting. Uther likewise, sniffing back a tear, kissed us and hugged us both—then turned hurriedly away lest we see him crying.

When they had gone, I asked my husband whether we should not also go. "You will be needed to ensure the garrison's survival once the plague has passed, and—"

Ari was already shaking his head. "I am needed here now. The legate must remain in place and in authority. With most of the legion gone, my position is more important than ever." He took my hand and looked sadly into my eyes. "But you, dear heart, should leave while you can. You and the priests should go. Stay safe. Those of us who are left will have need of comfort and consolation when this plague has passed over."

I considered the wisdom of his counsel and rejected it. My duty was clear. "No," I told him, squeezing his hand in return. "I will not leave. If your place is here, my place is by your side. If you are to stay, then I am staying with you."

That is what we did. Aridius filled his days marshaling the few soldiers left behind for our protection—sending them out on little errands each day just to get them out of the garrison for a while. That man strove day and night, often beyond fatigue, shouldering all the duties that normally fell to others.

As for myself, I filled my days in much the same way—taking on any task that needed doing. I rarely ventured beyond the gates of the villa; all my care was for the house and servants. When Nona, our good cook and kitchener, fell to the plague, I saw to the meals and, with my three serving girls' help, prepared them. We made countless tureens of bone broth and lentil stew for the sick, and more sustaining meals for anyone else who needed to eat.

The plague worsened. Many of those we counted on to maintain the ordered life of the garrison became too ill to work. With some regret and many misgivings, I granted Deidre permission to return to her people; the poor girl was so beside herself with worry about her family, it was cruelty to keep her in the villa. Junia and Jason returned to their homes, promising to come back as soon as the disease abated. Only Tatiana remained by my side—and if I did not already have cause to bless her, I did soon enough. Every aspect of garrison life that was not strictly necessary was abandoned as one soul after another fell to the plague.

I quickly came to know the hateful signs: first came the dry throat and thirst that nothing could satisfy, this was followed by mounting fever that bathed the body in sweat, a booming throb in the head, and the onset of deep lethargy that left the limbs weak and aching. Then came the nausea and vomiting of whatever could be eaten or drunk; often the bowels loosened, fouling garments and bedding with a bloody, black ooze that stank to heaven. The sufferer lingered in this way before lapsing into a fevered sleep which often heralded the end. Many who closed their eyes on one day did not wake the next. Sometimes, the victim would linger on, groaning and gnashing their teeth for days. For others, the end came more quickly. I even heard of one or two who went to their nightly rest feeling well, but were found the next morning dead in their sleep.

God help us, it was horrific!

Very soon, dealing with the dead became our most pressing problem. Theo and his few priests, who had been ministering to as many of the sick as humanly possible, were also responsible for the Christian burial of the dead as well. Although they strove mightily, the floodtide of death surged over them and mounted high against the church's stout walls. Those good priests toiled each day and by torchlight far into the night: digging graves, burying the dead—often two or even three family members to a grave. Still, the corpses piled up. The good brothers simply could not inter them fast enough and even the most simple service of prayer taxed the time.

"We cannot allow you to continue like this," Aridius told Theo one night. "You are killing yourselves, digging graves."

Gray faced, swaying on his feet, and ready to topple over at the next puff of wind, the priest offered a rueful smile at the absurdity of this remark. I poured a little watered wine into a cup and handed it to him, then passed one to Aridius as they sat for a much needed respite in the courtyard at another grim day's end. "Ari is right," I said, pouring a cup for myself. "Listen to your legate. You and your priests have battled beyond all endurance, but you cannot go on like this. It is the sick who need you most right now, not the dead."

Aridius, nodding in agreement, said, "In normal times, yes, your duty is to bury and bless the dead, to see them carried into their eternal rest. But these are not normal times. Aurelia is right, it is the living who need you now, not the dead."

A thoughtful silence claimed the courtyard as we sipped our weak wine.

"When did you last sleep?" I asked Theo.

He shrugged. "Yesterday, maybe? The day before?"

"You must sleep tonight," Ari told him. "And tomorrow morning I will send soldiers to prepare a large pit—"

Theo saw where this suggestion was going and reacted immediately. "A mass grave? Not on sacred ground!"

"A mass grave, yes." Ari told him. "The soldiers will dig it for you—wide and deep—and wagons will transport the bodies to you."

Theo wearily shook his head as the legate finished. "I cannot find it in me to like this solution, but neither do I have a better idea."

"It is the only way," I added, "and let it serve the living in our need."

"You will be freed from the digging and the burying," continued Aridius gently. "This will allow you to perform prayers and service for the dead—"

"And free you to better aid the sick," I offered.

"Yes, yes," Theo agreed finally. "It is not a perfect solution, but perfection is not within our reach. Let it be as you say, and we will make the best of it."

Talk moved on to how many of the lesser details might be worked out, and I left to prepare the evening's table. The meals were getting ever more modest as the days wore on and it became ever more difficult to secure provisions—*or those who could provide them.*

One day soon, I thought, *this hideous plague will be over and life as we've known it will return.*

Well, the plague *would* end right enough, and life *would*, in time, return. But it would be a life I did not recognize and never would have chosen.

For, only five days after that last meal with our good friend, Aridius fell victim to the plague. It came on in the night and I marked the onset: awakened by my husband's thrashing about, I touched his back and my hand came away wet with sweat. The poor man was burning with fever. He had kicked off all his bedding and was moaning softly.

"Ari," I said, giving him a gentle shake, "wake up."

By way of response, he groaned and gradually opened his eyes. "My head," he mumbled, wiping sweat from his face. "Why is it so hot in here?"

"You have a fever," I told him, swinging my legs out of bed. "I'll fetch some water."

On my way to the kitchen to fetch a jar and cup, it was all I could do to put one foot in front of the other without collapsing in despair. We were surrounded by the vile pestilence morning to night and had been for weeks, but I had kept myself from imagining the worst. The doom so many others faced had now arrived at our door and, like all those others, my husband had fallen to the disease.

I flew back to our bed chamber and helped Ari sit up so he could drink. Then I wet a cloth and folded it so he could place it on his brow and help cool himself somewhat. He closed his eyes and slowly went back to sleep; I stayed awake and watched him through the little left of the night, my heart torn between hope and despair.

The next day, he attempted to rally somewhat. "I should go," he said, throwing off the newly changed bedding. "There is so much to do."

"All the more reason to give yourself a little time to regain your strength. Rest—at least for a day, my love. If you feel better tomorrow, you can return to your duties and you will return refreshed."

Neither one of us mentioned plague. We pretended that this was some complaint brought on by overwork and the cares of the garrison, and would yield to rest.

Tomorrow came and went and Aridius did not feel better, did not regain his strength. He grew weaker and the ache in his head spread to his joints; he complained of pain in his knees and throughout his body. He could not eat solid food. After a few bites he would gag and throw it up again. At best, he could but sip a little tepid broth—but at least that was something. And all the time the fever came and went, leaving him cold and shivering—only to return again as hot and fierce as ever.

At midday the third day of his illness, I made a brief foray out of the villa and hurried to the church to inform Setonius, that stalwart man, that the legate had surrendered to the plague. I found Setonius near the door of the *infirmarium* as two more invalids were carried into the yard. "I will come at once," he told me, snatching up the bag in which he kept his tinctures and potions at the ready. He went off to tend Aridius, and I went on to inform Brother Theo, who also offered to come at once.

"No, my friend. I did not come to summon you from your duties. I only wanted you to know so that you could pray for him when you offer prayers for the other sick among us."

"But—" He regarded me with a taut expression.

I could see he was torn between staying to help those before him and running to his friend's aid. "You are needed here," I told him, "and Aridius will not thank me for pulling you away from your valuable work here—or you for deserting it."

"Not even for him?"

I shook my head. "*Especially* not for him." Turning away, I started for home once more. "Let it be this way, please."

"Send word when you can," he told me. "I must know how he fares."

"Pray for us, Theo," I called behind me. "You have the ear of our Good Lord. He hears you, I know."

I hastened back to the villa and marked how very quiet it was in the garrison town. Ordinarily, the noise of the place reached me as a confused jumble—like that of a burbling brook: a perpetual stream of meaningless sound, a low din that rarely resolved into anything significant. But now that low clamor was gone—along with those who made it.

On my return, I went at once to Ari's bedside and saw that he was sleeping. I decided to take a little rest myself while I had the chance, and found a comfortable corner in one of the empty chambers where I curled up in a shawl, and was soon blissfully asleep.

I must have slept longer than I intended, because when I rose the sun had sunk low and the shadows in the courtyard were already stretched long. I threw off the coverlet and hurried to Ari's chamber.

He roused himself when I entered the room. "Good," he said, his voice a dry croak. "You're here."

"Don't talk," I told him. "I'll get you some water."

A jar stood on a tray beside the bed, and I poured him a cup and helped him drink it down. When he did, he gave me a weak smile and lay back, his eyes bright with fever.

"How do you feel, my love?" I asked, stroking his hand.

"Much better," he lied—as if I could not see how utterly wan and waxy his skin had become, as if I could not see how his flesh seemed to hang on him—limp as clothes on a carpenter's scaffold.

"You do look a little better," I told him, repaying his lie with a small one of my own.

"I think I could eat something—maybe some more of that bone broth?"

"Of course," I replied. "I'll have Tatiana warm some for you right away."

I hurried to the kitchen which was deserted, but there was broth still in the big pot so I stirred up the embers and stoked the flame and soon had enough heat to take off the chill. While the pot warmed, I made up a tray and filled a jar with fresh water, then filled the bowl, crumbling a bit of dried bread into it. By the time I returned to the sickroom, Aridius was asleep once more.

Loathe as I was to rouse him, I nevertheless brought him out of his sleep and sat next to him on the bed and held the bowl while he ate. The poor man was so weary, it was all he could do to keep himself awake long enough to swallow down the food. I spoke to him, telling him all that was being done within the garrison and what I knew about life outside the walls. "One of the generals—Severus, I think—sent a messenger yesterday. The soldier stood outside the walls and shouted up at the gateman. He said that all was well and that their cohort was hale and able to forage for what they required. We need not be concerned for them." I gave Ari a smile of encouragement. "It appears your decision to send them away has proven a boon, my love. You were right."

He nodded and slumped back once more. "Good," he said, closing his eyes once more. "That's good..."

I left him to his rest and returned to my duties, filling the remainder of the day dealing with the various little emergencies that came my way. I looked in on my husband from time to time—twice rousing him to drink—and at last fell into my own bed tired and vaguely unsettled...by the unnatural quiet in the house and garrison...by the growing sense of fear that we would soon be running out of necessary food and supplies...that the plague was taking too long to dissipate and was instead growing worse...and any number of things.

With all this on my mind, sleep was long in coming. I woke again in the middle of the night with a raging ache in my head and a throat that seemed to be on fire.

BOOK FIVE

YNYS AVALLACH

"IT WAS THE PLAGUE," I say, stating the obvious.

"Aye, it was. Maybe. It may have been something else. Who knows?" Aurelia's head drops at the dreadful memory. "I was laid low. I clearly recall...I recall rising early to relieve myself then returning to see how Aridius had fared through the night. I opened the door to his sickroom and thought it stuffy and rank. Ari was sunk deep in sleep, so still. I went to fetch his jar to fill it with fresh water..."

She gives a little shudder at the memory.

"And then?" I ask, urging her gently back across the years.

When she speaks again, it is from that far-off place. "I am told I was found in the corridor amidst the shards of a broken jar, or in the cookhouse—or was it somewhere else? My next memory was waking up in a bed drenched in sweat with a raging thirst. Setonius was standing over me and so was my faithful servant and friend Tatiana.

"Then Theo appeared. I awoke much confused and with no clear understanding of where I was or what was happening."

"Did you learn how long you were abed?"

"Five or six days, I think," she sighs, "and little memory of it even now. Oh, little snatches of this and that came back to me over time—starting up out of sleep in the middle of the night to see a candle burning at my bedside and someone, I don't know who, slumped in a chair, asleep beside me...being offered a drink of water and almost choking on it...the deep, dull ache in my belly and my bones...of feeling that I had not the strength to lift hand to head...and such like. "

She draws a deep breath and then faces once more the pain she carries deep in her soul. "It was not until the next day—the day my fever broke, or maybe the day after—that I was considered well enough to receive the news that Ari had died."

Silence falls between us again. Aware that I am treading on a sort of sacred ground, I allow this revelation the respect it deserves. In a moment, she nods and continues, "Everything changed after that. Everything."

"I can well imagine," I agree.

"My poor husband had died alone in the night—the self-same night I awoke with fever and went in to him," she says. "So Tatiana told me—indeed, I think the moment of his passing is what roused me from my bed that night." She bends her head and closes her eyes on the everlasting grief of that moment. "I did not see him again—not even in death could I hold his hand and tell him my love."

"No?"

"He had been buried by then, you see," she replies softly. "Just another corpse in the burial pit he had himself ordered to be dug." She offers a grim smile. "A small justice that—the man who commanded such a grave for others becomes just another occupant."

I let this assertion settle, then say, "I am sorry to hear it but, in truth, I don't suppose it could have been otherwise."

"No," she replies slowly, "and I do not think I would have done anything different in any case—not that I could have. But it would have been nice to at least write a few words for Theo to speak over the bodies at the funeral. There were nine others buried with Aridius that day—six men and three women." She shrugs lightly. "That is what Theo told me. As soon as I could rise and leave the villa, Tatiana and I went to the grave."

Aurelia lowers her head and sighs. "There was little enough to see—a simple wooden marker carved with a cross and the names of those buried beneath. He was gone. The only man I had ever loved was gone."

We sit for a time. Each of us turning over in our heads the tragic events of that cruel season. Aurelia weeps for the misery and waste she witnessed and the dreadful aftermath as the world moved on and she, along with everyone still alive, moved with it.

After a time, she dabs her eyes and glances out across the far southern hills. Something prompts me to ask, "There is someone you have not mentioned," I say. "Someone I worry about."

Aurelia comes out of her reverie. "Who is that?"

"Ursa!"

With a shake of her head and a smile, she replies, "Ah, yes. Ursa—my faithful protector, companion, and friend." Aurelia turns a wondering gaze on me. "Do you believe in guardian angels, Merlin?"

"I do," I affirm. How could I not? I had met at least one that I could call by name, and likely more that I never recognized.

"I believe in them, too," Aurelia says, and laughs. "I just never thought mine would be a dog!"

I give her a wondering look. "Truly?"

She nods her assurance. "When Uther was born, Ursa lay by my side through the birth—I'll not pretend that it was an easy delivery, it wasn't. But, when the travail had passed and the baby was swaddled and safe in my arms, Ursa came padding back into the room. She looked at me and at the infant, and then came to the bed and rested her head on my arm. I stroked her for a moment and thanked her for her watch-care. Then she licked my hand and left the room, pausing to look back one last time." Aurelia regards me with a little half smile. "I never saw her again after that."

"No?"

"I did not know it then, but I believe she had come to bid me farewell," replies Aurelia. "That is how it is with guardian angels, you see? They only stay as long as they are needed."

1

HOW LONG I STOOD AT THAT GRAVE I cannot say. All I know is that a day begun bright and fair had gone gray and cold by the time I turned away from that awful pit of half-buried corpses with its pathetic wooden marker, tears streaming down my face as I was swept away by the surging floodtide of grief. I wept for the cruelty, the futility, the frailty of all flesh and the brevity of life.

I wept not only for Aridius, but for all those lost to this hideous disease and whose lives would be buried with their bones in this noisome tomb. I wept for Aurelius and Uther who would return—if they did return—to a life without a father's care and strong hand to guide them. I wept for myself and my bewildering predicament. Where was I to go? What was I to do? What would become of me without my rock, the one who had long been the solid anchor of my life? What was I to do without Aridius? How could I raise my two boys to manhood without him?

Sobbing, I turned away from that saddest of sights and moved to rejoin Tatiana who was standing a respectful few paces away, solemn, her hands tightly clasped, her lips moving in silent prayer.

Grief was no stranger to me, God knows. I bore it then as I had before, and there came a morning when I rose, washed in the basin, put on fresh clothes, and returned to my duties. Despite the ache in my soul, I forced myself to remain busy as I went about my chores—to keep the surge of grief from overwhelming me again, and hold the darker thoughts at bay. Though often exhausted as I slumped into bed

349

at night, this strategy worked. Little by little, as the days slowly dragged away, I began to find my way to the light again. Brother Theo helped in this and, of course, Tatiana, faithful as a shadow. Both of these good friends had somehow come through the plague without yielding to it. So many others—such as Bishop Gosselyn, good man and upright churchman—was not so fortunate. The plague ravaged the town, killing street by street, with the same ruthless efficiency that had spread it through the garrison.

But, the season turned and the hateful scourge abated at last— thank God—or there would have been none of us left alive. For those of us who survived, the ordeal was not over yet.

The scarcity that had long been looming, finally began to bite. One of the commanders ordered a company of soldiers to go into the town and search among the dwellings of the deceased for any supplies and foodstuffs that might be of use. Of course, the undertaking raised an outcry—not only from those of more delicate sensibilities, but from other scavengers who were doing the same thing. Nevertheless, cartloads of gleanings began rolling into the garrison to be distributed among the living. All the items—grain, cheese, butter, dried meat, hard bread, wine, olive oil, clothing, and anything else of immediate use— were stored in one of the vacated barracks and a tribune put in charge of keeping and allocating the supplies. From the moment the garrison gates were opened each day, the hungry lined up to receive a ration and soldiers kept order in the ranks.

The change, when it came, seemed to happen all at once. One day, the fortress lay swathed in that odd, unnatural silence of disease and death'... the next day the streets were once more ringing with the shouts and clatter of noisy soldiers. Even I could hear it.

I ran out the gate and into the street to see that the first cohorts to leave Constantia and escape the plague were now returning to rousing welcome. The gates were flung wide and as the first company streamed through, I caught sight of Aurelius and Uther, riding side by side up the street leading to the garrison. Oh! They looked as if they had aged years since I had last seen them. They were men now—young men, yes, but they carried themselves with military bearing and wore the confidence of Roman legionaries. I shouted and waved. Aurelius somehow heard me through the clamor and an enormous grin spread across his lean, handsome face. Handing Uther the reins, he threw himself from his mount and instantly I was folded into a crushing embrace. I marveled at the strength of his hands and arms. The months away had indeed changed more than their aspect and bearing; time spent with the soldiers had also made them sinewy and strong.

No sooner had Aurelius released me than Uther gathered me up. I felt his wet kiss on my cheek and the tiny, cold cinder of my heart rekindled and began to glow a little. But then Aurelius, still grinning, glanced around. "Our Da?" he said, keen dark eyes sweeping across the gathered throng. "Where is he?" He looked to me. "Where's our Da?"

The stark reality of what I had to tell them struck me with like a blow to the stomach. "Oh, Aurelius," I moaned, taking his hand.

Uther, still holding me, sensed what was to come. He pulled back. "What's happened to our Da?"

I took Uther's hand, too, and holding both my boys, I struggled for the words. "He...he is—"

"He's dead!" cried Aurelius.

Uther recoiled and gulped a breath. Then, straightening himself, said, "When did he die?" He glanced at his brother. "We didn't know."

"Where is he?" said Aurelius. "I want to see the grave."

"Yes, of course. I'll take you when you're ready and we'll bring..."

"No," Uther said flatly. "Now. We want to see him now."

I glanced at Aurelius and saw that the two were of one mind. "Very well," I agreed. "I'll take you now."

2

THE CHURCH YARD BORE STARK WITNESS to the pestilence: countless patches of overturned earth, many with temporary wooden markers—the individual graves that had been dug in the early days of the desolation. The massive charnel pit dug at Aridius' insistence was now a large muddy depression. Mostly full, covered in soft earth, but unmistakably a mass grave of recent use, awaiting closure. Here and there, a bit of burial shroud could be seen—often the cloak the victim died in—poked through the soft dirt and, God help us, a stench unlike any other emanated from the depths.

I allowed the two their moment of reckoning and then said, "I had hoped to prepare you better."

Uther shook his head in disbelief. Aurelius, moist eyed, murmured, "I didn't . . . We didn't *know*." He turned to me and, in a small, shaken tone, said, "We didn't think it was this bad. We had no idea."

How could they? Purposefully kept away from the worst ravages of the disease and its hideous progress, they could not begin to know what we were suffering at the garrison.

"Which one is his?" Uther asked, regarding the grim array of grave markers spreading across the churchyard. "Where is our Da?"

"It's here," I said, indicating the mass grave before us. "This is his place."

Instantly angry, Uther turned on me. "Not good enough!" he shouted.

Aurelius echoed his brother's outrage. "How could you—" He flung a hand at the great, gaping hole with its heap of dirt beside it. "How could you allow this . . . this *travesty?*"

"Travesty?" Stunned by the accusation, I stared at him. "I don't know what you mean."

"He was legate of the legion, for God's sake!" Aurelius charged.

"He was somebody!" cried Uther. "And you've thrown him into a stinking pit like just . . . *anybody.*"

Their indignation provoked me something fierce. The words surged up hot and sharp. "How dare you!" I shouted. "How dare you accuse me! Were you here? No! You were not here when we dragged the dead out of their houses and piled them on the burial carts! You were not here when the sick lay moaning in the streets, soiling themselves, too weak to move! You were not here when the shrieks and wails of breaking hearts filled the day and night!"

Both shut their mouths and looked away.

"Have a care before you start throwing accusations. Brother Theo nearly killed himself digging graves by torchlight. I was awake days on end comforting the dying, and once they had passed, taking care of those left behind too sick to look after themselves. And still they kept dying—and dying—they all kept dying! We could not even pray for their souls fast enough, let alone bury them. What would you have done? Left them to rot in their beds? Piled them in the street like firewood?"

Heaven help me, all the rage I had stored up came rushing out in a torrent. "You look down from your lofty thrones and imagine that I have somehow dishonored your father by allowing him to share a common grave?" I continued, my voice shaking. "Look at it! Look at it! Do you think any of this is what I wanted? Do you think that this— *this* is what I would have chosen of my own volition? Do you imagine there was some better choice I refused to take?"

Uther drew breath a protest, but I did not relent "There was no better choice. Death was all around us and we did what we had to do. If you know a better way, then I stand ready to hear it! Well? Tell me if you can."

I could see them being crushed by my ferocity—Aurelius' wide shoulders were sagging and he had turned away, Uther stood staring at me face-on, his expression one of utter shock.

"Hear me now, both of you—you that are so keen to join the legion and kill your enemy to protect your home. Hear one speak about death and life who knows. If you are ever to rule, ever to command, know that this—this stinking pit, is what awaits you. No, don't act so bashful now, Aurelius—don't look so affronted, Uther. If you believe yourselves to be better than those that lie in this churchyard, then you will be worthy of nothing in this life.

"And if you believe that Aridius desired a pompous monument of stone as the crowning achievement of his life, then you did not ever truly spend even a day with him. Your father did not place himself above others—he lived to serve everyone around him, and *you two* most of all. He did not believe himself better than those he served. He was happy enough to share his table with all—why not also his grave?"

Both boys were weeping now. I was still weak from recovery and my voice, scraped raw from shouting, was now so low that even I struggled to hear myself. I put out a hand to the mass grave. "This was your father's decision. He ordered the grave pit to be dug. I fought him on it, Brother Theo fought him on it, but he insisted and supervised the work himself.

"Yes, Aurelius, your father was legate of the legion. And yes, Uther, he was *somebody*, and worthy of all the care and attention we gave him. But if he rests here it is not with just *anybody*, as you have it. He rests here with people he knew, people he loved, people he served. Aridius is laid to rest among friends in holy ground. I tell you, every living soul among us should aspire to as much and hope for no less.

"I will leave you to make your peace," I said, and returned to the villa alone.

By the time they returned home, both boys were chastened. Aurelius found me where I was at work in the dining room. He came quietly into the hall and, without a word, sank to his knees before me. Hands at his side, he hung his head. "You have a fool for a son, Mother," he said. "You have every right to be angry. I was wrong and I am mightily sorry."

So abject in his remorse, I was moved to comfort him. I rested my hand on his head. "This is not how I imagined this day," I told him.

He glanced up, eyes full of hope. "Forgive me?"

"Have I not already forgiven you in my heart?" I glanced around and saw Uther standing in the doorway, watching, uncertain what kind of reception he would receive. "And you, too, Uther. I forgive you. Come here."

Like a pup that has been punished, he shuffled over to stand beside his brother. Aurelius stood up and I embraced them both. "I have missed you so much," I said, my voice catching. "So very, very much."

They both mumbled something in reply. Wiping a tear from my eye, I stepped back, holding them both at arm's length. "Stand there and let me look at you." I took in the sight, shaking my head in disbelief. "You're both so tall—and thin! Didn't they feed you at all?"

Both boys grinned with relief. "We ate, yes," Aurelius said. "Only one meal a day most days."

"And we had to work for it," offered Uther, assuming something of his usual boyishness.

"I'm sorry about Da," said Aurelius, suddenly thoughtful again. "We didn't know..."

"I wish we could have been here," added Uther sadly.

"What would you have done?" I asked, then answered: "Nothing that was not done—except get sick yourselves."

"We did not know you got sick, too," said Aurelius.

I nodded. "Your father died in the night with Brother Klerwi by his side. I was not there with him because, by that time, I was stricken. When I came to myself again, he was gone." I sighed. "They showed me his grave as I showed you today."

We talked more after that, mostly about how they had occupied themselves in camp while waiting out the plague. Supper that evening was a melancholy affair; both boys kept stealing glances at the empty chair where their father would have sat at the end of the table. Bless them, they felt so bad—for me, for behaving the way they had, for themselves and the grief they now felt, for the hardship everyone had endured, for the cruel injustice of it all.

I did not doubt the depth of their feeling; I know they grieved in their own way and would forever feel their father's absence, even as I felt it. But, youthful spirits do not remain low for long. It was impossible for them not to return to their chief pursuit: becoming soldiers.

Joining the legion was not a decision either one of them made as a considered, deliberate choice; it was merely accepted as a self-evident fact. That they would be anything *other* than soldiers never occurred to them; or, I must say, to anyone else who knew them. Certainly, I was never consulted and any misgivings I might have had went unspoken. So, a day or two after their homecoming, both boys dashed off to speak to the commander of their adopted cohort—rather, the cohort that had adopted them—as if legionaries seeking new orders. And I began the task I had been dreading—and putting off doing—for weeks but could not put off any longer: finding a new home for myself and my boys.

The death of Aridius left the legion without a legate, obviously. In the ordinary run of things, a new *Legatus Legionis* would be swiftly appointed. The governor, procurator, or maybe even the emperor for all I know—some official somewhere—would select from among men of rank and experience a man suitable for the position. And that would be that.

But this was not the ordinary run of things and, truly, had not been for some time. The vicious plague altered any sense of normality in the region, along with nearly everything else. Throughout Armorica, Gaul, and the wider world of the empire and beyond, the pestilence had carved vast swathes of death and desolation. I expect that many a contender suitable for the job of legate had been removed from consideration by his recent demise, and any others with higher aspirations to power were unwilling to make the move to a plague-ravaged outpost of little importance and less hope of advancement.

So, it was determined by the powers that be that the new legate would be chosen from among those already in command in Flavia Gallicana. This threw the garrison into convulsions of indecision. The governing authority lay with the most senior commander in the region: Dux Riothamus. However, he—as ever and always—had other garrisons and more pressing matters to worry about and made it clear that, so long as the next legate was loyal and capable, he would accept the decision of the garrison commanders. This did little to aid the actual decision-making process; choosing the next legate remained as much a dilemma as ever. The problem, as I came to understand it, was that the generals considered taking on the administrative duties and title of legate to be something of a demotion, a loss of rank, status, and authority. Aside from that, each considered his services much more useful, if not required, in the field—especially when defending against yet another attack or barbarian incursion.

I'm not suggesting that they were mistaken in this belief. No doubt they were right. Who was I to say? But it did mean that the office remained vacant. The outcome concerned me, of course, but there was nothing I could do about it one way or another. Even so, my own path was clear. Whoever the new legate might be, he would take possession of the legate's house and official quarters. I had little choice but to begin making plans to vacate the villa, a task that I approached with a heart full of dread.

Our modest garrison villa may not have been as grand as that at Deva, but it had nevertheless been our home. Here, we four had been a family, the place where Aridius and I had raised our boys, and the only home the two of them had ever known. To leave it like this was, to me, a sorrow sharp as a knife in the gut.

Aching with regret, I considered which of the paths before me I might choose. Should I return to Deva, where I would find folk who knew me and, more to the point, where the name Aridius Verica still commanded respect? Or, should I go back to Venta, my father's home and the home of my birth? Then again, why return to an old haunt at all? Maybe better to go somewhere new—but where? Maybe we should stay in Constantia: prosperous, in its own way, and secure enough because of the garrison that dominated the town. Also, my boys' pursuit of their military careers could proceed unhindered, their place in the legion was assured. Stability, security, and continuity had much in their favor in a world increasingly unstable, insecure, and lurching from one cruel upheaval to another.

It was with this in mind that I began making little trips to the town round about, exploring the areas near the garrison to see which might offer a modest house for purchase or rent. What I discovered, however, fair took my breath away. Though I knew the plague had devastated the town—how well I knew it!—and I imagined myself prepared, the damage I witnessed was far worse than anything I imagined. In street after street, house after house stood vacant, the owners dead or fled. No area remained untouched. I quickly concluded, as I went about my rambling search, that I would have my choice of dwelling from a wide range of possibilities.

That is, *if* I chose to stay in poor, sad Constantia.

3

AURELIUS AND UTHER had been at their training all day—the same as every other day since their return to the garrison. They burst into the villa just before sunset, shouting at the top of their lungs for me to come running. Fearing something terrible had happened, I dropped the linen I was folding and ran to the courtyard.

"Mother!" cried Aurelius, rushing to meet me.

"What is it?" I cried, seizing him and searching him for injuries. "Are you hurt?" I looked to Uther and did not see any blood or broken bones. "What has happened?"

"There's to be a new legate!"

I met this assertion with somewhat confounded relief. "I know this," I told them. "Did you not—" Then, I remembered that this might well be the first they had heard. So, I began to explain. "You see, the generals have been trying to decide and—"

"They've decided," Uther crowed cheerfully. "The choice has been made!"

"Has it now?" I confess, I felt the ground shift slightly beneath my feet. "Come," I said, leading them to the little bench where Aridius and I used to sit of an evening to discuss the day's events. "Sit, both of you, and tell me all about it."

Too excited to sit, both boys stood together before me, nudging one another, almost hopping from foot to foot.

"Well?" I said, composing myself to receive the news. "Who is it to be? Tell me."

"You'll never guess!" cried Uther.

I laughed, caught up in their childlike enthusiasm. "No—and at the speed of your telling, I suspect I'll never know."

Both boys looked at each other and Uther blurted out: "It's Vitus!"

"Vitus?" I said, thinking I could not have heard correctly. "You mean *our* Vitus?"

"He was with the generals most all day and they announced their decision just a little while ago," explained Aurelius. "We came to tell you as soon as we heard. Isn't that good news!"

"Vitus is to be legate? You're sure?"

"It's true! He told us himself," shouted Uther. "There's going to be a ceremony and everything."

Well, I was stunned. Uther was right: I never would have guessed that our dear friend Vitus would be chosen to replace Aridius. The two boys, still bubbling with the news, ran off to tell others, leaving me to contemplate what this turn might mean. It did not take long before I began to tease out the logic of the choice and then, of course, it made good sense. Indeed, Vitus was the perfect choice. A seasoned veteran and an able soldier, he knew each and every legionary and servant in the garrison from general to stable groom—most of them by name and tribe. Then, inasmuch as he was a centurion, the appointment to legate would be seen as a rare promotion and not a step down in rank and status such as the generals feared. Also, he knew as well as anyone, and more intimately than most, how the garrison worked and how it should be ordered. He had known Aridius and was well acquainted with the legate's duties and responsibilities and could follow them. As legate, he could ensure the efficient functioning of the garrison and its various parts. Added to all this, Vitus was a man known and trusted by one and all, and promoting him meant that some unknown outsider would not be thrust upon the garrison.

Clearly, the commanders could not have chosen a better man for the job. Aurelius was right, this was good news—*very* good news.

It was not until the house was settled for the night and I was blowing out the candles that the realization hit me: now that next occupant had been chosen and would be eager to set up his own household, I would have to move out—and that right soon. The decision was made: I would stay in Constantia.

The next day, I redoubled my efforts to find a place to live. I took myself off to the plain stone building that served as the Civitas House for the town to speak to Magistrate Martinus, whom I had known from various business dealings between the town and garrison. He had been to visit Aridius at our villa several times and attended the occasional function with other dignitaries.

Upon arriving at the house I was received somewhat grudgingly by the magistrate's *adiutor*—a fellow I had never met before. "You can wait here," said the man, waving me to a bench beside the door.

And there I waited. The *adiutor* left the room and another entered—barely of an age to shave, with a shock of black hair and sad dark eyes in a long face. He glanced at me and barked, "Come!"

I rose and followed him into what I took to be the magistrate's chamber—a small, spare room dominated by a large table, with a chair on either side. The entire table top was taken up by a crude map of Constantia someone had drawn in charcoal on the bare boards.

The lad introduced himself as Solinus and took his place behind the table, but did not sit. He began abruptly, almost dismissively. "What is your business with the magistrate, madam?"

I touched my ear and asked him to speak more loudly and plainly. With an air of someone put upon, he repeated his curt request to which I replied, "I am the wife—I mean, widow of the previous legate, who was—"

His dark brows lowered. "*You* are the wife of Aridius Verica?" He paused and thought hard. "Ah, Renea . . . isn't it?"

"Aurelia," I corrected. "Have I seen you before—at the legate's villa, maybe?"

"Of course!" he said, the light of recognition blooming across his smooth face; he extended his hand and gave me a shame-faced smile. "I was sorry to hear about your husband. It is a loss for the garrison and for the town." He shook his head. "A very great loss. I know he and my father became good friends over the years."

I agreed that this was so, and said, "Speaking of your father," I said, "it is him I have come to see."

"Ah, well, if it is the *magistrate* you have come to see, then you are looking at him."

"You, Solinus?"

"None other." He gave me a modest little bow. "The plague, you see . . ." He left the rest unsaid. I knew. It did not need saying. Then, as if admitting a guilty secret, he confided, "There was no one else—at least until the governor appoints another."

"It has been a hard year for so many of us."

He nodded, then sat down in his father's chair. "Now then, what can I do for you, Aurelia?"

I explained briefly about Vitus' appointment and my consequent need to find new accommodations. "Since my sons are still in training with the legion, I think taking a house here in Constantia would be best for all of us."

"Do you mean to say you will settle here?" I nodded and, to my utter amazement, he slapped the table in front of him and cried, "But that is the best news I have heard all day!"

His reaction and, moreover, the sudden shedding of whatever officious demeanor he had managed to maintain until then showed his true self: a boy trying very hard to do a man's job.

"Oh, indeed? And why is that?" I wondered. "You must have more pressing matters claiming your attention."

"Pressing, yes—that is one way to put it. Demands! That's what they are. All day long, every day, citizens flow through this house with a flood of requests and petitions: Fix this! Fix that! I need this, that, and the other. I have rats, send the rat catcher! My water is tainted! What are you going to do about cleaning the streets? When will the market resume?"

I nodded with more than a little sympathy. "How well I know it!" I replied. "My father was Magistrate of Venta Silurum and I grew up working in his office. I know how difficult"—I nodded toward the crude outline of Constantia—"all this can be."

"It never ends," he allowed. "Just now, deciding what to do with all the empty dwellings consumes most of my attention. See here. This is Constantia and the garrison." He waved a charcoal-smudged hand across the simple tabletop map. "We have been charting all of the abandoned houses within the boundary of the *civitas*. Some of the property passes to the family, but in some cases—too many cases, there is no family, or none we can locate. Each of those empty houses is marked with a black spot." Solinus pointed to a row of sketched boxes of various sizes, more than a third of which bore a big, black splotch in the center.

I glanced at the map. It was one thing to note the vacant dwellings on my informal rambles, but quite another to see all the black marks spread out before me. "There are so many."

The young magistrate nodded sadly. "So very many." He regarded his handiwork for a moment, then glanced up. "Are you saying you could be induced to take one of these?"

"Induced?" I said, not sure I had heard correctly. "But this is the very thing I came to ask—indeed, to beg if necessary."

"I could offer you your choice of houses," he said. "Within reason."

"And I will gladly accept." I smiled, and added, "Within reason. I do have a little money," I told him. "I can pay."

Solinus was already shaking his head. "No, no, we would not require payment. You would be doing the town a service. Abandoned properties are a very menace. A danger. Rats, to begin with. And looting—there is already some of that going on. The city elders—the few that survived and those newly appointed—are desperate to fill these abandoned houses and build up the population again."

"Increase the tax base—that's how it was often put to my Aridius."

"I would not be so crass, but it is a fact that the streets must be cleaned and vermin exterminated and water . . . well, everything takes money." He shook his head. "It is an enormous task in the best of times."

I studied the map intently and located one or two areas I had noted on my previous visits. "What would happen if I chose a house where the owner expected to come back? What then?"

"I can assure you that would not happen. My father, before he died, kept very good records. We know that some owners have fled the town and taken refuge elsewhere in order to escape the pestilence, and we assume that they will eventually return to take up residence again. I hope they do, and soon. But we also know those dwellings where the owner is, shall we say, *never* coming back." He regarded me hopefully. "All you need do is tell me which house you have in mind and I will have Julius search out the record." He spread his hands over his charcoal drawing once more. "That is why we made this map."

The sensible solution to this problem impressed me as much as Solinus' generous attitude, and I told him so, adding, "Your father would be proud of you, I'm sure."

"Coming from you, Aurelia, that is high praise indeed."

We parted as friends and the young official bade me to make short work of finding a house and securing it before it was claimed by someone else or, worse, fell to looters and into ruin. I promised I would do just that. I went away feeling confirmed in my decision to remain in Constantia, and determined to make a good home here for myself and my sons.

4

VITUS CAME TO SEE ME LATER that same day. He appeared at the villa at day's end and, with a reluctance and deference unusual for him, asked if he might speak to me in private. "Are we not already speaking in private?" I asked lightly, looking around the empty courtyard. Only Tatiana was in and out as she prepared for the evening meal. "I assure you we are quite alone, my friend."

"Please," he said. "I would not like what I have to say to be overheard."

I led him inside to the room Aridius had preferred when conducting garrison business or meeting with one of the commanders so as not to disturb the rest of the household. It was a tidy room off the courtyard, its only furniture a table and two chairs set on a thick rug of woven wool; one wall featured a fresco depicting a willow by a riverside with a group of nymphs cavorting in the water. "We can speak freely in here," I said, ushering him in and closing the door.

I took one of the chairs, but Vitus remained standing.

"Oh, Vitus, do sit down," I told him. "You're making me nervous hovering over me like that."

With a distracted nod, he glanced at the closed door and then took the chair across from me. I waited for him to speak first, but a moment passed and he sat silently regarding his hands. Finally, I said, "Am I right in thinking that this is something to do with your splendid new promotion?"

364

He glanced up sharply. "You know about that?" Before I could reply, he rushed on. "Of course, you do. How could you not? The whole world knows by now."

This odd assertion surprised me because, more than anything, he seemed embarrassed to admit it. "But surely this is very good news," I told him. "Good news for you and for the garrison. You have to be very pleased."

He shook his head. "You'll not think it good news when you hear what I have to say."

I raised an eyebrow. "Perhaps, you better say it then—and let me be the judge."

"This is not my idea. I want you to know that..." He made an apologetic motion with his rough hands.

"Spit it out, man! Whatever you have to say cannot be made sweeter for waiting."

He sighed. "I have been ordered to take possession of the villa." He said this as if making a guilty confession.

"Of course," I replied. "I expected nothing less. What of it?"

He looked shocked. "They told you?"

I laughed. "No one told me! This is the way of things—as I should know better than anyone. I was daughter to a magistrate and wife of a legate, remember. How do you think *we* got this house?" Seeing as this clearly caused him some anguish, I softened my tone. "I have been living in official dwellings all my life. The new magistrate comes, the old one goes. That is how it is and I have never questioned it."

His anguish only deepened. "But I don't *want* you to go!"

There it was. Though why this should cause him such torment, I could not imagine. I was still trying make sense of it when he said, "See, here, I have been thinking about this—"

"I can see that."

"—and I have found a solution to this problem. We can share the villa." He spread his hands as if revealing his plan on a silver plate.

"*Share* the villa, did you say?"

"Aye, just so," he said, relieved to have it out at last. "See here, I will take a room or two, and you and the lads can have all the rest. I am only one man and I don't need so much space. I would rattle around in this big house like a bean in a box."

I sat for a moment taking this in and trying to decide how best to respond. Unable to abide the silence any longer, Vitus said, "Well? What do you think?"

"You dear man," I said finally, "that you even consider making such an offer is tribute to your care and compassion." Reaching across the gap between us, I leaned forward and gripped his hand. "You are a true friend, and I bless God for you."

"Then you'll do it?"

"No, Vitus," I replied, shaking my head gently. "As tempting as your offer may be, I cannot agree to it."

His mouth tightened and he looked down again. "Is it because of what people will say—us living together, I mean?"

"I care nothing for what the gossips say! I've heard as much and worse. No, it is not that. Rather, it is *you* I am thinking of—you and the duties you have taken on. See here. You have stepped into some very big shoes, my friend. The demands of the office are very great—even greater now that the town and garrison are struggling to return to life. You will face tremendous difficulties in the days ahead. You will be needed everywhere—coming and going all day and working into the night. You need a place of quiet, a haven, a refuge of peace. You will want to meet privately with garrison commanders, and on occasion entertain them. You have a garrison to order and oversee, and you cannot have a widow woman and two noisy boys knocking around and under your feet."

I paused to allow him to absorb this, then continued, "However well-intentioned we both were, we'd soon tire of such an arrangement and then it would begin to chafe. Sooner or later, we'd be resenting each other and that would be the end of our friendship and I, for one, could not bear that."

Gripping his hand harder for emphasis, I added, "Hear me, Vitus, and believe me when I say I never want to lose you as a friend."

He accepted my decision with a nod. "Then you're set on leaving?"

"Yes, I'm leaving. But I won't go far," I quickly reassured him. "I'm leaving the villa, but not Constantia." It told him about my discussion with the magistrate and how I have my pick of places to live.

"You'll stay?" he said, brightening a little. "You'll live in the town."

"Within sight of the garrison walls. Aurelius and Uther have no other desire than to serve the legion. Their home is here now, and it would be folly to interrupt their training—much less take them away from the man who has already taught them so much, the man who has faithfully stood by them from the beginning—who is like a father to them now."

. This, I think cheered him more than anything else I could have said. "Uther and Aurelius are among the best recruits I have," he told me then. "Maybe the best I have ever seen."

I smiled at his assertion. "And you thought you were about to lose them, is that it?"

"Well, yes," he confessed. "That was in my mind." Then, adopting a more solemn tone, he said, "Aurelia, I will do all I can to make them not only soldiers but true leaders of men. This is my pledge to you."

"I accept your pledge," I told him. "And I will hold you to it."

We talked a little more about when I would leave the villa, and when he would take up residence. Our business concluded, he rose and took his leave. I walked with him to the gate and, before he could walk away, I said, "Your offer to share the villa was generously made—most generously and graciously made—and I thank you for it. I thank you most of all for your kindness, your love for Aurelius and Uther, and your concern for my well-being." I leaned forward, took his hand and gave him a quick peck on the cheek. "You are a good man, Vitus."

Smiling with his whole being, he put his hand over mine, let it rest there for a moment and then walked away, lighter in step than when he first arrived.

5

"THIS IS THE HOUSE YOU MEAN?" Solinus asked as we stood before the arched gate of a whitewashed stone dwelling with an old-fashioned red-tiled roof. Its small courtyard was full of leaves and bits of rubbish; a stray animal or two had taken residence and left filth all over the paving stones, even in the short time it had been unoccupied. A tile beside the gate bore the name: *Alba*.

"The very one," I said. "Do you know it?"

"Oh, yes, I know it very well. It belonged to Livius Drusus."

"The lead and tin merchant?" I had met the man once or twice at some official function or other. "I thought he lived in Britannia."

"He does," affirmed Solinus. "That is, he *did*. He and his wife Claudia had a large villa in Eboracum, but they used to winter here." The young magistrate nodded toward the empty house. "And here they both died in the first days of the plague."

He lifted a hand to the gate. "Shall we go in and have a closer look?"

It was one thing viewing a vacant house from the street, but quite another to stand in a room where the inhabitants had died suddenly and, as I imagine, mostly alone.

And now, I stood in a room where everything was much as Livius and Claudia had left it: a chair furnished with fine cushions still bearing the indent of the body that had last used it; a plate with bits of dried bread on the table; a rumpled rug on the smooth, stone floor. In sleeping chambers the same thing: a bed with coverings strewn aside, and a cloak on the floor—as if someone had risen quickly and rushed

368

out of the room only moments before; an overturned jar in the corner, an expensive woolen shawl dropped in a doorway.

The sense of their lingering presence was so strong, it was difficult to believe we were not trespassing. I half expected Claudia to walk into the room at any moment and find us there, or to see Livius stooping to rekindle the fire in the hearth that had long since become cold ash. It was all so, so sad.

We stood for awhile, silent amidst the oppressive stillness of the place. Then, shaking off the gloom lest it overwhelm us, we quickly examined other rooms—three sleeping chambers, a dining room, the tidy little cookhouse out back, and the common rooms—then made our respectful retreat. Once more in the courtyard, Solinus turned to me. "What do you think? Will Alba House serve?"

I smiled at this somewhat whimsical name and replied, "Yes, the Alba House will serve most admirably well." I looked back at the house with its white walls and quaint red roof. "It is a fine house and I am happy do whatever I must do to lay claim to it."

"Easily done," he said, turning to go. "We will go now and record the change in ownership."

On our return to the Civitas House, my name was duly entered as the new owner of record, and now all my energy was directed toward the move. The next morning, taking each room of the villa in turn, Tatiana and I surveyed its contents, reckoning what we owned and could take with us, and what must be left behind; and then we began packing. We were still hard at work when Vitus appeared, striding into the courtyard and calling my name. I dropped the bedding I was folding and hurried to greet him and asked if he would take a sip of wine with me. I brought him into the villa's dining room and he saw the chests and crates—some we were still filling and some ready to go.

"Uther told me you have already found a house and have begun to pack your belongings," he said.

"As you see," I put out a hand to a half-filled crate, "we've already made a good start."

"That is why I have come," he said. "I want to offer my services and—" He smiled, adding, "I brought help." Turning back toward the courtyard, he beckoned me to follow. "Come and see."

We went to the gate and looked outside to see a crew of young legionaries—Uther and Aurelius among them—trooping down the street, a mule-drawn wagon rattling along behind. "You brought a whole cohort!" I exclaimed. "But—"

Vitus raised his hands. "No need to thank me. It pleases me to be of service."

Before I could explain that I was not ready to have my personal things mauled by rough-handed soldiers, Vitus, adopting a serious tone, said, "Aurelia, I have put you out of your home. This is the least I can do."

Seeing that this was how it was to be, I accepted his thoughtful offer with good grace. After all, strong, willing hands are not to be refused when heavy lifting is required. "Very well, we can start by making Alba House fit to live in." He raised his eyebrows at this, and I explained. "It is a good house, Vitus, but it is full of ghosts and the clutter of other lives. I want it all gone. I am minded to clear out all of the previous owner's personal belongings and anything else that will be of no use to me—and that includes the hangings on the walls and rugs on the floors. I want everything washed—top to bottom—scoured with sand and hot water. You can fill the wagon with everything to be discarded and take it to the market square for anyone who wants it."

He was smiling when I finished. "My men and I are at your command," he proclaimed and hailed me with a mock salute, then went off to instruct his crew.

With the help of Vitus and his soldiers the work progressed at a pace that made my head spin. With so many hands employed, it was difficult to keep up. I made myself dizzy, darting from room to room, directing, cajoling, pleading, answering a dozen queries at once. "To the cart!" became a chant.

Fortunately, legionaries are used to being yelled at, so all took my protestations in good humor. I could but marvel at the speed and efficiency of well-trained soldiers. I expressed as much to Vitus, who nodded knowingly as we watched the fully-loaded wagon trundle off to deposit its load of useable objects and furniture in the marketplace. "You are not wrong," he replied, with not a little pride. "I trained them myself."

We turned back toward the house, now nearly ready for my own furnishings. Halfway across the courtyard, Vitus stopped. "Did you hear that?"

I confessed that I did not hear anything, as is so often the case.

"There!" he said, cocking his head toward the garrison on the low rise above the town. "That was the call to arms," he said. "The troops are mustering. I have to go!"

He dashed into the house and called to those of his men who were still at work. A moment later, they all came out on the run, dashed across the courtyard and out the gate and were gone, disappearing into the street. I started toward the house and then even I heard it—a short, sharp trumpet blast in a rapid succession of rising notes—repeated once and then . . . an ominous silence.

6

WORD RACED THROUGH THE TOWN on the wings of the wind: a large Saecsen warhost had crossed the eastern border. Dux Riothamus had sent fast riders to all the garrisons under his command and ordered the legions to march. This time there would be no parlay with the chieftains. This time there would be war.

Tatiana and I closed up Alba House and hurried up to the garrison, passing knots of worried citizens on the way. By the time we reached the walls, the first cohorts were already marshalling in the field—Uther and Aurelius with them. I met them in the stable yard where they and other solders were readying their mounts. I called to Aurelius. He saw me and came to me, taking my hands in his. "The entire legion is called out," he said. "We're leaving at once."

Stunned, I blurted the first thing that came into my head. "Where?"

"Near a place called Autricum," he shrugged. "That's all I know." He gave me a quick hug and kiss, and pressed my hand. "I've got to go."

He rushed off again and I stood on stiff legs and watched as they finished their preparation and took their mounts. They paused as they passed me. Uther leaned down and took my hand, kissed it, and bade me farewell. I accepted then what had long been true: Uther and Aurelius were warriors blood and bone. They were soldiers true—no longer my children, they were Rome's. As I stood there in the courtyard, the day suddenly seemed a little colder, the light a little dimmer, as I came face-to-face with the grimmest of realities: my sons, the children I had loved and cared for, placing their every need above my own every day since birth, were among those who would live and die with a blade in their hands.

And there was not a thing I could do about it, except pray. This is what I did. Returning to the villa, I found a candle stub and hurried to the church, passing soldiers, wives, and children making their farewells. The church was empty when I entered the dim coolness of the sanctuary. I lit my candle from the one burning on the altar, and then knelt on the stone floor and prayed before the cross on the wall. I prayed to the One who held all beginnings and ends in His hands that He would draw this latest catastrophe to an end worthy of His good name, and that the men who rode to defend us would survive the battle to come and live to see their loved ones on their return. I might have prayed longer, but my mind was heaving with turmoil and my thoughts kept darting off on other paths. Finally, I gave up and said my Amens.

Leaving my candle flickering on the step before the altar, I walked back to the villa and was met on the way by Solinus. "The legion is marching out," he told me. Realising that he was stating the screaming obvious, he added, "Some of the citizens and soldier's wives are to follow."

At first I did not understand his meaning and my first thought was that I had not heard him correctly. He said it again and removed any doubt: the townsfolk and families of the legionaries were following the army to the battle.

This rarely, if ever, happened in Britannia. But it happened in Gaul and elsewhere in the empire—that wives and relations, or those merely close to the combatants in some way, would travel behind the army with the baggage carts, and maintain a camp of their own to support the troops so that those bearing arms could put all their efforts and energies into their combat with the enemy.

"I will go." The decision was made the instant I spoke the words.

He shook his head. "I didn't mean that—"

"Then why tell me?" I demanded.

"I didn't want you to learn about it later," he said. "And, yes, in case you wanted to join them."

"If my sons are to take any part in this battle, I want to be there—for them, and for all those who must put their lives at risk." I was thinking about Aurelius and Uther of course, but also all the families of fighting men. "If I can be useful to them, then I want to be there."

"Then you will come with me," he declared. "I'm taking a wagon."

"But you are magistrate now," I countered. "You will be needed here. With everyone else gone, someone must keep the town in good order."

"I'm going," he said. "You can school me on the duties of a magistrate on the way."

I don't know if he meant that as a rebuke or not, but I accepted his offer to accompany him in the wagon, and ran to fetch a few things to take with me. Tatiana helped me gather a small bundle of items I would need for the journey. She assembled her own bundle, too, informing me that her place was by my side and there was no way she would remain behind. So, we joined the troop of camp followers and, as the sun went down on that fraught and harried day, our straggling parade of wagons and walkers set off.

7

A MILITARY CAMP is a marvel of order and efficiency. Leather tents run in rigid straight lines with paths wide enough between opposite rows for wagons and horses to move through quickly; each sleeping tent shelters four to six soldiers, and there are kitchen tents at either end of the camp. Commanders' tents are clustered in the center to be among their men the better to direct them; weapons are neatly stacked at intervals along the central path so that they are ready to hand, the same with vats of water. Long picket lines of horses run along behind this array so the mounts are never far from their riders. In every detail, the camp is designed to best serve the purposes of warriors and of war.

Compared to the military camp, that of the followers was more akin to chaos—at least such was our sprawling huddle of tents and makeshift dwellings. Be that as it may, we had our purpose, too: caring for those who fought and who, inevitably, would be wounded.

Gossip coursing through the civilian camp had it that Riothamus intended to crush the Saecsen warhost utterly—not only halting the current incursion, but dealing a blow of such dispiriting devastation that barbarian aggression would be curtailed for years to come.

The Flavia Gallicana cohorts occupied the spine of a low ridge with light wood and meadowland sloping away below it. Our camp lay a short distance behind that of the soldiers—far enough away not to hinder, but close enough to be of help when needed. Other legions—at least three others it was said—occupied similar encampments spread out along the ridge top. A prime position, some called it. Here, our Dux Bellorum displayed a portion of the skill that made him such a successful commander. He had not only chosen the battlefield, but had taken and secured the high ground—in a stroke giving his troops a considerable advantage. It was a clever tactic, yes, but not without its limitations—as Uther explained when he and Aurelius came down to see me in the little tent Vitus had provided for Tatiana and me.

"The barbarians can always choose to ignore us and continue raiding somewhere else," he said, and added that had been known to happen. "Usually, they'd rather fight."

That made no sense to me. "Why?" I wondered.

He shrugged. "Who knows? It's their way."

"Maybe their craving for blood and the chance to defeat the defenders overcomes all reason," Aurelius offered.

Uther gave a little laugh. "Ha! They have little enough of that for a start!"

"Victory in battle gives them renown and high status among their tribes," Aurelius continued. "To the Saecsen kind, the will to power is all but irresistible."

"So, the dux will get the battle he foresees," I concluded. The dread I had held off for the last few days washed over me anew. In travelling to and establishing our camp, I had been able to occupy my thoughts with other things. Now, on the eve of battle, fear reasserted itself in force.

"When the battle starts," I said, "where will you be?" I looked to Uther for an answer.

"With Vitus," he replied.

Aurelius explained, "Vitus is commanding a cohort and we are in it. So, wherever Vitus is, we will be." He forced a thin smile meant to reassure me. "So, you see? Nothing to worry about."

Well, I did worry and nothing he or anyone else could say would lessen that burden. I did not tell them this; instead, I made them promise to look after one another, not to take unnecessary risks, to obey Vitus in everything. We talked a little more and then they had to go. I embraced them both and pledged to hold them close to my heart and my heart close to the Good Lord in prayer for their safe return.

I followed them out to the edge of the camp and then stood

watching as they hurried away in the shadowed moonlight. I watched and wondered ... *would I see them alive this time tomorrow?*

Tatiana found me there, wearing a path between our tent and the next, as I murmured my prayers for the safety of my sons. She told me she had prepared a little bone broth and bread, and bade me to come in and eat. I assured her I would when I had finished my prayers. I thought she would be back inside, but she stood and waited with me, adding her prayers to mine. After I had prayed all I could think to pray, we went back into the little tent and sat together in the dim light of a single candle to sip our broth and eat our bread before curling up in our cloaks and sheepskin mats.

Though I closed my eyes, I knew I would not sleep.

Twice during the night, I stirred and, wrapped in my cloak, went out to gaze at the hilltop where, just below the crest, the soldiers lay in camp. All was quiet, all calm. Only the winking of sentry fires could be seen here and there along the ridge, marking the position of other legions' encampments.

My second visit was just before dawn. The sun had not risen, but the sky in the east was pale with the promise of a cloudless sky—light enough to make out the path leading up to the camp above. There were others up and about by then, and we all stood at the edge of the camp and gazed up at the hilltop. "I think some activity up there," one of the young wives said. I saw nothing and was about to say as much when into the early morning quiet a distant trumpet blast signaled the commencement of combat.

Jolted from our survey of the ridge, those of us gathered there looked at one another and, as if some decision had been made, we all charged off at once. Before I knew it, my feet were moving up the hill. I heard a noise behind me and glanced back to see Tatiana following me. I paused and waited for her to catch up. "I want to see—*need* to see how the battle fares," I told her. "You should stay here where it's safe and help prepare for the wounded."

"Where you go, I go," she replied. She fell into step beside me and we scrambled up the slope to the legion's camp with the others. Through it we ran, passing empty tents and picket lines, to the crest of the hill.

What I saw when I looked down brought me to my knees.

"God in heaven!" I gasped, pressing my hand to my mouth.

"*Dei Maria!*" echoed Tatiana, crossing herself as she sank down beside me.

The early morning mist rising from the valley and feeble light lent everything a strange, ghostly quality. The battle was already joined and a snaking double line of legionaries was advancing down the slope, shoulder to shoulder behind their shields and lowered spears and into a writhing, churning mass of Saecsens.

Though the fighting had only begun, already the slope behind the advancing legionaries was strewn with bodies of dead and wounded—both men and horses, barbarian and Briton sprawled side by side. Here and there, a body quivered, or limbs flailed as life ebbed away. Horses screamed, thrashing out their death throes, trying vainly to rise; riderless horses whinnied and trotted away from the carnage, or stood with heads low in silent suffering.

Out on the plain below the hill, we could see the Saecsen camp as a dark smudge in the indistinct light and—God help us! Was it possible?—another dark mass of enemy warriors rushing up to join the howling barbarians hurling themselves at the shield wall. Amidst this surging swarm I searched for our mounted troops. The cavalry—where were they? Where were my boys? I could not see them. In the faint light of a beclouded morning I could see nothing clearly—only a heaving hellscape of shadowy shapes in desperate, tumultuous motion.

As if that was not terrible enough, rising up the hill and up to heaven thundered an unholy cacophony: steel on steel, and clatter and crash of battle axe and sword, the bellows of commanders, shouts of soldiers, cries of men and horses. The sound swirled around and merged into a roar—harsh, dissonant, and unnatural—and underpinning it all, the dull, throbbing thunder of war drums.

It was all too terrible to hear and to behold. I closed my eyes and turned away. Reaching out, I caught Tatiana by the sleeve. "Come away," I told her. "There is nothing we can do here. We will be needed soon enough to help the wounded."

Tatiana and I retreated. Arm in arm, we fled back down the hill to the followers' camp. Many others, awake now and milling about, came running to learn what we had seen. I had not the heart to tell them how our brave soldiers were so woefully outnumbered, or that already the field was strewn with bodies of the fallen. Instead, I told them only that the battle was well begun. Then Tatiana and I went to help ready the camp to offer whatever aid would be required. There would be soldiers—wounded, hungry, in many kinds of distress—to comfort before long.

With some of the other women, I helped build up a fire, adding fresh wood to the coals of the night before until we had a goodly blaze going. Meanwhile, Tatiana fetched an iron pot, filled it with water and set it on the flames to boil. This work occupied our idle hands and took our minds away from the horror beyond the hill. We gathered a few things to add to the pot, and made up loaves of camp bread to bake on a slate amongst the coals.

I was chopping up a beet when the first cry went up—a single scream. Cut short. Then more screams—and suddenly there were horses coursing through the camp and riders with long beards and braids.

"Saecsens!" cried one of the women. "Run!"

8

THE CAMP ERUPTED IN TURMOIL—people scattering every-where, fleeing, trying to avoid the hooves and blades of mounted barbarians that came howling as they burst from the surrounding wood.

"Tatiana!" I shouted, and grabbed for her. "To the tent!"

Before we could take two steps, a Saecsen warrior loomed up before us. Swinging a double-edged war axe, long braids flying as he ran. Eyes wild, mouth wide, bellowing in his uncouth tongue as he closed on us.

I spun on my heel and made for the nearest tent, pulling Tatiana with me. I made but half a step and felt something snag the trailing edge of my cloak and pull hard, yanking me off my feet. I fell and lay squirming on the ground, trying to rise.

My attacker stamped down on my cloak and stood leering down at me. I kicked at him, but he put back his head and loosed a wild cry of triumph, his teeth a yellow gash in his dark, bearded face. He raised the wicked axe high above his head to deliver the killing stroke. I screamed and threw my hands before me to fend off the blow. My mind whirled. I saw the sky and the sneering face of my attacker and thought, *This is how I die.* My next sensation would be the cold bite of steel piercing my soft flesh.

I felt a burning sensation in my hand. I had landed on my back beside the cooking fire and my flailing hand had touched the iron poker used to stir up the coals. Without thinking, my fingers closed on it and I waved it before me. The brute stepped back, seized my ankle, and started dragging me away from the fire. I screamed. I kicked. I held on to the red hot iron, furiously swinging it like a fiery club. I struck him a glancing blow on the arm. He dropped my foot and jumped back, gathering himself for another attack.

Out of the corner of my eye, I saw a flash of motion.

There was Tatiana with the pot, fresh from the fire, gripped between her hands. She swung her arms to her side and with a mighty heave dashed the boiling contents into the brute's ugly face. A scream of agony tore from his throat. The axe spun from his hand as he threw his hands over his eyes. He stumbled back, screaming, pawing away at his face in a futile attempt to wipe away the scalding liquid.

I struggled to my knees and swung the hot poker into his leg, catching him just below the knee. He shrieked and tottered. I lunged forward and held the poker to his ribs. It smouldered and the odor of singed hair filled my nostrils as tiny tongues of flame ignited the rough pelt hanging from his shoulders.

Screaming, he staggered away, half-blinded, batting at the burgeoning flames as he fled.

Tatiana appeared beside me then, the pot still in her hands. I threw my iron club back into the fire and reached out to take the pot from her and recoiled from the touch. The vessel was still searing hot. "Let it go," I told her and, taking her arm, we ran to the tent. My only thought then was to remain out of sight.

Once inside, I took Tatiana's hands in mine and turned them over to examine the palms. Already, blisters were forming from where she had gripped the heated iron of the pot. She looked at her scorched palms and shook her head. "I didn't feel anything," she said. "I only thought—" It was then the agony began. Her face crumpled and she cradled her hands to her breast, her eyes squeezed tight against the pain, stifling her cries.

We stayed like this for an eternity of uncertainty. Would we be found again? Would we be killed? Raped? Taken captive and sold as slaves? These and a hundred other thoughts spun through my head and I prayed for Jesu and his angel army to protect us. Or, if that was not to be, a quick death.

How long we stayed cowering in the tent listening to the screams and cries outside, I cannot say. The commotion gradually decreased and diminished, and then faded away altogether—only to be replaced by the sound of other voices shouting, and horses galloping into camp. These voices were familiar. "Stay here," I told Tatiana.

I crept to the tent opening and peered out. There, among the wreckage of flattened tents and scattered clothing and utensils, I saw legionaries. I stepped out from hiding and into the path of a horse coming up behind me. I whirled around and stared up into the face of my own dear son. "Aurelius!"

"Mother!" he threw himself down from his mount and gathered me to him. "Are you hurt?"

"No, no," I assured him quickly. "Is it over?"

"We've driven them off," he said. "General Marcus sent a company down to help prepare a place for the wounded."

"Is Uther here, too?"

Aurelius shook his head. "No—the last I saw him, he was helping retrieve the wounded from the battleground."

"The wounded—are there many?" I asked.

Aurelius nodded. "Enough. Not as many as there might have been if the battle had gone on longer—but enough." He glanced around at the devastation of the camp. "I'm sorry we were not here sooner. We could have prevented this."

I put my arms around his neck and held him close for a moment. "You're here now and safe, thank God. That's all that matters."

We turned then to assess the devastation. Bodies lay where they had fallen. One poor woman had been ridden down, her tangled corpse speared where she lay. Another had been viciously slashed across the breast with an axe; a man lay beside her, his arms flung out as if he had tried to protect her. I shivered. It could so easily have been me lying there staring up empty eyed at an unheeding sky.

Others were stumbling around, sifting through the wreckage with dazed expressions on their faces. From here and there, I could hear the soft moans of the injured and wounded.

"Why do they do it?" I murmured beneath my breath. It all seemed so senseless, so meaningless. "Why?"

9

THE FIRST OF THE WOUNDED ARRIVED almost immediately. Those who could not be moved were treated up in the military camp; those who could walk made their way down to the followers' camp. I was busy applying a soothing salve made from pig fat and honey to Tatiana's burns, when Vitus and his company arrived. They had been rounding up the loose horses and dragging away the barbarian dead whose corpses were to be piled into a heap and burned. Any wounded barbarian was quickly dispatched to join their kinsmen wherever it is they go in the afterlife.

"But it's over?" I said, hope rising once again.

"For us, aye." Vitus regarded me carefully. "Riothamus and two other legions from the east are giving chase and will continue on to secure the border. Are you certain you're unharmed?"

"I am," I assured him and, gripping Uther's arm, added, "Thanks to Tatiana's quick thinking. Her hands are burned, but I can help her with that." I followed his gaze across the camp. "There are not many wounded," I suggested.

"There will be more," Vitus said. "Be ready to receive them."

Indeed, a wagon arrived a short time later carrying five bleeding men, and I suddenly found myself stretched in every direction at once. As the former legate's wife, I became the person others looked to in organizing relief—a notion aided, I suppose, because it was also known that I had some skill or knowledge of treating wounds. God knows, I had done enough of it in the past. Vitus directed cloaks and skins to be spread on the ground for the injured men so their injuries could be treated in an orderly manner. The first of these wounded soldiers suffered from lacerations of one kind or another; slashes produced by a blade. Three of the mounted legionaries had suffered cuts to their lower legs. Two of these were easily bandaged and the soldiers given water and bread and, after a little rest, sent back to their camp; the third man's wound was sufficient to lay him low for a while, so he remained with us in camp. Of the two remaining, one had sustained a deep cut to the inside of his thigh that was not only bleeding profusely—just staunching it was fraught—but even bandaged threatened to reopen at the slightest movement. And the fifth was a foot soldier who had suffered a blade thrust through his hand that had cut deep and broken several bones.

Thus it began. Those first were joined by others, and all too soon what started as a trickle became a steady stream of wounded men coming for aid. The few able to walk hobbled down the hillside, leaning on the shafts of their spears; others were brought by one of the wagons, fresh blood seeping through the cracks. One wagon and then another, leaving a sticky crimson trail all down the slope.

Tatiana, her hands bandaged, helped as much as she was able. Once, we paused to look up from our work and saw a long double row of wounded men lying on the ground. Dear God, there were so many—and still they kept coming.

"We'll soon run out of places to put them," I told her.

"Then we'll make more places," the young woman, ever practical, replied. She looked around at yet another oncoming wagon, and then at me. "What else can we do?"

All through that long day we worked—battling pain and death and fatigue. There was no escape—save, for some, in the empty oblivion of unconsciousness, or the finality of death. Benumbed by the suffering around us, we did what we could to relieve it. Our own relief would not come until the wounded stopped coming and even then it would go on for some time after. I remember stepping away from the side of a dying soldier to stand blinking in the full bright light of a brilliant sunset. It had been early morning when we returned to the camp from our survey of the battlefield. Where had the time gone?

I looked up the hillside toward the legion camp, expecting to see the yet another wagon coming to deliver more battle casualties. But there was no wagon in sight—only a trio of soldiers limping wearily down the hill to us. Tired as I was, I hurried to meet them. "Where is it?" I blurted, without thinking what I was saying. "Where's the wagon?"

The soldier—wincing in pain, but still resolute—looked groggily around. "There's just us," he said.

"You're the last?"

"I don't know," he said. "Ahh!" He pressed a hand to his side as a spasm gripped him; his hand came away sticky and wet.

Taking his arm, I sat him down. "Let me see it," I ordered, and sent one of the women nearby to fetch some cloths and vinegar to bind the gash. That done, I helped him to his feet and found him a place to lie down. Weary to the bone, I turned again to the trail leading up to the legion camp and saw only a single rider. A few moments later, Vitus was beside me. He had been up to the soldiers' camp to confer with the commanders who confirmed there were no more injured or wounded soldiers coming down to us.

There was no more blood to staunch, or wounds to bind. Sadly, for some, these ministrations would be the last kindness they would know in this worlds-realm. And it broke my heart to say that more than one wife received the cruelest shock when she stooped to tend a soldier only to see her husband lying there. But the worst was over.

"God be thanked," I sighed, almost collapsing with relief. "Tell me what happens next."

He nodded, and said, "I need a drink first."

Aurelius came galloping up with Uther right behind him. "It's all over!" he shouted. Uther whooped a victory cry, and Aurelius raised a fist and shouted in triumph. "We won! You should have seen it, Mother! We won!"

Vitus leapt forward and seized the reins of Aurelius' horse. "We won?" he shouted, his voice an accusation. "Just what do you think *we* won?"

Aurelius sat there stunned, unable to speak.

Instantly angry, Vitus roared, "We won nothing! Nothing! Do you understand?" He flung out a hand and pointed up the hill. "There are no winners lying out there on the battleground—only losers! Those who lost their lives, yes—but many another not here to witness the loss. Mothers who have now lost a son, fathers who have lost an heir, wives who have lost husbands, children now without a father."

Red-faced now, spittle flying from his mouth, he raged, "And all of them—every single one of them will reckon the loss for years to come! We lost fewer than the barbarians, as may be, but we lost all the same." He wiped his chin with the back of his hand and continued on. "We defended our lands and drove off the enemy—that is all. Good men lie dead on that accursed field. Damn the man who calls it winning!"

Aurelius shrank down into himself under the heat of Vitus' rage. Humbled, humiliated to be shouted at in front of the others, he nevertheless took the bitter draught and swallowed it. My heart went out to him, of course, but Vitus was right: there are no winners in war—only those who lose and, those who live to bear the loss.

Vitus sent a chastened Aurelius back up the hill to help with clearing the battlefield, to retrieve weapons and armor from the fallen and bury the dead—for many would forever lie in the ground they had shed their blood to protect.

Uther knew well enough to keep his mouth shut. He hesitated, looking to Vitus and me for a word of absolution, but did not get it. He wheeled his mount and galloped after his brother. Vitus turned to me, somewhat shamefaced, and apologized for his outburst.

I had never seen him so enraged, but this flare-up was entirely justified. I told him so, and I told him that he was right to be angry. "If they are to be the leaders of men that you and I expect them to be," I said, "they must learn that lesson, however hard they find it."

MERLIN AND AURELIA

"DID YOU NEVER THINK of marrying Vitus?"

Aurelia smiles and I catch a fleeting glimpse of the young woman she still is beneath her illness. "Marry Vitus?" She considers the question for a moment, then replies, "I did—once. Yes, I did. But only for a season. He never knew because I never told him, never let on."

"He would have welcomed the prospect, would he not?" I suggest. "Perhaps, when he asked you to stay and share the villa with him, he was proposing something more."

"Perhaps," she allows, "but we never spoke of it. In my heart I knew it would only be a union of convenience, and I knew it would not work in a way that would please either of us in the end. I loved Aridius so very much. That is, I grew to love him more than I could have thought possible. I love him still. And though I did esteem Vitus greatly, there was nothing like the great affection I had for Aridius. I could not imagine ever giving his place in my heart to another."

"I think that is often the way of it," I say. "For me also. After Ganieda there will never be another. She will be forever part of me."

Aurelia nods in affirmation of this sentiment, then continues, "In any event, marriage to me would not have been fair to Vitus. He deserved so much more than that—" She laughs suddenly, adding, "Not that I didn't try to procure for him what I could not supply." I raise my eyebrows at this and she hoots. "Time and again, I introduced him to women I thought he would like." Smiling, she shakes her head at the memory. "It always ended in disaster. I was a pathetic matchmaker."

She smiles at the memory and continues, "No, no, that life was not for Vitus. Anyway, he was legate now and he had more than enough to do without a wife to please. The demands of a garrison, you would not believe! I think he little guessed what rough waters he had plunged into when he became the legion's legate. If he had, he would have deserted the post altogether—and I, for one, would not have blamed him." She laughs again and it cheers me to hear that happy sound. But her laughter ends in a rattling cough that dispels any gladness.

Aurelia dabs at her mouth and glances at her hand where a glistening spot of bright red blood has appeared, and I see both pain and resignation in her look as she rubs it quickly away before she thinks I can see it.

"I was happy enough to order my own little house in the town—the only one I had ever owned. Tatiana and I moved into Alba House a day or so after that appalling battle with the Saecsens. We furnished it well with this and that, and it became our happy home. Aurelius and Uther would stay there when they were not required up in the garrison, and it was a boon to live somewhere that held no memories of my life with Aridius.

"Still, they were difficult times, precarious times. Barbarian raids continually taxed our survival—almost daily, it seemed. And if that was not enough, divisions within the imperial court and elsewhere grew ever more fraught and fractious."

"The trials of life are what make us," I tell her.

"Ah, now, that's just what Brother Theo was fond of saying," Aurelia recalls. For me, it was another—my old friend and teacher, Blaise—so long ago it seems another life entirely.

"You endured," I tell her. "You survived."

She folds her hands, entwining her fingers. "We did, yes... we survived—when so many others did not. I don't know why..."

"You were telling me about the battle—the first for Aurelius and Uther."

"Ah, yes, well, Autricum..." Her voice falls and her gaze softens as the memories come winging back. "Our return from that bloody battle was more akin to a funeral procession than any kind of triumphal march. I was riding in a wagon with some of the wounded too ill to be left unattended. We came trailing a long shadow of grief for those we had lost.

"Something about that day has remained with me ever since. Maybe it was seeing Constantia sprawling before us, spreading up the low hills—an untidy straggle of houses, small holdings, little more than hovels some of them, and that's being kind—and the garrison fortress sitting squat in the center. Not what anyone would call attractive but, for us on that day, a welcome sight all the same, and it lifted our doleful spirits.

"I remember feeling a great surge of relief sweep through me as the carriage crested the hill and started rolling down the long, stone-paved road into the town. Nothing there had changed at all. How could it? We had not been away very long—or even very far away, come to that. That first glimpse cheered my heart the all the same. If I had traveled the length and breadth of the empire, I don't imagine I would have felt any different. I remember thinking, 'Here is where I belong.'"

Aurelia glances at me as if I might take issue with this. "Unlikely, I know, for a girl born in proud south Britain. Yet, Constantia had become my home: where I was married, where I raised my boys, where I owned my first house . . . and where, in the graveyard of my church, I will have my resting place."

"I know well how you feel," I murmur, thinking of my home in Celyddon.

Aurelia has not heard me, but knows I have spoken. She taps her ear as she must have done ten thousand times, her gestured request that I speak clearly. I shake my head. "It was nothing," I tell her. "Please, continue."

"All the same, the move to Armorica was not easy. When I left Deva, I thought I would die of longing for home. Indeed, there is that part of me that will always remain as deep rooted in Britain as any oak. Nothing will change that." I hear again, the echo of the old complaint she voiced when first we met.

"Armorica is part of Britannia," I point out.

"You know what I mean," she says. "But, following that gruesome battle, just seeing the welcoming walls of Constantia inspired a feeling of homecoming like no other I had ever known—so strong that it removed any further thought I might have had of leaving. At the crossroads of the town, as I remember, I waved a brief farewell to Aurelius and Uther, and the boys continued on up to the garrison with the other soldiers. I lingered a moment, watching until they passed through the garrison gate. In that moment, I knew the garrison was where they belonged—as I knew where I belonged as well."

"They were soldiers—legionaries now," I observe. "And, from what I have seen, among the finest of their kind."

"True enough. Yet, I did wonder sometimes . . ." She drifts off in her thoughts.

"About them becoming soldiers?" I prompt.

"That and more," she replies, coming back to herself. "The life of a soldier I knew well enough, but was there more? *Could* there be more? Could they better follow their father and grandfather as legate or magistrate and better prove their worth that way? I did often wonder. And as much as I pondered, I prayed—for their feet to find the path best suited to their natures and abilities. And so"—she lifts her chin with motherly pride—"when it came time to choose, they chose Britain."

"What brought that about?" This is something I have wondered about since I heard the two young warriors had returned from their long sojourn in Armorica. "Can you tell me?"

Aurelia ponders the question for a moment, then says, "There was a change in the garrison command. I think that must be where it began." She nods, confirming the notion to herself. "Vitus had people back in Britain—mother and two sisters, I think it was. And he felt he had a duty of care for them, too. At the time, the region was quiet, the borders secure enough. He saw his chance to remove himself gracefully and without too much inconvenience, so he did. A smooth handover of responsibilities—that was his plan. And it might well have worked as he hoped. Vitus stepped down. He was feted and honored for his good service, and a new *Legatus Legionis* was duly appointed. The provincial governor..." she pauses, thinking. "Ah, I can't remember his name. Anyway, the governor promoted an official of his acquaintance that he thought could do the job. And that was that." She pauses again and, mouth pursed, shakes her head. "So far as the governor was concerned, all was well. If only it had been that easy. The problem, as I came to see it, stemmed from the fact that this man— Marcellus, his name was—had not been drawn from the ranks."

"He was not a legionary?"

"Nor a leader of any kind," Aurelia confirms. "He might have been a competent enough official in the governor's appraisal—there were those who thought so and argued the point—but this Marcellus assumed he'd been appointed to return the legion to some state of former glory. He acted as if he'd been chosen to impose discipline on an unruly house, to expose corruption, or incompetence, or misconduct, or something." Her mouth squirms with distaste. "As I say, there were some who agreed with him. 'The garrison must be saved!' they shouted. I never understood why. Under Aridius and Vitus, affairs ran honestly, fairly—if not always smoothly. There was never even a hint of corruption. They were scrupulous in all their dealings within the garrison and the town. I tell you truly, Merlin, both those men lived on their proper salaries and never sought or accepted a bribe, or rewarded a friend who did not deserve it with a favor of any kind. Corruption? They would have squashed it like a cockroach without a second thought. And that's the truth!"

"But Marcellus..."

"I don't know why, but he never bothered to get the measure of the office to which he'd been appointed. He did not know the men, or his generals and commanders. He never paused long enough to learn a thing about the garrison or the town, so far as I could tell. He seemed to me to be a man who wanted to be seen to be doing something important, and desperate to please his superiors. He made changes—not for any purpose other than to be seen making changes. Most of his policies made no sense at all, and of the others... let us say the best were of no consequence, and the worst were disastrous.

"Well, the garrison lurched along and it seemed as if every day some new outrage was perpetrated."

"How long did this last?"

"Too long, if you ask me," she says. "But the troops, who often bore the brunt of bureaucratic foolishness, did not accept their lot quietly. And when the grumbling grew too loud to ignore, the commanders acted. By then everyone had decided they had finally had their fill of this officious outsider, and they undertook a delegation to the governor. Their pleas fell on deaf ears. The governor backed his man—now, *there* was corruption, if you ask me—and he demanded complete, unquestioning loyalty to Marcellus and threatened reprisals for even airing complaints."

"Curious, how often those in power confuse disagreement with disloyalty."

"Well, the commanders came home, more aggrieved than ever that their case had not been heard. They put another plan in motion and Marcellus was deposed."

"Assassinated?"

Aurelia laughs at the thought. "Good heavens, no!" She shakes her head. "They sent another delegation—this time to Vitus. See, he may have retired, and was soon to return to Britain, but he had eyes in his head and he'd seen what was happening. Lord knows, the generals were not the first to bend his ear! I think he waited until things came to a head."

"Then he stepped in?"

"Vitus still had the support of the legionaries and influence enough to bring a little power to bear. He gathered the commanders and they met with the legate. I don't know what was said, but the next day Marcellus packed up and left Constantia for good—he and his household.

"Well, that created a vacancy in the garrison command. Vitus was asked and agreed to return to the position—but only until a new legate could be chosen and installed. He proposed Aurelius. Many of the legionaries also wanted him for the job. They had fought alongside him, they knew him. But the older command held that he lacked experience—though he was the son a legate and steeped in it from birth. The campaign grew heated, I can tell you. Oh! The things they said about Aurelius... and about *me*! Vile things, awful things, wicked things..."

Here it is again, I think, *the source of the complaint she voiced to me the night we first met.* The malicious rumors faced by her son must have rekindled the grievances she had labored half a life to silence. *Great light, the pain of an unjust accusation, I know only too well!*

"And Aurelius did not become legate," I say.

"Aurelius—unlike his brother—is ever the diplomat. Uther may be the better commander, the best when blood is flowing; but Aurelius is much the better peacemaker. When he saw the forces arrayed against him, Aurelius chose the wiser path. He was too young still, and he knew it. In the end, he withdrew from consideration and one of the generals was elected."

"Which then created a place among the elite command," I surmise.

"Yes, and Aurelius graciously filled that place. As I think on it now, that was what he really wanted. And he was better suited to it in any case."

"He used the leadership struggle to his ultimate advantage," I say. "Very shrewd."

Aurelia nods in agreement. "He was given command of a cohort, and immediately made Uther his second."

"This legion cohort," I say. "These are the warriors he and Uther have brought with them to Britain."

"The same—and likely more. As time goes on, they gain both experience and loyalty among the troops. Soldiers want to follow them. You see how it is."

Yes, things have fallen into place.

"Ah, but in the years those gangly boys were growing into men, did I ever imagine they would become kings in Britain? Did it once cross my mind that such a thing might happen?" Aurelia gives her head an emphatic shake. "No. It did not. The very idea—it never occurred to me. And if anyone would have suggested such a thing, I think I might have said it was far more likely that they would grow golden wings and fly."

"We live in hope, do we not?" I suggest lightly.

"That's what Brother Theo used to say." She smiles at the memory. "He also said, 'The fires of Hell have been stoked high and rage unchecked throughout the world. God alone is our only hope and refuge.' Brother Theo . . . that dear, dear man."

She sighs, and falls silent. I think she will not speak again, but then continues, "Once I had moved from the garrison into Alba House, I found myself more taken up with the church and its many doings. This was in no small part due to Theo's growing influence in the region. He was a good and capable man. Much of his time was devoted to the various duties and concerns of the diocese, to be sure, but he refused to move from the priest house near the church at Constantia. Consequently, we came to see much of one another as my own place among the faithful grew ever more firmly rooted."

"You served the church," I observe.

"I served God!" she declares, then softens, "and yes, I served that little church—and Theo." She smiles at the memory. "That man—gentle as a lamb, but stubborn as a ram. It was impossible to say no to Theo. So, yes, I took on duties I would not have imagined—some of them I did not even know about until I was given them! He found me one day tending to the graves in the churchyard—pulling away weeds and grass from the markers, placing a few flowers—small chores, out of remembrance for those I loved. The next thing I know I am dressing the altar in the church!

"I told him that I thought only priests were allowed to do that, but Theo said, 'The brothers might perform the service out of duty. But you, I think, would do it out of love.' That was Theo, you see? Well, how could I refuse after that? And I suppose I was just a little flattered to be thought worthy to serve in the Lord's house. Dressing the altar was not much of a task at all—setting out the cloth, cleaning it when necessary, polishing the sconces, arranging the candles and trimming the wicks—and none of it difficult, much less onerous."

"You took it on."

"That and more. A simple enough beginning, perhaps, but from that day my involvement in church affairs grew."

"That is often all it takes," I say, thinking how things that are meant to be have a way of catching us up one way or another.

"Well, over the next years, as Theo's obligations and burdens increased, so did my own. There was no denying it, the barbarian upheavals were everywhere wreaking havoc and more people were moving into Constantia to escape the attacks, but you know? I learned a curious thing: The greater the chaos and confusion of the world, the greater grows the congregation of God."

How not? I think. Is it any wonder that in times of turmoil and upheaval folk do often lift their eyes to Heaven for the solace and strength offered by the faith? Great Light, it was ever thus. For where else to find the refuge and relief that only the Good Lord can provide?

Clouds have crowded out the sun and a chill has crept into the air. Aurelia pulls the robe around her and reaches out to give my hand a pat. "You are so kind to listen to an old woman ramble on about times often forgotten."

I hear in her tone a lament for this fast-receding age, for her fear that she will be cheated of the promise of today delivered tomorrow. How it is now her time to leave—and leave too soon, just as her father and Helena and husband before her, without seeing Britain united again and her son ascend to the throne? And yet, I see Aurelia is a solid link to a time, not so very long ago, when Britannia was a valued and functioning part of Imperial Rome. Here was a woman whose life bridged the ever-growing chasm between the old world order and the teeming chaos of the present age. The granddaughter of a British queen, daughter of a magistrate, and wife of a legate of a border garrison, she had known both the stability and strength of the empire and the anarchy and turmoil of a world drifting toward destruction. I remind myself that when Constantine in desperation proclaimed Britannia's freedom from Rome, Aurelia was there; when Valentinian took up the wreath of empire, she was there; when titles such as magistrate, proconsul, and legate still conferred a modicum of power and respect, she was there. Aurelia remembered all of it and more.

I look at the person before me and see not an ailing woman old before her time, but a woman of courage whose steadfast faith evinces the best of the human spirit. I see before me not a Roman subject, but a true citizen of the Island of the Mighty.

"Rambling?" I say. "Never that. But, I see that I am tiring you just now. I will leave you in peace, and we will speak again later."

"My boys," she says, suddenly earnest. "You *will* look after them, won't you? They need you, Merlin. There are difficult days ahead."

"While I have life and breath, my sole work in this world will be to serve them," I vow, and if ever I meant those words, I mean them now.

A smile flickers across her dry lips. "Then I am content." She drifts into silence once more. I allow her this moment, and when she speaks again it is from the depths of weariness, and I watch fatigue stealing over her.

"What is it, Aurelia?" I ask. "What is in your mind?"

She glances up at me, hesitates, then decides to speak it out. "You know full well that I am dying, Merlin." She holds up a thin hand quickly, lest I protest this blunt assertion. "It is the real reason I came back to Britain—to see my sons, to visit my home in Venta one last time, just to see if..." She shrugs, letting the forlorn thought go. "I have known since we journeyed to Armorica that Constantia was the right place to live, for my boys to grow up, and now I know that it is the right place for me to die. There is no longer any doubt whatsoever; there is nothing here for me."

"There may be healing," I object. "Charis and the priests—"

"Your mother and the good brothers here are a balm and a blessing—truly, they are. And Ynys Avallach is a wonderful place. I cherish every moment here. But nature will have her way in the end. You and I both know nothing can prevent that." She offers a faint, but perceptive smile, and adds, "I am not of your race, Merlin. I'll not live forever." With a gentle shake of her head, she turns her eyes to a horizon grown misty in the falling light. "No, my friend, I want to go home while I still can. Tatiana is there, keeping the house—she will have it when I am gone."

I see how it is with her and do not try to persuade her otherwise.

When she turns to me again, there is unflinching honesty in her faded eyes. "I want to die in my own bed. More than anything else, I want to be buried beside my dear husband—not in a solitary grave in the corner of some unknown churchyard."

"I understand," I assure her, though it is not at all where my heart is just now. "Aurelius and Uther will be devastated when they learn you are returning to Armorica."

"You must not tell them!" She reaches out and takes my hand in a hard, bony grasp. "Promise me you will not tell them."

"They have a right to know, dear lady. I cannot be the one to keep it from them, or they will hate me for it. I care nothing for that—I am loathed and lauded in equal measure, so be it. But if I keep from them such as I know, then neither of those men would ever trust me with a whole heart again, and that would ruin our work before it has rightly begun."

"Wise words, I'm sure. They have important work to do uniting Britain—yes, I agree. If I am to die, let it be away from them. The last thing I want is for my death to become a distraction in their battle for the throne."

"They must know, Aurelia. I won't keep it from them."

She sinks even further into her chair. The discussion is tiring her. I see it in the lines and creases in her face and know I should let her rest, but I cannot leave before this matter is resolved.

Just then, Brother Ruan appears on the terrace. He has been spending time at the abbey with the priests there, learning something of the healing craft. He smiles uncertainly when he sees us and approaches hesitantly.

"Yes? What is it that cannot wait?" I demand, irritated by the intrusion.

"I am sorry to disturb you, Emrys," he says. "Pelleas is looking for you. He told me to say that a messenger has come from Lord Tewdrig. He says it is urgent."

Now I am the one feeling apologetic. "Forgive me," I mumble quickly. "Of course, I will be there directly—as soon as Aurelia and I have concluded our discussion." I turn back to her, but already my mind is on Tewdrig and whatever his message may contain. Torn between two competing demands, I quickly weigh the implications of delaying my return to Aurelius' and Uther's war camp.

"Well, there it is, you see?" Aurelia says, seizing on the interruption. "You are needed elsewhere. You must go. Do not worry about me. I got myself here and I can get myself home. After all, I am not dead yet." As she says this, a light kindles in her eyes at a sudden thought. "And *that* is what you will tell my boys—that I have taken their advice and have gone home to await their victory."

"It will be as you say," I tell her. "When will you go?"

"Soon—as soon as preparations can be made."

It would, no doubt, be well for her to remain in Ynys Avallach, but I see her determination, and do not attempt to persuade her otherwise. All the same, I also own the obligation I have taken on to look after her welfare. I dare not leave her alone and I tell her so.

Aurelia counters quickly. "Alone? Hardly that. I'm never alone, Merlin." She smiles at the thought. "I have Mairenn, don't forget. She helped me get here, after all."

"I am certain your maidservant is more than capable," I reply. "But, if anything happened to you on the way, Aurelius would never forgive me—and rightly so. Indeed, I would never forgive myself."

"Hear me when I say that *if* anything barred my son succeeding to the throne that you could have prevented, *I* would never forgive *myself*. Or, you, either."

There is a shuffling behind me and Brother Ruan clears his throat. "Excuse me," he says stepping forward. "Am I to understand that Aurelia wishes to return to Armorica?"

Before I can answer, she says, "That is the nut of it. And the Good Lord willing, that is what I am going to do."

Ruan regards her thoughtfully. "If you will allow me, I will gladly accompany you. I will see you safely home."

His offer, unexpected as it is, takes me aback. "You, Brother Ruan? You would do this?"

"Have I not already vowed to be at her service until I am dismissed?" he replies. "Armorica is not unknown to me. My brother and I grew up there, if you recall? I can easily make the necessary arrangements."

I regard the sturdy young man and again something I noticed the night we met—the span of his shoulders, the breadth of chest and strength of hands, his assured bearing—and I make a guess: "Would I be wrong in thinking you also know your way with a sword and spear, brother?"

"Not wrong in the least!" he laughs, the sound easing the strain we have all been feeling just now. "I rode with Lord Hoel's warband for two years before taking the cloth. Both Rónán and I trained with Hoel's warriors."

"But a life in the saddle was not for you, is that it?"

"I was called to the priesthood and, in short, was sent to Caer Myrddin to begin my service and learn from the bothers there. Rónán followed me," Ruan explained simply, adding, "My brother rides with Tewdrig's warband, and I serve the king in his church."

"There it is, you see?" exclaims Aurelia happily. "Heaven itself has not only supplied the solution, but smoothed the path. Who are we to object?"

"Who are we, indeed?" I tell her. Turning once more to Ruan, I say, "Thank you, Brother. Now, if you would, please go find Pelleas and tell him that I will join him when I've finished here. And see that Tewdrig's messenger is given something to eat and drink, and that the horses are watered and readied. I have a feeling we will be leaving shortly."

Ruan offers a small bow in acknowledgement, and then hurries away. As soon as he is gone, I return to my place beside Aurelia. "You see how it is..."

"Even the great Emrys cannot be two places at once," she says lightly, "and I have kept you long enough. You must go."

I stand and then kneel before her. I take her hands in mine. Her grip lacks strength and her fingers are cold. "It has been an honor to spend time in your presence these last few days," I tell her, gazing into those pale eyes that have seen so much. "I know how painful it can be to stir up the past, but I thank you for it. Your experience, your knowledge, your memories are gold to me. Know they will be enriching for many in days to come. Thank you, my friend, for entrusting me with such treasure."

My little declaration embarrasses her and she waves it aside impatiently. "Oh, get on with you. It is nothing of the sort."

Though she protests, I can tell that some part of her rejoices to have her life so acknowledged. I raise her hand to my lips, kiss it, and return it to her lap. "I must go now," I tell her. "Unless I am much mistaken, the Island of the Mighty will soon have a new High King. The Good Lord willing, his name will be Aurelius."

"If anyone can make that happen, it is you," she tells me. "Thank you, Merlin. I know that Aurelius and Uther are right to trust you. So, I will trust you, too." Extending her hands to me, she invites a last embrace then pushes me gently away. "You must go. So, off with you. Do convey to my boys my undying love and let them know that whatever happens, I am in good hands."

"As you have been from the beginning," I tell her. Then, with pangs of regret I have not felt in a very long time, I commend her to the care of Brother Ruan. The events of a wider world are calling me away, and I cannot stay.

"Until we meet again, Aurelia."

"In this world or the next," she replies and, raising her fingertips to her lips, wishes me on my way with a kiss. "Go, and may God go before you."

This is her favorite benediction. It will, I think, also be her last word to me.

I make my way through the palace to find Charis and take my leave—caught in the traveler's quandary: anxious to be gone but sad to be going. I suspect Pelleas will soon be waiting for me in the courtyard and with him, no doubt, is Tewdrig's man bearing whatever urgency has prompted his arrival. That I will learn soon enough. Just now, my thoughts are filled with all that Aurelia has told me.

It breaks upon me that the reason for this dear lady's survival and long endurance—through attack and plague and slavery and grief and bereavement and every other trial visited upon her—is, like so much else, bound up in the ever-mysterious purposes of God. Why Aurelia, one might ask? Perhaps it was for this: that the feet of those two young men, on whom so much now depends, should remain securely on the path ordained for them. It was for the raising and rearing of Aurelius and Uther—men called to take up the burden of redeeming this time and place, men chosen to keep the flame of civilization alive in this small corner of the world. It was for the saving of whatever is good and worth preserving from the unholy barbarism plundering this worlds-realm that she was chosen.

Aurelia, then, was the instrument perfectly crafted and fitted for that very purpose. Aurelia is not only the mother of the next High King, God willing; she is one of the last witnesses to an elder time and also a handmaid of the age to come. One of those specially endowed to receive the virtue of the past, maintain it, and pass it on to those who would have need of its saving grace in the turbulent years to come. And who better?

Who but an unassuming, unpretentious, half-deaf girl from an unimportant backwater on the edge of a fading empire could be trusted to protect the best of her inheritance and ensure its survival? It was not the emperors, God knows! It was not the procurators, the governors, or even the legates and magistrates—forever chasing their own dreams of power and glory—who could be entrusted with such a sacred charge. As all who follow the Way should know by now, it is the humble folk of this world that God chooses to advance his purposes. Amen.

As I consider this—turning it over and over again in my mind like a miller sifting his grain—I begin to glimpse a shape, the form of a tender leading, subtle guiding and directing, occasionally bending the incidents of a lifetime toward an inexorable will. The believing Celts of an earlier age would have called this the undeniable action of the Swift Sure Hand: that steady and steadfast presence, eternally vigilant and endlessly resourceful and, above all, monumentally determined to ensure that its purposes triumph in this worlds-realm.

In thinking this, I also offer up a prayer that Aurelia—the essential guarantor of our future leaders' formation and upbringing—will survive long enough to see her work brought to fruition.

Well and well, these are musings to be taken up another time. The day is moving on and we must be moving with it if we are to rejoin Aurelius and Uther in time to make good my pledge to be their counselor and their guide in the storm-fretted days ahead. I turn my thoughts to the struggle before me—better armed now with the knowledge I have gained from time spent with Aurelia—and more certain than ever that we can prevail and our work at last begun. I turn my thoughts to the next High King of All Britain.

 # CODA

There is a land shining with goodness where each man protects his brother's dignity as his own, where war and want have ceased and all races live under the same law of love and honor. It is a land bright with truth, where a man's word is his pledge, and falsehood is banished, where children sleep safe in their mothers arms and never know fear or pain. It is a land where kings extend their hands in justice rather than reach for the sword; where mercy, kindness and compassion flow like deep water over the land, and men revere virtue, revere truth, revere beauty, above comfort, pleasure, or selfish gain. A land where peace reigns in the hearts of men, where faith blazes like a beacon from every hill, and love like a fire from every hearth, where the True God is worshiped and his ways acclaimed by all.

—The Dream of Taliesin, Chief Bard of Britain